THE HOMECOMING OF BUBBLES O'LEARY

JEAN GRAINGER

For more information or to download a free book go to www.jeangrainger.com

❀ Created with Vellum

To my sister Aisling,
The funniest person I know.

CHAPTER 1

'Very well, of course.' Katherine paused and gestured with her hand for Conor to stay beside her until she finished the call.

He tried to hide his impatience. Katherine was normally very efficient, keeping the day-to-day details of running the hotel under her control. He needed to get out of there.

'I'll tell you what, I'm sure we can accommodate you, but if I can call you back in just a moment, I'll confirm it all with the manager. Yes – Conor, that's right.' She laughed, a surprisingly girlish sound for someone so austere.

Conor looked at her quizzically. Katherine O'Brien managed the front desk at Castle Dysert effortlessly, allowing him to focus on other aspects of running the hotel. Initially, Corlene, the other owner, was worried that someone as forbidding as Ms O'Brien would put guests off. He had to agree that the dark suit, rail-thin body and severely coiffed hair pulled back off her pale face in a tight bun was not exactly the welcome look they were going for, but she was excellent at the job. She didn't suffer fools, and she struck fear into most of the staff, but underneath the hard exterior, she was unfailingly kind. She was invaluable and everyone knew it. He understood a lot of her nature

1

came from finding some social interaction difficult. She didn't engage in idle gossip or chit-chat. If she had something to say, she said it, but silence didn't unsettle her. She was loyal to the last, and he would trust her with his life.

Since the fire last year that almost destroyed everything they had worked so hard to build, the business had gone from strength to strength, and there was rarely a night that they weren't fully booked.

Conor gave her a pleading look, tapping his watch with his finger, wishing she would just let him go. The way she held her palm up, ordering him to wait, brooked no argument, and he knew better than to defy her. If she was insisting he stay, it must be important.

It was Ana's birthday, and he wanted to get home early. The twins had made her a cake with the help of their beloved Babusya, Ana's mother, and Conor was taking her out to dinner. Things had been so busy lately, he felt like he hardly saw her or Joe and Artie.

Eventually, Katherine hung up. 'Can we go to your office?' she asked. Then, turning to Meghan, the junior receptionist, she said, 'Meghan, please attend the desk.' She pointed to a neatly arranged in tray. 'And ensure all those invoices are in correct date order.'

Meghan got straight to it; when Ms O'Brien gave an instruction, she expected it to be followed to the letter without question or delay.

'Be my guest.' Conor smiled, ushering Katherine ahead of him. He caught Meghan's eye behind the older woman's back and made a funny face. She giggled and blushed.

'I saw that,' Katherine said tartly as she closed the door, though she couldn't possibly have. 'Right. That was a man from America, and he wants to book in a large group. They're all patrons of an Irish bar or something apparently, and they want to come here to attend the Lisdoonvarna Matchmaking Festival.'

Conor was confused – normally she wouldn't involve him, she'd just take the booking if they had availability. He wished she would get to the point, but she was not a woman to be rushed.

'Fine, and can we do it?' he asked.

'Yes, we can.'

'And so...' He smiled encouragingly.

'They want you to take them around, be their guide and so on.' Katherine did not give anything away in her expression, but Conor was used to that.

'Ah, but sure I don't do that any more. But ring them back and tell them we'll find them someone else, someone great, and that'll be fine.' He grabbed his car keys.

'No. That won't be acceptable this time, I'm afraid – it has to be you. The booking would be very useful to us, and they would stay for six nights, so it's a significant saving on housekeeping and so on, not turning the rooms around. The person who rang, his name was Kevin Wilson, and he insisted that you should be the one to do it. Apparently, someone he knows remembers you from a previous tour. The reason I'm suggesting it, apart from the fact that they would be far too enthusiastic and chirpy for me to be dealing with every day – you know how I can't really do small talk, and Americans always seem to want to chat – Sheila Dillon's son is getting married that week and she wants the week off. If we had one large group in rather than lots of singles, the housekeeping team could hold the fort till she gets back. But if it's lots of one- and two-night guests, then we'll need a substitute for Sheila, and getting staff is proving impossible, as you know.'

Conor sighed heavily and sat down. Katherine was right – the Irish economy was booming again and getting staff was a huge issue. Sheila was invaluable as head of housekeeping, and she really needed her holidays.

'Is there no other way?'

'None,' she said with certainty.

'Sure maybe you could hit the matchmaking festival yourself, Katherine?' He winked at her.

Apart from a never-mentioned romance that went wrong years ago, to the best of his knowledge, Katherine had never had a relationship of any kind. She lived alone and was dedicated to her job. He knew she read a lot and studied online courses in history and philosophy all the time, but he would have liked her to have a bit of joy in her life. Though what kind of man would be suitable for her was anyone's guess. She wasn't everyone's cup of tea.

'Utter nonsense. The idea that a farmer with a big dirty book could arrange weddings, for goodness sake.' She rolled her eyes. 'No, Conor, I have no interest whatsoever in such foolishness. Now, can I telephone Mr Wilson back and tell him you are available?'

He sighed, knowing he would never wriggle out of it. 'Look, I'll ring him tomorrow and see what he wants to do. I might be able to swing it – I'll see. Now, I've got to go. I'm taking Ana out for her birthday.'

He had been for a swim in the hotel pool as he did every day, and got dressed and ready to go out afterwards. He was back in his casual clothes: dark jeans and a pale-pink shirt. He was tanned and muscular, and his silver hair was neatly cut. 'Do I look all right?' he asked with a grin.

Katherine raised a perfectly arched eyebrow. 'Yes, you look very presentable.'

He chuckled. Presentable was as far as she would go.

As he drove away from the castle, he planned the evening. Artur and Danika were looking after the boys, who at eight were full of energy. Luckily, their grandparents adored them. Conor thought having his parents-in-law living near them full time might be a bit of a strain, but he couldn't have been more wrong. They'd moved to Ireland two years ago from Kiev. Artur quickly made himself indispensable as head of maintenance, and Danika was a huge help to Ana with the boys.

He was taking his wife to a new fish restaurant out at Spanish Point, and he was really looking forward to spending a whole evening with her uninterrupted. She'd been so tired lately, what with the boys on summer holidays, and she really needed a break. They hadn't managed to take a vacation since the fire last year as there was so much to do.

He pulled into the driveway and was surprised that Joe and Artie weren't in the garden. They lived outside, playing football or hurling. He let himself in, glancing at the clock on the wall over the big stove. At ten past six, the place was usually a hive of activity with dinner and bath time, but the house was silent.

'Ana!' he called. 'Are you here?'

Something was wrong. If she wasn't going to be there when he got home, she would have texted him.

He looked out back; her car was there. He took the stairs two at a time and opened their bedroom door. There she was, in bed. Relieved but perplexed – she never took a nap during the day – he walked over to where she lay on her side. She was awake.

'Ana, what's wrong?' He bent down so he was level with her head. Her eyes were puffy and swollen; she'd been crying.

'Ana, please, are you all right? Where are the boys?' A growing sense of dread threatened to engulf him. She was not a drama queen – something was really wrong.

'They are with my mother. They went over to her house for dinner. My dad picked them up.' Her voice was not normal; it was as if every word was an effort. Her Ukrainian accent was more pronounced than usual.

'So what's the matter?' He felt his mouth go dry. This was so out of character for his wife.

She sat up and took a deep breath that seemed to come from her toes and threw back the covers. She was still dressed.

'Conor, I… Today I was going in the hospital. Last week, I find a lump here' – she pointed to the side of her breast – 'and so I go to see doctor. I know you will say why I don't tell you, but everything so busy in the hotel, and I think is nothing. But Doctor Moriarty make appointment for me, and tell me to go in hospital today just for to make check. They did a test, and they say there is something there. They take some out with a needle to test – I forget the name of that thing – and now I must wait.'

Conor could feel the blood thundering in his ears, his heart thumping in his chest. *This can't be happening.* His beautiful, lovely Ana couldn't have cancer. *It's just not possible.* He struggled to say the right thing.

'Oh, Ana, my love.' He drew her into his arms, and she rested her head on his chest. 'I'm in shock. I…I feel terrible, I should have gone with you. To get news like that on your own… You're so much more important to me than any hotel. I'm so, so sorry, pet.' He was struggling to keep his voice normal. His darling girl – she was so young, and so fit and healthy. 'How long before we get the results of the test – was it a biopsy?'

'Yes, this. A biopsy. They say to come back on Friday, but the other doctor, the special one for breast cancer, say she think it look suspicious. She said to call you, but my phone was dead, and anyway, I was not able to talk. I didn't want to tell you this on the phone, so I come home and wait.'

It was Tuesday. Friday seemed forever away.

'Oh, my darling, I should have noticed something. Can you see the lump or feel it?' He tried to keep the anguish he felt out of his voice; the last thing she needed was a hysterical husband.

'I just feel it in the shower. I was shaving under my arm, and I feel it. Look here.'

She took his hand and placed it along the side of her right breast. He pressed gently, and sure enough, there was a hard little lump. He swallowed.

Memories of his own mother, in bed and fading away from cancer when he was just sixteen, flashed before him. It was as if she had been erased before his eyes. It was horrible. He couldn't bear that to happen to his darling wife. He felt his chest constrict with panic and fear, but he tried to breathe through it. He needed to be strong for Ana.

'I will be right beside you, I promise. We'll do this together. We don't know what we're facing, but I love you so much, and the boys love you...' His voice cracked, and he couldn't go on.

She nodded sadly. 'I can't leave you all, Conor.' Her eyes filled with tears. 'I don't want to die.'

'You are not going anywhere, do you hear me? You're going to be fine. Things are so much more advanced now, technology and all of that, and they've caught it early.' He prayed he was right. He felt so guilty; if he'd been paying more attention to his wife and less to the hotel, maybe he'd have spotted it. 'How long has it been there, do you think? I should have noticed.'

'I think two weeks, not more.' She swallowed. 'Is okay, Conor, you don't have to be so strong. It's bad news.'

His eyes locked on hers. He felt the moisture on his face before he knew the tears had come, and they sat on their bed, clinging to each other, crying.

CHAPTER 2

*T*hree days later, Corlene stood in his office, fuming. She had cleaned up her act considerably from the time he first met her years ago, a desperate five-time divorcee on a tour looking for her next victim. The leopard-print dresses and over-the-top make-up had been replaced by chic designer suits and perfectly done hair and nails. She was all right, and she was the senior partner in the hotel, but he did all the work, and he had no patience for anyone today.

'Conor, are you even listening to me? I've left voice messages, sent texts, and nothing back from you. This is just not good enough.'

'I'm listening. I've no choice,' he replied, checking his phone for the tenth time for a text from Ana. He was picking her up at noon to go to the hospital, but he'd reluctantly come in to deal with urgent matters that Katherine had been plaguing him with since Wednesday morning. He should probably tell them – Katherine would make sure nothing to do with the castle would bother him if he did – but even saying the words 'Ana might have cancer' out loud was so gut-wrenching.

'Well, what are you going to do about it?' Corlene was not used to being dismissed like that, and she didn't like it.

'Nothing. We're full all the time, so I don't see what your

problem is. Anything urgent, you can call Katherine. If you're that concerned, why don't *you* do something? We are meant to be running this place together, but there's not been a hair or hide of you here for weeks. So don't bother coming down now shouting the odds at me, Corlene, because frankly, I'm not going to take it from you. And don't give me that you're totally flat out with work. Dylan and Laoise were over last weekend, and they said you were on a cruise.'

He picked up the phone on his desk. 'Katherine, can you get Carlos and can both of you come in here now, please.' He replaced the receiver.

Corlene's face was a picture of shock. Conor realised he had never spoken to her in that tone before.

'What is going on? You're not yourself. Seriously, you're not on top of things, and it's not like you. I know we've been so busy and you are managing mostly on your own, but I need to be able to rely on you. I just need you to call me back...'

She was off again, but Conor tuned her out. She was hardly ever there, as she was running another business in Dublin. She only showed up in Castle Dysert once a month or so. It suited him in general – Ana didn't like the way Corlene flirted with him, and her overbearing manner and Alabama drawl seemed to put the staff on edge. The truth was, things worked much better when Corlene wasn't there.

Katherine and Carlos Manner, the deputy manager, appeared together, and Corlene caught Carlos's eye. Conor knew he had summoned her.

'Okay, I'm leaving shortly. I wanted to tell all three of you together, but I want your assurance that what I say remains between us.' He met each of their eyes in turn.

'Ana found a lump in her breast, and it's suspicious according to the doctors. We are going to the hospital today for the results of the biopsy, so I'm focusing on my family from now on.'

All three of them stared at him, speechless.

'I'm sorry for being ratty, and for not returning calls and all the rest of it, but I'm worried sick. We are just trying to keep everything ticking over for now, so I'd appreciate your support.'

Corlene walked over and drew him into a hug. Her strong perfume was nauseating. He caught Katherine's eye over her shoulder and saw the empathy and sadness there. All he could think was how Ana would hate to see Corlene's arms around him.

Katherine sensed his discomfort and stepped forward to break up the hug. 'Of course, you must go. Take care of Ana. We'll manage everything here.'

Katherine's cool voice was just what he needed to hear. Corlene was going on about some doctor she knew in Dublin who was a miracle worker. She meant well, he knew, but he didn't need anything except for Ana to be okay.

Katherine distracted Corlene – mid-tale about someone who was cured by a guy after a terminal diagnosis – with some detail of the grand opening of the new wing.

Carlos nodded as Conor left. 'Everything will be kept under control here.' He'd never lost his clipped South African accent, and while he wasn't popular or particularly friendly, he had a meticulous eye for detail. One of the reasons the hotel had five-star reviews all over the internet was because of how well Carlos managed the whole operation from behind the scenes. It was not cheap to stay at Castle Dysert, but it was luxurious, and every whim of the guest was seen to.

'Thank you, Carlos,' Conor said.

HIS WIFE WAS ready when he pulled up at the house. The boys were inside with Danika, who knew nothing of the trips to the hospital. Ana knew her mother – if she told her, she would go straight into doom mode. Danika was lovely, and Conor really liked her, but there was a melancholy to her that was always threatening to take over her cheery disposition. Ana said it was something to do with the Soviets, but then she blamed them for everything. Artur, he suspected, knew something was wrong with his daughter as they were extremely close, and if it had been anything else, his father-in-law would have been there when he made his announcement to Katherine, Carlos and Corlene. Artur was the operations and maintenance manager of the castle, and there was nothing he couldn't fix. But they had decided to say nothing to anyone until they knew more. They told Danika and Artur a white lie that they had a meeting; they didn't say where.

'Okay?' he asked as she got into the car beside him. He leaned over and gave her a kiss.

She nodded and held his hand. 'Was it okay for you to leave the hotel?'

He nodded as he turned the car onto the main road. 'I told Katherine, Carlos and Corlene, but swore them to secrecy. They know I'm concentrating on you from now on, so they'll just have to manage on their own. If they ring me today, I swear I'll swing at one of them. Corlene came all the way down from Dublin to have a go at me for not ringing her back. She didn't know how to take it when I nearly took the head off her.'

Ana gave a weak smile; she could just imagine it. It took a lot to rile Conor. He seemed to have endless patience, but even he had a breaking point.

'Anyway, don't mind about them. Let's just focus on you, all right?'

They drove the short distance to the hospital, and he held her hand as they walked into the new oncology suite. The staff there were friendly and efficient and directed them to a waiting room where they would be called.

Ana tried to leaf through a magazine, and Conor glanced at the morning paper, but they were both too agitated to concentrate. After what felt like an hour but in reality was ten minutes, a nurse popped her head round the door.

'Anastasia O'Shea?'

She smiled pleasantly, and Conor and Ana followed her to a consulting room. 'I'm one of the oncology nurses here – Katie is my name. I'm just going to take you down to the consultant first, and then you'll be back to us, okay?'

Conor squeezed his wife's hand. 'Thanks,' he answered.

Poor Ana looked terrified.

The doctor was there ahead of them, and she stood up to shake hands. She greeted Ana first and then turned to Conor.

'I'm Dr Sunita Khatri. It's nice to meet you. You're Anastasia's husband, I take it?'

'Yes, I am. Conor.' He shook her hand. Something about her gave him confidence. She seemed kind and gentle but efficient.

'Now, we have the results of the biopsy, which we did with a core needle. We took a piece of the suspicious tissue and examined it under a microscope, and I'm sorry to tell you that the cells are cancerous. It is stage 2, and there is a negative margin, which means as far as we know now, the cancer has not spread further than the borders of the tumour. Your lymph nodes are clear, but we will need to do more tests to be sure and determine a plan of treatment. Your cancer is called an invasive ductal carcinoma, often found in older women actually, but it can occur in younger women such as yourself. I am going to suggest a lumpectomy as soon as possible because you have stage 2B, which means the tumour is larger than five centimetres, but does not, at this stage, appear to have spread. We'll follow that with a course of chemotherapy, then radiation, and we'll take it from there. I'm sorry the news is not better, but please try to stay positive at this stage – survival rates are very high.'

Conor knew that Ana would not have got all of that information. Her English was fluent but accented, and when it came to medical things, she had trouble understanding because of the unfamiliar jargon. That, added to the fact that she was upset, meant he needed to pay very close attention.

'By very high, what do you mean?' he asked, dreading the answer. Anything less than 100 percent was less than he would hope.

'Ninety percent?' The doctor smiled. 'Look, I understand this is a shock. Nobody wants to hear this news. But please trust me, I am confident that we can have a very good outcome here. Anastasia, you are young and strong with no other underlying medical issues – you stand an excellent chance of recovery.'

She gave them as much time as they needed, and they asked more questions: how the treatment was likely to affect her, the time scale, the drugs. She answered each one patiently and as fully as she could. Conor liked her; she didn't sugarcoat it, but she had a nice manner.

Afterwards, they had lunch and discussed everything. Conor was enraged to see six missed calls from Castle Dysert – how could they? They knew he needed to be with Ana today. He dismissed the notifications in frustration.

A message popped up: *Conor, ring me. It's urgent. I wouldn't call if it wasn't. Its personal, not hotel business. K*

Ana was in the bathroom, so he scrolled to Katherine's personal mobile number and pressed Call. Instantly, she answered. 'Conor, how is Ana?'

'It's cancer. We hoped it wasn't but it is. What do you need me for?' He didn't want Ana to come back to find him discussing her health with Katherine.

'A man has turned up. He has a reservation and everything, but he's looking for you.'

He sighed in exasperation. 'Well, I'm not available. Can't you take a message?' This wasn't like her. She normally guarded him like a pet Rottweiler, hardly allowing anyone to take up his time. She knew better than anyone what Ana meant to him, so why was she bothering him like this?

'I've tried, but he knows where you live – don't ask me how – and he's threatening to go over there. Conor, he says his name is James O'Shea and that he's your father.'

He was speechless. Surely it couldn't be. His father had walked out when Conor was eight years old, never to be heard from again. Rumours he'd heard growing up were that his father had left with some young woman he'd gotten pregnant, but his family in Cork never knew for sure. For so long, he raged at his father for leaving them, for not caring, for forcing his abandoned wife to face the humiliation of a small town where everyone was stuck in everyone's business. But he'd not thought about him for years, and if his father ever entered his head, he assumed the man was dead. He'd be in his seventies now, he supposed.

'Conor, are you there?' He heard Katherine's voice. 'What do you want us to do?'

Conor thought quickly. 'Tell him I'll come up to the hotel when I'm ready and I'll see him then. I have to go.' He hung up. Ana was on her way back from the bathroom. She had enough on her plate without knowing about this.

CHAPTER 3

*H*e stood in front of the mirror in the downstairs bathroom. Ana was sleeping upstairs; she was physically and emotionally exhausted after the morning in the hospital. He did not want to leave, but he had to go and deal with his father – if that's who this guy really was – before he showed up on the doorstep.

He was tired too; all he wanted to do was climb into bed and hold his darling wife while she slept. He hated the idea that she went through the beginnings of this on her own because she thought he was too busy. He should not have put anything before her and the boys, especially not a job.

He splashed some cold water on his face to revive himself.

He didn't feel fifty-three, and people said he didn't look it either. But he suspected that was because he'd had silver hair since his early forties, so maybe he'd looked older for years. He wondered if his father would recognise him. He had no mental picture of Jamsie O'Shea. There was one old photo that his mother had kept in the back of a drawer – his leaving broke her heart – but Conor had thrown it in the fire after she died.

He went into the kitchen to see the boys before he left. He needed to spend more time with them, especially now.

'Dad,' Joe piped up as he entered the kitchen. His eight-year-old son looked so cute in his Man United jersey and shorts. 'Are you going to be late? 'Cause we've a blitz down in the club at six and Mammy said she can't go, so can you go instead? Me and Artie are the whole back line on our own 'cause Sean Dullea is after fracturing his ankle, so we're a man down.'

He ruffled his son's hair and helped him open the box of crackers he was struggling with. 'I'll be there.' He kissed Joe on the head.

He went to the bottom of the stairs to look for his other son, but Artie was already on the bottom step. He leapt like a cat up into his father's arms.

'Did Joe talk to you about the blitz?' he asked.

Conor smiled. Artie's blonde hair was flopping over his eyes and shaved tight at the back. While not exactly identical, the twins were very alike, and they liked to dress the same and have the same hair-cuts. Ana and he had laughed when they saw the latest style they wanted – apparently, they wanted to look like Angel Gomes, the Manchester United midfielder. The fact that Gomes was black and they were white didn't seem to enter into the debate.

'He did and I'm going. Now come here, the pair of you.' He knelt down in front of his sons and put his arms around their waists.

'Poor Mammy isn't feeling too good, so she must be allowed to stay in bed as long as possible. So no noise and definitely no going up to ask her anything. Babusya is here to look after you, so ask her for whatever you need, okay? Promise me?'

'We promise,' they chorused.

Conor felt his heart melt. He adored his boys, and the idea that he would just take off one day and leave them was so inconceivable, it made the idea of meeting his father again even more repugnant.

They were going to tell Danika and Artur that night when the boys were in bed. He knew Ana was dreading it, especially informing her mother, but it had to be done.

He drove towards the castle, trying to envisage how the meeting with his father would go. Only one thought popped into his head since he heard the news – that he wanted him gone. He had absolutely no interest whatsoever in meeting him again. As far as he was concerned, Jamsie O'Shea was dead – and good riddance too.

As he turned off the coast road, the sun sparkled off the azure Atlantic and the gardens of the castle were a riot of colour. It was hard to believe anything could go wrong when the world looked so perfect. The builders were putting the finishing touches on the restored wing. He didn't like to go there. His children had almost died in that fire, set malevolently by a man who wanted revenge on Corlene. If he had not been warned by a little boy in Edwardian clothes – a boy he fully believed was the ghost of Grenville King, who perished in a fire in that very castle in 1920 – he would never have known to run into the building and save his children. Grenville was at peace now, and Joe and Artie were safe. And despite Conor having a lot of scarring on his back, all he felt was gratitude.

As he parked, he saw his father-in-law coming towards him. Artur was wiry and small but strong as an ox and efficient like nobody else. Conor had taken him on to give him a hand in the early days of the renovations, but everyone agreed now that they could not be without him.

'Artur, how are things?' he said as he locked the car. He tried to stay cheerful and friendly despite all he had on his mind. Artur had learned English from Joe and did not do small talk. He fell into step beside Conor as they walked through the landscaped grounds.

'I want you tell to me what is wrong. I see something with my eyes for my daughter – she is not happy. Please, we are worried, Danika and me. If something is wrong, please tell to me.'

Conor thought for a second. Perhaps it would be best to tell Artur first; then he might be better able to handle Danika. He stopped and turned to face Ana's father. He took a deep breath.

'Okay, Artur, we were going to tell you both tonight anyway. Ana has been diagnosed with breast cancer. The prognosis is good...' He saw the confusion on the older man's face. 'The doctors say she will be fine. They can take it away.'

'Anastasia have the cancer? I... I... Here?' He pointed to his own chest.

17

'Breast.' Conor gave him the word. 'Yes, she does. I know it's a shock, but she's in the early stages, and she is going to be well – the doctors say so.'

Artur exhaled a ragged breath. 'My little girl... It should be me. I am old, she is not. Artie and Joe need her, and you need her... Is not right. Is not right...' He shook his head.

Conor put his hand on the older man's shoulder. 'They need us to be strong now. I know Danika will take this badly, and between you and me, I'm sick with worry over Ana too. But we have to be strong for them.'

His father-in-law nodded. 'Yes, of course. Will you tell the boys?' He exhaled, steadying himself, and gradually the capable man appeared again.

'Not yet. We'll just say she's not well, but I don't want to scare them.'

Artur patted him on the back. 'Good. Yes, we don't say, not now anyway.' He turned to go back to the builders' yard, concealed from the rest of the hotel behind landscaped hoardings.

Conor walked to the side entrance beside his office. He liked to wander around the hotel from time to time. The staff were used to him, and it did no harm to pop in unannounced in the various areas just to keep everyone on their toes. But today, he needed to deal with this new development and move on to what really mattered.

He called Katherine in. 'So is he still here?'

'He is. Said he'd stay as long as necessary to talk to you.' Her cheeks turned red with indignation. 'I tried to take a number and have you ring him, but he just kept saying he would wait.'

'What's he like?' Forewarned was forearmed. He could trust Katherine. If he could hear him out, let him say whatever he wanted to say and then get rid of him, Ana need never know.

'Very like you, actually, an older version. You are similar to him in appearance, and he goes on with all that old rubbish, trying to charm people, just like you. The waitresses are eating out of his hand. He's had lunch and a few coffees.'

Conor sighed. 'Right, send him in to me. I'd better get this over with. I need this now like a hole in the head.'

'Take a moment to compose yourself – I'll send him in then. And I won't keep asking about Ana, but you know that if either of you need anything, anything at all, please just ask. She is such a young woman, with a family. It's not fair.'

He smiled. 'I know that, Katherine. We count you among our closest friends, and we really appreciate everything. It's going to be a rocky few months ahead, but please God, she'll come out the other end. The prognosis is as good as it can be with cancer, and she trusts the doctor, which is good. So we'll just have to take one day at a time.'

'Indeed. Right. Well, I'll have Mr O'Shea called then.'

CHAPTER 4

*C*onor sat behind his desk, something he rarely did. Corlene had insisted he have a large walnut desk and a fancy leather chair for those occasions when he needed to be 'managerial,' but Conor found it much easier just to chat with the staff informally when there was an issue. Today he was glad of it. He had to admit that when he first saw the architect's plans for his office, a beautiful room downstairs with a huge bay window overlooking the front lawns, it felt like too much. The cream deep-pile carpet, the antique filing cabinets, the twin sofas facing each other over a rosewood coffee table – it all felt vaguely ridiculous and very ostentatious, but Katherine and Ana had backed Corlene, and they won out.

Had Bert lived to see what his legacy achieved, Conor felt he would have taken his view. He smiled at Bert's photo on the wall. The man who made all of this possible. It felt like a lifetime ago that he took Bert Cooper and Corlene and a whole bunch of others on a tour of Ireland. He was only a lowly tour bus driver in those days, and he could never have envisaged how his life would change. He'd met the love of his life, had twin boys, and inherited a legacy from Bert that allowed him and Corlene to bring Castle Dysert back from dereliction to Ireland's finest five-star resort. He thought about his father, landing back after so many years. How dare he? Who did he think he was showing up out of the blue like this?

There was a gentle knock on the door, and then it opened. Katherine ushered a tall, silver-haired man inside. His hair was longish and swept back from his forehead. He wore a cream suit and had a silk scarf tied at his throat, and in his hands, he held a panama hat. He was deeply tanned and certainly looked very exotic.

'Hello, Conor, it's nice to see you again.' The man's accent was neutral, not Irish or British or American, but he sounded cultured, something Conor wasn't expecting. He presumed his father would be some kind of a down-and-out looking for a handout, and maybe he was and this was an act. Whatever he was after, he wasn't getting it anyway.

'What do you want?' he asked, neither rising from the chair nor offering his father a seat.

The man gave a small, sad smile. 'I wasn't expecting the fatted calf, son. I suspect you never thought you'd lay eyes on me again. How have you been?'

Conor sat back and gazed at the man who had abandoned his family over forty years earlier and tried to formulate an appropriate response. The anger and frustration, buried for decades, bubbled to the surface, and he said much more than he intended.

'I haven't thought about you for years. I assumed you were dead actually, not that it matters. You made your choice the day you left me and Gerry and Mam – and you killed her by doing that, by the way, in case you're interested. I was sixteen when she died. Having suffered years of humiliation and people whispering behind her back, she got cancer. I had to rear Gerry on my own, and if it weren't for Mary Harrington, he'd have wound up in care. But none of that mattered to you then, so you don't matter to me now. I don't know why you're here, or what you want or hope to achieve, but if some happy reunion is what you had in mind, that's not going to happen.' Conor felt the loss of both his parents blindside him.

'May I?' Jamsie asked, pointing at the chair on the other side of the desk. Without waiting for an answer, he sat down.

'I understand why you're angry. I behaved appallingly, and you'd be dead right to throw me out on my ear – nobody would blame you if you did. But if you could hear me out, then maybe I can convince you that I am truly sorry.' He wrung his hat as he spoke.

Conor didn't have time for this. 'Look, whether you're sorry or not is frankly of no interest to me. As far as I'm concerned, Jamsie O'Shea left and never returned. The reasons why, or how you feel about it now, mean nothing to me. Now if that's all you have to say, can I suggest you go back to wherever you came from and let me be?'

He knew he sounded harsh, but he just didn't care. He was out of his mind with worry about Ana, and this eejit showing up was the last thing he needed. The man's open smile and manner that seemed to think they were two old buddies meeting up for a friendly chat got under Conor's skin.

'I hear you're married and you've two little boys – that's just wonderful. I'm so happy for you that life worked out so well. I'd love to meet them. I bet you're a great dad, not like me. You always were a conscientious little lad. And this place… Well, I'm very impressed. It's absolutely beautiful.'

Conor stood. On his desk was a framed photo of Joe and Artie, who smiled up at him. He was their age when Jamsie left. *How does a man do that?* He could never imagine any situation that would make him abandon his sons.

'Thanks. Now, if you'll excuse me?' Conor opened the door, hoping Jamsie would just walk back out of his life.

'I know you're angry – of course you are – but I would really like it if we could have a chat?' His voice was quieter now, and he looked more vulnerable. But Conor had been around people all his life and had a sense of the genuine, and this guy was a fake. Whatever his reason for showing up, it was selfish. At first, he thought his father was looking for money; however, on the face of it at least, he seemed well turned out – but that meant nothing. A little part of him might have been curious years ago, but that ship had sailed and he genuinely no longer cared. His mother was dead, his brother Gerry long gone – he'd lost touch with him years ago. Ana, Joe and Artie were his family and he had great friends, so he had no need of this man whose blood flowed in his veins but who was not his father, not in any real sense.

He remembered vividly the confusion. He had been only eight years old. His mother always said that he was like a miniature Jamsie, following him everywhere. Gerry was too small to remember him, and Conor learned quickly to stop asking where his daddy was when he saw the pain on his mother's face. All those happy memories had been obliterated by the abandonment. He watched his mother struggle financially, working her fingers to the bone to keep a roof over their heads and enduring the whispers from the neighbours who in some kind of twisted logic seemed to blame his wife for Jamsie's flit.

Mary Harrington, their old neighbour and his mother's friend, told Conor what a charmer Jamsie O'Shea was, how the women in the small town they lived in vied for his attention. He played hurling and football for the parish and was the star of the team, and, according to Mary, he was the best-looking man for miles around.

'No.'

The short, blunt answer hung between them.

'I'm going to America. I'm trying to track Gerry down. I was hoping you might have a number or an address...'

Conor was astonished at the audacity of the man. Did he really think for one second they could have a happy family reunion? Anyway, last he heard of his brother, he had a hard-drinking lifestyle, so it was very likely he was dead. Gerry was an ungrateful spoiled brat of a child, an indolent teenager and a waste of space as an adult. He took off with the girl Conor was about to marry nearly thirty years ago and disappeared into thin air. The girl, Sinead, made contact a few years back, but Ana was on the scene then, and Sinead soon realised that there was no chance of rekindling anything.

He never discussed his family – or lack thereof – with anyone apart from Ana. He'd told her everything in one go years earlier, and she had the good sense not to raise the matter again. They had no taboo subjects in their marriage, but there was nothing to say, and so they just left it. The boys asked why they had grandparents on their mother's side and not on their dad's, and he told them the truth: Their Granny O'Shea was dead, and he had not seen his father for years. They thought it odd at the time, but Conor said he didn't mind really, and they were happy enough with that explanation.

'I don't. I haven't heard from him in twenty-five years. I don't know. But look, I have a lot on at the moment and I just don't have the time for this, so I'd appreciate it if you'd just let me be.' Conor gestured to the open door, a wave of exhaustion crashing over him.

Reluctantly, Jamsie stood and placed his hat on his head. He stopped beside his son.

'I'm sorry you feel that way, and I suppose I can't blame you. But I'm happy to see the man you've become – without my help.' He opened his wallet. 'Here is my card anyway, in case you ever change your mind. I'd love to hear from you anytime.'

Jamsie patted his son's shoulder, sighed sadly and left the hotel.

Conor looked down at the embossed business card. James O'Shea, with an address in Dublin and an Irish mobile phone number. Had his father been in Ireland all these years? Something about that struck him. He'd always assumed that if his father was alive, he lived in England.

He looked at the card one more time, ripped it in half and cast it into the wastepaper basket.

CHAPTER 5

*K*evin Wilson parked his car up the street from Bubbles O'Leary's bar in Woodside, Queens. Being a Saturday, there was parking off the Grand Central Parkway. Kevin headed towards the green-painted building with the hanging baskets of flowers outside. Someone had watered them at least. The bar was open, Miguel and the rest of the staff trying to keep things ticking over until someone came and told them what to do, he guessed.

Bubbles had no family it seemed, or at least not a family that anyone had ever heard of, and he'd been in New York since the early '80s. To the best of anyone's recollection, nobody from his native Ireland ever visited, nor did he go there. It was weird – Bubbles was the most Irish guy anyone knew. And yet most of the regulars had been over there at least once, and he'd given them recommendations and helped them plan itineraries, but he hadn't been back to his native country in nearly 40 years.

Kevin pushed open the large door, its glass panels engraved with a caricature of Bubbles himself. He stopped, his hand on the door, and felt an unfamiliar prickling at the back of his eyes. Bubbles's flaming-red beard and mad mop of curly hair, his ever-present grin, his dancing eyes that giggled back at him. The artist had given him a huge head and a small body, wearing a leprechaun suit, 'for the craic,' as Bubbles explained. That was his motivation for most things – just for the fun of it.

He was relieved to see Bubbles's main gang of friends there. Miguel had put out coffee and bagels. It was a bit early for booze, even for this lot.

'Hey, Kevin.' Marianne greeted him first. A few others murmured their greetings, but the whole group was subdued. In shock really. Was it only last Friday? It was a moment Kevin knew they would all carry in their memories forever. The usual sing-song was happening, being MC'd by the *fear an tí*, as Bubbles insisted everyone call him. He explained it meant "the man of the house" in Irish. Bubbles refused to allow anyone to call the native Irish language Gaelic, explaining patiently but firmly that in Ireland, the language was called Irish – it only became Gaelic when it came to America.

He held court every night, but Fridays were special. He'd gather musicians, usually young Irish kids on student visas, and they'd play, and people would sing. Bubbles himself had a gorgeous voice, but he liked to let others shine while he managed the whole session. The only song he could be relied upon to sing every night was 'Danny Boy.' He would stand at his bar, and in a slightly growling tenor voice, he would sing that sad lament. Every regular knew the chorus.

'But come ye back when summer's in the meadow, and when the valley's hushed and white with snow, 'tis I'll be there in sunshine or in shadow, oh Danny Boy, oh Danny Boy, I love you so.'

Last Friday was like every other. The usual crowd, a mixed bag. Lawyers and nurses rubbing shoulders with Department of Sanitation workers and pizza delivery guys. Bubbles didn't allow cell phones or work meetings of any kind. He ran a very strict house – craic only. Kevin smiled as he looked at the sign over the bar. On it was a large green flag with the words 'Craic Addict' emblazoned in gold. Newcomers were shocked sometimes, until it was explained to them that in Ireland, 'the craic' is a good thing. That summed up Bubbles O'Leary's – fun and friendship and a place people felt they fit in. In a city like New York, that sense of belonging really was rare, and the regulars cherished the bar and its owner. For some reason, though it was not a singles bar as such, there always seemed to be a lot of single people there, and looking around on this Saturday morning, he recognised everyone – all single, all bereft. It was as if their world stopped turning last Friday.

Bubbles had been teaching everyone a new song. It was about a tree in a bog or something, and you had to keep adding new things in each verse and remember it for the next time. Everyone joined in, the drinks were flowing, and all were in great spirits. Bubbles was surrounded by the crowd – behind him, people were playing fiddles and guitars and uilleann pipes – when he stopped, grabbed his chest and collapsed. At first, everyone thought it was a joke, but as he fell first to his knees and then forward onto his face, one of the customers yelled, 'Call an ambulance!'

Beth Anderson, a doctor at Mount Sinai, tried her best to do CPR, and someone ran to the hotel up the street where there was a defibrillator, but it was too late. Before his friends and customers, Bubbles O'Leary died.

The ambulance arrived and took him away. Most of the people left, but the gang, the inner circle, those people he considered his personal friends, stayed. They didn't have anyone to go home to, and besides, they were all Bubbles had.

Kevin was the natural leader. He didn't really know why that was, maybe because he was a social worker, but the group seemed to look to him for guidance.

They'd had a few more drinks and pooled what information they had about Bubbles, his background and his family. It didn't amount to much.

Kevin sat down, greeting each person with a smile. They were hardly ever in the bar in the mornings, and never without Bubbles. It all felt so wrong.

'What are we going to do?' Marianne Peterson asked, tears in her eyes. 'I don't think he has anyone. It's just us.'

Marianne was in her forties, divorced, no kids. Her husband,

Warren, took off out west two years ago, and she hadn't heard from him since.

'I keep expecting him to come out from the storeroom and joke about how he fooled us all,' Will Munro drawled in his Southern accent. He was a new face in the bar. Bubbles met people and invited them all the time, and the girls were happy with this new addition. Will looked like one of those country singers you see nowadays, Kevin always thought. Not scruffy like Willie Nelson or outdoorsy like Kris Kristofferson – the country singers nowadays looked like supermodels. All tanned, ripped and polished. Will was like that. Kevin guessed he was just jealous – nobody ever looked at him the way they looked at Will.

'I know. Me too,' Kevin agreed.

'Should we call the hospital, or go down there or something?' Annie deLancey asked. 'As Marianne says, there's nobody else as far as we know. I don't know what they do in those circumstances.' Annie was an all-American girl with her blonde hair and white teeth. She looked more like someone you'd find hanging out in a cocktail bar in Manhattan, but she loved Bubbles just like everyone else did.

'Do you know, Jimmy?' Marianne turned to the man sitting at the bar. He worked as a road sweeper on the Lower East Side. He was older than most of them, possibly around sixty. He didn't encourage chat, but once you got to know him, he was a very well-read man. He held a doctorate in philosophy from Molloy College but never left the city's sanitation department. He was a conundrum, but those who knew him liked him.

'Well,' he drawled. Jimmy Burns always spoke slowly. It gave the impression that he wasn't the sharpest, but nothing could have been further from the truth. 'Bodies of vagrants or victims of crimes usually go to the Chief Medical Examiner's morgue until someone claims them…if they do. If nobody shows up, then the body is buried, no ceremony or anything. But they don't cremate them either – too many religions are against cremation, and a body can always be exhumed at a later date.'

28

'Okay, well, should we claim him then? Can you do that if you're not a relative?' Marianne wondered.

'The cops will try to find a family member,' Kevin explained. 'But I think they'll let us claim him. Unless there is something among his things mentioning a family member?'

'Should we look?' Beth seemed unsure. She'd tried her very best to save him, but she knew, even when she was working on him, that it was futile. Bubbles died within seconds of the myocardial infarction.

They looked uncertainly from one to the other.

Bubbles was such a hospitable man, so welcoming and gentle, but none of them, except Miguel, had ever been upstairs in his private rooms. It felt wrong somehow to go poking about up there.

'Not now anyway,' Kevin decided. 'Let's give the cops a few days to do what they need to do. I can call someone I know in this precinct and explain the situation as far as we understand it. Let's take it from there, are we agreed?'

Kevin would never forget the look on Miguel's face. He was the Mexican bar manager, and he and Bubbles were very close. Kevin suspected for a long time that Miguel, and possibly even Bubbles, were in the United States illegally. It was never said, and Bubbles was on good terms with the local police, but it would explain why neither man ever seemed to go back home.

Annie and Marianne were sitting together, both stricken. Jimmy leaned on the bar, sipping coffee, and Will was standing, studying the huge photo montage of Bubbles and all his customers that covered one wall.

Erin and her sister, Shannon, hadn't said a word. They met Bubbles when they took a conversational Irish class at the Irish Center on Long Island. Bubbles was helping out at the Senior Lunch Club, and he suggested they do the same. Erin worked as a secretary in a law firm, and Shannon was a doctor's receptionist. Neither had ever married. Their parents were Irish but both dead. They took him up on the idea and found it very rewarding. Though they didn't drink, Bubbles gradually coaxed them into coming to his bar, and soon their lives opened up in a way they could never have imagined. They were middle-aged, quiet and timid, but over time, people got to know them, and now they were part of the gang.

Kevin suddenly had an idea. 'Y'know what would be cool? I don't know if we could, or even if you guys would want to, but how about – if no family members show up obviously – we have Bubbles cremated and we take him back to Ireland and scatter his ashes?'

He looked around, and while the group seemed surprised, there was general positivity towards the idea.

'We've never been abroad,' Erin admitted. 'But if we were to go anywhere, Ireland would be top of the list.'

Shannon nodded encouragingly.

'Sounds like a great idea,' Marianne said. 'I could use a vacation, and it would be so nice to do that for Bubbles.'

'I'm in.' Annie was excited. 'Bubbles was always telling us we should go there. I wish we could take him in life, but if not, then this is something we could do for him after all he's done for us.'

The idea grew on them, and soon they were discussing it like it was a done deal.

'Okay, folks,' Kevin interrupted. 'Let's see if it's a runner first. If it is, I think if we just put a notice up, anyone who wants to go?'

Everyone agreed.

'So will we meet again?' Erin asked.

Kevin nodded. 'Same time next Saturday? Miguel can let the cops deal with whatever they need to do.'

Miguel sat down to join them, pouring himself a coffee. 'I know where Bubbles kept his papers. I've sent everything to his lawyer. I'll just keep this place going until I know more. I don't think Bubbles had any relatives here, and he wasn't in touch with anyone in Ireland, so maybe we should think about his funeral. I think it's just going to be us.'

* * *

MIGUEL SANCHEZ LOCKED the door as the last customers left. He'd cleared up around them, so the bar was clean and tidy; the brass and glass behind the bar shone. Bubbles had loved this place, and made sure it was always looking its best. He went behind the bar and poured himself a beer. Before he drank it, he went to the back to his locker and extracted his camera. It was a Nikon D850 DSLR, top of the range. Bubbles had bought it for him for his birthday years ago.

He snapped the bar from every angle. He even took a few of the outside of the building. Bubbles had a really nice printer, and he encouraged Miguel to make photo postcards to send home to his mother back in San Luis de la Paz. Miguel had always sent her post-cards since the day he left, but being illegal, he had to be careful. He had told Bubbles how he sent hundreds of postcards to his mother as he travelled through America but how he wished he could send her real pictures of his life – not just the Statue of Liberty or the Brooklyn Bridge, but of Bubbles's bar and the streets he walked every day. It was after that conversation that Bubbles gave him the camera.

For years, Bubbles would take a picture of Miguel at various land-marks and then Miguel would print them as postcards and send them. He tried to picture his mama with all the postcards now – over the years there must have been hundreds – seeing her son in New York City. He wondered, was she proud or was she just lonely? Her letters came every single month, addressed to Bubbles as a precaution in case ICE were monitoring post from Mexico, and she told him about life in the village, about his family, the births and deaths. They were cheerful and full of news, but every letter ended with the same thing: *Take care of yourself, my* chiquito. *I pray that someday I will see your face again. Your loving mother.*

The idea for the postcards was Bubbles's. He too was illegal, though nobody knew that – Bubbles went about like he owned the place; nothing frightened him. He would take the train or even fly someplace once a year, take a photo of himself, turn it into a postcard and send it home to his mother. Each one said the same three words, nothing more. *I love you.*

Miguel scrolled back in his camera, looking at photos he'd taken of himself and Bubbles just two weeks ago. His heart was breaking.

CHAPTER 6

'That man Kevin Wilson has rung again. I told him you'd call him back. I explained that you were really very busy and that you might not be available to take them – he seemed upset by that. There have been some changes to the booking, adding someone, removing another. I don't know why people can't just be organised to begin with and save everyone all this palaver.' Katherine listed off all the messages she'd gathered for Conor in the days he'd been away from the hotel. They were standing at the reception desk, which was quiet for once.

'I know he wants me to take a tour,' Conor said, 'and I know we could do with having one big group, but I've been thinking. How about we compromise? I won't go away around the country – I can't leave Ana, obviously – but if they want to do day tours and base themselves here, then I can take them out and about?'

'I think that would work beautifully. Especially since they want to go to the matchmaking festival in Lisdoonvarna, though why that would appeal to anyone is totally beyond me. It's something to do with a publican with the ridiculous name of Bubbles who died. Anyway, can you please call him back and arrange it? You know much more about this sort of thing than me.'

He smiled. 'I don't know, Katherine... You're still not tempted to head up to Lisdoon? You never know your luck!' He winked at her and thought he caught a glimpse of a smile.

'Oh, let me assure you that some farmer with a plastic bag in his pocket to keep the tractor seat dry will not lure me to some cottage on the side of a mountain to be his slave.'

'Ah, that's not a very romantic attitude now, is it?' He chuckled.

Katherine was glad to see him in better spirits. 'Romance? For goodness sake, would you have sense. The road to misery and nothing more. Anyway, more importantly, how's Ana?'

'Do you know what? She's doing okay. They did the lumpectomy – they didn't need to take the whole breast – and it's stage 2, but they are happy they got it all. She's sore and not looking forward to the chemotherapy that's starting next week, but her spirits are good. We were in with the oncology team yesterday, and they are really happy with how she's responded to everything so far. I'm thinking of taking her away somewhere nice for a night or two before the chemo starts, just the two of us. Dylan and Laoise are around to mind the lads, which is brilliant. They were on tour in the States for the last month – packed out the Irish centres and pubs of New York and Boston, as you can only imagine – but they are taking a break from touring for a bit while they prepare for the new album. If it was anyone other than that pair of lunatics offering to babysit, the lads would be whining to come with us, but they are stone mad about both of them.'

Dylan was Corlene's son. He'd gone on that first tour with her as a surly teenager and fell in love with Irish music and a wild Irish girl called Laoise, and now they were fast becoming household names in the music world.

'How did Joe and Artie take the news about the cancer?' Katherine asked directly. Other people skirted around the word, but she was not one for euphemisms.

'We did tell them. Sure, in the hospital you meet everyone, so they would have heard it anyway. But they were okay about it. We toned it down, just said that Ana was sick and that she would get better but it would take a while. Once we reassured them, they were fine. They've been so great actually, really taking care of her. And even in the weeks since this whole thing started, they've grown up and are doing more things for themselves. They're great boys.' Conor's pride in his children shone from his face.

Katherine beamed, a rare event. 'Oh, they really are. Ana is so lucky to have you three. I'm so relieved. Father Eddie said he is inundated with locals asking him to say Mass for Ana, and people are constantly asking if they can help, but I've deliberately kept them away from you. You had enough to deal with, and though people mean well, it's easier to just paddle your own canoe.'

'Ah, sure, people are very good,' Conor said as he leafed through a bundle of post she had sorted for him. 'I might ring Eddie, actually. Ana told me to play golf this weekend – I think she's getting sick of me hanging around her, to be honest.' He looked up and smiled. 'Dylan and Laoise are playing at that festival near Athlone at the end of the month, and Ana says she's going with Valentina and a few more women. I think Corlene is going too. She's so proud of Dylan now – it's great to see. If anything, they are even closer than your average mother and son after all they've been through. Anyway, I don't know if Ana should go, but she's determined, and once that wife of mine gets a notion in her head, you can't lead nor drive her.'

'She's a wonderful woman, and you're so lucky to have her,' Katherine said, pretending to be stern; she knew how much he loved his wife. 'And yes, Corlene is finally taking to motherhood in a way none of us could have envisaged. Now by all means, play golf, but you have a mountain of work to get through first, so get into that office now and get cracking.'

Conor rolled his eyes, nudging Meghan who had just arrived for her shift. 'Do you ever wonder who the boss is here, me or her?' He jerked his thumb in Katherine's direction, joking with the head receptionist in a way nobody else dared.

'No, Conor,' Meghan answered. 'I never wonder. We all know Miss O'Brien is the boss.' She giggled, and Katherine shot her a glance, at which she reddened. She took off her jacket and went straight to work.

* * *

THE DAY FLEW BY. He did a round of the hotel, calling on the kitchens, housekeeping, office staff, and maintenance team, stopping for a cup of Ukrainian coffee with his father-in-law. They talked about the progress of Ana's treatment, and Conor reassured him that everything was going to plan. Artur seemed visibly relieved.

'I know I don't need to thank you, Artur, but you and Danika have just been incredible. Taking care of the boys and the house and Ana. We'd be lost without you both – I mean it.'

'You are right,' Artur said, rinsing the coffee cups. 'You don't need. Anastasia is our daughter, and you and Joe and Artie are our family also. You give us chance, Danika and me. When in Ukraine, it seem so bad, no work, no money. We nearly lose our apartment. We should thank you.'

'It's worked out great for all of us.' Conor smiled and patted the other man on the back. 'Now I better get back to it or Katherine will string me up.'

'She protect you like lion.' Artur laughed.

'I know.' He nodded. 'But that doesn't mean I'm not scared of her!'

As he was returning to his office, having admired photos of a barman's new baby and commiserated with the porter on the death of his elderly mother, he caught up with Carlos outside on the lawn that led to the ocean. The deputy manager was berating one of the younger gardeners for putting out his cigarette on the gravel drive-way. He was holding the offending butt between finger and thumb like it was a dead mouse. He found the item days ago but had checked back on the CCTV to find the culprit. The unfortunate lad was caught red-handed, and Carlos was giving him holy hell.

Though Conor was the general manager and Carlos only the deputy, everyone addressed Conor by his first name but everyone except Conor and Katherine called Carlos 'Mr Manner'. The young gardener looked relieved to see the boss approach, but Conor stood back until Carlos was finished. They didn't undermine each other. Carlos initially had been inclined to be too harsh on the staff, but he

35

had mellowed a little, so Conor didn't interfere too much. And as Corlene pointed out, if Conor wanted to be Mr Nice Guy, someone had to crack the whip.

When the gardener had been dismissed with dire warnings that it was never to happen again, Conor approached.

'Hi, Carlos,' he began. The other man did not enjoy chit-chat, so he got right to the point. 'Thanks for holding down the fort so well this past while. Ana is doing okay considering everything, so I appreciate it.'

'Of course, and I'm glad your wife's health is being taken care of appropriately.'

Conor often wondered what on earth had drawn the man into the hospitality industry. There was no doubting his efficiency or attention to detail, but he was possibly the most inhospitable person Conor had ever met. Luckily, he left customer relations mostly to his boss and Katherine, and he handled the smooth running of the hotel behind the scenes, something he did with aplomb.

'It is, and it's been hard on her, but she is such a trooper. She starts chemotherapy next week, so of course she's not looking forward to it. But the sooner they start, the sooner it will hopefully be all over and she can get her life back.' He ventured a smile, but this level of intimacy was clearly outside Carlos's comfort zone.

'Yes, indeed. Now, I must get back to work.' The deputy manager nodded curtly and walked away.

Conor watched him go. He might be very competent, he thought, but Carlos Manner was one peculiar puppy.

CHAPTER 7

'Child Protective Services, how may I direct your call?'

'Good afternoon. My name is Conor O'Shea from Castle Dysert in Ireland. I'd like to speak to Mr Kevin Wilson, please.'

'One moment, please.' The tinny-sounding receptionist put him on hold.

'Hello, Conor?' A deep rumbling voice came on the line. Though he was in New York, he had the long, slow vowels of Boston. 'Kaah-naah' – the way this man said his name reminded him of his old friend Ellen O'Donovan.

'Hi, Kevin. Apologies for the delay in getting back to you. Now, Katherine tells me you want to come over here with a group in September?' Conor glanced at his watch. He hoped to wind this conversation up quickly as he had a lot to catch up on.

'Yes. There's a group of eight of us. We'd like to stay at your hotel, and we were hoping you could be our guide? Your reputation precedes you.' The other man chuckled.

'Oh really? And who recommended me?' Conor hoped he'd remember the name. He'd taken so many groups on tours of Ireland in his long career, he couldn't remember them all.

'My old history teacher actually. Her name was Ellen O'Donovan.'

His heart sank. Kevin's use of the past tense could only mean one thing.

'I remember Ellen very well, and her incredible story. I was privileged to be with her when she went back to Inchigeelagh to discover the story of her life and to visit her family there. A very special lady.'

'She sure was. She taught at my high school, and that was not easy, I can assure you. But you know, everyone liked her and treated her with respect. I guess she treated us the same way, and that wasn't the norm for professional college-educated people dealing with kids from Southie. She kind of set the tone. She expected us to be respectful to her and to each other, and in return, she was the same way. We loved her, and I stayed in touch with her when I left school, even after I moved to New York. I'd always visit when I was home in Boston, and my daughter loved her house. It was always full of interesting things, and she let her explore to her heart's content while we talked.'

Conor sighed sadly. 'I'm taking from the way you're talking that Ellen has passed on? I didn't hear.'

'Oh, I'm so sorry. I thought you knew. Yes, she died seven months ago, in her sleep. She wasn't really sick or anything, though she did have heart trouble, and the autopsy said a heart attack. She wouldn't have known a thing. Her family came over from Ireland for the memorial service, and we got to meet them. It was lovely, a real celebration of her life.'

Conor thought about Ellen often and how she had extended an invitation in her annual Christmas card for him and Ana and the boys to visit her in Boston. He had fully intended to go; now it was too late. He felt so sad. She and Bert had been on the same tour years ago, and they had been firm friends ever since. Bert died two years ago, and now Ellen. Conor judged she must have been in her mid-eighties.

'No, I didn't know. I would have liked to pay my respects. As I said, she was a wonderful person, and she invited my family to visit many times, but we never got round to it. I really wish I had now.'

'Well, she spoke very highly of you, and she talked so fondly of Ireland. One evening, she told me her story, about her dad being in the IRA on the run from the British and how he took her as a newborn over here. That whole story about her mother's murder and her uncle Michael and the wedding and the coat and everything – wow, truth really is stranger than fiction sometimes, isn't it?'

Conor warmed to this man. He seemed so genuine and he clearly loved Ellen.

'It certainly is. I'll never forget that day for as long as I live. Now, so on Ellen's recommendation, you're coming to visit Ireland, so I'll have to make sure you're taken good care of. What did you have in mind?'

'Well…' Kevin sounded a bit doubtful. 'This might sound crazy, but we are a bunch of regulars from a bar here in New York called Bubbles O'Leary's. The guy who owned it, Bubbles, was a real larger-than-life character. His real name was Finbarr – I only found that out after he died, as everyone just called him Bubbles. His bar was a kind of home for so many people, and sadly, a few months back, he died. He doesn't have any family here, and he has had no contact from his family in Ireland for many decades as far as we can make out, so we – his friends, I mean – were all he had. We weren't sure what to do, but in the end, we had him cremated. Though he had no contact with Ireland and he never went back – I'm not sure exactly, but I think he might have been illegal over here or something, but anyway – he was the most Irish guy you could meet. He loved the country, and he had so many stories, so much advice for anyone visiting. If you heard him, you'd think the guy left last week.'

Conor knew by the way Kevin was talking that he had great personal affection for this Bubbles character.

'We want to bring him home, scatter his ashes there.'

Conor smiled. 'That's a lovely idea. Do you know where he came from?'

'No, we don't know anything about him really. Miguel Sanchez – he's the bar manager, and he and Bubbles were very close – thought he was from near Dingle. He was definitely from Kerry, we know that for sure. It's so funny and kind of sad too. We all saw him all the time, had so many talks and jokes and everything. He really was a fun guy, everyone loved him. But only now that he's gone, we all realise he never talked about himself. He never married, and he's been single for as long as anyone knows him. He lived up over the bar.'

Kevin paused, perhaps a bit choked up. It was hard to tell on the phone.

Conor spoke. 'That's okay, though. We can find somewhere to scatter his ashes – you'll know the place when we find it. Now, I have to be honest, I was going to try to wriggle out of this one. Nothing personal, but my wife is not well at the moment, and we have twin boys who are just eight, so they need me to be around and not tearing off around the country. But especially because you're a friend of Ellen's, I can offer you two options. First one is take a tour of Ireland, and I'll find you a really good guide, someone handpicked by me, and I'll guarantee you'll have a great time. The other possibility is you can base yourselves here at this hotel, and we can do day trips and get back here every night. I'm happy to do either, but I can't stay away overnight right now.' Conor hoped he'd understand.

'Oh, well, that's a no-brainer for us.' Kevin sounded relieved. 'We want you, so if we have to slum it in a five-star Irish castle for a week, then so be it.' He chuckled. 'I know we won't get to see all of the country, but that doesn't matter. Anyone who wants to do more can arrive before the main group or stay after we leave. Now, as well as Bubbles, we have...um...another request.'

Conor noted the change in his tone from confident to sheepish. 'Go on. If it can be done, we'll do it.'

'Well,' Kevin went on, 'the other thing that all of our group have in common, apart from our connection to Bubbles, is that we are all single. And well, we heard Bubbles often talking about the matchmaking festival someplace near you, and we thought he'd get a kick out of it if we tied it in with our trip, just for the craic, as Bubbles would say.'

'Of course we can. It's on for the whole month of September, and what you need to do is make an application ahead of time. I think you can download the application form now, if you go to their website. Be warned though, that's where the high-tech ends. The whole show is run by the matchmaker, a man called Paudie Mac, and he'll see who might suit you. They have remarkable success actually, and as you so fluently say it in our Hiberno-English, it's great craic.'

They talked for a few more minutes, Kevin telling Conor about the 'Craic Addict' sign in Bubbles's bar. Conor suggested they bring that flag as their emblem for the trip.

'Okay, I'll put you onto Katherine on reception. She'll deal with the details, and I'll see you all in September.'

He hung up and sat back. He hadn't taken a tour for four years – after the last one, he swore he was done. A priest on the run from the mob, Ana's friend Valentina who lived there now had been trafficked by an American who was now serving a long sentence in an Irish prison, and a nice old lady who went there to die. *And yet here we go again*, he thought. He wondered what this next one held.

CHAPTER 8

*K*evin saw the incoming call and his heart sank. If Debbie was calling him, it was bad. He could hear his mother's voice in his head. 'You'll regret it, Kevin. She's not right for you. She's not the one.'

The child support probably ran out again and she needed more money, or someone had told her there was a way to make him pay for something else. It was never anything else with her. Try as he might, he could not recall a time when things were good. There must have been, surely, but he just couldn't remember it. Eight years of miserable marriage, followed by a miserable divorce. He had his daughter to show for it, and he loved Tess with all his heart, but he wondered how long it would be before Debbie poisoned her little mind against him. She only let him take her at the weekends without a fuss because it suited her. She was unpredictable and used Tess as a bargaining chip. The woman was a total nightmare, and he could not believe they had stayed together so long. She hated him and constantly criticised his weight. He was carrying some extra pounds, no doubt about it, but she was a gym bunny who existed on kale and protein shakes.

He picked Tess up every Saturday morning and took her back on

Sunday afternoon. Most weeks, he would take her to the park. They would ride their bikes, and then they'd call on Bubbles for lunch. Tess loved the big Irishman, with his flaming-red hair and bushy red beard – she said he was like Santa Claus – and he loved her. A wave of sadness at the loss of his friend threatened to engulf Kevin once more.

People should listen to their mothers. He put his cell in his pocket; he'd call her back. He picked up the desk phone and asked Natalie the receptionist to send in the mother and son who were waiting to see him. The door buzzed and clicked open. They'd had security doors fitted last year to stop people marching in and demanding that children who had been taken into care be returned.

A weary, overweight black woman stood before him with a mutinous boy beside her. Kevin guessed he was around fourteen. He was all gangster, from the haircut to the clothes. Kevin had seen it a million times before.

He looked at the file Natalie had placed on his desk. This mother had taken the unusual step of contacting them. His job meant he was almost always dealing with hostile parents who were resisting having their children taken into state care, no matter how negligent or abusive they were. Those were one type, but this woman was the other type. He'd seen that look in mothers' eyes so many times before as they did everything they could for their kid not to be one of the statistics, to go to school, get a job, stay out of jail. According to the file, this woman and her son had new information about a drug crime. Nobody in her community trusted the cops. It would probably turn out to be nothing, but someone had called him. He'd listen to what they had to say, pass it on to the cops and send them on their way.

Deshane, the kid, seemed less than enthusiastic and managed with much prompting from his mother to say there were people dealing drugs in his neighbourhood. This was hardly news to anyone. He had no names, nor could he give any specific information.

Kevin took a few notes. 'Okay, Deshane, thanks for letting us know. But I must tell you that without any definite details, I doubt law enforcement will be able to do anything.'

The kid shrugged, and Kevin got the impression there was something else going on. His mother ordered him to wait outside.

Once the door was shut, the mother pleaded. 'He's a good boy, Mr Wilson, he is. I know he's comin' over all snarky now, but he jes don't want to rat on his friends. But those guys ain't his friends. They no good, but he won't listen to me.' She burned with intensity.

'I know, Mrs Fisher. It's the toughest age, thirteen to seventeen. If you can keep him on the straight and narrow in those years…'

'Can you give him a fright?' she whispered, standing close to him.

He looked at her quizzically. 'How?'

'Get him arrested, throw him in jail, in juvie even. I want him to see the future, and maybe it'll scare him enough to stay clean. Some people I know said you are good with these kids. I don't want to go to the cops.'

Kevin looked at her, wishing it were that simple.

'I know where you're coming from, and I understand why you want me to do that. I'm not saying it's a bad idea, but that's not how the law works, I'm afraid. He hasn't committed a crime, I –'

'There's drugs in my house. He says he's not dealing, that they belong to someone else, but if you send the cops over… Here's the address.' She shoved a piece of paper into his hand. 'You send the cops, they'll find it, and then they can arrest him. He'll only be charged with possession and it's a first offence, but he needs to see the road he's taking…' He could see the desperation in her eyes.

'Mrs Fisher, I can't do that.' He was firm even though he felt very sorry for her. 'I'm a social worker. My job is not to get kids in jail. Putting your son into the prison system might have the effect you want, but I have to tell you from years of experience, it's much more likely to have the opposite result. They meet people in prison who make the punks he knows now look like choir boys, and they use and abuse kids like Deshane.'

Tears shone in the woman's eyes, and Kevin wished he could do something, but it was the grim reality of life. The area they lived in was notorious. The schools tried, but with very limited resources, poorly paid, demoralised teachers and every single social demographic stacked against the people there, Deshane and all of his classmates would have to be exceptional to escape. And Deshane didn't appear to be exceptional.

'He was first in his class every year, but they made life so hard for him… They beat him up, they even…' She started to cry. 'He's a smart kid. He could read before he went to school. But the world we live in, it's crushing down on him. He's bein' like this just to survive.'

Kevin had spent his entire career in social services; he knew when people were lying. He sighed and opened the door. 'Deshane, can you come in here, please?'

The boy stood, his pants halfway down his backside, a tattoo on his neck, his hair shaved on the sides and arranged in some kind of gang style on top. He ambled in, exuding boredom and defiance simultaneously.

'Do you have any interests or hobbies?' Kevin knew better than to try to pander to him.

'Huh?' His face said it all.

'Look, Deshane, I'm a busy man. Your mother here seems to believe that you are not like those other kids you hang out with, who will, as sure as I'm standing here, wind up in juvie and then jail. So if you want to go a different route, then this is your one chance. I won't be offering it again. There's a community scholarship scheme, and I can suggest people to put into the programme. It's full tuition at a school upstate. You'd live there, and the scholarship covers all school fees and books and a tiny stipend. You'd be living on cereal and bread – you wouldn't be able to afford fancy sneakers or a cell phone or any of the things the other kids have. The thing is, there are lots of people like you who would cut their arm off for this chance, so I won't waste it on someone who won't appreciate it. It could be your ticket out of all of this.' He pointed to the projects that towered outside the social services building. 'But if I give them your name, you have to swear to me and to your mother that you won't screw it up.'

The boy's whole face seemed to change – the scowl was gone, the attitude melted away. Beneath the clothes and haircut, Kevin caught a glimpse of what his mother believed to be true about her son.

Mrs Fisher's eyes pleaded with her son to say the right thing.

'What would I have to do?'

Kevin caught his mother's glance. 'What you need to do is this. There's an exam in July for the September intake. It's hard – math, English, science, history, geography, everything. The curriculum and past exam papers are online. You need to get yourself to the library, download the past papers, take out the books you need and lock yourself in your room between now and then and study day and night. If you ace the exam, and I endorse you, then you're in. What do you say?'

Deshane looked from Kevin to his mother and back again. Kevin could see him weighing the options in his head. He knew the kid wanted the chance – he could see it in his eyes – but could he stand up to the bullies long enough to escape?

'I'd like to try.' His voice was unsure, but there was a confidence there.

'Okay, here's the website.' He scribbled the address on a piece of paper and handed it to Deshane. 'Don't let us down.'

'I'll try not to,' the boy answered.

'Thank you, Mr Wilson. You might just have saved both our lives.' Mrs Fisher held his hand, her eyes bright. 'You're a good man.'

As Kevin watched them leave, he felt his phone buzz in his pocket.

'Hello, Debbie,' he said, trying not to sound confrontational.

'I'm going to Puerto Rico for ten days in September – you need to take Tess.' Her tone was clipped. No preamble, no greeting, straight to the point.

'Sure, I'd love to.' He hardly ever got more than an overnight with his daughter.

'Okay.' She sounded almost disappointed that she was making him happy, even though she was getting what she wanted. 'I'll drop her over on the tenth, and I'll collect her on the twenty-third.'

He smiled. That wasn't ten days, it was thirteen, but that was great. Then a thought struck him: They'd booked to go to Ireland on the twelfth till the twenty-second. He thought quickly.

'Well, that's even better because I'm going on vacation myself at that time and I'd love to take Tess.' He hadn't thought this through, but it would be fine.

'Where?' Debbie sounded belligerent again. He'd need to tread carefully.

'Ireland.' He didn't want her to have any more details.

'Ireland? What the hell you wanna go there for? It's cold and all full of drunks, isn't it? Isn't there a war going on there?'

Kevin wondered, for the millionth time, how he married this woman. 'No. There was a conflict in Northern Ireland years ago, but it's over now.' The complexities of the politics of Ireland were going to be beyond her interest or comprehension. 'And Ireland is a beautiful country. Tess will love it.'

'I dunno. I mean, is it safe, like…'

Kevin needed to cut off this line of thought immediately. 'Well, I'm all booked to go, and I am going at that time. I'm delighted that I can bring Tess with me, so if you want me to take her, then she's going to Ireland. I promise you she will be perfectly safe.'

Kevin tried to not let her hear the annoyance in his voice. She treated him like he was some kind of deadbeat dad who'd let her play with knives.

'Are you going with a woman?' That sharpness again. The weird thing about Debbie was that even though she definitely didn't want him, she made it clear in a myriad of ways since they split that she hated the idea of him seeing anyone else.

'I'm going with a group of friends, men and women, but I'm not seeing anyone if that's what you're asking.' *Not that it's any of your business*, he wanted to add, but he kept it in.

'See who you want, Kevin, I don't care, but I don't want my daughter around the kind of people you know. She told me about the guy in the bar. I mean, seriously, you are taking our eight-year-old to a bar? And he gave her some kind of potato chips or something – have you any idea how much saturated fat, not to mention salt, is in those?'

The irony that Debbie left Tess with anyone who'd have her so she could frequent the bars of Manhattan's Lower East Side was lost on her. She only drank vodka and soda – very few calories.

'My friend owned that place. During the day, it's more of a café. People go there for lunch – it's fine.' He didn't want to hear her opinion on Bubbles.

'So you say, but Tess told me a big man with a beard was tickling her. How do I know he's not some kind of a sicko?'

Kevin snapped. 'Because, as I told you if you'd listen for one second, he is my friend, and he died, and we are all grieving for him. So don't say anything about him because you never met him. He was a great guy, and he was great to Tess, and she loved visiting him. Now do you want me to take Tess to Ireland or not? Make up your mind.'

'I'll think about it.' And she hung up.

Immediately the call-waiting light lit up – two calls waiting.

'Kevin Wilson,' he barked.

'I'm sorry, Kevin, it's Erin. Have I got you at a bad time?' She sounded worried, but then she always did.

'No, Erin, I'm sorry, just a busy morning. What can I do to help?' He tried to sound friendly.

'Oh, I just wanted to tell you that Shannon and I have paid for the trip this morning, and we are so looking forward to it. And we were wondering if should meet up before we go, or will we just meet in the airport?'

He could hear the uncertainty. He would bet the two sisters had never left the state of New York before, let alone the country.

'Let's have brunch on Saturday at Bubbles. Everyone should be paid up by then, and we can make a plan. Can you call the others? I'm kind of busy here.'

'Of course, we'd be happy to do that. Shall we say eleven on Saturday then?'

He melted at the excitement in her voice. Bubbles would have loved this idea, he was sure of it.

'Perfect.' He hung up.

He didn't know how this trip was going to go. That Conor O'Shea guy seemed like a nice man, and Miss O'Donovan had spoken so highly of him, he felt confident in his ability. The castle he ran looked amazing. A bit expensive, but Conor had made them a really great deal, and for the group, it really was a once-in-a-lifetime trip. He just hoped he was going to be able to take Tess.

CHAPTER 9

*E*rin hung up the phone. She wasn't supposed to make personal calls at the office, but she hoped it would be okay this one time. Her boss, trial attorney Candice Browne, was a formidable woman to say the very least, and if Erin were honest, she was a little nervous around her.

Shannon's employer, Dr Mills, was a nice man, and he always made sure his wife bought Shannon a thoughtful little gift at Christmas. Erin and Shannon would wait patiently for the day the gift would be given, and then that evening, they'd feel it and try to guess what it might be. In recent years, they'd taken to having a glass of sherry when they did it. It was usually soap or a nice candle, and for the Glavin sisters, the day the gift from Dr Mills arrived, Christmas began. They placed it under their tree, which stood on a small table in the living room, along with their gifts for each other. Mammy didn't go much for gifts – she thought it a waste of money – but Erin and Shannon had always bought each other something for Christmas. When their mother was alive, they hid it in their bedroom, each making the other promise not to peep if she found it. When Mammy died, they could be more open, and Erin often smiled when she remembered the first time they put their gifts under a tree.

Mammy would have been horrified to see her girls drinking sherry, but they were in their fifties now, and they thought they should be at least a little bit sophisticated. When Mammy was alive, they weren't allowed, but she was dead over ten years now. Shannon and Erin visited her grave twice a week, and they always made sure both her and Daddy's plots were well tended and cared for.

Daddy was gone to heaven since they were twenty, but Mammy ensured he was remembered every year on his birthday and on the anniversary of his death. She got a Mass said specially, and then they would all go down to Battery Park and look out towards Ellis Island. Their father had been one of the last people through the arrivals hall there in 1941, as a boy of sixteen. They would have loved to go out to the island, to sail by Lady Liberty and her lamp and to stand in the hall where Daddy must have stood all on his own, only a boy, but the tickets were expensive and really only for tourists.

She wondered what they would think about their daughters going all the way over to Ireland. She and Shannon had to keep reminding each other that this was really happening. From the moment Kevin suggested it, it had been their main topic of conversation. They'd had to apply for passports, take money out of their savings to pay for the trip and plan what to pack. It was in equal measure exhilarating and terrifying. Apart from an overnight trip to Niagara Falls once when they were in their twenties, they had never really left the city. They had a map of Ireland on the wall, and Shannon had asked Dr Mills if she could take ten small Post-its from the stationery closet to mark where they would be on the map.

She and Shannon prayed for their parents every night before bed, asking God to keep their souls safe until they saw each other again. And now they added Bubbles as well. What Mammy would think of her girls having a friend called Bubbles O'Leary who ran a bar they dreaded to think, but then as Shannon pointed out, if Mammy had met Bubbles, he'd have charmed even her. They missed him so much; it was hard to believe such a larger-than-life person was gone.

* * *

BETH ANDERSON WISHED the alarm would just stop. She was exhausted. She should have gone home, but by the time her shift finished last night and she did the handover, she would only have had a few hours before she had to get back to work. So she opted to nap in the on-call room, telling nobody she was there.

Half-blind with sleep, she found the phone and realised it wasn't the alarm but an incoming call – she should have switched it to silent. She didn't recognise the number, but she always answered unknown numbers in case it was Maddie.

'Hello? Is that Beth?' Not Maddie.

'Yes, who's calling?' She sat up and tried to focus.

'It's Erin Glavin. I'm sorry if I'm calling at a bad time?' Erin trailed off nervously.

'No, I'm sorry. I was working late, but go on, Erin. I'm sorry.'

'I was just calling to let you know we are getting together on Saturday morning for brunch at Bubbles just to discuss the trip, and all of…well, everything, I suppose…'

Beth felt sorry for the other woman. When she met them, she was never sure if she was speaking to Shannon or Erin, as they looked almost identical. They always struck her as kind of quaint, like something from a novel of a hundred years ago.

'Sure…I'll be there. What time?' She had no idea if she was working or not, but she'd manage to sort something out.

'Eleven?' Erin sounded relieved.

'Great, see you then.' Beth hung up and lay back down, but it was no good – she was awake now. She wasn't due back on the ward for another hour, so she'd get up and shower and maybe get something to eat.

The familiar feeling of despair threatened to smother her again. 'Where the hell are you, Maddie?' she whispered.

Maddie was officially missing now, though it took the cops weeks to accept that. She was wild, and she was known for taking off, sometimes for months at a time, but never without making contact with Beth – a text or a voicemail or something. She would never worry her sister like this.

Beth had done all the usual stuff, calling friends that she had contact numbers for and all of that, but nobody had seen her. Her passport was still in the drawer in the kitchen of their modest two-bedroom apartment in Queens. She had taken some of her stuff, but Beth knew in her bones something wasn't right.

This trip to Ireland was going to have to be cancelled. She'd agreed to it on the spur of the moment, but there was no way she could go with Maddie missing. She was hoping she wouldn't have to cancel, assuming her sister would just turn up like she always did, but she was worried now. She'd tell them at the brunch that she couldn't go. She needed to find her.

She had no idea where to even start looking. She went from being furious with her to being worried sick about fifty times a day. Maddie was able to take care of herself, she knew that, but this was not like her. She had taken off before but with her friends or a guy. And despite how they looked – hairy, dreadlocked, pierced – Beth knew her sister's friends were good people for the most part, and nobody seemed to have a clue where she was.

She was disappointed that she couldn't go to Ireland, had wanted so badly to bring Bubbles home, but she knew he'd understand.

She would never forget the night she met him. He'd brought an old guy who'd been sleeping rough into the emergency room. It was the depths of winter, and the man was suffering from hypothermia. Bubbles seemed agitated and kept asking him why he didn't go to the Center.They obviously knew each other. The old man died later that night, a few minutes before her shift ended. Bubbles just stood there, looking so bereft and alone, and something made her offer to buy him a cup of coffee. He accepted, and over horrible coffee in plastic cups in the hospital cafeteria, he told her how he had been volunteering at the Irish Centre for many years, mainly helping old guys like the one he brought in. He'd explained how so many came over from Ireland but never really made a go of it. They were too ashamed to go home, so they descended further and further into poverty. The Irish Centre was one of the few places they were welcome. It seemed to Beth like Bubbles was taking the responsibility for his fellow countrymen personally. He was heartbroken, and she just let him talk. The old man had come from Kerry, where Bubbles was from, and Bubbles knew of his family. He'd tried to convince him to go home, but the man, Mick, wouldn't hear of it.

They walked the seven blocks to Bubbles's bar that night. It was long closed, but he invited her in, and they sat there for hours just talking.

Something about Bubbles made her confide in him that night, something she never did with anyone. It was the anniversary of her dad's death, and she had a pain in her heart thinking about how much she missed him. She told Bubbles stories all about him, and when they went outside to the little beer garden at the back for him to have a cigarette, she cried and Bubbles held her in his arms, letting her weep for her darling father.

He'd invited her back, and she went the following Friday with Maddie. It became a ritual, going to Bubbles's every Friday she was off, up until Maddie disappeared. He was like a father to them, insisting they take a cab home if it was late, or telling Beth she was working too hard. He joked around with Maddie about her ever-changing appearance – she had different hair, piercings and tattoos all the time. Beth was the total opposite – she thought she was the boring one – but they both felt so welcome and loved by him.

She could tell from Bubbles's colour that he needed cardiac care, but he shooed her away every time she tried to talk to him about his health. He was overweight, drank a bit too much – though she never saw him drunk – and smoked lots of cigarettes. All of those things together were a recipe for disaster, but he wouldn't listen.

* * *

Miguel Sanchez wrote the specials on the blackboard and placed it on the pavement outside. He was on autopilot since Bubbles died. He kept the bar open, served people, answered a million questions about Bubbles and his death and the future of the bar, and worked so hard that at night he just fell into bed too tired to think.

The group taking Bubbles back to Ireland were meeting for brunch tomorrow, and he wanted everything to be right.

Miguel thought how strange life was as he emptied last night's bottles into the recycling bins. Since he was a kid, he dreamed about getting out, getting to America – it was the only future he could envisage. So one day, he said goodbye to his parents and his sisters and set out with two friends, Fidel and Francisco, to do whatever it took to enter the USA. It turned out to be reasonably easy. They paid a guy who knew a way to sneak over the border, and one night they did it. They laid low for the first day or two – those border towns were full of cops – but soon they managed to move north and blend in.

Fidel met a woman in Dallas and decided to stay there with her, so he and Francisco went on. They worked picking fruit, cutting lawns, cleaning windows – anything that paid cash – to make the next Greyhound bus fare to move up through the vast country. He sent a postcard back home of everywhere he passed through. He tried not to think about his mother. She was heartbroken when he left but knew that a poor kid with no real education had no future in San Luis de la Paz.

It amazed them that nobody asked for papers. There were just so many people, he guessed, and he and Francisco didn't say much. They kept away from cops and anyone official looking. And at night, though they were bone tired, they practised their English together. It was the subject Miguel had really tried hard at in school, the only one he could see a use for. His parents ran a small café, and he worked there as a cook. His culinary skills kept them alive, and they lived on tomatoes, beans, onions and rice. They slept rough sometimes; other times, they stayed in hostels where they'd shower and shave and wash their clothes. It was hard, and some people were kind, but to most, they were invisible. There was one goal: New York City. He never imagined how his life in that city would be; he just knew he wanted to be there.

He started out offering to clean windows and take care of buildings. He took out the map of the city and did one street each day, looking for any kind of work. Bubbles gave him a job watering the hanging baskets of flowers and cleaning his bar before it opened in the morning. He knew Bubbles was different when he paid him the going rate and insisted he stop and have a cup of coffee and a bagel once he'd finished. They would talk, and Bubbles would offer advice about who to go to for work, or places to avoid where he might be caught and deported.

'How come you know so much about it?' Miguel asked him one day.

Bubbles laughed, and it seemed like his whole body shook. 'Well, Miguel, my old buddy, I'm in the same boat as you. Though I've been here so long in this melting-pot country, these days, nobody asks any more. All the cops drink in here, and they just assume I've a green card, but I was ducking and diving the same as you for a long time.'

Miguel never considered that white guys like Bubbles had the same trouble.

He'd been working in the kitchen of a busy diner on Seventh Avenue at night, sharing a room upstairs with ten others, when immigration officers burst in. He managed to get out the back, but he had to leave all he possessed there. He was one of the lucky ones. Tony, the owner, only employed illegals and paid them a pittance, so they got ten or fifteen guys that day.

Standing on the street, without a penny in his pocket or even his coat, Miguel had nobody else. Francisco would be of no use – he was in the same position as Miguel – so he walked for almost two hours, from Seventh Avenue to Queens, and told Bubbles his story.

Bubbles gave him a full-time job and helped him find a small apartment. He paid the going rate, he didn't exploit anyone, and as Bubbles often put it, between the jigs and the reels, Miguel became part of the furniture. He owed Bubbles his life.

He went back inside, savouring every minute. Those times when the place was full and buzzing were exhilarating and fun for sure, but now he just wanted to sit and take it all in. He was going to ask Kevin if he could join in the trip to take Bubbles home. His ashes were in an urn upstairs in the apartment. So many people showed up to

Bubbles's service, held at the Irish Centre. The musicians who played in the bar all performed, and people said lovely things about him. It was very moving. Miguel was unsure of his role at first, but he and Kevin and the rest of the gang seemed to be cast as chief mourners, so in the absence of any family, that's what they became.

Since Bubbles died, he'd been mulling it over, and he was happy with his decision. He would take his personal things, his camera, some books and a few photographs. He had a lovely one of him and Bubbles out at Coney Island at a wedding of one of Bubbles's friends. He had so many, he knew everyone, but he let Miguel in, and for that, Miguel was so grateful.

He knew the whole story – why Bubbles never went home, why none of his family could visit – and he knew how much it hurt the big Irishman. Listening to Bubbles talk about his home, his mother and his sister made Miguel tear up too. He was adamant that he could not put them in danger by making contact. Bubbles was so kind and so gentle and wanted to help everyone, but he lived with such sadness.

Miguel knew he would never get back into the United States again – once he left, it would be for good – but without Bubbles, there was nothing there for him any more. Maybe he'd just go home, see his mother and take it from there. Luckily, he still had his Mexican passport. It would get him out, but not back in.

* * *

The group gathered: Jimmy and Will, the Glavin sisters, Beth, Kevin, Marianne and Annie.

As they were served coffee and the platter of pastries Miguel had prepared, Beth made her announcement.

'I'm so sorry, guys, but I'm going to have to pull out. Maddie is still missing, and I'm really starting to worry. The cops say she's done it before, and she has, but she has never gone this long without calling me. I need to stay here.'

Everyone was very sympathetic, and Kevin offered to use his

connections with the cops to see if he could get anything more out of them.

'But you not going isn't going to help, though, is it?' Will Munro asked. 'Like, you've tried all her friends and everything... What more can you do?'

Beth looked a little taken aback. Will was only a recent regular to the bar – Bubbles met him someplace and invited him just like he did with everyone – and they were surprised when he approached Kevin a few weeks back when he heard about the trip and asked to go. There was no reason why not of course, the more the better, and he was very fond of Bubbles.

'I don't know, Will, but I don't want to be thousands of miles away if my sister turns up or the police find something or whatever...'

'Of course.' He smiled. 'I'm so sorry. I didn't mean... Of course you should stay here.'

Miguel saw his opportunity. 'I was wondering, guys, if I could come?' All eyes turned to him.

Nobody suggested it before, even though Miguel and Bubbles worked together and were very close friends, because they assumed he was illegal and didn't want to draw attention to it and embarrass him.

'Of course, Miguel. We'd love to have you, wouldn't we, guys?' Kevin beamed and everyone agreed.

'Thank you. I... I think Bubbles would want us to bring him home.'

Annie leaned over and placed her hand on Miguel's. 'I think he would too.'

The conversation became animated as everyone discussed the upcoming trip. For the Glavins, it was their first time doing anything remotely impetuous, and they were as nervous as they were excited. Annie was full of information about the matchmaking festival, which filled the sisters with horror, but apart from that, it sounded like a lovely trip. Jimmy too said he hadn't travelled much, but they knew him well enough not to press for details.

Beth glanced at her phone to check the time. She needed to get going, as she was due on shift in forty minutes. She stood up.

'I'm so sorry, guys. I've got to take off – I'm working at twelve. We'll talk soon, okay?'

They all hugged her and she left. Before she got to the end of the block, she heard her phone beep in her pocket.

'Maddie Cell' flashed on her screen. She pressed Open, relieved.

Hi B – sorry for silence. Phone is trashed – fell in john (again! – I know) – so speaker broken, text only. Am fine anyway, on road trip with a friend. Might stop by Mom's. Talk soon, M xx

Beth read and reread the text as the city went on around her. Maddie was okay. She just broke her phone. The only strange thing was suggesting the visit to their mother. Beth hadn't spoken to their mother in over ten years. She knew that Maddie had a little bit more contact, but she was surprised to hear her offering to visit. Still, the main thing was she was okay. The friend was no doubt some guy she'd picked up.

She turned and ran back to the bar.

'Everything okay?' Will asked, seeing her come in.

'Fine.' She grinned. 'Better than fine, actually. Maddie just texted – she's fine. She just broke her phone.'

Everyone was thrilled.

'So you can come?' Kevin asked.

Beth looked around at the motley crew, united by one thing only – their love of Bubbles – and smiled.

'Sure, why not?'

Miguel looked worried; maybe now there would be no room for him.

Marianne spotted his consternation. 'The more the merrier. We'll have some craic, won't we, Miguel? Bubbles will be watching.'

'It is still okay, now that Beth is going again?' He didn't want to impose.

'Of course. I'll call the hotel tomorrow, and we'll get everything arranged.' Kevin clapped him on the back.

'Okay, thanks.' Miguel was relieved.

CHAPTER 10

*C*onor lay in bed on Sunday morning, Ana beside him. Danika and Artur had taken the boys to Mass. They went without a fuss, mainly because they knew that ice cream and cake back at Babusya's was on the menu afterwards.

She was managing the chemo all right, though she had shaved her head as soon as her hair started to fall out. He'd found her in the shower, crying, holding her blonde hair. She said she hated the idea of a wig, so she just wore hats or scarves, and she looked even younger and smaller than before.

He decided to tell her about his father's visit. Katherine would take it to the grave, so he wasn't afraid of it getting back to her, but he wanted to always be honest with her. He told her quickly about how he reacted and assumed she would understand.

Ana surprisingly took the opposite view. 'This is your family, Conor. I know you say me and the boys is this for you, and I know that, but this is your father. Are you not just a bit... I forget the word... You know, like you want to know?'

'Curious?' he asked.

'Yes, this.'

'No, I'm not. I've enough to be worrying about without adding him into it after all these years.'

She looked at him with those eyes that could see into his soul.

'Okay, well, a bit,' he admitted. 'A little bit maybe, but I just want everything to stay the same, and it feels like letting him in would be opening a can of worms, you know?'

Ana rolled her eyes. 'A can of worms, ugh. That is so disgusting. I now know what it means, but really you have such terrible sayings.'

Conor chuckled and held her closer, and for a second, life was normal again. She delighted him and had done since the day they met.

As he held her in his arms, he was reminded again of her diagnosis. She'd lost a lot of weight. The first few days after a chemo treatment, she would be okay, but then she'd be blindsided by crushing tiredness and nausea and feel miserable. She would recover just in time to start the next dose. It was gruelling for her, and Conor wished he could take it from her, but he felt so helpless. She tried to stay cheerful, especially when the boys were around, but the skin under her eyes seemed to have become translucent and her little wrists looked like they could just snap. It broke his heart to see her ill.

'I just thinking,' she said, her head on his chest, 'this is not just about your father. It is about your brother too if he can be found. Your father is old, so it is not for long-time relationship, but he want to see you, and if you don't take this chance, maybe you won't never get another one and it will be too late? I just don't want you regret later. Having this, cancer, it makes me think about all of the things, and how nobody knows what will happen. Sometimes is good, some-times is not. But we don't know what time we have.'

He sighed. 'I don't know. Maybe you're right, but I keep coming back to the same thing. If I took off today,' Conor said, leaning up on one elbow, looking into her face, 'seriously, if I just walked out that door and never came back, and you had to explain to Joe and Artie that their dad just left, no note, nothing. And you were not only alone, but you were financially in ruins and everyone was talking because I'd got some girl pregnant, would you really be telling our boys to welcome me back when they were men and had families of their own?'

Ana reached up and laid her hand on his face. 'No,' she said. 'I would not. I'm sorry, I just don't think really about it like this.'

He lay back down, drawing her into his arms once more. 'I know I told you about how gutted I was when Sinead took off with Gerry, but that was not the first time my heart was broken.' Conor's eyes were fixed on the ceiling. 'I was Joe and Artie's age, and I adored my dad. He was the most popular man in our town, and he was great at sports, and he had time for me, talking to me about cars and all of that. I couldn't believe he'd leave me. I remember even thinking, like, how he might have wanted to leave Mam and Gerry but he'd never have left me. He took off two weeks before my ninth birthday, and I was totally convinced he'd send me something, a card or instructions on how to find him. And I'd have gone, you know. I'd have left Mam and Gerry and gone off with my dad. But he never did. Christmas, birthdays, even when Mam died, a part of me hoped he'd turn up. I'd probably have beat him up I was so angry, but I still wanted to see him.'

Ana kissed his bare shoulder and ran her hand over his chest.

'I can't forgive him, Ana, and I don't want to. I'm a good dad, or at least I try my best, and I hope I'm a good husband to you. And that means everything to me. I just don't understand people who get married and have kids and then screw around. I stayed single for years, as you know, and a lot of it was I was afraid that if I got involved with someone, I'd end up hurting them like my father did to us. But then you came along, and you believed I could be a good husband and father. And I don't know... That belief gave me courage or something.'

'You are not your father, Conor,' Ana said quietly. 'You are a wonderful man, and we love you so much, and you are not him. But people make mistakes, and he is sorry. Sometimes, when we don't forgive, it hurt the person again, you know what I mean? Like the first hurt, it still goes on. Because when we forgive, we can let it go and it don't hurt us more. I think you should try to forgive him – not for him, for you.'

Conor smiled at his wife. 'You're very wise this morning.'

'Oh yes, I am Ukrainian version of Dalai Lama.' She chuckled. 'I even get the hairstyle.' She patted her bald head.

'Well, you are much more beautiful than the Dalai Lama. How about I get up and make you some breakfast? Can you eat?' Sometimes she was ravenous, other times unable to even look at food.

'I think so. I feel bad sometimes you making me something and I just can't...'

'That's okay, sweetheart. I would go through this for you if I could, but since I can't, I just want to make this as manageable as possible for you. Eggs? Toast? A ring of black pudding?' He chuckled. Ana thought the Irish blood sausage was the most disgusting thing she had ever seen or tasted.

'Ugh, not that. Artie took that for his lunch yesterday, just cut up, disgusting.' She grimaced. 'Just some tea and toast and a yoghurt, please.'

'Coming right up, madam.' He kissed her and rose to make her breakfast.

CHAPTER 11

*C*onor stood at the arrivals gate at Shannon Airport. The flight was down.

The usual collection of drivers and guides began to assemble at the gate awaiting their groups. Conor was surprised to see so many faces he didn't know. There was a time when he was acquainted with every single person in the business, but his life had changed so much over the last decade, it was almost unrecognisable.

He got a takeaway coffee and the paper. It would be at least forty minutes before they were out by the time they got their bags and cleared customs.

'Well, well, well, the dead arose and appeared to many.'

Conor's heart sank; he knew that voice. He looked up from the paper reluctantly. 'Mike, how are you?'

Mad Mike, as he was known, was standing before him, large as life and twice as ugly. His ever-receding hair was arranged on top of his bald pate in a ridiculous fashion, fooling nobody, and his teeth were yellow from years of smoking cigarettes. His pot belly hung over his belt, and his wrists jangled with gold bracelets. Despite his obvious physical flaws, the man believed he was God's gift to women and bored to tears anyone who would listen with his entirely imagined romantic exploits. He was married to Mags Murphy, who terrified everyone she met, regardless of age or gender. Conor and Mike worked for the same tour company for years, so the guy had to be endured. But when Conor left the tour business and bumped into him a few years back in the wrong place at the wrong time, he told him exactly what he thought of him. Mike refused to speak to him for ages afterwards. It was bliss. Unfortunately, Mad Mike was a regular at the castle, taking groups there to stay. He seemed to have forgiven Conor, more's the pity.

'What has you out here in the airport mixing with the mere mortals now that you're a high flier with no time for your old friends?' Mike sneered, scanning the area for someone to join him in his hilarious banter.

Conor suppressed the urge to point out that the two were never friends and merely answered. 'Well, I don't have my own personal airport, so I suppose I'm meeting someone.' He tried to return to his paper, not caring if it looked rude.

'You're not back on the road, are you? I thought your days behind the wheel were over now that the little woman has you on a tight leash and that yank left you the money for the castle? Stroke of luck that, wasn't it? Trust you to get the tour with your man on it, and he only looking for someone to give his millions to? You must have spun him some yarn, boy, I'll give you that. But if I'da had him, I'd have got two castles out of him!' He clapped Conor on the shoulder, almost causing him to spill his coffee.

The idea that he had somehow swindled Bert Cooper made him smile. That old Texan was one of the sharpest men he had ever met and could spot a chancer a mile off. Conor had been surprised at the legacy, and at first, he'd felt he shouldn't take it, but Corlene convinced him. Bert had turned Corlene's and her son Dylan's lives around by setting them up in Ireland, and he liked to do that with his money. Bert's legacy had allowed Conor to give up driving tours and take on the huge renovation of Castle Dysert in partnership with Corlene. He was home with his family each night, he was on a very generous salary, plus he had shares in the business – and it drove Mike out of his mind with jealousy.

'I'm sure you would.' Conor sighed.

'So you never said, who're you meeting?' Mike persisted.

'That's right, I never said.' He'd had had enough of this clown. 'Now, I'm going to read the paper and finish my coffee if you don't mind. I'll see you around.'

'Jays, that young wan has you fierce cranky altogether, Conor. You must be after getting too old to keep up with her, is that it? Them foreign wans so be mad for road in the bedroom department, if you know what I mean. I had a Lithuanian wan two weeks ago, a fashion designer she was. Jays, I wasn't right for a fortnight after her, swinging from the chandeliers, she was!' He guffawed, and one or two other guides and drivers shot Conor a look of sympathy but moved away. Everyone avoided Mad Mike as much as possible.

'How's Mags?' Conor asked pointedly.

Mike looked disgruntled. He would have much rather waxed lyrical about this fantasy woman he had.

'She's grand. Anyway, this Lithuanian – or was she Latvian? I don't know, there do be so many of them, I forgets – anyway, she was into all the kinky stuff, you know. She –'

Conor interrupted him before he could wander any further down this disturbing conversational path. 'I'll have to go there. I must ring Ana.' He took out his phone and called his wife. The other man stood beside him, listening.

'Hi, love, how're you feeling?'

'Okay. A bit tired.' She sounded exhausted. She wasn't sleeping, and the drugs were playing havoc with her appetite. This was day four after her chemo, and that was always the worst day.

'I left some breakfast on the tray for you. Artie said he'd bring it up when you woke?' He hoped his son remembered.

'Thank you, he did, and him and Joe pick me flower too for little vase on the tray. They are so nice, my little boys, and I did eat a little.'

He looked up. Mike was still there.

'Could you give me a bit of privacy, please? I want to talk to my wife.'

'Who's there?' Ana asked, shocked that Conor would be so rude.

'Mad Mike,' Conor murmured into the phone.

'Oh no, poor you, getting stuck with him... Always I think he is kind of creepy,' Ana sympathised. When she was a waitress at the Dunshane, she and the other female staff knew to give the man a wide berth.

Mike moved away a little.

'Creepy doesn't cover it,' Conor said with a grin, glad to hear her perk up. 'He always was a class A eejit, and he hasn't changed a bit.'

'So have the group arrived?' she asked.

'No.' He checked the board again. 'They should be out in the next twenty minutes or so. I'll load them up, go straight to the castle, then pop back home for a coffee to see you, is that okay?'

'I'm fine, you know,' she admonished him. 'I don't need to be babysitting.'

He smiled. Her English was improving all the time, but when she was tired or a bit stressed out, the sentence structure went out the window. She wanted him to correct her, but he never did; he thought it was adorable. His Ukrainian was coming on as well under the tough taskmasters, his bilingual sons, who insisted he learn five new words every day. Over dinner now, they could have at least a rudimentary conversation in Ukrainian. And while speaking it was still hard, Conor understood a lot of what his parents-in-law or Ana said to the boys.

'I know, but I just want to check in, okay? I'm allowed to do that aren't I?'

She laughed. 'Okay, okay. See you later. I love you.'

'I love you too,' he replied, and hung up.

Kevin was the first to come through the arrivals hall, and he found Conor right away.

'I knew who I was looking for from your picture on the hotel website. Nice to meet you, Conor.' The men shook hands.

It was unusual for Conor to meet someone taller, as he was over six feet, but Kevin Wilson was six foot six with what was once probably a very strong athletic build. Now he had a belly where once he'd had a six-pack. Beside him was a little girl wearing denim dungarees and a pink T-shirt.

'This is my daughter, Tess. She's eight.' Kevin introduced her.

Conor bent down to make himself eye level with her. 'Well, Tess, I must say it's a great honour that you came over to visit us. It's lovely to meet you.'

'Do you have a leprechaun in your garden?' she asked. Her huge brown eyes and dark curly hair captivated him.

'Well…' Conor looked very serious. 'I don't have one in my garden because they don't live in people's gardens – they live in the woods and forests and under hills and by riverbanks and all sorts of places in Ireland. You see, Tess, Ireland isn't like New York. There's lots of empty space, and the leprechauns like to stay away from humans as much as possible. That said, I do know one of them – and my boys have met him too – called Seamus O'Flaherty. But he's a tricky little lad, so we might keep our eyes open for him. Grownups can't see them because they are too high up, so it's only children can see them usually.'

'Hmm.' Tess looked doubtful. 'My mommy says they aren't real, that they are just invented to make stupid tourists spend more money.' She was pure New York despite her tender years.

He smiled. 'Well, I'm not saying your mammy is wrong, but they are not real in America, that's for sure. But here in Ireland, well, that's a different place altogether, and all sorts of unusual things happen here.'

'Can you show me one?' the little girl asked.

'Well, if it were as easy as that, Tess, my love, I'd be a very rich man, but unfortunately it's not. But we can certainly look anyway. Now,' he whispered, 'I better say hello to all these grownups in case they get lost, but we'll talk again, okay?'

Tess nodded and smiled.

Kevin introduced Conor to each of the group as they emerged.

The wide-eyed Erin and Shannon arrived, looking like they were coming for six months rather than ten days, they had so much luggage. A young woman called Beth, who looked tired, greeted him. She was tall and athletic with short brown hair and dark almond-shaped eyes.

'And these are Annie and Marianne. They're friends of Bubbles as well.' Kevin continued around the little group.

'He's trying to say we were regulars of Bubbles's bar, but that sounds bad for a first impression.' Annie grinned at Conor, eyeing him up and down.

She was in her thirties and quite attractive, but there was something about her – trying too hard or something, he wasn't sure. She held his gaze a little too long. He was used to American ladies finding him attractive – it had happened so often when he was a tour driver. But he was convinced it wasn't because of him as such, it was because he symbolised Ireland and vacations and something different. Ana always teased him about that, saying that he was just being modest – women fancied him because he was gorgeous. That kind of chat was lovely to hear from his young wife, but in general, it embarrassed him, and anyway, he was sure it wasn't true.

'Oh, don't worry your head, Annie.' He smiled. 'That's not taken badly in Ireland at all.' He shook her hand warmly.

Marianne shook his hand as well, and he noticed she had tears in her eyes. 'I'm sorry,' she began, wiping her tears. 'I just never thought I'd get here. I always wanted to go… And now to come here with Bubbles… I'm sorry.' She smiled through her tears. Kevin stood beside her and gave her a friendly squeeze.

'Nothing to apologise for, Marianne. Kevin told me the story, and I think what ye are doing is just wonderful. I'm sure Bubbles is looking down now, and he's delighted that so many of his friends could make it to give him a send-off.'

'Conor,' Kevin continued, 'this is Will Munro and Jimmy Burns and, finally, Miguel Sanchez.'

He took the last three men in. Will was dressed in a Ralph Lauren pale-blue shirt and black jeans, and his longish blonde hair shone. He looked like an advertisement for Gillette. Jimmy was older, with thinning grey hair, and looked much more sedate than the others with his old tweed jacket, shirt and trousers. He could have been in a photo from the fifties, Conor thought. Miguel was Mexican, and he manoeuvred his trolley with one hand and carried a pewter urn in his other arm. The ashes, he assumed. They all shook hands, and then they were off.

Within ten minutes it was like old times. He had the bags loaded and his band of travellers aboard the bus.

CHAPTER 12

*M*iguel sat on the bed in his hotel room. It was the most beautiful bedroom he'd ever been in. When he thought of the rat-infested hovels he'd slept in over the years, it made him smile to look around at the plush carpet and green and gold upholstery. He stood up and went to the window. Below, a verdant green lawn gave way to the glittering Atlantic Ocean. He tried to imagine what his family back in San Luis de la Paz would say if they saw him now. He took his camera out of its case and took a few shots. It was the nicest thing he owned, made more precious because Bubbles had given it to him.

Miguel smiled sadly at the memory, and tears stung his eyes. In typical Bubbles style, he'd just left the camera on the bar for Miguel on the morning of his birthday. Bubbles was out, and when Miguel tried to thank him, he just brushed it aside. Bubbles was a mystery really. So emotional on one level – he would cry at the drop of a hat – but when people tried to thank him or tell him how much what he had done meant to them, he was embarrassed and ended the conversation abruptly.

He never imagined for one second the way his life would have turned out, and it was all down to Bubbles. If it wasn't for his intervention, Miguel would have found himself back in San Luis de la Paz with no prospects and no hope. But because the big Irishman took a shine to him, it changed everything. After the meeting in the bar where he'd asked to join the group, Kevin had approached him to say how much his coming on the trip would have meant to Bubbles.

He wasn't just an employee – he was a friend. It made him feel good, and it was the first happy feeling he'd had since Bubbles died. Miguel was proud that he had saved enough money to pay for the trip. He wanted to go; he needed to say goodbye to Bubbles.

He pulled out the letter from his wallet. Miguel had found it when he went up to get the spare keys to unlock the cellar – he knew Bubbles kept an extra set behind the locker in his bedroom. Bubbles told him once in case they were ever held up or broken into. Along with the keys, there was the letter. Miguel thought that Bubbles might have left it for him to find, knowing he was the only one who knew where the spare keys were.

He held it in his hands and looked down at the loopy handwriting on the faded blue envelope.

Mr F O'Leary,

525 Tumbler St

Brooklyn, NY 11217

It was postmarked Ireland, and there were two identical stamps, each with a picture of a monk. They said "De La Salle in Eireann 1880–1980" and cost twelve pounds. He could just make out the year on the postmark: 1980. There was no address or name on the back. He extracted the sheet from its envelope again. The first time he read it, it felt wrong, like he was prying into the private affairs of a man who had shown him nothing but kindness.

He almost knew the words by heart now, he'd read them so often. Bubbles had told him the story years ago.

Bubbles never opened the bar on the twelfth of September. One year, he came back late. Miguel was doing some painting, taking advantage of the fact that there were no customers. He'd never forget the way his friend looked at him that night; it was the memory he held closest to his heart.

'Are you okay?' he asked. Bubbles was in his horrible hairy suit and looked tired and beaten down somehow.

He rubbed his flaming-red beard and didn't answer that question, instead asking, 'Will you have a drink with me?'

Miguel nodded and went behind the bar, washed his hands, placed a bottle of Irish whiskey on the counter – Jameson Very Rare, the stuff Bubbles didn't waste on customers – and poured two glasses.

Gazing into the amber liquid, Bubbles began to speak unprompted, and Miguel knew, though later his friend confirmed it, that he was the only person in America Bubbles had told his story to.

'On the twelfth of September, I go to Mass. I'm not a religious man, but I do believe, and I've done a terrible thing. I know I will have to pay for what I did. I killed someone.'

The words hung in the air between them.

Miguel didn't interrupt; he knew Bubbles needed to say whatever he was going to say.

'A family who lived near us, the Mahers, had a son – Jack was his name – and he was a grand lad. But his mother's brother, a fella called Kit Mulligan, lived with them, and he was a violent man. Jack's mother adored him, and she was married to a right mouse of a man altogether. Anyway, I was in there doing a bit of work when this fella gets stuck in the young lad, really battering him, and the poor boy was a small, thin little thing. Anyway, I intervened – I was always a big lump – but then he turned on me. I hit him a clatter into the jaw, but he fell sideways and went down like a bag of spuds.' Bubbles inhaled as if to gather strength for what he was about to say. 'He hit his head on the kerb of the fireplace and…there and then, he died in front of us.'

Miguel didn't know what to say.

'I had to go, leave my home and everyone and everything I knew that night. Maybe I should have stayed and faced the music, but I panicked. Bridie Maher was well connected, and she was threatening all sorts. I can't ever go home – I'm a wanted man – and apart from one postcard to my mother every year, I've no contact with my family. I don't want to risk putting them in danger. If Bridie Maher knew they were in touch with me, well, it would be bad for them, so I took off and I never saw them again.'

'Do you want to go home now?' Miguel asked gently.

'I would, but I'd be put in jail. I'm wanted for murder. And I'm too scared. Kit Mulligan was not a person worth doing a life sentence for. It was an accident, and he was a vicious man. I try to do good, inasmuch as I can, to make up for it.' Bubbles lit a cigarette and exhaled a long plume of blueish smoke. The no-smoking ban only applied during open hours. 'Besides, I'm as illegal as yourself, Miguel, so if I left, I'd risk never getting back in again.'

Miguel picked up the letter once more.

Dear Finbarr,

I hope this letter reaches you in New York. It seems so far away, and I try to picture you there, but I can't. We're all okay. Daddy and Mammy refuse to mention anything about that night, and Fr Horgan is keeping a very close eye on everything and everyone.

The Mahers totally ignored us at Mass last Sunday. Bridie looked like a woman on a mission, sat in the front row, and poor old Con looking sheepish beside her. I'd say he's mortified about everything. I always liked him. Why he ever married that auld dragon, I'll never know. She marched Fidelma and Jack up the aisle in front of her like they were five years old, not fully grown adults. And they all decked out – I'd swear the whole family was in new rig-outs for the occasion. Fr Horgan made some reference to respectable families and all of that. He never said anything outright, but everyone knew what he meant.

I wish you didn't have to leave. Mammy and Daddy are heartbroken too. What happened wasn't your fault, Finbarr – he hit his head, you didn't kill him. I don't care if this is bad to say, but Kit Mulligan was a thug and he was going to hurt poor Jack if you didn't step in. Kit was Jack's uncle for God's sake. I don't know how Bridie can take her brother's side over her own son's.

Daddy told me what Bridie Maher threatened, about her other brother being high up in the guards as well in case we'd forgotten, as if you could. She's a horrible woman, Finbarr. How someone as lovely as Jack could have her for a mother, I'll never know.

I'll never forget that night as long as I live, Bridie screaming and Mammy crying and Fr Horgan threatening everyone. Poor Mammy and Daddy are afraid of him, you know? (I'll have to post this in Tralee now in case certain eyes decide to go snooping.)

I just want to say, none of us blame you. You were standing up for Jack against that brute Kit Mulligan, and Bridie should see that. But she is a dangerous woman, Finbarr, so maybe it's best you stay away.

I miss you, and I hope to see you again someday.

Your loving sister,

Kathleen xx

Miguel folded the letter.

* * *

KEVIN'S PHONE beeped in Tess's hands as he lay on one of the beds and she on the other. The room was beautifully decorated and huge. He'd been warned to expect small hotel rooms in Ireland, but this one was perfect.

'I need that, honey.' He held his hand out.

She ignored him.

'Tess, the phone please,' he said, this time a little more forcefully.

Still no response.

He went to take the phone out of her little hands.

'Hey, I'm in the middle of that,' she squawked. 'You made me die! That's not fair!'

Kevin looked down at her angry face and saw Debbie. His heart sank. Was his darling little girl turning into her mother? Debbie indulged her with things. His daughter had every new toy the moment it came out, and to Kevin's horror, his ex-wife had even bought Tess an iPad of her own to play games on. Debbie had packed the tablet with the girl's clothes and a list of instructions as long as his arm, but Kevin had deliberately left the device behind. He wanted to interact with his daughter, and he was sure all that time spent staring at a screen could not be good for her.

He'd only given her the phone to play a game she'd insisted he download because she was jet-lagged and refused to eat anything but candy bars since she left home. Debbie had been most adamant about Tess's diet; 'no candy' was written on the list of instructions in big black letters. No soda, no ice cream and no chips were also part of the dictate.

He knew the rest of the group were meeting in the bar for something to eat and a few beers, but he hoped Tess might fall asleep, so he had planned to order room service for them both.

'I just need to read this text, honey.' He tried to keep his voice light.

'Give me the phone when you're through.' She sighed, her little hand outstretched, palm upwards. It might have been funny if he weren't so tired and hungry.

The text was from Marianne.

Do you want something brought up?

He replied. *No thanks, getting room service. See you tomorrow. X*

He looked at it and went back, deleted the X.

He dutifully handed his daughter the phone. He'd start proper parenting tomorrow.

CHAPTER 13

*A*nnie and Marianne were not close friends. In fact, it was even a stretch to call them friends at all. They just knew each other from going to Bubbles's bar, but when Annie suggested that they share a room to keep the costs down, Marianne felt she couldn't refuse.

Talking when they bumped into each other in a bar was one thing; staying together in a foreign country for a whole week was quite another.

Beth had insisted on having her own room, and Marianne wished she'd had the courage to do the same. Splitting the cost was a considerable savings, but it felt weird. She hadn't shared a bedroom with anyone since Warren. She mentally rushed to put up the big stop sign in her head. That's what her therapist said she should do every time her husband popped into her mind.

Her husband… Well, to call him that now was a joke. Warren had moved on in every single way imaginable, and even in some ways that defied imagination, and she would just have to accept it and move on. It was hard, though.

She told Deanna, her therapist, that she'd deleted his number, but that was a lie. She didn't even know if he was still using that number.

He probably wasn't, but she just could not make herself do it. She didn't know where he was, though she imagined somewhere like Vegas or Atlantic City – someplace glitzy anyway. Then she dismissed that thought. Just because he told her he identified as a woman and had felt like he was a woman all his life didn't mean he was suddenly Priscilla, Queen of the Desert. She berated herself for being so uncool. That was one of the hardest parts about this... Well, the humiliation was the hardest part – that and the broken heart – but the fact that she was expected to be fine about it was so hard to take.

If Warren had had an affair, or if he'd just left her, then everyone would be rallying round, supporting her, being kind. But when your husband says he's a woman, you're expected to either have known about it – and that makes you a total weirdo – or you must be all sympathetic and understanding. She was so sick of the constant platitudes. He told everyone his news – their families, their friends – and never even consulted her. Then he took off, leaving her to deal with the fallout. Luckily, he didn't enjoy going to Bubbles's. He came with her once or twice but declared it wasn't his scene. She'd started going there with a gang from work for Bubbles's famous Friday night sessions. She loved Irish music, and Warren seemed happy to let her do her thing. Little did she know that while she was innocently enjoying the tunes and the camaraderie at Bubbles's, he was transforming into Samantha. And yet, since he left, she'd had to listen to how hard it must have been for him all those years, it's not his fault, he was just born that way, isn't he so brave? She wanted to scream into their stupid faces. 'He's a man – he's *my* man – and no, I had no idea he was a woman inside because he always seemed perfectly manly to me.'

She felt the tears sting her eyes again. Oh God, there was no way she could cry in front of Annie. Nobody in the group had mentioned Warren. She assumed they knew – everyone else did – but she could not talk about it. She wanted just one part of her life that was free of Warren or Samantha or whoever he was.

Annie happily unpacked; she had lovely clothes. Marianne felt very dowdy beside her in her jeans and T-shirts.

Annie was stunning. She was slim and had long blonde hair and that sweet little-girl-lost look about her. Marianne thought she was like a prize pig by comparison. She'd tried to lose some weight before coming on the trip, and all day she was so good, miserably eating undressed salads and drinking sparkling water. But at night, when she closed the door on the home she shared with Warren, she found refuge from her pain not in a gin bottle, though that might have been better from the weight perspective at least, but in the bottom of a Ben & Jerry's tub, or a family-sized pack of potato chips.

'I'm going to take a shower, unless you'd like to go first?' Annie asked her roommate, who looked on the verge of tears.

'No,' Marianne said in a strangled voice. 'You go ahead.' She recovered and gave a fake beam.

ANNIE STOOD under the lovely rain shower. Castle Dysert was as magnificent as it looked on the website. The décor was an eclectic mix of modern and sleek, with the odd antique dotted around to give a sense of time. It had every modern convenience, but still you felt like you were staying in a castle. She was so excited to be there; it was where she was going to meet 'the one', she just knew it. She thought initially that sharing with Marianne was exactly what she wanted. The other woman was really chatty and easy-going, and because she wasn't exactly model material, she would be an ideal wing-woman. Marianne could lure the guys in with her easy charm, and then they would fall for Annie – it was perfect.

Her mother had laughed when she told her about the matchmaking festival. 'Are you telling me that you can't find a man in the entire city of New York, but you think you'll find one in some village in the west of Ireland?' She'd rolled her eyes and sighed. Just another of Annie's crazy schemes.

But she would prove them all wrong. Her three sisters were all married and had kids and a mortgage and an SUV. In her mother's eyes, that was the pinnacle of success. It was all they asked her about at family get-togethers: Had she met anyone yet? She tried to laugh it off, make out like she didn't care, that she was single by choice, that she was married to her career. And she fervently wished that were true, but it wasn't. She wanted it. The whole lot – the husband, the kids, everything. But that was such a pathetic thing to admit to nowadays. She longed to have someone of her own. She looked at families in the park or at the movies and she yearned for that, to feel like she belonged to someone and they belonged to her. If you even uttered such a desire out loud, people looked at you like you were a sad and pitiable creature. But it was how she felt.

She wondered what was wrong with Marianne. She seemed a bit upset now that she was here. Annie hoped she wasn't going to be all mopey; she only had one shot at making this work. Maybe this wasn't the best idea in hindsight. Marianne seemed a bit emotionally unstable.

She always seemed like a nice person whenever they met at Bubbles. Annie recalled she came a few times with a smallish, skinny guy, bald, but she hadn't seen him in a while. Maybe they'd split up. She thought they looked odd together. Marianne didn't mention she had anyone when they were talking about the matchmaking festival, so she assumed that was over.

She wished she could just go up and talk to people – well, guys, if she was honest – the way Marianne could. She was so outgoing and funny, and even though she was at least thirty pounds heavier than Annie, she seemed to have them eating out of her hands. It must be true that men loved curves. She gazed ruefully at her flat stomach, her bony hips and her almost non-existent breasts. Marianne was so lucky – those boobs of hers were magnificent, and she made it look so effortless. She just wore jeans and shirts, hardly any make-up, and yet she managed to look great and everyone wanted to talk to her.

That guy – Conor – that picked them up was her perfect man actually, she mused as she washed her hair. Tall, muscular and with that gorgeous silver hair. But he must have mentioned his wife four times between the airport and the hotel, so he was not on the cards. She was a lucky woman whoever she was. Maybe there were more like him; that Irish accent melted her. It was what drew her to Bubbles actually. Not that he was attractive in that way – he was more like a big red-haired bear – but his accent swept her away. She wondered if she had any Irish in her; she must have to explain the connection she felt with Ireland. Her mother hadn't a clue about her roots and couldn't have cared less, and Annie didn't remember her dad, as he left when she was five.

* * *

WILL WENT FOR A WALK OUTSIDE, passing Jimmy in the lobby, but he just said hi. He had never actually spoken to Jimmy before Bubbles died. Jimmy always had his nose in a book, his NYC Sanitation Department hi-vis jacket hanging on the seat behind him, a glass of red wine in front of him. He was an unusual kind of guy, that was for sure.

Will, or at least Todd, had been in Ireland before, what seemed like a lifetime ago, but he'd never stayed someplace like this. He was backpacking and slept in hostels or camped to save money. He had a great time, what he remembered of it, but he was back now as a grown-up and determined to experience the culture. This was a new start, the reinvention of Will Munro. He'd moved to New York just six months earlier, as far from San Antonio, Texas, as he could get.

He wasn't Todd Munroe any more – Todd was dead, and good riddance.

He thought about Beth, in her room now, unpacking. She was the reason he'd come, though he was very fond of Bubbles. He wanted to get close to Beth.

Meeting Bubbles in the hospital was the best thing that could have happened. The big Irishman was in for a check-up, and health and safety laws meant that all patients needed to be transferred between departments in a wheelchair, though as Bubbles pointed out, he was perfectly capable of walking. It was only Will's second day on the job at Mount Sinai, where he'd been hired as a porter. All non-medical staffing was handled by a private company, and he'd managed to falsify his paperwork and references well enough to pass their not-too-vigorous recruitment process. He and Bubbles hit it off that day, and Bubbles said that Will should stop by his bar one night. He did, and it was the best move he could have made.

It was like Bubbles's bar gave him a life, and identity. He was so sad that Bubbles was gone. He really was a remarkable man, and so many people owed him something, but the Irish guy never took any credit. But for all of the improvements Bubbles brought to Will's life, he got to meet Beth, and that was the best thing.

* * *

Jimmy Burns sat in the garden of the hotel, admiring his surroundings. His book, *Nicomachean Ethics* by Aristotle, lay unopened beside him. It didn't matter if he read it or not; he knew it almost word for word anyway.

He leaned back and inhaled. The fresh clean air, with the slight tang of salt from the sea, was such a contrast to the pollution in New York, though things had improved considerably since the monitoring of the air quality began a decade ago. The people had Mayor Bill de Blasio to thank for that, though New Yorkers didn't tend to notice improvements, just deteriorations. In his forty years in the sanitation department, he'd seen huge changes – recycling, reducing waste, cleaning the air – but he lived closer to the heart and guts and bowels of the city than most people. That and the fact that he was quiet. He listened rather than talked.

He surveyed his surroundings. The landscaping was truly exquisite. The plant species were not native to Ireland; in fact, he recognised several Antipodean varieties growing in profusion. They were a long way from home, but they seemed to like it there. The heat from the Gulf Stream hit the coast of Ireland, warming the sea and the land a little so tropical plants could thrive there. It was one of the many anomalies that made up Ireland.

This was Jimmy's first time out of the United States, though he had a valid passport all his life, renewed each time it went out of date. He had no desire over the years to leave; he liked his life. He needed to keep on an even keel all the time. It was how he coped. He worked alone for the most part, in a job that required virtually no emotional investment. And while he enjoyed being in company, hence spending time at Bubbles's bar, he avoided intimate situations. He could talk about philosophy or chemistry with anyone, but when people struck up conversations about the weather or baseball, he was awkward. It made life difficult, but it was how he was, and he had come to accept it. His mother had understood. She didn't have the words for it, but she knew he felt things more deeply than other kids. He would cry so easily and felt the pain of others. His father called him a crybaby and frequently beat him to 'really give him something to cry about', so he learned to bottle it up. He was drawn to philosophy – the ancient Greeks understood humans in a way that seemed to have been lost in this time. He dedicated his life to the study of the human condition, what made people what they were, the study of empathy and how it was the path to greater and deeper understanding of themselves and others. His graduation from Molloy, when he was conferred with a PhD, was a great day. Others had family there, photographs and all of that, but Jimmy went alone. If his mother had been alive, he would have asked her, but she died, and he wasn't close to his siblings. But he went up and accepted his scroll as he was conferred with his degree, and his heart sang. He was officially Dr James Burns, but he never mentioned it to anyone. He did it for himself, and it was a rewarding way to live. He was hoping to catch up on some reading this week for his new course of study, Ethics and Practical Theology.

He had a small apartment in Forest Hills, Queens, worked a full week in the sanitation department and relaxed with a book when he wasn't working, eating or sleeping. He travelled the world in books, from ancient Greece and Rome to fiction set two centuries in the future. He read books on botany, criminology, philosophy, astronomy, sport, chemistry... The list was endless. He rarely bought books as he didn't like clutter, so he used the library.

He admired this place, glad he'd come. It was so different from the landscape of his daily life.

So this was the land that created Bubbles, he thought. It made sense; the land was like the man. He was big and warm and welcoming, with a wild streak, and then other times, he could be so melancholy it would break your heart. There was a terrible sadness in Bubbles, and when Jimmy was around him, he could feel it, almost as if the despair was his own.

CHAPTER 14

$\mathscr{B}$eth insisted on a room on her own. She needed to be alone sometimes. She could have shared with Marianne and Annie, but she would have been uncomfortable. Besides, she needed to keep her phone on loud all the time in case Maddie called.

She sat on the bed, her clothes neatly unpacked, and decided the time had come – she'd have to call home. She'd tried calling Maddie several times since the text, but her calls were going straight to voice-mail. She had been putting off phoning her mother.

She scrolled and found the number, not one she used frequently, and pressed the green Call button. The familiar feeling of dread filled her.

'Hello?' That voice.

'Hi, Mom, it's Beth.' She tried to keep her voice steady.

'Elizabeth… How nice to hear from you. How are you?' The cold, haughty New England tone hadn't changed.

She hated being called Elizabeth. And her mother knew it.

'Fine, thank you. I was just wondering if I could speak to Maddie. She's there with you, right?' She could hear her heart thumping in her ears.

A pause. Did that mean something?

'I haven't heard from or seen Madison for over two years, Elizabeth.' That coldness, how she managed to infuse every sentence with that depth of bitterness, brought Beth back to her childhood.

Poor Maddie looked just like their dad; it was as if every time their mother looked at her, she saw her husband. No wonder Maddie went off the rails and Beth hid in the library. She studied so hard, day and night, and finally got to Harvard. The money her father left her paid for it – another reason for her mother to hate her. Beth had accepted there was no future for her and her mother, but poor Maddie kept trying, like a little puppy, to get their mother's affection. They had long ago agreed not to discuss it as it just upset them.

'Oh… Okay then.' She was fourteen again.

'Is there anything else I can do for you?' Melanie Anderson asked.

'Um…no. That's all I wanted to know.'

Silence. Her mother was going to make her end the call.

'Well, take care, Mom, and…well…bye.' She longed for something else to say.

'Goodbye, Elizabeth.'

She pressed the red End Call button and threw the phone on the bed like it was on fire.

It was the most unlikely thing in the world that Maddie would have gone back to Norfolk, Virginia, but it was what she said in the text. Beth mentally shook herself. Maddie *had* texted. She said she was all right and she'd get in touch again soon. She always did. Beth repeated the words like a mantra, forcing herself to believe them.

'Eventually'. The word popped unbidden into her head. She had to admit it was true. One time, Maddie moved to some kind of a commune out west, a cult almost, and Beth heard nothing for five months. But afterwards, she made Maddie swear she would never do that again. The cops warned her too about wasting police time and all of that, and she seemed contrite, but then with Maddie, you never really knew. She was regaling some people in the bar one night about the number of times she'd just taken off, and everyone was delighted with her. She came across as such a free spirit, but that wasn't really how she was. She was broken and searching, and sometimes she just couldn't cope so she checked out. Whenever she crashed, it was Beth who had to pick up the pieces.

She booked this trip almost to spite her sister. She was so mad at her, thinking she could take off without a word, knowing that Beth would be out of her mind. But she wished she could just feel angry. The overwhelming feeling was not anger, it was worry.

She decided to check out the hotel. They were all meeting in the bar later for food and a drink, but she needed some time before that. The building itself was incredible – a gorgeous castle, separated from the ocean's edge by a long, sweeping lawn. Conor explained that last year there had been a fire on the opening night, and one wing was totally destroyed. But the insurance paid out, and now it was good as new. He was a nice guy, that Conor; he seemed a restful sort of person to be around. Annie put her eye on him, but he was definitely not on the market. Apart from the white-gold wedding ring he wore, he mentioned his wife and children a lot.

She should make more of an effort with Marianne and Annie. They were nice people. Marianne especially was great fun, and she had something nice to say to everyone. They were both single and excited about this matchmaking thing, but Beth dreaded it. She knew it would just be awkward.

She walked in the grounds. There were incredible gardens, fountains and ponds all around the castle and what looked like a wooded area behind. Conor explained how they had a marquee in a clearing in the woods where they held weddings and big crowd functions. There were stables as well, and she found herself drawn there. The half-doors were open in the eight stables around a cobbled courtyard, and in four of them, horses watched her enter the yard.

She went to the first one, a shiny bay with those melted-chocolate eyes, and she stroked his muzzle. He gazed at her, and she leaned her face to his and inhaled that gorgeous horsey smell. That wonderful aroma of horse sweat, sweet hay, linseed and old leather. She was back with her dad, in their stables, able to ride almost before she could walk. Memories came flooding back, the hours she and Maddie spent with him, then that night. She hadn't sat on a horse since; that was fifteen years ago.

She turned and ran from the stables – it was all too much. She couldn't deal with that, not with everything else as well. She went back into the gardens surrounding the castle and found Jimmy sitting on a bench. She half wished she hadn't seen him, but it would be rude not to stop. She found him difficult to speak to, as he allowed the other person to do all the talking.

'Hi, Jimmy.'

'Hello, Beth.' He smiled, holding his hand up to his eyes to shield them from the evening sun as it began to set over the Atlantic.

There was an awkward silence. She didn't know whether to move on or sit or wait for him to say something else.

'Would you like to join me?' he said eventually. The invitation seemed genuine.

'Sure.' She sat beside him.

They sat in silence, and she tried not to feel like she should fill the space between them with talk.

The birds were singing in the nearby trees, and two red admiral butterflies danced near a fragrant lilac tree to their left. In the distance, one could just about hear the gentle lapping of the waves on the rocky shore. A seagull squawked overhead, disturbing the peace.

The world seemed so perfect – everything in harmony, nature doing its thing, the sun sinking slowly, sure to rise again tomorrow – but nothing was right. Absolutely nothing. Her dad was dead, and he shouldn't be. If only she hadn't been so stupid, he'd still be there, their mother wouldn't hate them, and Maddie wouldn't be the way she was. Tears flowed silently down her cheeks, and without saying a word, Jimmy reached over and held her hand. She looked down at his age-spotted hand, with the calluses from years of physical work, resting gently on her small white one. And for a reason she couldn't explain, it gave her peace.

They sat together for a while, but the silence was no longer awkward.

Eventually, Jimmy spoke. 'Why are you so sad, Beth?'

The question was so direct, so gentle yet forthright, it took her aback. She was naturally a very reserved person, but she found that she wanted to share with him. Jimmy had always talked to her and Maddie when they met, mainly because they spoke to him. He was so interesting on a wide range of topics, and she always enjoyed their conversations, but they'd never discussed anything personal before.

'My dad was a really good trial attorney. He was well respected and always fought for the underdog. He drowned trying to save me and my sister when he was only fifty. We were kidding around on our horses near a flooded river. It was really dumb and dangerous, but I was fifteen and Maddie was only ten. I should have known better – we'd been warned about that river over and over. She went out too far, and her horse lost his footing, and she was swept downstream. I went after her, but the current was too fast, and the same thing happened to me. Someone must have seen us and raised the alarm. My dad came running and jumped in to save us. Maddie hit a rock but managed to get on top of it, and I grabbed a low-hanging branch and held on until someone got to me, but my dad died.'

Jimmy kept his hand on hers, never flinching, never reacting. 'Keep talking if it helps,' he said quietly.

'My mother blames me and Maddie. She…she hates us for taking him from her. And after that, Maddie went kind of crazy. She flunked out of school, always in trouble with the teachers and all of that, and she's lived a kind of nomadic life since then – she can't settle to anything. And now she's gone missing, and I'm so worried. I think this time something bad may have happened to her.'

Beth turned her head to look at Jimmy. His eyes were bright. There was something about him, something that made her feel not so alone.

'But she has been in touch?' he asked.

'Yes, I got a text from her, but in it, she said she was going to our mother's house. Maddie would never go there. And then I called, spoke to my mother for the first time in years, and she's not there. My mother hasn't seen her in two years.' Beth's brow was furrowed.

'Trust your instinct. If you believe some harm may have come to your sister, then trust that,' he said quietly.

'But she's done this before. The cops are fed up of me reporting her missing. She's probably off living in a tent with some hairy guy and not giving a damn what this is doing to me.' She heard the bitterness in her voice.

'Did you feel that strong sense of foreboding the last times?' he asked.

'No... Maybe... I don't know.' She struggled to answer him honestly. Was she this worried the last time?

'Trust your instinct,' was all he said.

A shadow crossed them, and they looked up. Will was standing there. 'Hi Beth, Jimmy. How are you doing? This is some place, right?'

Beth shielded her eyes from the sun, but he could see she'd been crying.

'Oh, Beth, what's wrong? Can I help?' He sat beside her.

'I'm just worried about Maddie...' she mumbled. She'd opened up to Jimmy, but she hardly knew this Will guy.

'But she got in touch, didn't she? She's fine?' Will's face was a picture of confusion.

'Yeah, she texted to say she was at our mother's house, but I called there, and she hasn't seen her. I don't get why she'd lie.' Beth frowned, and Will thought she'd never looked more beautiful.

'Well, maybe she's with some guy or something and she didn't want you to worry, so she just said that?' he suggested, and the other two looked at him.

'But why would she lie?' she asked. 'What if someone has her phone?' A horrible thought occurred to Beth. Since receiving the text, she'd tried to quell the feeling that something didn't add up, but it was back with a vengeance now.

Will shrugged. 'I don't know. I guess I'm just trying to make you feel better. But y'know, most people who go missing do show up. I watched a show about it on PBS.'

She gave a weak smile. 'Thanks. You're probably right. I'm going to text her again and then try the cops, tell them that she's not at our mother's.'

As she got up to leave, Jimmy had an idea. 'How about you ask her a question in the text, nothing suspicious, but something only she would know the answer to?'

Beth's face lit up. 'That's a great idea. Like I could ask her… I don't know…' She thought hard.

'Your second-grade teacher? You could say you ran into someone who knew her or something and you couldn't think of her name?' Will suggested.

Beth smiled for the first time. 'My second-grade teacher taught Maddie as well. She was a really scary lady, Mrs Bell. She'd definitely remember her. Thanks, guys. I just need to not freak out here. As you say, Will, there's probably a perfectly innocent explanation.'

CHAPTER 15

'What you doing today? I think maybe I will come to hotel for lunch?' Ana asked as she and Conor ate breakfast together alone. The boys were at a hurling camp all week, and Artur had dropped them before he went to work. The remains of their cereal and toast were still on the table, but Conor just moved everything to one end and made space for himself and Ana at the other. He'd clear it all up together when they were finished.

He smiled across the table at her. He noticed she'd taken off her wedding and engagement rings because they were too big. She was always chilled, but they were warned that the constant feeling of cold was a side effect of one of the drugs. They had the heating on full blast day and night, so much so that it made the house really stuffy. But Conor explained to the twins why it had to be like that, and they didn't complain; they just wore as little as possible.

He frequently came home to Ana on the sofa, wearing flannel pyjamas, fluffy socks and Conor's sweaters and wrapped in blankets, still shivering, as the boys stripped down to their underwear. The cold, the aching joints, the nausea – it was all gruelling, but she rarely complained. After each session of chemo, she would have a good two days, have enough energy to hang out with the boys or do some housework though Conor begged her not to, but the next three days were awful for her. She hadn't the energy to get up, and she felt nauseous and hungry simultaneously and just depleted completely. She looked exhausted, and while the doctors were very positive about the progression of her treatment, she had a long road ahead of her. The thought of losing her tormented his dreams as well as his waking hours. Now that he knew love like this, he couldn't function without her. He could do little except watch and try to keep her as comfortable as he could. Sometimes she just wanted him to lie beside her and hold her.

Artie and Joe were worried too. They came to him with their concerns, and it broke his heart to see his boys' carefree lives altered so suddenly. He and Ana were honest and called the cancer what it was. They told them that their mammy was definitely going to get better, but it might take a little while longer. They were great though. They helped out as much as they could and lay on the bed with Ana watching movies on Netflix when she was able. They never complained about the sauna-like house or spending so much time with Danika and Artur, and Conor did his best to allay their fears.

'I've to pick up that group, take them out to Lisdoonvarna this morning and collect them this afternoon, then it's the same old ding-dong. Katherine and Carlos are really managing everything. I just need to show my face and sometimes smooth a few ruffled feathers. Our Mr Manner can be a bit over the top, as you know. I'd love to see you, you know I would, but your immunity is compromised, and maybe in a public place, people sneezing and coughing...'

'Ding-dong, feathers, how is this silly language the biggest in the world, I don't know.'

Conor chuckled. It was a recurring theme with her, the madness of the English language.

'Seriously, today is a good day. I feeling okay, you know, and I can't stay all day in this house. It making me crazy.'

He thought for a moment. She *was* good today, relatively speaking. It was one of her strong days, and she did need to get out of the house, but he was still worried.

'All right, but no driving, okay? I'll come back here for you, and we can have lunch in my office, and then I'll take you home. Deal?' He smiled.

'Deal, but I want to see Katherine and my father and go for a walk in the grounds too, okay? Deal?'

She stuck out her hand and he took it, bringing it to his lips and kissing it gently.

'Deal,' he said huskily. She looked so fragile, so vulnerable. He was terrified.

* * *

HE CAUGHT up on paperwork and calls while the group enjoyed breakfast. He knew that while they had kept everything ticking over, neither Katherine nor Carlos was what you'd call a people person.

He'd made contact with a film company earlier in the year that wanted to use the castle in a movie as well as for accommodation next winter. It would be a very lucrative deal if he managed to set it up, so he called the producer. He also called Corlene, assured her all was well and filled her in on everything. She ran a business helping older women who had reason to believe their husbands were after young ones. It sounded ludicrous to Conor, but apparently it was very successful. He checked in with several tour operators, who were the mainstay of the business. Luxury tours in Ireland were clamouring to stay at Castle Dysert because it had the right combination of ancient charm and modern convenience.

He would have liked to go for a swim – he swam most days – but there would not be time. He finished up and gathered his phone, keys and wallet. the hotel had its own minibus, a really luxurious one, which he used a lot. Though the timing wasn't ideal, he loved being back driving a tour again. He'd had many happy years in that business, and it was how he'd met Ana.

Katherine raised one eyebrow as she saw him head out to the coach. 'It's just like old times. I remember you coming into the Dunshane, getting housekeeping to do your laundry for you, using the reception desk as your personal office – you were the bane of our lives.' Though her tone was serious, he knew she was joking. Katherine and he had been friends for well over thirty years.

'Ah, you loved me then, and you love me more now.' He winked and smiled at her. Carlos was at the desk looking impatient.

'Morning, Carlos, how's everything? Thanks again for all the extra hours you're doing with Ana being sick. It's a great weight off my mind that you and Katherine have the place running like a mouse's heart. I'll make it up to you once the season is over and we have time to draw breath.'

Carlos looked uncomfortable. He was a man who was meticulous in every way and fastidious in his personal appearance. Ana said he looked like an old-fashioned toy soldier.

'Yes, well, we will discuss that in due course, and *in private.'* He bristled. Conor was used to him now, but he knew Carlos Manner found Conor's style of management – casual and personable – to be entirely unsuitable and inappropriate.

'Righteo. I'm off, on the road again, as if nothing has changed.' He tapped the beautiful oak reception desk and was gone.

The group were punctual, and they sat gathered outside the castle on the benches and chairs placed there for guests' use.

'Ok, folks, will we get this show on the road?' he asked as they followed him to where the bus was parked.

'Hi, Tess.' He addressed the little girl as they all followed.

'Hey.' She looked glum, and her pigtails were uneven.

'What's up?' he asked as they walked. Her father was deep in chat with Marianne, an attractive woman with a kind, open face.

'Daddy can't do my hair, and I look really messy. And he won't let me play on his phone, and he forgot my iPad, and there's nothing to do here.' She kicked some gravel with the toe of her expensive-looking sneaker.

'Well, let's solve one problem right now.' He smiled as a car pulled erratically into the car park and a girl with violet hair and lots of piercings jumped out.

'Conor!' She launched herself on him in a big hug. Behind her stood a man in his twenties carrying two music cases.

'Laoise, great to see you! How was Japan?' He hugged her back. 'Hi, Dylan.' He smiled at the young man.

'A-*may*-zing!' Laoise announced. 'So, so cool, like not a bit like I imagined. But then I thought the whole place would be full of geisha girls or sushi bars or something. But anyway, it's not, but such a cool place. And they loved the music, which is so weird 'cause it's nothing like theirs. Like I can't imagine Japanese music going down a bomb over here, but sure, there you have it. It's a mad but cool and brilliant place.'

Conor laughed. Laoise was always the same, like a thunderclap, full of chat and dramatics, but she had a heart of gold. Her boyfriend, Corlene's son Dylan, had come to Ireland when he was just a teenager, and he fell in love with the uilleann pipes – and with Laoise – and nothing had changed in the intervening years.

'Well, I'm looking forward to hearing all about it, and the boys will be over the moon you two are back, but I've got to go now. How about you call over to us tonight – we'll get takeaway. Before I do though, can you help me and my little friend out here?'

'Of course, and yes to the takeaway too. We need some junk food. Those Japanese are so healthy... I nearly died of hunger over there.'

Dylan caught his eye and grinned.

Conor hunkered down in front of Tess. 'Tess, this is my friend Laoise, and she is brilliant at doing hair.'

Tess didn't look convinced. Laoise's own hair was long on one side and shaved on the other and dyed an alarming colour.

'Honestly, she used to have long hair, but she changes it every week. Now, Laoise, this is Tess, and she's on her holidays from America with her daddy. He's like most daddies – terrible at doing girls' hair – so we have a bit of a predicament.'

Laoise responded by going down on her hunkers in front of the little girl and making a funny face, which made Tess giggle while the group looked on.

'I thought it wasn't too bad!' Kevin exclaimed with mock hurt.

'Daddy, look, I'm all wonky.' Tess pointed to her head of curls.

'Not for long. Come here to me, Tess. Watch and learn, Daddy.' Laoise winked at Kevin. Then she gave Tess her full attention.

'I know exactly. My dad tried to do my hair once, and I looked so silly, like a poodle!' Laoise made a face and Tess giggled. 'Now, I have a brush here somewhere.' Laoise started digging in what looked to Conor like the world's biggest handbag. She extracted tuning forks and phone chargers and packets of chewing gum, throwing them up on the bonnet of the car until eventually extracting a hairbrush.

'Now, let's get these pigtails down and we'll start again, shall we?'

Dylan gazed on in adoration. He appeared very conservative in a white shirt and black trousers, but nobody could doubt how he felt about the very exotic-looking Laoise. She worked quickly, not pulling on Tess's hair, and soon had it in two cute French plaits.

'I like your sleeve,' Tess said, pointing to Laoise's fully tattooed arms adorned with women's faces and Irish script.

'Thanks, Tess, so do I. But my mammy and daddy went a bit crazy when they saw it.' Laoise pulled another face and Tess laughed. 'See here?' Laoise pointed to a woman's head on her upper arm. 'That's Grainne Uaile – she was an Irish pirate queen. And this other one is Maire Rua, a woman who killed bad soldiers to protect her sons. And this one here' – she raised her arm to show Tess the woman on the underside – 'is Dr Kathleen Lynn. She fought for Ireland to be free and looked after all the poor people when they had no money for a doctor. And this other woman here is Countess Markievicz. She was a lovely lady, but she led the women of Ireland to fight the British too. There was a whole army of women called Cumann na mBan, and that's written here, see?' Tess was mesmerised.

'Okay.' Conor grinned, putting his arm around Laoise and planting a kiss on the top of her head. 'Thanks, Laoise, you're a lifesaver,' he whispered.

CHAPTER 16

'So, folks, this is County Clare, on the western seaboard of the island of Ireland, and it really is a rich and rare land. A bit further north is the Burren, a hundred square miles of limestone, where the most wonderful arctic and alpine and even Mediterranean flowers grow in the cracks in the stone. It's also where the greatest concentration of prehistoric monuments in Ireland can be found. Maybe if ye like, on one of the days, we could take a tour around to see dolmens and ring forts and standing stones?'

The crowd answered enthusiastically that they'd love it.

Conor chatted away, telling them stories and bits of history here and there. He stopped at St Brigid's Well and everyone got out.

'Now,' he said, as they stood in front of what looked like a small cave, 'this is a special place. It's a shrine dedicated to St Brigid, who is the female patron saint of Ireland. Legend has it that she was asking the king of Leinster for land for a monastery – anyway, he refused. But she was like most Irish women, not to be thwarted. She'll get her way in the end and it's best to give in early, I've always found.'

The group laughed.

'Anyway, she asked again and said she only needed as much land as her cloak could cover. Well, the king looked and saw her small cloak and said that she could have that much land. But Brigid asked her followers to each take a corner of the cloak and begin to walk. As they did, the cloak grew and soon covered many acres, plenty of space for a monastery, so the king had to give her the land.'

Conor went on, knowing his audience was listening carefully.

'But Brigid wasn't always a Christian deity. You see, when the Christians came here, in around the fifth century, they found here a Celtic, pagan people. And rather than create trouble by insisting they abandon all of their beliefs, they simply laid the Christian beliefs on top, as it were. So Celtic festivals and deities of the pagan world simply became Christian ones. The Celtic cross – the one with the crucifix and the circle in the top – is the best example of that. The cross symbolises Christianity obviously, but the circle in the top is there to represent the sun and the moon, important symbols of the pagan tradition.'

He led them into the small cave, and to their astonishment, they found it to be full of things: bars of chocolate, walking sticks, CDs, clothing, photographs and so much more.

'What are all these things?' Erin asked shyly.

'This is a place sacred to the travelling people. The travellers are nomadic people who move around the country, and they have a very deep faith. They leave these things here as offerings to St Brigid, as remembrances for people who have passed on, or as intentions, something they are praying for.'

The group read the little notes and prayers and messages on every available space on the cave walls. Things were stacked in every corner, and the whole place was full.

'On St Brigid's feast day, the first of February, called Imbolc in the Celtic tradition, the festival heralding the beginning of spring, people tie a piece of cloth to a tree or a bush – we call it a brat – and it is believed that St Brigid flies through the country that night blessing these pieces of cloth. Then people use those as good luck charms, or they might put it in the cot with a sick baby or something.'

Conor noticed that Jimmy walked quickly out of the cave back towards the bus.

The group pottered around the cave for a few minutes before Conor announced it was time to go. As they walked out, he fell into step with Shannon and Erin, who were almost identical. They were dressed conservatively, in beige walking trousers and sturdy shoes, and each had a navy Polartec fleece.

'So, ladies, is everything to your liking in the hotel?' he asked as they strolled back to the bus.

Both women reddened, but Erin spoke. 'Oh yes, thank you. It's a beautiful place, really amazing. I've never seen anything like it. And the staff are so friendly, nothing is too much trouble.'

'Ah, that's great to hear,' he said. 'I'll pass that on to them. So is it your first time to Ireland? With names like Shannon and Erin, you must have some Irish blood in you?'

Erin answered again. 'Yes, we do. Both our parents are Irish – well, they've both passed on now, but yes, they were from the west of Ireland. They met in America, and our father was one of the last people through the immigration hall at Ellis Island before they closed it in 1943. They never got the opportunity to return, so I'm sure they'd be happy that we are getting to see the beautiful island they came from.'

She looked embarrassed to have made such a long speech, but Conor had a way of putting people at their ease.

'I'm sure they would.' He smiled, looking up at the blue sky with puffy white clouds scudding across it. 'I'd say they're looking down now, delighted to see their daughters in Ireland. It was a terrible hardship for people to leave their home, but back in those days, there wasn't much to keep them here. There are over forty million Irish Americans I believe, incredible when you consider there are only four million of us here. You'll have a great time, and sure you never know, you might meet the man of your dreams at the matchmaking and stay here.' He winked to show he was joking.

The matchmaking element of the trip terrified Erin. What would they be expected to do? Neither of them had ever been on a date. Mammy would not have allowed it when they were younger and might have attracted some man's attention, and now that they were older, well, that ship had sailed, for her at least. Still the others, Annie and Marianne, and even Kevin and Miguel, seemed to think it all a bit of a lark, so they had to go along with it. Of the two sisters, Erin knew Shannon to be the prettier one. She loved her sister and was happy with their life together. What if Shannon met someone and Erin was left all alone? She tried to dismiss the thought. She should be happy for her sister, but the prospect was horrible. She didn't want to sound negative since her sister seemed interested in it. Her heart sank when she heard Shannon speak.

'About that, Conor. We have never been to a festival of that nature, and we wondered what the procedure was?'

Erin saw her sister flush with embarrassment.

'Well, ladies, there is a matchmaker there. His name is Paudie Mac, and he is a third-generation matchmaker. Long ago in Ireland, most weddings were a made match, where the families would put two young people together, and sometimes not so young either.' He smiled gently, realising these were fragile ladies, unused to banter.

'And anyway, he has an office in a pub in the town, and there he meets with people looking for love. He has a lucky book, and once you fill out the application form, he places it in the book. Now the story goes that if you close your eyes and hold the book for seven seconds, then you'll be in love within six months.'

They looked at him wide-eyed, taking every word seriously.

'But if that's not for you, then there is plenty to enjoy during the festival. There's music and dancing and great craic around the streets...' He paused. 'Craic has a different meaning here –' he began, but Erin interrupted.

'We know.' She giggled. 'Bubbles explained, and he had a sign up in his bar with "Craic Addict" written on it. He loved that sign.'

Conor saw the sadness on their faces at the loss of this man.

'He sounded like a character all right. Forgive me for being so nosey, but you two don't strike me as a pair of hardened drinkers, so how did you know Bubbles?'

They giggled.

'You're right. We're both teetotallers. We met him at the Irish

Centre. He was such a good man, you know, always helping others. He used to cook and serve at – and probably fund – the seniors' lunch club,' Erin said.

Shannon continued. 'They bought a building a few years ago – Bubbles was involved from the start, I believe – in Long Island, where Irish people could congregate. They do Irish language classes, music, dancing, all that sort of thing. They have a lunch club once a week, and it's a way for older Irish people to get a good meal and a cup of tea and a biscuit. We call them that in the Irish Centre, not cookies.' She laughed, and Conor was delighted to see them relax a bit.

'And so we were taking an Irish language class there, and we ran into Bubbles. He suggested that we volunteer at the lunch club, so we did, and then he invited us to come to his bar. And you're right, we are not real bar-goers, but Bubbles's place was different. It was more like a family,' Erin finished, her voice catching with emotion as she spoke.

'He was obviously a special man much loved by his friends,' Conor said, offering them his hand to get up the step into the bus. They took it in turn, and each gave him a radiant smile.

Jimmy was already in his seat, gazing pensively out at the stunning vista. He found the cave overwhelming. So many sad stories – it was exactly that sort of thing he tried to avoid.

Beth followed with Will, who seemed to be doing his best to chat her up, but she seemed distracted somehow. Conor had seen that many times before; the person comes to Ireland to get away from something, but they are only physically there – their mind and spirit are elsewhere.

'Hi, Beth, how's everything going?' he asked as she entered the bus.

'Oh...um...great, thank you. It's a beautiful country,' she responded, but it sounded hollow to his ears. Something was on her mind.

Taking tours for over twenty years meant he met so many people and observed them all. He found he had a natural talent for seeing what lay beneath. He'd had so many wonderful and bizarre and downright unpleasant experiences as a tour driver, he reckoned he'd seen a lot of what human nature had to offer. Every type of person had shown up on his bus at one time or another.

Marianne and Annie were deep in chat as they approached the bus.

'Hi, ladies, all okay?' he asked, helping them up.

'Oh, we're more than okay.' Annie smiled. 'The view is just spectacular.' She smirked at Marianne, clearly indicating she wasn't just referring to the glittering sea and tall cliffs.

A robin landed on the stone wall right beside them.

'In Ireland, we say that the robins are the souls –' Conor began.

'Of loved ones who have passed on,' Annie interrupted. 'Bubbles always said that. He used to have a birdbath out on the deck behind the bar, and he loved the robins coming in particular.'

'That's right. It's them dropping by to say they are okay.'

Marianne and Annie looked at the robin for a moment. 'Hi, Bubbles,' Annie whispered, almost to herself.

Marianne smiled at the idea and silently said hi to Bubbles too. Annie was a conundrum. Sometimes she could seem so confident and downright intimidating; other times she seemed vulnerable.

Miguel was taking photos further along the road, and he stood on a mossy bank getting a panoramic shot of the bay. He was entirely lost in his own world. He had an actual camera with a big zoom lens, not a phone like so many people used nowadays.

'Miguel,' Conor called. 'We're taking off now.'

Miguel waved and began to walk back to the bus.

Conor looked back towards the grotto where Kevin and Tess looked like they were having another argument. The little girl was standing with her arms folded and a scowl on her face, undoubtedly because her father was refusing to give her his phone.

Kevin was trying to reason with her. He wanted her to see the scenery, experience Ireland, but she just wanted to play games on his iPhone.

Conor discussed this problem often with Ana – the boys were the same. They loved playing football or making things with Lego, but the moment the option to use a device presented itself, they dropped what they were doing. He got that screens could be a really useful tool when parents needed a bit of peace and quiet, but Conor had his doubts about whether they were good for them. His heart went out to Kevin. He couldn't imagine single parenting; it must be so hard.

'No!' He could hear Tess yelling now. 'I'm not going on that stupid bus, and I want to go home. I want to go back to Mommy. I hate it here, and I hate you!'

She took off at a speed that belied her little legs out onto the road, her father running behind her. Conor heard the roar of an engine seconds before a car came around the bend at speed. He ran into the middle of the road, forcing the vehicle to swerve. Kevin grabbed Tess. The driver screeched to a stop, skidding to a halt inches from where Conor stood. The air was instantly filled with the smell of burning rubber where the tyres had clung to the road. Tess, once she recovered from the shock, started screaming in her father's arms.

Marianne and Annie ran out of the bus and were trying to comfort the little girl. Kevin was white with shock.

Shaking, Conor went over to the driver's window, where a boy no older than twenty sat, with a girl around the same age in the passenger seat beside him. Conor leaned down as the lad lowered the window. He was dressed in a tracksuit with a baseball cap down over his eyes. He looked belligerent but shocked.

'Get out,' Conor ordered. The boy did as he was told – Conor's tone brooked no argument. He stood beside the car, and Conor felt his heart rate return to normal.

'Nothing happened this time, thank God, but that is a ridiculous speed to be doing on narrow roads with bends like this. Slow down, for God's sake, or you might actually kill someone next time.'

The boy looked up as the girl got out and came around to where they were standing.

'I'm sorry, you're right… He wasn't concentrating. Is the little girl all right?' She looked sheepishly to where Kevin and Tess were being soothed by Marianne. Tess's screams had subsided to sobs now, and her little arms were wound tightly around Kevin's neck.

The boy still said nothing; he was in shock.

'She is, but learn from this, will you? One second later and you could be looking at your life changing forever. You could have killed her, or me.'

The boy just nodded, still unable to speak.

'Can you drive this car?' he asked the girl.

'Yes, I'm insured on it as well,' she replied. She was shaken but not as bad as the driver.

'Okay. Get in the driver's seat, go back to the road there. There's a café. Take him in and give him a hot drink and something to eat and take him home. He's had a shock.' Conor opened the driver's door, and the girl got in. The young man walked around to the passenger side, but then changed his mind and approached Kevin.

'I'm so sorry... I was going too fast...' He was as white as a sheet.

'It's okay. She's fine. She shouldn't have run out, but you need to slow down, all right?' Kevin said.

The boy nodded and went back to his car, and they drove away.

'Conor, I... If you hadn't stopped him... I... Thank you.' Kevin could hardly express what he felt.

Marianne had found some chocolate in her bag and gave it to Tess, who was still crying, albeit more quietly now. She was sitting on Marianne's lap, and Kevin stood beside them.

'No problem. I'd say that lad got a right fright as well, so hopefully it will teach him a lesson.' He bent down in front of Tess.

'Are you okay now, pet?' he asked gently.

She nodded, her eyes still wet with tears.

Conor patted her head. 'You're a brave little girl, but you must promise me that no matter how cross you get – and we all get cross sometimes – that you'll never run onto the road like that again, okay?'

'Okay,' she whispered. She hopped off Marianne's lap and went to her father. 'I'm sorry, Daddy. I shouldn't have run off...and I don't hate you.'

Kevin swept her up in his arms and held her tight, fighting the tears.

'I know you don't, sweetheart, and I love you so, so much, so we'll never do that again, okay? Conor is very brave and very fast, but there may not be someone like Conor around next time.'

She leaned back a little and gazed up at him. She held his face in her two little hands and said, 'But you saved me, Daddy, and you'll always be there, won't you?'

He smiled. 'I will, sweetheart. I will always be there.'

CHAPTER 17

*M*iguel went up the Cliffs of Moher with his camera like a shot out of a gun before Conor had even finished explaining that they were the highest cliffs in Europe and home to thousands of gulls, gannets, razorbills and even peregrine falcons. There were lots of tour buses and people milling about, but in the sunshine, it didn't feel crowded, and the salty breeze from the ocean was refreshing.

Jimmy climbed down out of the bus. Conor was surprised at how spritely he was. It was hard to put an age on him. He could be anything between fifty and seventy; he looked ageless. He wore dark trousers, a cream-coloured shirt and a jacket, and he was one of those people who would be hard to describe, as nothing about him stood out. He seemed perfectly content, but he didn't go much for small talk, and people seemed to respect that. He sat alone on the bus, and Conor noticed he seemed to always have a book in his pocket.

'Will you walk to the top, do you think, Jimmy?' he asked as the man surveyed the scene: tall dark-coloured cliffs topped with mossy green grass and an azure sea punctuated by white horses as the waves endlessly battered the west coast of Ireland.

Jimmy turned to Conor and held his gaze. His eyes were gentle and somehow knowing, and he said nothing. It was a little disconcerting, Conor thought, but he'd give him time.

'Pedro Calderón de la Barca. He was a Spanish dramatist from the seventeenth century, said green is the prime colour of the world and that from which its loveliness arises.'

He paused and Conor remained silent. He surely wasn't finished?

'I doubt he travelled to Ireland, I don't know. Perhaps he did, but he could have been describing this land, couldn't he?'

'He could indeed.' Conor smiled and turned his face to the sun, exhaling deeply.

'Then there's the great philosopher Johnny Cash.' Jimmy smiled and nodded sagely. 'He was a smart guy, especially as he aged. But his song about the forty shades of green always made me smile.'

'I have his last-ever album. You can hear the regret and the pain and the faith he had, it's all there in his gravelly old voice. It's one of the most moving collections I ever listened to. *A Hundred Highways*, do you know it?' Conor asked. He was getting used to the older man's style of talking – he went straight to the meaningful stuff, no fluff.

'I heard it in the library. I agree – it's raw and bare, and it's like he's done with all pretence.'

Jimmy wandered off up the cliff, no further talk.

Beth and Will were chatting, and Conor observed them. She seemed a little more animated today; perhaps jet lag made her lacklustre before. Will was certainly doing his best to ingratiate himself, laughing at her jokes and being very attentive. He might have a chance with her if she ever put that phone down, Conor thought to himself. She was constantly checking it.

He'd overheard her telling the group that she'd had another text from her sister who was on the missing list, answering some question she asked, so everything was okay again. Kevin had filled him in briefly on the situation the first night they arrived.

As he watched the group walk off towards the cliffs, he got back into the coach. He'd made a flask of coffee in the morning so that he didn't need to endure instant in the café, but also because he needed some peace and quiet. Word was out among the drivers and guides that Ana was sick, and while he knew they all meant well, he just didn't want to talk about it with them. People either wanted to tell him about miracle cures or special prayers or having Masses said, and none of it meant anything to him. He could see what people got from religion – he envied them sometimes – but it wasn't for him.

He was good friends with Eddie the local priest; they played golf fairly regularly. But Conor's days of being involved in organised religion were over. He had his own quiet kind of spirituality based on kindness and acceptance of people regardless. He thought there was a God and heaven – he hoped there was as he'd love to see his mam again – but people who were adamant about their faith being the only one irritated him.

He sipped his coffee and sat in the back. If he sat in the driver's seat, he would only attract other guides for a chat, and he wasn't in the mood; he had too much on his mind.

At night, he lay awake for hours, just listening to Ana breathe. He'd had a nightmare that he woke up and she was dead beside him. He didn't dare share it with anyone, but it was a recurring dream, and he was exhausted. He finished his coffee, stretched his legs out onto the seat in front of him and nodded off.

The sound of voices outside woke him. The group were back. He got up and opened the door.

Everyone was deep in chat or licking ice cream cones with a chocolate stick stuck in them, inexplicably called ninety-nines in Ireland.

He grinned at Tess, whose entire face seemed covered with ice cream, but she looked like a much happier little girl and none the worse for her ordeal earlier.

'Did you get me one?' he asked jokingly.

Tess looked up at her dad. 'We forgot to get one for Conor, Daddy.'

Kevin chuckled. 'Conor doesn't look like a guy who likes ninety-nines, honey, not like your old dad.' He patted his belly.

'Well, he's probably right. They are full of sugar and saturated fat, Conor. My mommy never allows me to eat ice cream. We just have zero-percent-fat frozen sorbet with stevia instead.'

The two men shared a glance over her head.

'Well, I think a little bit of ice cream now and then won't do us any harm. My boys are your age, and they love mint chocolate chip and salted caramel.'

'Sounds good.' She grinned. 'Can you get me some of that next time, Daddy?'

'Sure.' He picked her up and gave her a tickle. 'But don't tell your mom, okay?'

Conor drove on to Lisdoonvarna, a picturesque village a few miles inland, and put the group into the safe hands of the matchmaker himself, Paudie Mac.

Paudie Mac greeted the group with much joking and laughing and promises of marvellous outcomes romantically speaking. Conor told them he would be back for them later and drove away to collect Ana.

CHAPTER 18

*J*immy enjoyed the day. The west coast of Ireland was spectacular, and while the others were joking around with the matchmaker in the bar, he went for a walk, found the local library and made himself at home.

He'd loved libraries ever since he was a child. His mom was never able to afford books, and if his dad thought his hard-earned money was being wasted on literature, he'd have had a fit, so Jimmy not only was a member, but he also read in the library. It was quiet and peaceful, and he met all sorts of people there who were happy to talk about what they were reading, which interested him, not the news or weather, which he hated.

When he was a child, he met immigrants trying to learn English by reading little kids' books in the children's section. That was how he discovered China, Russia, South America. He learned about the Vietnam War, not from schoolbooks but from a veteran who was homeless, so damaged by PTSD he couldn't hold down a job. Lieutenant David Rafter spent his days in the library. It was warm and welcoming, and Jimmy used to take two sandwiches each day for all the years he knew Dave – one for him and one for his vet friend.

His usual reticence was somewhat dissipated among the books, and while he would never be considered chatty, he interacted differently with people in libraries.

He was browsing the local history section when he came across an entry pertaining to Castle Dysert in a newish book about the area. The story said that the house had a tragic past. A little boy lost his life in a fire there in 1922, a fire set deliberately by the local IRA because the private house, as it was, was seen as a symbol of British imperialism. The family, the Kings, abandoned the castle then, and one of them returned to rejuvenate the place in the 1950s with his Australian wife and daughters.

That explained the Antipodean plants he'd seen growing abundantly in the garden.

The piece went on to explain that there were rumours about a perfectly preserved playroom and even ghostly happenings at the hotel, but the details were sketchy. Jimmy got the feeling that it hadn't been written with approval from the management of Castle Dysert.

'A load of old rubbish.' A voice came from behind him.

Jimmy turned and saw a vaguely familiar woman, a stack of books in her arms ready to either return or check out.

'I'm sorry. I'm not one to normally interrupt someone reading, but that piece is written by a journalist from one of the tabloid rags. He came to Castle Dysert looking to do some kind of salacious piece on the recent fire, and when he was refused outright, he came up with that drivel.'

Jimmy took in some of the titles she carried and was impressed.

A Portrait of the Artist as a Young Man by James Joyce. *The Maltese Falcon* by Dashiell Hammett. And *A Year in Provence* by Peter Mayle. He'd read them all.

She also held a book on archaeology, and the others appeared to be in German.

He replaced the book on the shelf with a small smile. 'I liked most of Joyce, but I didn't enjoy *Ulysses* so much. "The Dead" is one of my favourite stories of all time.'

She glanced at her bundle. 'I like *A Portrait of the Artist*, and I agree with you about *Ulysses*, though trying to read it is perhaps a folly. I had the great fortune to be in Dublin many years ago and heard an Irish senator, a man called David Norris, himself a Joycean scholar, perform extracts, and it was mesmerising. The lack of punctuation, for me, means reading it is too subject to interpretation, and I tire of it, but having it performed gave it much more meaning.'

'Interesting point. I never heard it read aloud. What did you think of *A Year in Provence?*'

'I enjoyed it. His writing is humorous and warm but very informative. I've never been to Provence, but after reading this, I think I would like to go.'

It was unusual to find someone who didn't feel the need to resort to platitudes and small talk when conversing with a stranger.

'Will you go then?' he asked.

She looked directly at him, appraising him at one glance. 'Perhaps I will in the off season. I work at Castle Dysert, so I must declare my interest in interrupting your reading.' She gave a slight smile.

He remembered where he'd seen her. She worked on the reception desk at the hotel. In her work uniform, he thought she looked quite old-fashioned and austere, very unlike Conor, who was very casual in both his manner and his dress. Today, her civilian clothes reminded him a lot of his mother's dress sense. Simple but elegant. She wore a navy skirt to the knee and a pink blouse with a tiny flower embroidered on the collar; over it she wore a wine-coloured cardigan. Her shoulder-length hair was held back from her face in a loose plait.

'I'm staying there,' he said.

'I know,' she replied. 'I'm Ms O'Brien on the reception desk.'

Jimmy nodded.

The conversation seemed to come to a natural end at that point, so she turned and approached the desk to return her books, and he moved, as he always did eventually, to the small philosophy section.

* * *

PAUDIE WAS GOING on about finding true love, and Kevin stood at the back of the group, Tess in his arms. He wanted to be close to his daughter today; the near accident really shook him. Tess had sat beside him on the bus and held his hand as they walked along the street. There hadn't been a meltdown since.

'Is this boring for you?' he whispered in her ear.

She turned and cupped his ear with both her little hands. 'Very boring 'cause I'm too small to get married.'

He grinned and whispered back, 'Let's get out of here and get another ice cream, what do you say?'

She nodded enthusiastically, and they quietly slipped out the door.

The town was bustling, and the main street was lined with street vendors selling all sorts of things. He bought Tess a bangle that glowed in the dark and a cute hat that had a leprechaun on it, and they strolled happily together. He tried not to think of the what if.

'Look, Daddy, an ice cream store!' Tess squealed in excitement as she dragged him along the street towards the pink building with three or four little tables and chairs outside.

They went in, and Tess decided on a frog on a log while Kevin ordered a coffee for himself.

They went to sit in the sun while the lady put their order together.

'Well, fancy meeting you two.' Marianne was strolling by and stopped. She had decided against the matchmaking as well. Annie tried to make her stay, but she had no interest.

'Hi, Marianne. I'm getting a frog on a log. It's mint chocolate chip ice cream and bubblegum-flavour blue ice cream to make the sea and a chocolate stick for the frog to sit on and then some gummy frogs on top,' Tess explained.

Marianne caught Kevin's eye and smiled. 'Sounds yummy!' she said.

'Daddy is just having coffee 'cause he is cutting his carbs,' Tess went on.

Kevin looked surprised. 'I'm what now?'

'Cutting carbs – refined sugars, white flour, that sort of thing, stuff that makes you fat. Mommy never ever eats carbs, and she only eats healthy fats and lots of lean protein. She stays under eight hundred calories on MyFitnessPal, so that's okay, and she only drinks green smoothies and whey protein shakes. She says it's the only way to fight the fat and to stop cellulite buildup. I think I've got a little cellulite on my thighs actually...' Tess was so matter-of-fact, but both Kevin and Marianne were secretly appalled.

'Well, honey...' Kevin didn't want to say anything negative about Debbie, but at the same time, he didn't want his little girl growing up with a head full of nonsense about diets and being fat and all of that. Debbie was obsessed with weight; it was one of the main reasons they couldn't be together. She tried to feed him like a rabbit and looked pained every time he ate anything that wasn't organic and vegetable based. She nearly had a nervous breakdown if she saw him drinking a beer. 'I'm not cutting carbs or anything like that. I eat a normal, healthy diet, but right now, I just feel more like a coffee than an ice cream. But I might have an ice cream later.' He turned to Marianne. 'Will you join us?'

'Sure.' She smiled. 'Maybe I'll have a frog on a log too?'

'You can if you want,' Tess said uncertainly. 'But I think it's over 500 calories with the chocolate and the gummy frogs...' She looked pointedly at Marianne's belly, which was definitely maintained on more than eight hundred calories a day.

Kevin was mortified. Marianne was a lovely woman, and while she wasn't a skinny misery like Debbie, she looked great.

'Tess!' he blurted. 'That's so rude. I'm sorry, she didn't mean...'

Marianne chose to see the bright side. She'd been through so much in the past year, she'd learned not to sweat the small stuff.

She looked at Tess directly. 'Well, maybe it is, Tess, but I'm on vacation, so all rules are broken on vacation, right? We'll worry about the calories in things when we get home, okay? I think there are no calories in Irish food anyway – I read that somewhere.'

Kevin looked relieved that she had taken it so well. It wasn't the kid's fault. She was obviously listening to this crap all day from her mother, so how could she be any different?

The owner came out with Tess's ice cream and Kevin's coffee and laid them on the table. Tess's eyes lit up, and she tucked in with vigour.

'Could I get one of those too, please?' Marianne asked. It did look delicious.

'Of course,' the woman replied.

'Are there really no calories in Irish food?' Tess asked before she turned.

'Not one,' the woman replied very seriously. 'But the trouble is it only applies to visitors. So Irish people have to take care, but people on their holidays can eat whatever they like and not worry about it for one second.'

'We should tell Mommy about this, Dad,' Tess said between spoonfuls.

Kevin tried to imagine Debbie's horror if she knew the junk Tess had been eating. 'Maybe, but I don't think she'd like Ireland, honey. It's too...' He tried to think of the right word.

'Far from the tanning salon?' Tess suggested.

'Yes, sweetheart, it's too far from a tanning salon.'

He caught Marianne's eye again as he suppressed a smile, and she tried to stifle a giggle.

CHAPTER 19

*A*nnie was enraptured. Paudie Mac showed them his book and promised all they needed to do was hold it for seven seconds, close their eyes and believe. After so long on stupid internet dating sites and speed-dating events and singles nights and weekends and holidays, she was going to throw her fate to the wind and trust this Paudie Mac. He was the seventh son of a seventh son, he told them, and the magic was passed on, generation to generation.

'I know there's many who say that the only cure for love is marriage, but they're wrong. Wedded bliss is the perfect form of human happiness.' Paudie pronounced. 'Now, there was a time long ago when people believed that if you couldn't see your intended from your own ditch, then you were doomed to a life of singledom. But that is not true either. I've matched people from the four corners of the globe, and it always works out beautifully because the ancient wisdom is behind it all.'

He held the floor, knowing the audience were eating out of his hand.

'Now, there's some would have you believe that as love grows old, then love grows cold, but again – wrong!' He was warming to his theme now. 'The old song says cupid is a cruel foe, but that is not the case. Falling in love is as simple as falling out of bed. Sometimes you just need a small kick in the right direction.' He chuckled and winked.

Beth and Will were to Annie's right, giggling at it all, Miguel looked amused too, and Erin and Shannon looked like rabbits caught in the headlights, dazzled and terrified. Annie was probably the only one taking it all seriously, but she was. This was her best shot of finding the right person. If this didn't work, well, she was all out of options.

Her job as a research scientist was fulfilling and well paid, she liked her colleagues and she was constantly challenged. But no matter how great her days, each night she opened the door on a small empty apartment, ate dinner alone and slept till morning with nobody by her side.

She could have one-night stands, she knew that. She often got hit on in Bubbles's place; sometimes Bubbles even stepped in if the men made her feel uncomfortable. One night, a really sleazy guy had been very insistent, and Bubbles had to throw him out. That night, he asked her to stay back and have a drink after closing time.

She found she could be more honest with him than she could with anyone else – maybe because he wasn't a threat; he had no romantic interest in her – and yet he could give her the man's perspective.

'The way I see it, Annie, is this,' he'd said once the place was closed up for the night. He'd light up a cigarette, and having poured them both a large beer, he'd make his pronouncement. Bubbles's pronouncements were famous, and everyone teased him good-naturedly about them. 'You're a smashing girl. You've a good disposition, a nice way about you, you're well able to earn your own living. You're smart, and you try to find the best in everyone. I see you there in the evenings giving the time of day to people who maybe others wouldn't bother with. You'd be a great wife and mother because you're loyal and kind. And you're not an auld trout either, so you're easy on the eye.' He winked and nudged her playfully. 'So there are three possible problems. One, you're trying too hard. Two, the kind of fella you're after isn't the kind of fella you attract. Or three, your standards are too high. So which is it?'

She thought seriously about the question. 'Well, number one' – she counted the options out on her fingers – 'as for trying too hard, when I do online dating and all that, nothing comes of it. If I like them, they don't call me back. If they like me, I'm calling the cops. So am I trying too hard? I don't know. When I stop looking for Mr Right, nothing happens.'

She raised her ring finger. 'Number two, hell yeah, the guys I attract are not the ones I want. I seem to only get sleazeballs, married men, convicted felons and potential sex offenders, so you're right about that. And number three, are my standards too high? Well, I want someone sane, solvent, single and without a criminal conviction, an axe-wielding ex or a history of psychotic episodes – after that, I'm flexible. Though an Irish accent would be high on the wish list.' She was only half joking. 'I think I'm too ordinary. Like, I look fine, blonde, blue eyes, skinny, whatever, but I look like a million others.'

'Okay.' Bubbles exhaled a long plume of cigarette smoke. 'So you are not attracting the guys you want, so how do you make yourself more attractive to those sane, smart guys?'

'I don't know. I have zero clue.' She laid her head on her arms despondently on the bar, and he patted her on the back.

'You know what I think?' he said with a devilish grin.

'What?' she asked, raising her head.

'Well, I can't do much about the other stuff, but you want an Irish accent? Well, there's only one place to go for that!'

'The Bronx?' she joked.

'No, smart-arse, that's for the plastic Paddies. If you want the real deal, you have to get your little Yankee Doodle dandy behind over to Ireland, where there's not a million of you – there's just you. Eliminate the competition. You'll be the novelty with your all-American cheerleader looks. You'll attract the right guy, and once he gets to know you and sees what a great girl you are, you'll be away for slates.' Bubbles took a sip of his beer.

'And that's a good thing, right?' She chuckled at another of his many Irishisms.

'Oh, that's as good as being on the pig's back.' He winked and lit up another cigarette.

'Y'know, you might just be onto something there. But if I meet an Irish guy, wouldn't I have to stay in Ireland?' Her mind was doing overtime.

Bubbles threw his head back and laughed, his guffaw infectious.

'Well, Annie, me love, the first thing is Ireland is God's own country. There's nowhere on this whole planet like it. Where I grew up was so beautiful, it would steal your heart away, and that's the truth. Green fields, stone walls, old ruins of castles everywhere, music spilling out of full pubs, fish fresh from the cold Atlantic, curlews and corncrakes and sheep and cattle... I'm telling you, it's like nowhere on earth. So if you dropped anchor there, it would be the best decision of your whole life. But even if you couldn't, the odd Paddy has made his way over here over the years, y'know?'

Annie heard the emotion in his voice. He loved his place so much, but yet he never went back and nobody visited him from home.

'Will you come with me, Bubbles? Show me around?' she asked, hoping she wasn't hitting a nerve.

'Yer a girleen – you're big and hairy enough to show yourself around. And sure if the Irish boys saw you with a big handsome man such as myself, they'd keep well back by the wall and wouldn't dare approach you. No, Annie, you'll have to fly solo now, little bird.' He winked.

'Why don't you ever go home?' she asked quietly.

He looked at her and raised his drink to his lips, finishing it in one gulp. He stood up. 'That's a story for another day.'

The night was over, and he was closing up, in every sense of the word.

Bubbles had told her to go there, that Ireland was where she'd finally meet him – the one.

'So, if you'd like to take this form and fill it out, give it back to me when you're finished, and I'll get the ball rolling, lads.' Paudie was dispensing clipboards with a single sheet attached.

Annie read through it.

Name, address, age, hobbies, drinker, smoker. She filled out the first section quickly.

Ideal character traits in your love? She smiled at the archaic turn of phrase.

She thought, and then wrote, *I would like to meet someone kind and funny who wants to get married and have kids and who would love me and never cheat or leave.* She felt ridiculous. It wasn't what you should write – it made her look pathetic, she knew – but it was the truth, and if this was going to work, she needed to be honest.

What would your best friend say about you? The next question caused her to pause again.

She knew what her mother or her sisters would say, that she was book smart but actually life clueless, that she was prone to getting crazy ideas, that men found her exhausting, that she could be pretty but her hair was too straight, her teeth weren't straight enough, she needed a boob job... *Enough!* She made herself stop. *Think about the question,* she demanded of herself. *What would your best friend say?*

She wasn't great with friends. She knew loads of people, and she was friendly with them, with her colleagues, with the people at Bubbles's, but she always seemed to screw up friendships. She either was too full on or not into the friendship enough. She sighed. Life was so hard to navigate. Since she was little, she felt she always judged it wrong. Other people seemed to just know how to do it, how to get a boyfriend, how to have a bunch of girlfriends, but she didn't. She glanced up at Paudie. Maybe this guy knew more than she did about what made relationships work. He was her best shot, so he'd better. Bubbles was the closest thing she'd had to a best friend, and he was everyone's friend. How sad was that?

What would Bubbles say? She tried to picture him right here in Lisdoonvarna, sitting in the pub with them. Here with Miguel and the Glavin sisters and Will and Beth. He'd sit beside her and take the form and write. Annie lifted her pen and let the words come.

Annie is kind and funny and loves animals and the outdoors. She is very smart and has a good job, so she is able to support herself. She doesn't care about stupid things like designer clothes. She is a nice person and sees the good in others and never the bad. She tries to make people happy. She would make a great wife because she is loyal and honest, and she will be a great mother. She is also a fine-looking girl.

She reddened with embarrassment as she read it back; even the sentence structure was Bubbles's. Suddenly, he didn't feel gone.

Without allowing herself a moment's hesitation, she handed the clipboard to Paudie, who unclipped the form and placed it in the book. He did the same for the others, and then he asked each of them to hold the book for seven seconds and close their eyes.

As Annie held it, she didn't wish for the man of her dreams. She spoke to Bubbles.

'I did it, Bubbles. I came to Ireland. You know what I want, so I'm leaving it up to you now, my old friend. If the man I'm going to marry is here, please do your best for me.'

Her seven seconds were up.

CHAPTER 20

*E*rin looked at Shannon as Paudie gave them the forms to fill out. She didn't want to answer a questionnaire to find a husband – in fact, a husband was the furthest thing from her mind – but she was too polite to excuse herself. She saw Shannon hesitate before lifting the pen. Erin's deepest fear was that Shannon would meet someone and she'd be left all alone. She felt mean for even thinking like that. She loved her sister with all her heart, and of course she should be allowed to find a man and be happy. But a future without Shannon by her side was a very lonely and scary one. Conor was gone off somewhere in the bus, and he'd mentioned that they need not be part of the matchmaking thing if they didn't want to, but it was difficult to imagine how to get out of it.

The town of Lisdoonvarna looked lovely as they drove through, and Shannon had pointed out a tea shop on a corner that looked just delightful. Erin would have loved to go in and have a cup of Irish tea and write the postcard to Dr Mills and his wife that they had bought. They'd spent ages selecting it at the Cliffs of Moher gift shop; they wanted to make sure it was the right one. As Shannon left work on the last evening before the vacation, Dr Mills stopped by her desk, told her he hoped she had a wonderful time and said, 'Send me a postcard.'

The Glavin sisters took him at his word and vowed to get the nicest postcard they could. They searched rack after rack. Should they select one with several scenes of Ireland or just one magnificent one? They dismissed the humorous ones out of hand; Dr Mills would like a nice, proper postcard. They speculated if he would put it up in the office or at home. If in the office, then a single image would be better because people might not be able to make out the smaller images in the montage-style cards.

Erin would have liked to send one to her office co-workers as well, but theirs was not an office that allowed things like that. Everything was very streamlined and professional looking, and people tended not to reveal details of their personal lives. She shared a cubicle with another legal secretary, Lois, and she had no idea where she lived or what her situation in life was. It just wasn't the done thing. Shannon was so lucky to have Dr Mills, and he was constantly saying how he would be lost without her. Erin even thought about trying to find another job, somewhere a little friendlier, but she was worried she would never get a position as good as the one she had with Weston, Weston and Brockley again, so she remained.

Meeting Bubbles and going to his bar filled the need for social contact though. They had both picked out a postcard that said 'Having the Craic' that had a picture of a sheep drinking a pint of Guinness. It made them so sad, as they would have loved to have sent it to Bubbles.

Erin wondered what Bubbles would do in this situation. He was always giving people ideas; he was such a dynamic person. She missed him every day. She looked around and saw everyone but Shannon writing. She would not stand in her sister's way, however painful it was. She had a right to her own life.

She stood and addressed Paudie Mac.

'Mr Mac, thank you very much, and I'm sure your services are much sought after for good reason, but I will not be needing them, so I'll give you back these forms. Thank you for sharing the fascinating story of your remarkable family, and I mean no offence.'

Shannon looked at her like she had taken leave of her senses, but she stood up too. 'Thank you, Mr Mac, but as my sister said, I don't think it's for me either.' She thrust the clipboard at him, and he accepted it with a smile.

'Not a bother in the wide world, ladies. Contentment with your lot in life, regardless with or without a mate, is the secret to being happy.' He beamed and planted a smacker of a kiss on first Erin's then Shannon's cheek. He went on. 'More power to your elbows!'

Neither Erin nor Shannon had the faintest idea what the last bit meant, but they took it as their cue to leave.

Once out on the sidewalk, they giggled.

'Erin, I don't know how you did it, but thank goodness you did. I didn't know how we were going to get out of it,' Shannon said with relief.

'Really? I was so scared you were excited to do it, and I was terrified you'd find someone and I wouldn't.'

'What? Are you nuts? What would I want to get married for at this time of life? No, we are perfectly happy as we are, the two of us. We've no space for a man.' She squeezed her sister's arm. 'I had no idea how to get out of there, but every sentence made me more nervous. How on earth did you get the guts to just stand up like that? I could never have done it.'

'I just thought of Bubbles and what he would do. To be honest, I doubt I could have done it if I'd planned it. It sort of just happened,' Erin replied with a smile.

'Mammy would have a stroke, as she used to say, if she saw us being so rude.'

'Not as bad as if she thought we were in the market for a husband.' Erin chortled.

They walked up the street arm in arm towards the tearoom, where they ordered tea and a slice of walnut-and-carrot cake topped with thick cream-cheese frosting. The tea was served in Royal Tara china, and the cake was succulent and flavoursome. The two sisters could not have been happier.

'Are ye identical twins or what?' An elderly man wearing farming clothes, with a very strong and unidentifiable body odour, stood in front of them as they ate. He had entered the tea room around ten minutes after they sat down and ordered tea and a slice of fruit cake. Their perfect afternoon was being ruined by the appalling stink as he ate and drank noisily.

They were unsure if he was speaking to them, but he must be, as they were the only other people in the room. The young lady who served them was gone into the back – to get away from the smell presumably.

The sisters exchanged a look.

'Excuse me?' Shannon began. 'We didn't quite catch that.'

'Twins,' he said now, very loudly. 'Are ye twins?'

'Oh, no… We are not. Sisters, yes, but not twins.' Shannon wished he would stop at that.

'Are ye married?' he asked. This time they understood him.

Erin spoke this time. 'No, we are not married.' She tried to return to her piece of cake, but their new friend didn't either care for or know about social cues.

'Will ye come dancing?' he asked, a lecherous grin showing big yellow teeth like tombstones. The sisters looked at him in horror and disgust. He was unshaven and had longish greasy-looking grey hair curling over his grubby collar. He wore a tweed coat that had seen many better days and dark trousers, shiny with dirt. On his feet he wore gumboots, turned down at the top. It was impossible to know if the smell came from him or his clothes, but the entire package was horrible.

'No thank you,' Shannon said firmly as she caught Erin's eye. They would just go. It would be easier and less nauseating.

'I'll give ye a lift.' He jingled a vehicle key on his finger and pointed outside to a filthy ancient tractor. He took a plastic bag out of the pocket of his coat.

'I've a bag an all, for fear 'twould rain on we dancing, to keep the seat dry. I've a nice farm up the hills there, and I wouldn't mind a bit if 'twas two of ye I had to keep the place going and to keep me warm at night. Two for the price of wan!' He cackled, delighted with his great find.

The idea of getting up on that deathtrap and going anywhere with him filled both Glavins with utter revulsion, but it would have been beyond their capabilities to simply turn their backs on him and leave.

'Again, thank you, sir.' Erin glanced at Shannon and tried to be as polite as she could. 'But I'm afraid we have to go – we are being collected.' They gathered their Gore-Tex jackets and handbags and ran out of the tearoom.

'Where are ye shtaying?' he called, swallowing down his tea to follow them.

As they emerged onto the street, they were relieved to bump into Conor.

'Oh, Conor, thank goodness,' Erin said.

'What's up, ladies? Is everything okay?' He asked, concerned, as they looked so flushed and distracted.

Before they had a moment to explain, their suitor appeared beside them.

'I saw them firsht,' he said. 'We're getting along grand, so you can shtay out of it...'

Conor immediately understood the situation. While lots of nice, normal people came to Lisdoonvarna for the matchmaking festival, there were still some ancient love-hungry farmers who were filled with untapped sexual energy, generally not presented with any degree of charisma or allure.

'These ladies are spoken for, I'm afraid,' he said, putting an arm around each of them.

'But they told me they weren't married or a bit?' the smelly man protested.

'Oh no. We all live in a free-love commune in the States, so I'm afraid they are unavailable. Cheerio now.' Conor grinned and escorted both ladies down the street. It was only when they turned the corner out of sight of their admirer did he let them go. Erin and Shannon didn't know how to react. They had never had so much excitement, albeit unwanted attention, in their lives. Erin started giggling, then Shannon started, and Conor looked on in amusement as both sisters descended into uncontrollable laughter.

CHAPTER 21

*W*ill tried to get a glance at what Beth was writing. She was only halfheartedly filling the form out, as if her mind wasn't really on it. He thought they were getting closer though. She'd walked up the cliff with him this morning and they chatted. She even told him about her sister being missing, which must mean she saw him as more than just someone from the bar?

She was lovely, just his type. Her dark hair was short, in a cute cut, so when she tucked it behind her ear, she looked adorable. She was slim but strong. He'd noticed that the night Bubbles died, how she was able to do CPR so well. He should have been focusing on Bubbles, but he deliberately stood behind Beth as she worked on the big guy – the view had been terrific.

He'd need to take it slowly. She was worried about her sister, and that was understandable. It was like she sensed something was wrong, even though Maddie had previously taken off without telling anyone.

He gave the guy the form he'd filled out and held the book with his eyes closed as he was told. He watched Beth as she did the same. Miguel was next, and Will wondered. In prison there were lots of gay guys, or guys who weren't gay exactly but had relations with men in the absence of any women, so his radar for that sort of thing was high. In San Antonio State Prison, not to have that ability could mean terrible consequences.

Will would put a million dollars on the fact that Miguel was gay, closet certainly. But if Will's instinct was right, and it nearly always was when it came to this, Miguel was definitely playing for the other team.

That pair of sisters who looked like twins but weren't apparently had bailed out, and Will thought he saw a flash of relief on the matchmaker's face. Some gigs were tougher than others, he guessed.

The meeting with Paudie came to an abrupt halt as he took a call on his iPhone, and judging from the one side of the conversation they heard, things were not going too well.

'I told you 'twill take time, and ringing me every second won't speed it up.'

A pause.

'I know I said it would, but let's face facts here, Johnny. You're not exactly the catch of the century, are you?' Paudie's frustrations were coming through.

Another long pause.

'Well, go on the internet if that's what you want! Bring the whole of Siberia or Thailand or Brazil over here if it makes you happy. Though you better be clear about what's on offer, Johnny, because I can't see any gorgeous young wan wanting to hitch her wagon to you, and you with four score years and ten under your belt and not a whole pile else!' Paudie was getting red in the face now, and Will and Beth exchanged an amused glance.

Another pause while Johnny no doubt vented about Paudie's poor service.

'And what do you want me to do?' Paudie was hopping mad now. 'Huh? You'd have to get a computer, learn how to turn the bloody thing on, do a course in internet studies and get yourself a credit card – and that's just for starters.'

Another silence until Paudie erupted.

'No indeed then, you cannot use my computer!' he spluttered before he pressed End.

'Apologies, folks.' He smiled beatifically as if nothing had happened. 'Another customer service issue dealt with there.'

Annie, Miguel, Beth and Will all stood there, not sure what to do next.

'Right. So I'll do my best for ye, and yer staying out at the Castle Dysert, that's a grand spot altogether. So I'll be in touch once I have a potential person for you. These things take time, so I'd urge a bit of patience, though fine handsome people such as yerselves should be much easier to pair up than some of my other clients, I can assure ye.' He rolled his eyes dramatically and they laughed.

Within moments, they were out once more on the street, and immediately, Beth was on her phone again.

'Is everything okay?' Will asked, concerned.

She looked up. 'Yeah, no... I don't know. I just hoped I'd get a text from Maddie.'

'But I thought you said she replied?'

Beth shook her head. 'She did. I texted her after I called our mother and found out she wasn't there, remember? So I texted, and I used the suggestion Jimmy came up with, asking the name of our old teacher. And she texted back the right answer – Mrs Bell. So I asked why she said she was going to our mother's, and she replied that she was going to but changed her mind, that she was just taking some time for herself, that she'd be in touch and for me not to worry. It's so weird. Look, this is probably nothing, but Maddie always covered her texts with emoticons and exclamation marks – I used to tease her about it – but the one she sent me back was very formal, or stiff-sounding or something.' She groaned in frustration. 'Ignore me, Will. I'm probably just paranoid.'

He smiled. 'It's okay. You guys are super close – of course you'd worry. I wish my siblings would take such an interest!'

'Do you have brothers or sisters or both?' she asked as they strolled along in the sunshine, the busy colourful town bustling about them.

'Two brothers, but we don't keep in touch much. No big drama, we're just very different. My parents are both dead.'

She nodded. 'I get it. My dad died, and my mother kind of blames me and Maddie for it – he drowned trying to save us – so we don't really talk. That's why it was so weird that Maddie said she was going to go to our mother's place.'

'Well, you two are lucky. I wish I had a sister like you looking out for me.'

Beth smiled. 'I need to take a chill pill, as the kids say. Say, I want to try a Guinness. Will you join me?'

'I'd love to.'

Will put his arm around her shoulder. It felt so nice to have her in his arms. He kissed the top of her head. It was a friendly gesture, and he hoped she wouldn't be freaked out.

She turned slightly, her beautiful face looking up at him. He thought he had never seen anything so lovely. Their eyes locked, and he tried to read the signs correctly.

She didn't look away or try to move on, so he took the chance, dipped his head and gently kissed her lips. To his relief, she responded, turned to face him and put her arms around his waist. On and on they kissed until eventually she drew back and smiled.

'I wasn't expecting that.' She spoke quietly.

'Neither was I. I hoped, but I didn't know…' Will looked shy all of a sudden.

'It must be Bubbles working his magic.' She grinned, and as they walked on, he felt her hand sneak into his.

* * *

BACK AT THE BUS, Kevin looked a lot calmer and Tess had chocolate all around her mouth; some had even dripped down her snow-white Ralph Lauren polo shirt, but she didn't seem perturbed. Marianne held Tess's hand as the little girl explained to Conor how the lady in the ice cream shop told them that she was related to the woman that his friend had tattooed on her arm, a pirate queen called Grainne

Uaile. Tess was delighted with the attention, telling everyone how when Grainne Uaile was stealing all the gold from Queen Elizabeth's ships years ago, the queen asked Grainne Uaile to visit her so they could make a deal. The only language they had in common was Latin, so they spoke in Latin, and Grainne Uaile threw a linen handkerchief in the fire. Tess was such a cutie and had the entire group eating out of her hand.

Will stood with his arm on Beth's shoulder.

The Glavin sisters were delighted with Tess, and when she was finished, they gave a hilarious account of their romantic encounter in the café. Neither sister was used to the limelight – they were mousey little people – but they were flourishing in the group.

Conor loaded everyone up, and they were in fine spirits as they went back to the hotel.

'Now, folks, I hope the matchmaker met yer expectations, those of you who are going to give it a whirl. We'll be back at the castle around five, dinner is at seven, and afterwards, I have a suggestion. The young woman you saw this morning driving like a lunatic is my friend Laoise, and she and her boyfriend and musical partner Dylan are playing in the hotel tonight. You should go to see them – they are incredible. He plays the uilleann pipes and flute, and she sings and plays the fiddle and harp. They are some duo, I can tell you. They travel all over the world and are doing great.

'But now, folks, I thought we might talk about the main reason you're here. The weather is going to be lovely tomorrow, so it might be the day to scatter Bubbles's ashes? I propose we have a little meeting about how you'd like this to go – if you want to scatter his ashes tomorrow, if you'd like to do anything else. I'll have some suggestions for you too. So how about I go home after dropping you back to the hotel, check in with the family, and then I'll come back to meet you all when you've finished dinner? Would that be okay?'

'But, Conor,' Marianne said, 'we don't want to drag you out again once you've gone home.'

Conor smiled at her in the rear-view mirror. 'That's very kind of you to be thinking about me, Marianne, but my wife, Ana, and Laoise are great buddies, so I'm hoping she might come with me. I might as well tell ye, she's going through cancer treatment at the moment, so it's very hard on her. But she's feeling not too bad today, and she just texted to say she'd like to get out of the house for an hour or two, so we'll come back together.'

CHAPTER 22

'Dad, Artie got a card from Aoife Cadogan, and she said she loved him, and now he's going to marry her!' Joe yelled the minute Conor entered the house.

'I am not, you eejit!' Artie thumped his brother, sending him flying off the couch.

'You are so, and she wants to kiss you… Kissy, kissy, kissy.' Joe made dramatic kissing sounds from the floor. Artie launched himself on top of his brother and started pummelling him mercilessly.

'Okay…okay… Enough.' Conor picked Artie off Joe by the jersey and then pulled his other son to his feet.

Artie tried to kick his brother as he made another kissing gesture.

'Enough,' Conor said, more firmly this time, without loosening his grip. Both boys stopped and looked belligerently at the other.

'I thought you two were going to behave?' He bent down so he was eye level with them. 'You know Mammy is sick, and she's not able for this nonsense.' He never lost his temper with them, but they knew that he wasn't joking around.

'I'm sick too,' Joe muttered. 'Sick of this family.'

'Well, why don't you go and live somewhere else if you're so sick of us? We'd be delighted,' Artie began, but a warning glance from their father stopped both of them.

'Come here.' He sat them both on the couch and knelt down in front of them. They were like a pair of grubby angels with their white-blonde hair cut in the style of the Premiership footballer they loved, their big blue eyes looking at him trustingly.

'I know it's hard.' He tried to sound upbeat, but he was exhausted. Ana had been awake most of the night, and he stayed up to be with her. 'Okay? I know. It's really hard for you because Mammy used to do loads of cool things with ye and take ye places, and she can't now. And I have to go to work, and when I'm here, I need to mind her. So that's not leaving much time for you two, and that's a bit rubbish…'

'That's not the worst thing,' Artie said quietly.

'Artie, don't…' Joe began.

Artie looked at his twin and stopped.

'Tell me,' Conor said gently.

They said nothing.

'Please, lads, ye can tell me anything, ask me anything…'

'Dara Kingston said Mammy is going to die!' Artie blurted, his voice cracking under the emotion of it all.

'And that you'd get married again to someone else…' Joe went on.

'And your new wife wouldn't want us…' Artie finished.

Conor exhaled. 'Right, listen to me and nobody else. Dara Kingston has a big mouth and a tiny brain. So has his father, Michael, and his uncle Dan, and every seed breed and generation of those Kingstons is as thick as a ditch – that's the first thing.' He was glad to see a slight smile on Joe's face.

'The second thing is Mammy is most definitely not going to die. No way. The doctors said she will be fine. It will take some time, but she will get better. We just need to be patient and helpful and gentle with her until she does, okay?'

They nodded, their eyes never leaving his.

'And the third thing is you're my boys and nobody would *ever* take you two away from me no matter what. And anyway, I only love one lady and that's your mammy, and that won't change until the day I die.'

'Do you promise, Dad? That Mammy won't die? She'll definitely one hundred percent get better?' Artie asked, and Conor sighed. He'd never lied to them, and he couldn't start now.

'I can't say one hundred percent because nobody knows what the future holds. But I will tell you that the doctors in the hospital are doing every single thing they can to make her better because they know how much we need her. And she is very tough, and she's very strong, and she won't leave us without a hell of a fight, so we must be strong too, okay?' He heard the catch in his voice.

'Are you worried too, Dad?' Joe asked quietly.

'I am. But we'll be okay. Whatever happens, we'll be okay.'

He put his arms around his boys and held them close.

* * *

CONOR PARKED the car and walked around to help Ana out. She looked lovely in a burnt-orange dress and her head wrapped in a cream-coloured scarf. She'd put some make-up on at the suggestion of her friend Valentina, something she very rarely did, and she tried to suppress a groan of pain as he eased her out of the passenger seat.

'Are you sure you're okay? We can go home anytime.'

'Conor, please don't do the fuss-making. I am okay, and if I not, I'll tell it to you,' she said through gritted teeth. She was stubborn and single-minded, which drove him daft sometimes over the years, but he was glad of these attributes now. She needed every weapon she had to fight this horrible thing.

'Okay, okay,' he said, hands held up in surrender. She punched him playfully.

She took his arm as they slowly walked to the castle. Katherine came out from behind the desk to greet her, and Conor could see she was shocked at how much Ana had changed in the few weeks since she'd seen her. Meghan watched the exchange, and Ms O'Brien was unusually animated.

'Anastasia Petrenko! *Laskavo prosimo!*' Katherine recovered quickly and smiled.

'*Dyakuyu,*' Ana replied, kissing the other woman on the cheek. 'You are also learning Ukrainian?'

'Oh, Artur teaches me a bit now and again, when things are quiet, which isn't often, I can assure you. Anyway, how lovely to see you again. This husband of yours has been driving us cracked with the gospel according to Ana on daily basis as usual, but it's wonderful to see you.'

'Conor tell to me the new wing is good now, totally fixed?' Ana glanced in the direction of the part of the castle that was destroyed in the fire last year. She shuddered. That fire would have claimed the lives of her children had Conor not gone into the burning building to get them out. She still had nightmares about those long minutes as she waited for him to emerge. Thankfully, he did, and Joe and Artie were unharmed. Conor was severely burned but healed well. The insurance paid out, the man who started the fire was in prison, and all was well, but Ana doubted if she could ever make herself go in there again.

'Yes, good as new. Nobody would ever guess what happened there.' Katherine kept her voice down.

After the fire, all sorts of stories and rumours abounded, but she refused to be drawn in and forbade staff from discussing it.

'Please, will you call for supper again some evening? It must be a month since you were at our house? I have been so tired, I didn't call anyone for the last few weeks, but I'm getting better now. We can have proper talk.' Ana couldn't believe how terrified she used to be of Ms O'Brien when she was a young waitress at the Dunshane and Katherine was head receptionist, but she was, just like everyone else. Katherine had proved to be a huge ally for Conor, and she became a friend of their family. The boys adored her and had no sense of how forbidding she could be. Conor remarked on it to Ana as they prepared dinner one evening while Katherine watched a soccer match with the boys. Ana explained it was because she didn't talk down to them or dismiss their opinion. They explained about the offside rule, or why Lionel Messi was worth the 853-million-euro fee Barcelona had paid for him. She asked them questions, but not about school or other things adults usually asked, and she talked to them about things they were interested in.

'I would love to, but you have enough to do, so how about I make supper and bring it with me? I know the boys like shepherd's pie, so perhaps I could make a large one?'

Conor stood back and watched his wife arrange the evening and the details. They were great women, both of them.

'Wonderful. I'll look forward to next Thursday.' Katherine noticed a guest waiting at the reception desk as Megan assisted another, so she left. Conor escorted Ana to the room where Laoise and Dylan were setting up. They were delighted to see each other again, so he left her there to squeals of greeting from Laoise and went to meet the group.

* * *

KATHERINE WATCHED them go and said a silent prayer that Ana would make a full recovery. Conor O'Shea was her best friend in the entire world, though she would never tell him that. All the years in the Dunshane, when he was a tour driver calling once or twice a week, he was the only one who treated her like a human being. She knew it was her own fault – she was standoffish – but Conor took the time to see past all of that and joked and teased her. She loved to see him coming.

She'd watched countless women over the years try their luck with him. He was very handsome, but more than that, he was a good man. However, none of them ever managed to get him into anything approximating a serious entanglement. She fielded calls from women looking for him before the days of mobile phones, held parcels sent to him from ladies in the United States and watched so many others fall for his easy charm. He was kind and polite to them all, but that was it. She suspected he might have had a few relationships over the years but nothing too serious.

Ana Petrenko came from the Ukraine – she was a teacher there. But because of the economy in that country, waitressing in Ireland was more lucrative than teaching in Kiev, so she took a job at the Dunshane. Katherine watched Conor get close to Ana. He was older than her by almost twenty years, and he resisted his feelings for her because of that. It was Ana who convinced him that they should be together. Katherine remembered how torn he was. He loved her, of that there was no doubt, but he didn't want to be seen as some lecherous old man preying on a girl. Katherine had been the one to assure him that he was nothing of the kind.

The whole relationship was almost scuppered before it began when Conor's old girlfriend Sinead turned up out of the blue from America, and again, it was Katherine's intervention that made him realise she was a charlatan, only out for what she could get.

He'd rescued Katherine from early retirement when the Dunshane was sold to a dreadful low-budget chain. This job at Castle Dysert meant everything to her. She was part of the senior management team, and while she didn't need the money – she was very wealthy, being the only beneficiary of her maiden aunt's estate – she needed the life the job gave her. She had Conor to thank for that.

He deserved to be happy, and those little boys needed their mother.

She turned to the man waiting at the desk, recognising him as the person she had spoken to in the library the other day. He was part of that group that had brought their friend home to scatter his ashes. Uncharacteristically, she had teared up when Conor told her the story.

'Good evening, sir. How may I help?' she asked.

Jimmy placed a book on the desk. He seemed shy and spoke slowly.

'I've finished this, and usually I get books from the library, but I found this at a thrift store and thought you might enjoy it.'

Katherine picked it up. It was a black book with a gold design of a rabbit on a plinth on the cover. *Sophie's World* by Jostein Gaarder.

'A novel about the history of philosophy,' she read aloud.

'Yes, it explores the big questions of life through the eyes of a Norwegian girl.'

'Thank you.' She placed the book on the desk beside her computer. 'I'm sure I will enjoy that.'

'You're welcome.' Jimmy turned to leave and hesitated. 'Perhaps if you finish it before I leave, we could discuss it?'

She looked at him directly. He was hard to make out, this American. She usually stopped any men in their tracks long before it got to anything approaching cordiality. Not that it was a frequent occurrence. She'd been burned once years ago, and she was not going to be burned again. He seemed perfectly pleasant and thankfully did not feel the need to blather on pointlessly as so many people did nowadays. Katherine was not one to make false arrangements. She heard that so often – 'Give me a call; we'll have lunch.' Or, 'It's been ages; we must get together soon.' – with nobody having the slightest intention of actually doing anything about it.

'You depart on the seventh, so I imagine I should finish it in that timeframe. So yes, we could. I will warn you, however, that if it does not grip me, I will abandon it.'

Jimmy smiled and his face totally changed. She got the impression that he was a serious person, but when he smiled, it was as if he lit up. His grey hair was brushed neatly back from his forehead, and he had a pleasant, open face.

'I understand. You can let me know.' He turned and walked in the direction of the small resident's bar where Conor was meeting the group.

She picked up the book just as Meghan was coming in to collect her phone as her shift was over. Katherine shoved the book quickly into her own bag.

CHAPTER 23

The group were all gathered and in good spirits after a delicious dinner when he arrived. The chefs tried when possible to use local ingredients and took an innovative approach to preparation, and their efforts had earned the restaurant a Michelin star.

'Hey, Conor. So we were talking just now about what we should do, and Miguel here has come up with something.' Kevin handed the floor to Miguel.

'Well, we all knew that Bubbles was from Kerry, and he often mentioned the town of Dingle. I don't know exactly where he was from, but looking at Google Images of the place, it looks stunning, just like Bubbles described. So we thought it would be the place to go?'

Conor liked Miguel from the start. He was a quiet kind of guy, but he had a tremendous affection for Bubbles, it was clear. He was typically Mexican looking – dark hair and eyes and skin that took the sun well – and while he had an American accent, you would know he wasn't born there. He kept himself a little separate from the others, and Conor wondered if it was because he worked for Bubbles while the others were his customers, but he didn't think so. He figured Miguel was just a bit of a loner.

'Well, the Dingle Peninsula is absolutely stunning. Dingle itself is a lovely little town, lots to see and do there. They even have their own bottle-nosed dolphin that has lived in the bay for years, called Fungi.'

Tess lit up at this. 'Can you see him?' she asked.

'Well, you'd need to go out in a boat, but yes, people see him all the time, and you can even get in the water and swim with him if you like,' Conor told her. 'He loves company.'

'That sounds so cool! Can we do that, Dad?' She turned to Kevin.

'We can look into it if we have time,' Kevin agreed, and Tess beamed.

'Anyway, when you leave Dingle, there is a coastal drive called Slea Head, and it is spectacular – cliffs, ocean, green fields, sheep, ancient stone monuments, beehive huts, ring forts, standing stones, dry stone walls. Every image you've ever seen of Ireland, you'll find it there.'

'That sounds perfect.' Annie was glad they were getting to lay Bubbles to rest somewhere as special as that.

Everyone agreed.

'I wonder,' Marianne said, 'should we have some kind of cere-mony? I don't think he was religious as such, but he did go to Mass sometimes and I know he was spiritual. What do you guys think?'

'It's a lovely idea, but I suppose we would have to do it ourselves. We could, I guess…' Erin was uncertain. In the Catholic Church, self-managed ceremonies were not the done thing.

'Well, I might be able to help you out there, if you think you'd like a priest to say a few words?' Conor suggested.

'You're not a priest as well, are you, Conor?' Will joked, and everyone laughed.

'No, Will, not at all, but I do have a friend who is. He's a grand man altogether – you'd enjoy him actually – and I think he might be able to join us tomorrow. Will I ask him?'

Everyone was on board with that idea, so they arranged to meet the following morning. Conor hung around for a few minutes, talking to individuals until eventually they left one by one.

He noticed Miguel holding back. Once the others had gone, he approached Conor.

'I wondered if I could ask you something. It might be a stupid question though.' Miguel sounded unsure.

'Fire away. If I can answer it, I will.' He tried to put the other man at ease.

'If you had a name of someone in Ireland, and just a general idea of where they lived – they might not even still live there – would there be a chance you could find them?'

Conor considered the question seriously. 'Well, stranger things have happened, so in general terms, I would say yes. Ireland is a small country, and especially in rural areas, people have long memories, so I would say you'd have a fighting chance. Now it depends on how long ago they were there and how common the name was and other factors like that, but let's just say it would be easier here than in New York.' He smiled. 'If you want to tell me who you might be looking for, I could probably point you in the right direction.'

Miguel considered it. He had nothing to lose, and he was sure if he asked Conor to keep it to himself, then he would keep his word. Bubbles chose not to tell his story, that was his right, so Miguel wasn't going to go blabbing about it now.

'Bubbles had a sister and a mother. The sister was named Kathleen, Kathleen O'Leary, and she wrote to him back in 1980. As far as I know, there was no contact between them since then apart from one postcard home to his mother each year, and it was always just a few words.' That was as much as he was willing to say. 'I think I should let them know.'

'Well,' said Conor pensively, 'was she younger or older than Bubbles?'

'Younger, I think.'

'Okay. She might have got married, so she would have a different surname now, but it's worth a shot to check the phone book, or the Register of Electors if you had a good idea of what political constituency the person lived in. So if she was living in the Dingle area, then she would be in the South Kerry constituency. If you have no luck with the phone book, then go to any library, ask to see the Register of Electors for South Kerry and check there.'

'Thanks, Conor.' Miguel smiled, suddenly hopeful. 'I'll do that.'

* * *

BETH LEFT the meeting and walked in the direction of the lifts. Will followed her.

'You don't want to hear the music?' he asked.

'I do. I just left my phone charging upstairs, so I'm going to get it.'

'Oh…okay.' He smiled, relieved she wasn't trying to get away from him.

'I'll see you in the bar then, shall I? Should I get you a drink?'

Beth locked eyes with him and he melted. She really was his perfect girl.

'How about you come up with me?' she asked quietly.

Will inhaled. Was this really happening?

'I'd love that,' he said hoarsely.

He stepped into the lift and felt awkward. What should he do? His heart was thumping in his chest with excitement. She slipped her hand in his once more and led him out into the corridor and down to her room. Once inside, she began to kiss him passionately and deeply, and he gave himself over to the sheer bliss of making love to the woman of his dreams.

Afterwards, they lay together, the sheets tangled around them.

'What would Bubbles say if he saw us?' She giggled, tracing her fingers across his bare chest.

'He'd probably have one of his crazy old Irish sayings.' Will chuckled. 'It's so hard to believe he's gone, isn't it? Where will we all go?'

She shrugged. 'Find another bar, I guess. But for me, it wasn't about the bar – it was Bubbles himself. He looked out for us, me and Maddie, and he made us feel safe. He loved Maddie, you know. He thought she was so funny. "You're a gas, Maddie," he'd say. The first time he said it, she thought it was an insult, like a fart or something, but when he saw her face, he explained that in Ireland that means someone is really funny.'

'He was special all right. I'll miss him, but then I guess we all will. Such an odd group we are, and the one person who connects us all is gone.'

'I like it though, all of us who loved him here together, in his country. It feels like a good way to celebrate him. It feels kind of like he's here.'

She leaned over and checked her phone that was charging on the nightstand.

'Nothing?' he asked, knowing she was hoping to hear from her sister.

'No.' Beth sighed. 'I'd love just one text, you know? One more, full of smiley faces and pictures of horses and spiders and all the other crazy symbols she used, even if it had nothing to do with the message. If I got one like that, I'd know for sure she's okay.' She snuggled up to him. 'You must think I'm crazy.'

'I think you're wonderful. In fact, I think you're the most amazing woman I've ever met.'

She leaned up on one elbow and looked into his face. 'I don't normally do this kind of thing, you know.' Suddenly it was important to her that Will knew it wasn't a meaningless encounter for her either. 'I don't know, I just feel very...' She blushed slightly.

'What?' he prompted gently.

'Safe around you,' she finished.

'I'm glad you do. Nothing could ever happen to you when I'm around, Beth, I promise you that.'

They never got to hear the band. They made love again and, afterwards, talked about everything. She talked about her father and mother and the hurt she felt at first losing her beloved dad and then the rejection by her mother. He talked about the loss of his parents, and the move to New York from Kentucky where he was from. They talked about work. He was a porter in a warehouse or something – she couldn't remember exactly what he said. She was a doctor, but that didn't matter. They had a connection.

146

* * *

CONOR HELPED Ana upstairs and went to check on the boys. The babysitter had her own car, so he paid her and let her go. He locked up and cleared away the boys' clothes and toys from the living room. Once the place looked tidy, he was about to head to bed when his phone pinged.

He opened the text from Fr Eddie.

No bother re tomorrow. See you at hotel at 9 E.

Delighted. Thanks Eddie. See you in the morning, he texted back.

He was surprised to see Ana still up, standing at the boys' bedroom door.

'I thought you'd be in bed,' he whispered, putting his arms around her waist. Together they stood and watched the boys sleeping. They refused to wear pyjamas now, insisting on sleeping in their underwear because they claimed it was too hot. The heating was on full blast as usual.

They walked across the landing to their bedroom, holding hands.

Once inside, she closed the door and put her arms around him. She was so thin now, he thought as he held her.

'I won't break,' she said quietly. 'You can hug me like you always do.'

'I know,' he answered. 'But I just don't want to hurt you.'

'You could never hurt me, Conor, but I miss you. I miss us...' she said, unbuttoning his shirt and running her hands over his chest.

He felt himself respond to her but held back. 'Ana, I don't think...'

She stopped him with a kiss. 'Don't think, just do.' She smiled and he grinned back at her. 'That's an order from your wife, so you must obey.'

'Well, you're the boss,' he murmured as he kissed her neck.

* * *

THE ALARM WENT off too soon, and he groaned as he tried to shut it off. Neither of them had such a good sleep in ages.

'I don't need sleeping medicine the doctor give. I know now what makes me sleep,' she said as she snuggled up to him. He wrapped his arms around her, wishing they could stay like that all day.

'That boring, was it?' He chuckled, giving her a cuddle.

'Well, not boring but...' She kissed his neck and he groaned.

'I would give a million quid to stay here now, I really would.' He sighed. They heard the boys stirring, and Conor dragged himself out of bed. He showered quickly and decided there was no need for formal work clothes today. He wore a suit most days, but today, he pulled on a pair of Levi's and a polo shirt, perfectly ironed by Danika, like all the family's clothes.

As he bent to kiss his wife goodbye, she said, 'But, Conor, you don't get breakfast...' She tried to get up.

'Ana, my love, I run a hotel. If there's one thing I can get, it's a breakfast.' He grinned. 'Stay in bed, have a rest.' He ran downstairs.

'Bye, lads, see ye tonight. Look after Mammy,' he called. And he was gone.

CHAPTER 24

The group were in a jubilant mood as he entered the main reception of the castle the next morning. Beth looked like a weight had been lifted from her, and Will's arm was casually around her shoulders.

She was showing everyone a text from her sister. It was made up of about ten words and a hundred emojis. Even though there had been contact before, this one really seemed to put her mind at rest.

'So it's good news on the sister front, I take it?' Conor asked as he led the group out to the bus.

'It sure is.' Beth's eyes shone. It was as if she had been physically holding herself together since he met her, and now she seemed so much more relaxed.

'And do my eyes deceive me, or is the matchmaker after doing his trick already?' Conor smiled.

'Who knew I had to come to Ireland to get with the guy I saw every week at Bubbles?' She laughed.

It was nice to see her happy.

'I'm delighted for you. Now, Beth, if you'll excuse me, I must go and talk to my friend over there.'

He'd spotted Eddie sitting in the lobby, reading the paper.

'Good morning, Eddie! Thanks for coming. It's a bit of an unusual one, I know.' He welcomed his friend. Fr Eddie was the parish priest, but he was in semi-retirement now, spending his days helping out the new parish priest, playing golf and eating cakes that the doctor told him were strictly off limits. Though Conor wasn't a Mass goer, they were firm friends.

'Not a bother. Sure who wouldn't love a spin around Kerry today? It's going to be a lovely day, thanks be to God.' Eddie rose, and when he was upright, he only reached Conor's shoulder. He had a round belly and a shock of white hair. Ana really liked him as well, and Danika was probably his Achilles heel when it came to cakes. He called to Conor and Ana's house a few times a week, and it gave the Petrenkos great comfort to be on friendly terms with the priest, as Artur and Danika were very devout. He was also not averse to mowing the lawn or bringing in fuel for the fire if Conor was at work.

Conor introduced him to everyone and watched as Eddie worked his magic. He had a special skill where he could put people at ease and make them feel like they were the most important person in the room. When he shook hands with Miguel, he noticed that the man was carrying the urn.

'I'm very honoured,' Eddie said, 'that you've invited me to play a small part in your ceremony today as you all say a last farewell to your friend Bubbles. Just from the little Conor has told me, and the fact that you all travelled so far to bring him home, is a testament to the man. But I'd love to hear your stories of Bubbles as we travel today.'

The group immediately relaxed. Eddie wasn't some kind of sanctimonious priest, preaching from on high; he was a really down-to-earth man, and Conor could tell they liked him instantly.

He led them all to the bus, and as they boarded, Tess piped up. 'Annie, you're good at science, right?'

Annie looked pleased. 'I guess I am.'

'So are people who are good at science good at math too?' Tess asked.

'Well, often they are. Not always of course, but a lot of science is to do with math as well. Why do you ask?'

"Cause Daddy bought me this kids' sudoku book because he won't give me his phone, but it's too hard for me, so I was hoping you could help me out with it.' The girl smiled sweetly and Annie melted.

'I would love to.' She grinned. 'I love sudoku.'

'Cool, then will you sit with me? And Marianne can sit with Daddy.'

Tess had it all worked out. Conor caught Kevin's eye but said nothing. He suspected the girl of a little matchmaking of her own. He wasn't surprised. Tess gravitated naturally to Marianne; she was a very warm person. And unless he was mistaken, there were the beginnings of a romance between her and Kevin, though neither of them was willing to show their hands yet.

Kevin stood up and allowed Marianne into the inside seat. 'You better get the window seat. I'm so big that if you sat on the outside, I'd block up the whole window and you wouldn't see anything,' he joked.

Marianne laughed. 'I'm not exactly a size zero myself, and I don't think that's going to change any time soon, especially now that I've discovered soda bread and scones and Irish butter and, oh my gosh, those Bailey's coffees. I'm glad they only weigh the luggage when we fly.'

Kevin wanted to say something about how she looked great but couldn't do it without looking totally lame. It was so nice to see a woman enjoying food and life compared to Debbie and her obsession with being thin. The woman had no joy: everything was measured in terms of calories, sugar, fat content. And she believed in sharing the misery too. Every single morsel he ever consumed for the duration of their marriage was analysed and commented upon. She was a nightmare. Marianne was the total opposite – she was funny and kind and loved socialising.

Conor eased the bus out of the car park, but before he could turn down the driveway, he noticed Meghan running across the lawn towards the bus, carrying a brown paper bag and a refillable coffee cup.

Conor stopped the bus and opened the door.

'Ms O'Brien,' she panted, 'said to give you this. Chef made it – it's a breakfast roll.'

Conor put the bus in neutral and got out to take the bag and drink from her.

'Meghan, you're a little star.' He smiled at her and she blushed.

As he was about to get back into the bus, his phone rang. It was a number he didn't recognise, and he walked away from the bus to take the call.

'Hello?'

'Hi, Conor. It's Jamsie.'

His heart sank. He thought he had heard the last of him.

'Hello.'

'I've found your brother.'

Silence. He fought the urge to just end the call. He could not deal with this on top of everything.

'I thought I made myself clear when we spoke. I'm not interested.' He exhaled slowly.

'But if you'll just hear me out. He's your brother, and I know what you said, but as your father...'

'Father?' He felt something snap. Anger, frustration and ancient hurt sprang up from deep inside him, with a ferocity that shocked him. 'You think you get to call yourself my father? You must be delusional. You're no more my father than the man on the moon. You left, Jamsie.' Conor could barely say his name. 'You left us for some woman, not before you humiliated my mother in front of the whole parish by chasing skirts. So you gave up the title of father that day, and it's not up for grabs again. I didn't need you then, and I most certainly don't need you now. I looked after Mam and Gerry – I did my best anyway – and it wasn't easy. I watched Mam die in front of me, a broken woman, because of what you did. So no. No way do you get to come back here and play happy families.'

'Okay, I deserve that. But the thing is, Gerry...' Jamsie began again.

'Oh my good God... Can you not get this into your thick skull? I don't care. I don't care about you, and I don't care about Gerry. I just want you to get out of my life and stay out.' He ran his hand through his silver hair in exasperation.

'He's sick, Conor. He's had a very hard life, but he's pulled himself out of the drink and drugs and all the rest of it, and he wants to say he's sorry to you. It's part of the recovery, to apologise to those you've hurt.' Jamsie spoke quietly. 'You loved him once, and he threw it back in your face. He told me everything, about how he took off with the girl you wanted to marry. He told me about you writing to him, telling him it was okay when it clearly wasn't. He knows what a terrible man he's been, and he wants to at least try to put it right.' He paused, and when Conor didn't respond, he went on.

'Gerry has spent most of his life in and out of jail, petty things, robbery and that, but all to feed his habit. He's out now, and he has worked so hard to turn his life around. He's in a kind of halfway house now, run by this charity. I know you're a good man, and he really feels strongly that he wants to do this.'

'Go on.'

'It's in Arizona, outside Phoenix, so I went and met him. Whatever about you, I had some memories of you, but he was only a toddler when I left Ireland…'

'When you left your wife and children. Let's not sugarcoat this,' Conor interjected.

'Okay, you're right. When I left my wife and children, Gerry was only small. So he was a stranger to me, as you can imagine.' Jamsie exhaled slowly. He paused. 'He's not in good shape, Conor. He looks bad, and he's in very poor health, but he's become religious, which seems to be giving him some comfort.

'His life, through his own fault one hundred percent, has been one of tragedy and loss and pain for him and everyone he came into contact with. He knows it, and now he's filled with remorse. He's just asking that he can see you, his brother, once more, to say he is sorry in person.'

Conor fixed his gaze on the lazy scudding clouds traversing the blue morning sky.

'I know he hurt you, and I hurt you,' Jamsie said, 'but you've a great life. Look at you, you're doing great – a family, you run a castle, you've a lovely home, enough money, plenty of friends. Can you afford to be a little bit generous to a man who never saw joy?'

Silence hung heavily between them. Eventually Conor responded. 'Ana is sick. She has cancer. We just can't deal with this at the moment. She doesn't need any more drama. Look, I'll think about it and get back to you, but at the moment, it's no.'

He pressed End.

* * *

MARIANNE GAZED OUT THE WINDOW, conscious that Kevin was so close. She knew him from coming into Bubbles's, but they had never really talked before this trip.

She wondered what Warren was doing now. *Stop!* She was getting better at this. What Warren was doing, where he was or who he was with was no longer her concern. She repeated the mantra over and over. It was still hard though.

In therapy, she tried to explore what hurt her the most. Was it that she missed Warren, or did she miss having a husband, or was she humiliated or embarrassed by the reason he left? Over and over, she and Deanna talked about it and always she came to the same conclusion. She was hurt and angry and humiliated all at the same time. Her family in Brooklyn were so supportive of Warren, it was sickening. Her parents were dead, and her brother and sister were so right-on liberal, they were almost delighted Warren decided he was a woman. His family too were worried about him, and his mother even went so far as to ask Marianne how come she never noticed anything. Was she a horrible person to say she didn't accept it? She didn't see how hard it must have been for poor Warren; she didn't have a clue. As far as she was concerned, he was a heterosexual man.

She wondered what would have happened if they'd managed to have a family. That was another thing that cut her to the bone. 'At least you guys didn't have kids.' Like that was some kind of a warped blessing. If they had managed to get pregnant, three financially, physically and emotionally crucifying rounds of IVF later, then maybe he would not have left, maybe he wouldn't have been transgender. She knew that was crazy – he was born that way, she supposed – but it was just so hard to take.

Nobody on the trip mentioned anything, but she was sure they all knew and were just too polite to say. She considered addressing it when they were all gathered together and just get it over with, but she couldn't summon up the courage. She cast a glance at Kevin, who was watching her. Everyone else was either chatting or sleeping. He looked embarrassed, and she heard herself say, 'Does everyone know about Warren?' She tried to keep her voice steady.

'What about him?' Kevin answered, looking perplexed.

'Why he left me?' she said quietly.

Kevin shrugged. 'To be honest, I thought it was you who did the breaking.'

'Why did you think that?' she asked, trying to determine if he was lying to spare her feelings.

'Just something Bubbles said. He gave the impression that you had ended it and that you probably didn't want to talk about it.'

Marianne thought back to a night, two nights before Warren left. He came home very late, smelling of booze, and he told her he had been at Bubbles's place after hours. She was surprised – Warren didn't even like the place – but she discovered why he went there when he said that he and Bubbles talked. Apparently, he told the Irishman the truth, that he was trans, but he had no idea how to tell his wife. Bubbles let him talk, sobered him up with coffee and sent him home. The news of her husband's new identity was such a bolt from the blue, she didn't dwell on how odd it was that he chose to confide in Bubbles. But now that it was all over, she did.

The next time she came in the bar, a few weeks after that, Bubbles gave her a warm hug and whispered, 'You'll be grand.' They never discussed it again.

She felt a profound sense of relief that her friend had spared her everyone knowing the truth. She had been worried and paranoid for months, sure everyone was talking about her behind her back, but thanks to Bubbles, they weren't. He put out the rumour that she had left Warren to spare her, and she wondered if Warren had been part of that effort. But then she remembered how he told everyone, even people she worked with, so she knew that the plan to lessen the blow was all Bubbles O'Leary's doing. She looked up at the Irish sky and whispered, 'Thanks, Bubbles,' to herself. She looked at Kevin and knew she could trust him.

'No, Bubbles just said that to protect me from gossip. Warren left me because he's transgender. He's living someplace else now – I've no idea where – as a woman.'

Kevin didn't react at first. He'd been a social worker for too long, and had seen and heard so much, that he was good at hiding what he was thinking. Something about her, though, the way she told him the truth, made him want to be honest with her as well.

'My ex is a neurotic psycho who hates me, so I guess neither one of us gets a prize for choosing good life partners.' He nudged her playfully, and she nudged him back before both of them started laughing.

CHAPTER 25

The Glavin sisters were regaling Fr Eddie with stories of Bubbles, with interjections from Annie and Miguel, who sat with Bubbles's urn on his lap all the way. The mood was buoyant, and all the stories illustrated just how full of fun but also kindness Bubbles O'Leary was.

Jimmy sat at the back, listening to Conor's entertaining and well-informed commentary and taking in the beautiful scenery. Across the aisle, Beth slept on Will's shoulder. She was exhausted. The nervous stress she had lived under daily since Maddie went missing had really begun to affect her health. He was so glad she was able to let all of that go now and relax. Of all the people on the trip, Jimmy felt closest to Beth.

By noon they were pulling into the car park in Dingle.

'Righteo, folks, this is Dingle. You'll find everything you might want or need if you take a right up there. There's lots of restaurants, pubs, shops, whatever you fancy, so I'll let ye off here to go exploring. I'll meet ye back here in an hour, and we'll head out onto the peninsula, okay?'

Tess squealed. 'Daddy, look! An aquarium, and they have penguins and turtles and loads of fish, even the *Finding Nemo* ones. Please, can we go, *please!*' She was hopping from one foot to the other in excitement.

Kevin was torn. He wanted to make Tess happy, and an aquarium was a lot better than a screen, but he was hoping to get to spend some time wandering around Bubbles's home town.

He bent down to talk to her. 'I would love that, but this place is kind of special. Remember Bubbles?'

'From the bar?' she asked.

'Yeah, him. Well –' Kevin began, but Tess interrupted.

'I really liked him, Daddy. He gave me soda and chips and he played games with me, remember? Mommy said Bubbles was a dumb name for an adult. She said the only Bubbles she ever heard of was some singer guy's monkey.'

'Well, Bubbles wasn't his real name. His real name was Finbarr, but everyone called him Bubbles, I don't know why. He was called that before any of us knew him, and it might sound like a funny name, but it really suited him, don't you think? He was so much fun, and we all miss him very much.' Kevin's voice cracked with emotion, and Marianne put her hand on his shoulder.

'Well, Bubbles is sure better than Finbarr,' Tess said gravely, and everyone laughed. 'So, can we go to the aquarium?'

Annie saw the dilemma Kevin was in, and she knew Marianne liked him, though she hadn't said anything. Annie's plan to use Marianne as a wing-woman hadn't worked out so far, but she could facilitate Marianne and Kevin getting some alone time.

'Hey, Tess, I love penguins and fish. How about you and I go there, and we can see Daddy back here afterwards?'

Kevin smiled. 'Are you sure, Annie? I don't want to take up your time.'

Marianne shot her a glance of gratitude.

'It's no problem. I'm happy to hang out with Tess. We'll see you guys later!'

The group began to disperse up the street. Erin and Shannon wanted to buy a knitting pattern to make two of those beautiful Irish sweaters. Nobody had the heart to suggest it would be so much easier just to buy two in one of the many gift stores. Will fell into step beside Beth, who announced that she was starving, something nobody had ever heard from her before, and Marianne and Kevin stopped outside the tourist office at a bronze statue of a bottle-nosed dolphin to read the inscription.

Jimmy walked off on his own as he always did but stopped when he heard Miguel call his name. Miguel was walking quickly towards him, still carrying the urn. Once he caught up to him, he said, 'If you'd rather be alone, I understand, but I thought we might take Bubbles on a walk around his town and maybe have some lunch and a beer with him?'

Miguel looked a little uncomfortable. Like Jimmy, he tended to keep a bit separate. He thought at first it might be because the other man was an employee of Bubbles while everyone else was a friend, but he soon realised that wasn't the reason.

'I'd like that.' Jimmy turned and followed Miguel, who was wearing a navy-blue suit with a peach shirt and a darker-coloured tie and pocket handkerchief, down the street. He had dressed up for the occasion.

They walked along, and Jimmy thought about Bubbles there as a boy, as a teenager, even as a young man. Nobody was really sure what age Bubbles was when he got to the States, but he was an adult, of that they were sure.

Off the main street with its busy restaurants and shops was a side street, and halfway down they spotted a pub – The Craic House.

'It's a sign,' Miguel said, smiling.

'It must be.'

They entered the pub, which was half-full, and a waitress saw them to a table and gave them some menus. Miguel placed the urn beside him; Jimmy sat opposite.

As Miguel perused the menu, he wrinkled his nose in disgust. 'Every single year on St Patrick's Day, Bubbles made this.' He pointed to an item on the menu. 'Boiled cabbage, boiled ham, boiled potatoes. In Mexico, we fry, we use spices, we give our food flavour, but this –

ugh. Every year he tried to make me eat it, but every year I said no. Maybe I should eat it today, for him.'

'Bubbles was such a joker. If he were here, he would probably tell you it was his dying wish and then laugh when you ate it.'

'He would. That's exactly what he would do.' Miguel smiled sadly.

'Let's both order it – for Bubbles – and if he's watching, we can give him a laugh.'

The server came and took their order: two plates of bacon and cabbage, washed down with a pint of local craft beer for Miguel and a red wine for Jimmy.

Once their drinks arrived, Miguel raised a toast. 'To you, Bubbles. We will miss you more than we can say.'

Jimmy raised his glass too. 'To Bubbles.'

Both men drank, and Jimmy waited for Miguel to speak.

'I won't be going back,' he said. 'I was illegal all these years, so I can't get back into the States even if I wanted to, but I... I don't want to be there without him anyway.'

Jimmy took another sip of his wine. The other man had confirmed what he always thought to be true.

'Are you shocked?'

Jimmy smiled and shook his head. 'I kind of suspected.'

'Bubbles was illegal too, not that it matters now.'

'No indeed. He's home now.' His eyes rested on the urn.

'Do you think he's somewhere, watching us spread his ashes on Irish soil, or is he just gone?' Miguel asked.

'I'm probably not the best person to ask. I'm not even sure that there is a life after death. I'd like to believe there was, but I think Bubbles might just be gone, no longer existing anywhere. So what we do with his ashes doesn't matter, except to us.'

The other man sighed. 'When I was young, back in Mexico, every week we went to Mass, and we prayed, at home, in school, in church, everywhere. All the time talking about this family of the Lord, the community, the place where we all belonged. But I never felt it. I always was outside – it's hard to explain. I have a nice family, all of that, but it was just that I felt like someone outside looking in.'

Jimmy watched him and said nothing but gave his undivided attention.

'That's why I was so anxious to get away from my village, I think. Not just because of the life in America. I don't care about money. I don't need too much, but I hoped that there would be somewhere I would not feel so...lonely, I think.'

He could sense the pain Miguel was in. For everyone else, the scattering of Bubbles's ashes was a sad thing, but they were glad to be able to do it as one last tribute to a wonderful man. However, for this man, it was something else.

'You loved him,' he said quietly, a statement not a question.

Miguel nodded sadly.

'Did you ever tell him?'

'No.'

'He knew,' Jimmy said with certainty. 'And he loved you too.'

Miguel sighed. 'I wish I could have said something, told him... I... He never said anything, and I never saw him with anyone in that way. He kept that part of himself so separate...'

Jimmy leaned over and placed his hand on the other man's shoulder. 'Don't ask me how I know this, but trust me, I do. He knew you loved him, and he loved you too.'

Tears shone unshed in Miguel's eyes as he smiled and nodded.

The food arrived, and Jimmy enjoyed it. It reminded him of the dinners his mother would make when he was a kid. Miguel tried it and wrinkled his nose.

He raised his glass of beer in a silent salute. 'I did try it, Bubbles,' he said with a smile.

CHAPTER 26

'So how are you bearing up?' Eddie asked Conor as they waited for their lunch.

'You know, Eddie,' Conor said with a sigh. 'Just keeping going, trying to mind Ana, look after the boys, run the hotel. I'm lucky though – I have great help. Danika and Artur are just wonderful. Honestly, I don't know how we'd manage without them. They look after the lads, there's always food in the fridge, they do a lot of the ferrying to and from training and matches and all of that. And then in the castle, I have Katherine and Carlos, so I'm managing.'

Eddie sat back as the fresh fish and chips were delivered, and Conor smiled. He'd ordered a salad.

'I know all about Danika and the cooking.' Eddie shook his head ruefully. 'She dropped in a cake the other week. You should have seen it – a piece of art it was, all cream and jam and chocolate sauce. You'd eat your fingers after it. Of course, Fr Scannell wouldn't look at cake – he's far too healthy for that.' He rolled his eyes.

Conor knew he and the new parish priest were like chalk and cheese.

'Did you see him in the Lycra get-up? Going around the parish terrifying pensioners with this skintight cat-sick-yellow cycling suit on him. He thinks he's Lance Armstrong. He has my heart broken going on and on about visceral fat and the dangers of diabetes.'

Conor laughed. The new parish priest and Eddie did not see eye to eye on most things. The new guy was a late vocation, having first worked in industry as an engineer, but he was called to serve the Lord in his mid-forties. He was conservative and very straight-laced, and he drove Eddie mad.

'I heard he told one of the Heffernans that she should get married before he would christen the baby,' Conor said. He wasn't one for gossip, but Fr Scannell had come to the hotel for lunch last week and another member of the Heffernan family refused to serve him.

'I know.' Eddie rolled his eyes. 'I think I've those feathers settled now, but he's a right plonker between you and me and the wall. I keep trying to tell him, those days are long gone when a priest could tell people how to live. Young Julie Heffernan and her boyfriend, Shane – he's one of the O'Donnells you know, out the Lahinch Road? They are the grandest pair of young people you could meet, and they might even get married sometime, but the fact that they even want the child christened is something we should be delighted with. Sure we're cancelling the second Mass on Sundays – there's so few go now.'

Conor was always honest with the priest, it was the secret of their friendship. 'Well, you can't blame people. The church has behaved despicably in the past, we all know that, but they continue to do it. Telling more lies, hiding their money so they won't have to compensate people whose lives were destroyed by them. No wonder people don't go to Mass in the numbers they used to.'

Eddie nodded. 'You'll get no argument from me on that score. I couldn't agree more. I remember when Declan came to me, Father Sullivan as he was then – remember that time? I said straight out to him, if what he was coming to confess was to do with kids or abuse of anyone, I'd be going straight to the guards. Of course, we could never have dreamed what his problem would be, mafia fellas after him and poor old Lucia out of her mind with worry.'

Conor did remember, very well. Declan Sullivan, a Catholic priest, and Lucia Sacco had come on one of his tours, and they were hiding from Lucia's father, the notorious organised crime figure Paulie Sacco, who wanted to string Declan up for getting Lucia pregnant. That was a particularly memorable tour.

'I'm going out to Italy to visit them in September. Lucia is due their third baby now, and life is going great for them,' Eddie said, then he tucked into the delicious golden-battered fish.

'Give them my regards when you see them.'

'So tell me to mind my own business if you like,' the priest said, 'but you seem out of sorts. I know you're worried about Ana, but is anything else bothering you?'

Conor hadn't discussed the situation with Jamsie – and now Gerry – with anyone. Only Katherine knew he had turned up, and she would not have breathed a word to anyone.

He sighed and sat back. The conversation with Jamsie this morning had really rattled him; he needed a friend to talk to.

'My father left my mother when me and my brother were kids. He got some young one in the village pregnant, and he took off with her.'

Eddie didn't react but listened carefully.

'I haven't seen hair nor hide of him for over forty years, and he turned up at the hotel a few months ago.'

'That must have been a shock. How did you feel?'

Conor gave a small laugh. He never knew if it was just Eddie's personality or the fact that he was a priest, but he was the most straight-talking man he knew, and he wasn't afraid of emotions like most Irish men his age.

'I was totally shocked, as you could imagine, but we had just had the diagnosis about Ana, and I told him that I didn't want anything to do with him. It was too late.'

'But now you're having second thoughts?' The priest took a sip of his drink.

'No, not at all. But it was him on the phone just before we left.'

Conor had told Eddie the story before, once, years ago, about Gerry and Sinead and all of that, so he filled him in on the latest developments.

'So you won't see your brother?' his friend asked. Despite the words, his tone wasn't accusatory.

He shrugged. 'I don't think so. I'm not happy he's had such a tough life, of course I'm not. But there's nothing I can do about that. And anyway, it's the life he chose, drink and drugs and crime. He had choices like everyone, and he made his. As I said, I don't hold any grudge at this stage, but he's a stranger to me.'

The priest nodded slowly. 'So you're fine with your decision?'

'Yeah, I suppose I am.'

Eddie continued eating his lunch and said nothing more.

'Okay. What?' Conor said eventually.

His friend smiled. 'You know what? You might be trying to convince me, but don't lie to yourself.'

'What are you on about?'

The other man sat back, having finished every morsel on the plate. He stopped a young waiter as he passed. 'I'll have a bowl of apple crumble with custard and ice cream, please.' He looked at Conor. 'Dessert?'

Conor gave a chuckle. 'No thanks, just a coffee for me, please.'

The waiter left and Conor tried again. 'So go on, what are you trying to say?'

Eddie gave him a look, then placed his hands together and tipped his fingers off his lips, as if trying to formulate the correct words.

'Well, you've told me all about how *you* don't need them, but I'm just wondering what about Gerry and your father. Maybe they have some needs here. It's very hard to kick an addiction, and it's an important part of the process to say you're sorry. Maybe they would love to meet the twins and Ana, and maybe they would like to spend some time with you. You have so much, and life has been so kind to you. Whatever about your father – that's more complicated, I suppose – but I think you should give your brother a chance. I know Gerry made choices, but there is such a thing as forgiveness, and it sounds to me like he was a victim of cruel circumstance. He made one foolish and selfish decision donkey's years ago, to betray you and take off with your girl, but nothing worked out for him after that. I just think maybe you could find a little compassion. You've so much good in your life, and it sounds like he has nothing.'

Conor exhaled. He didn't need this, but the priest was a friend and he knew he probably meant well. He didn't snap. 'I've enough on my plate, and so do Ana and the boys at the moment, so what Gerry might want or need isn't very high up the list of things I can give my attention to right now.' He couldn't keep the coldness out of his voice.

'What does Ana say?'

'She thought I should see him – Jamsie, that is. She doesn't know about Gerry. I only just found that out myself.' He sighed.

'And you didn't listen to her? That's unusual for you,' Eddie said mildly.

'I did listen, but I just think she has enough to be dealing with. We all do.'

'Are we going to fall out over this?' The priest was always straight to the point. 'We're good friends, and for me, a big part of friendship is telling the truth, even if it's not what the person wants to hear. It won't make one iota of difference to Ana's cancer treatment whether she meets Gerry and your father or not, and your lads are no delicate little flowers. You don't need to give them all the gory details, but just let them meet their uncle and their granddad. No harm can come of it.' He smiled. 'And it might do some good.'

Conor stood up; he really didn't want to have this conversation. 'We'd better get back – they'll be waiting.' He put some money on the table for lunch, and the other man did the same.

'Will you think about it at least?' Eddie asked, refusing to be put off even by his friend's clear lack of interest in pursuing the conversation.

'Will you stop pecking my head about it if I do?' Conor asked, exasperated.

'I will,' the priest agreed with a grin. 'For a day or two anyway.'

CHAPTER 27

*B*eth was happily browsing in a bookstore when Will appeared at her shoulder. She liked him and knew he was into her, but she wasn't used to having so much time off for starters. She worked a ninety-hour week usually, and she'd been single for years, so this new attentive boyfriend thing was a little hard to get used to.

'Hey.' He put his arms around her, his hands wandering up inside her sweater, and kissed her neck.

She wriggled out of his arms, a little embarrassed at the disapproving glances she got from an elderly lady. 'Hi.'

'Where'd you go? I was looking for you everywhere.' He tried to nuzzle her again.

She stepped away, more forcefully this time.

'I wanted some time alone. I want to buy some gifts and just browse, you know?'

'I could help you – what do you want to buy?' He looked eager, like a slightly annoying puppy. Beth looked at him. He was a nice guy, but in hindsight, maybe the whole thing about Maddie had her a bit emotionally needy. She shouldn't have let things go as far as they did. He seemed too full on for her in the cold light of day. He was constantly trying to touch her, hold her hand, kiss her neck, and it wasn't what she was into at all. Public displays of affection were definitely not her style, and she suspected that Will was way more into this than she was. Tough as it might be, she decided then and there to be honest about how she felt.

'I don't know, but Will...' She paused. 'Look, I do like you – you're a great guy – but I'm not really looking for...well, a relationship or anything right now.'

They were in a quiet corner of the bookstore, and thankfully, the man behind the counter was on the phone.

Will looked taken aback, and something unfamiliar flashed in his eyes. 'What do you mean?' His voice was suddenly cold.

'Just, well, I think it's better to be straight, and I didn't want you thinking that we were, well, together in any kind of a permanent way.' She stumbled over the words, and his blue eyes never left her face.

'So what? Last night meant nothing? Is that what you're telling me?'

Beth felt awful; she'd obviously really hurt him. 'No, of course not, but I'm just not –' she began.

'Yeah, I heard you the first time. Not in the market for a boyfriend. But you thought you'd make a fool of me in front of everyone?'

'That wasn't my intention. I just was...'

'Was what? Using me? I really liked you, Beth. You're the reason I came on this trip. I've liked you for ages, and I really thought we had a connection, you know? I thought we had something, but obviously I was wrong. They blame men for behaving like this, treating women like commodities to be cast aside when they've outlived their usefulness, but some women are just as bad.'

There were tears in his eyes, and she felt awful. Was he right? Had she just used him? She didn't think so. She did like him, but he was a bit too full on. This outburst confirmed it.

'Will, I'm sorry if I hurt you. I didn't mean to, and yes, maybe I should have thought a bit more before sleeping with you – it just felt right at the time. But I've had such emotional turmoil in my life lately, I guess I just wanted...' She struggled to find the right words.

'Oh, I know what you wanted. Thanks – thanks a lot.' He stormed off, and she was left standing in the middle of the shop alone.

* * *

KEVIN AND MARIANNE were sitting on the wall outside the aquarium, waiting for Tess and Annie.

'Mmm… This is so good. It tastes different than ice cream at home. It's much creamier or something,' Marianne said as they licked their soft-serve cones with a chocolate stick stuck in the top. 'I don't think one day has gone by since we got here that I haven't had ice cream or a drink!'

'It's all the rain on those green fields, makes for happy cows,' Kevin said. 'Happy cows, creamy milk.'

'Oh, listen to the farmer. I thought you lived either in Boston or New York all your life, and you're suddenly an expert.' She grinned.

'I watch nature shows on TV!' he protested.

'Do they do nature shows on cows?' She pretended to be perplexed, and they both laughed.

She wasn't sure what was happening. Since the near miss with Tess the other day, she and Kevin kind of naturally went wherever they were going. Tess was definitely pushing them together, which was nice; at least the little girl liked her, and now that she was not staring at a screen all day, she was a sweet kid. Her mother allowed her unlimited screen time, it would seem, but absolutely no sugar or white carbs, so Kevin was doing the opposite. No screens, but she was allowed to have candy and ice cream. The sweet treats would have to be cut back when they got home, but the child was on vacation, so she supported Kevin completely. Still, she wished she had some of that Debbie's willpower. She was definitely after gaining at least four pounds since landing in Ireland.

'Why couldn't Bubbles have come from somewhere with horrible food?' Marianne asked.

'Why? I love the food here – it's all so flavoursome. No spices really, but carrots taste like carrots and the meat is delicious. Debbie the vegan would have to be sedated right about now if she heard me.' He grinned.

'Oh, I love it too. That's what I mean – it's too good, and I can feel my pants getting tighter every day.' She sighed ruefully.

'Then buy bigger pants, and anyway, I think you look great.' Kevin didn't look at her as he said it; he kept his eyes on the aquarium door.

Her stomach did a flip, a sensation she'd not felt in years. Her confidence as well as her heart had taken such a bashing when Warren left, it was hard to believe anyone would ever find her attractive again. Kevin was different from Warren in every way, and she found herself drawn to him. While Warren was slim and short-ish, Kevin was huge. He was well over six feet tall, and he wasn't hugely overweight, but he was definitely not skinny. Chunky, she'd call it, and standing beside him, she felt small. She always hated the fact that Warren wore smaller jeans than she did. Kevin was more straightforward too; he saw things in practical terms, and she found herself in agreement with him a lot of the time.

Warren tended to overanalyse. She had gotten used to it, but it was nice to talk to someone who accepted things on face value and didn't overcomplicate everything.

Maybe he didn't mean anything by that remark. If she said anything in return, she might make him feel awkward, and it would be so embarrassing.

Kevin dared not look at Marianne's face. He wondered what she made of his compliment. He really liked her, more than he'd liked anyone for ages, but she seemed kind of hung up on her ex, and anyway, he was nothing like Warren. He was a short string of misery, as Bubbles might say. If that was the kind of guy she went for, then he was definitely barking up the wrong tree.

He decided to leave it. It would just be weird for the rest of the trip if he said something and she wasn't interested.

Annie and Tess were on the steps, and they held hands as they walked to the side of the kerb. Tess stopped and looked carefully up and down before checking with Annie that it was safe to cross. Once safely on the other side, she ran into Kevin's arms.

'Daddy, there was this cool thing where you could walk into a tunnel and you were in the penguin place, and they were all around. And the guy that worked there let me feed the sharks, and there were Nemo fish and Dory fish and octopus and rays and so much cool stuff. He told me to look really carefully at the bay there and I might see Fungi, 'cause he's very close to the shore these days 'cause the water is warm.' She paused to take a breath, and they all laughed.

'That sounds so cool.' Kevin kissed her on the cheek and tickled her, which made her giggle. 'I'm happy you had such a great time. Now what do you say to Annie for taking you?'

'Thank you, Annie. It was so much fun.'

'Now we better get you some lunch before Conor wants us all back on the bus,' Kevin said.

Tess cast a conspiratorial glance at Annie, who shook her head theatrically.

'Tell me,' Kevin said, with mock seriousness.

'We had potato chips, Irish ones called Tayto, and they were delicious. And we had a slushie and a chocolate bar with popping candy in it. The guy who was giving us the tour told us it was what all Irish people had for lunch.' She looked innocently at the group and once again had everyone laughing.

'And,' she went on, pleased to have everyone's attention, 'the guy friended Annie on Facebook, so I think he likes her!'

Annie made a funny face at Tess, and both of them giggled.

Conor and Eddie approached from one side, and shortly afterwards, the Glavin sisters and Miguel and Jimmy came from the other. Of Will and Beth, there was no sign. They all walked to the bus, Miguel still holding the urn.

'You look sharp today, Miguel,' Marianne remarked. 'I wish I'd dressed up a bit more now.'

Miguel smiled at her; he'd always liked Marianne. 'Today I say goodbye to Bubbles, and he always joked with me that I like clothes. He didn't care what he wore, but I like to dress nice, so it was kind of a thing with us.'

Marianne had always wondered about Miguel and Bubbles's relationship. The Mexican man was almost certainly gay, but she'd never seen him with anyone, but with Bubbles, it was hard to know. He wasn't at all camp or anything like that; if anything, he came across as kind of asexual. He loved people, men and women, he loved kids, he loved animals, but you never got the feeling that he was into anyone on a personal level.

She doubted there was anything between Miguel and Bubbles apart from friendship, but then who knew anything?

'Do you remember that tweed suit he had?' Marianne asked as they strolled back to the bus beside each other.

'Oh yes, a horrible hairy thing, and he wore it with that mustard tie and the wine shirt? That was a car crash.' Miguel chuckled. 'But Bubbles loved it.'

'And we all loved him,' Marianne said quietly.

'We did. We all sure did.'

When they arrived back, Beth was standing at the bus alone.

'Is Will not with you?' Conor asked.

'No, he…um… I thought he might be here,' she replied.

'Oh, sorry, I just thought you two were together.'

'No. No, we're not,' she said firmly.

Everyone else was climbing aboard when Conor took Beth aside. 'Is everything okay, Beth?'

'Yeah, I think so…' she said, though her body language disagreed.

'Okay. Well, if you need anything…' he said, not sure how to continue.

They waited for fifteen minutes, but Will never showed.

'What do you want to do?' Conor asked. 'We can wait another bit if you like, but we will need to crack on if you want to get out to Slea Head.'

Beth said nothing, just stared out the window, and Kevin finally said, 'I'll try his cell once more.'

He called, and this time Will answered.

'Hi, Will, it's Kevin. Yeah, we are about to get going to the place we're going to scatter Bubbles…' He paused. 'Oh, okay, sure. If that's what you want.' Another pause. 'Okay, see you then.' He hung up.

'He said he's going to make his own way back to the hotel – I don't know why, he didn't say – but for us to go on ahead without him.' Kevin shrugged.

They were all perplexed, but Conor said nothing and started the engine.

Tess sat beside Kevin this time, so Marianne sat with Annie.

'So how about the guy in the aquarium?' Marianne knew how much Annie wanted to meet someone.

'He was funny and sweet,' Annie admitted. 'A bit of a player, I think though. I had a look on Facebook, and he's got a lot of women friends. So no, not the one, but a nice guy. I had fun talking to him.'

Marianne was warming to her roommate. She wasn't as confident as she looked, and she seemed to genuinely think Marianne was so cool and together. If only she knew.

CHAPTER 28

$\mathcal{E}$rin and Shannon sat beside each other looking out at the Irish coastline as they drove out onto the Dingle Peninsula. The sea glittered in the sunshine, and while there were plenty of tourists about and some newly built houses, one got the impression that nothing much had changed over the centuries. Erin wondered if her parents ever came down this way.

Mammy was from Limerick and Daddy from Leitrim, and the sisters had toyed with the idea of extending their trip to go to the places their parents came from but almost immediately decided against it. Dr Mills couldn't manage without Shannon all that time, and Erin's line manager didn't understand why anybody needed a vacation. The woman was like a robot. Erin had never taken any time off before, and when she had asked for ten days, the woman looked at her as if she'd asked for a kidney.

Work was one reason, but though neither of them said it, the other reason was neither Mammy nor Daddy had much to do with their Irish families and maybe they would not be welcoming. Their mother had two sisters living, if not three, but they had totally lost contact. Daddy had a brother and a sister and several nieces and nephews. There were the obligatory cards at Christmas, both from and to

Ireland. The girls would open the cards from Seamus, Eileen and family, or Tony, Cait, Olivia and Tadhg, and wonder what they looked like, how old they were. Mammy hated talking about Ireland and always told them they were Americans now and that they should behave like Americans. She even hated the way the girls called her Mammy, the Irish way, but Daddy always did, and the girls just followed his lead. Once, when Erin was in the third grade, the teacher asked each kid to bring in something from their culture, and Erin asked her mother for something Irish. Mammy snapped crossly that her culture was American and made poor Erin take a stars-and-stripes mug that had come free with cereal or something one fourth of July. Everyone laughed and made fun of her that day, and when Shannon and she walked home, they tried to understand why Mammy was so set against Ireland. They never found out.

Whenever they asked her about Ireland, she would just say, 'There's nothing back there, only rocks and sea and hard work.'

They soon learned not to ask.

Daddy, on the other hand, always talked about his homeland and wished he could go back. At least he did when his wife wasn't within earshot. He'd sit the girls on his knee and tell them the stories of Fionn mac Cumhaill and the Fianna, the bravest warriors the world had ever seen, or of Oisín who followed Niamh to Tír na nÓg, the land of eternal youth, but when he came back, hundreds of years had passed. He told them about naughty leprechauns and talking fish and a king with donkey's ears. The girls loved their daddy with all their heart, and when they were twenty and he died of a heart attack one March evening while walking home from the subway station where he worked, they were crushed with grief.

Mammy hid her pain from her daughters, but they heard her sobbing at night through the thin walls of their apartment off 143rd Street. Their mother was a good person who did the best she could for her daughters, but her heart was broken when she lost her husband, and the only way she could cope was to wrap herself in steely determination, with no room for softness or emotions.

Daddy's family did write for a while after he died, but the letters were never acknowledged, and a cheap, thin Christmas card from New York every year, signed simply 'Shelia, Erin and Shannon', was the only contact. No 'x' or 'with love' or a note about how things were going – just the three names every year.

The Glavin family home was a small farm. As far as the girls knew, their Uncle Seamus still lived there, though they remembered Daddy saying that Seamus had written to say he'd bought the neighbouring farm as well and built a bigger house on the land. Seamus and their aunt Cait were still in Carrick-on-Shannon, County Leitrim, and they wondered what they would be like. Mammy kind of hinted that they were a bit rough, that Daddy didn't drink but it was not due to any good influence from his family, and that keeping them at arm's length was the thing to do.

'I had no idea it would be so magical looking,' Erin said as they rounded a bend on the road to reveal a huge expanse of crashing ocean and emerald-green fields. A narrow road off to the left snaked its way down from the main road to the sea, and it looked too tight even for a car.

'This is called the Devil's Elbow,' Conor explained as he expertly manoeuvred the big bus around what seemed like a hairpin bend, with a sheer cliff on one side and a steep drop to the sea on the other. 'And here we have the river running over the road. The river flow is determined by the amount of rainfall – it's coming from a lake on the top of that mountain there – and when we have a lot of rain, then those glacial lakes overflow and the result is waterfalls everywhere. That really only happens in the wintertime though.'

Everyone took out their phones and cameras to capture the incredible view.

'I'll stop in a while where the road widens a small bit, and ye can get out and stretch yer legs,' Conor said as they tried to stand up and balance as the bus wound its way around the sharp corners and steep hills.

The next stop was the beehive huts, small stone huts in the shape of a beehive where monks lived their entire lives.

Erin and Shannon had both read *How the Irish Saved Civilization* by

Thomas Cahill, so this was an exciting day for them. They had discussed it with Conor over coffee the previous day, and they were not surprised that he was really knowledgeable about the history and culture of his country. It was nice to be able to talk to him and know a little bit of it anyway. Apart from Dr Mills and Bubbles, the sisters had never had much to do with men. Conor was lovely, and very handsome too, they decided. His wife was a very lucky woman.

He stopped the bus, and the group followed him through a gate and up a steep field. It amazed them how something so ancient and precious would just be sitting in a field – no security, no visitor centre, just the huts themselves there where they had been since the sixth century.

'So...' Conor began to explain when his phone rang in his pocket; it was that same number again. He considered rejecting it, but something told him not to.

'I'm sorry about this, folks. I actually have a family situation at the moment, so I have to take this call, but Erin and Shannon here know all about this. We had a big chat about it yesterday, so maybe they could take over?'

The sisters looked like rabbits in the headlights, especially as people who were not part of their group were now waiting to hear the story as well.

They looked at each other, and Shannon took a deep breath. 'Well, we only read a book, but if you want to know...'

'Go, Glavin sisters!' Annie called, and everyone laughed and gave them an encouraging round of applause.

Erin began. 'Well, you know Ireland is called the land of saints and scholars. It's because of the monastic settlements here...'

Conor walked away, leaving the group listening to the stories of the monks who lived alone and, through their diligence, managed to save the manuscripts of Western civilisation during the dark ages in Europe.

He had allowed Jamsie's call to go to voicemail, but he returned it once he was out of earshot.

'Jamsie?'

'Hi, Conor. I wanted to let you know – I should have said it earlier – but we're here in Ireland, Gerry and I. I said he was sick, but he's taken a turn for the worse. We were about to go back to Dublin after you refused to see him. He was going to stay with me, but to be honest with you, he's too ill to travel. We were in the train station, and he collapsed on the platform – they had to get an ambulance. He's in the hospital in Ennis now, and I'm here with him.'

'What? You came back and brought Gerry with you?'

'I did. He's bad, worse than I thought. I…' Conor heard the anguish in his father's voice. 'I don't know what to do for the best.'

'Right, and is he conscious?'

'Oh yes, he's fully alert. He's stable again. They gave him some oxygen, so he's all right for now, but they ran all kinds of tests. He's dying, Conor. He has cirrhosis of the liver and hepatitis as well. The doctors said it might have been treatable if it had been caught earlier, but that didn't happen. The doctor just spoke to me and said he needs to go to the hospice really, because they'll be able to manage his pain and all of that better, but he doesn't want to go. I suppose I could take him back to Dublin with me, but I don't know if he's strong enough even for that. I'm not sure what to do. He's very religious now, and he says he wants a priest. The nurse here was going to contact the parish priest.'

Conor thought of Fr Scanlon in his Lycra. 'No, don't do that. I'll bring someone in to him if there's no immediate rush.' He sighed. 'Look, I'm working now, and I'm below in Kerry with a group, but I'll be home around six and I'll ring you then, all right?'

'Grand, son. I'll look forward to hearing from you.'

Conor felt a maelstrom of emotions. Frustration and resentment certainly, that he was dragged into this, but also guilt at how selfish he was being. He also found he was so sad to hear Gerry was dying. Even after all these years, and all that had happened, he was still his brother. Eddie's words were ringing in his ears, how life was great for him and he could afford to show a little compassion. Jamsie was an old man, and he was trying to deal with Gerry on his own on the other side of the country from where he lived. Gerry was his brother no matter what, and their mother would want him to do right by him. Ana thought he should see his father. Maybe it was time to let it all go and help them out.

'Everything all right?' Eddie asked as he walked towards Conor.

Conor exhaled deeply. 'My father is after bringing my brother back here. He was here when we spoke this morning but never mentioned it. Anyway, Gerry is very ill, cirrhosis of the liver and other complications it seems, and he had to be shifted into Ennis Hospital when he collapsed on the platform of the train station. He's stable again now, but they're saying he should be in a hospice. Jamsie doesn't know what to do because Gerry is refusing to go, and he was going to bring him back to Dublin, but he's too sick to travel.'

The priest placed his hand on his friend's shoulder. 'I'm sorry for being so hard on you – you do have a lot on your plate at the moment. How can I help?'

Conor gave a rueful smile. 'Thanks, Eddie. Nah, you're probably right. My mam would have wanted me to step in and help. Jamsie is getting on, and sure, he doesn't know Gerry any more than I do, but it's not fair to leave him handling everything. I'll give him a call when I get back, and we'll see what can be done.'

'You said Gerry is a man of faith now?'

'He is apparently, since he took on the twelve steps. Sure whatever works I suppose?'

'Do not judge lest ye yerselves be judged,' Eddie said with a chuckle. 'Will I call in to see him with you when we get back?'

Conor thrust his hands in his pockets and gazed out to sea. The sharp pointed island of Skellig Michael stood starkly against the horizon; curlews and gulls squawked and circled overhead. The monastic settlement had been used as a location in the new Star Wars film, so the area had been a hive of activity for a few weeks, but it was returned to a place of serene inhospitality once again, as it should be. Conor wished life could be like that.

'So I'm doing this now, am I?' The question was as much to himself as to Eddie.

The priest stood beside him, gazing out to sea too. 'You are, but you'll have Ana and me and the grace of your mam to help you.'

* * *

THE GROUP WERE TAKING PHOTOS, and Miguel got a group shot of everyone together, the urn down on the grass in front of them.

'Right, let's send Bubbles O'Leary on his way first anyway, will we?' Eddie said, smiling as the group joked around. They had loved this man Bubbles, of that there was no doubt, and Eddie prayed that he knew in his lifetime how much. He had been formulating a little homily all day based on the stories shared with him.

They strolled towards the bus when all of a sudden, the heavens opened. Huge fat raindrops soaked them all to the skin in moments. Conor ran to the bus, opening both the front and side doors, and everyone got in as quickly as they could.

He had a spare shirt in the boot, so he went to get it, and some of the others had spare clothes too. Kevin had a cute T-shirt for Tess, with a picture of a girl leprechaun on it saying, 'The leprechauns made me do it!' It was a little too big, so she wore it as a dress. Marianne had bought T-shirts for friends back home while they were in Dingle, so she offered them to Erin, Shannon and Annie. Beth had a dry hoodie on the bus, so the ladies went to the back of the bus and did the best they could to change.

Erin thought she looked ridiculous, but Shannon assured her that a Guinness T-shirt looked quite nice on her. Annie nudged Shannon and nodded for them to look out the back window of the bus.

The rain stopped as abruptly as it started. Conor was at the boot, where he kept spare clothes. Years of touring had taught him that it was always necessary in Ireland to have a plan B.

He stripped off his T-shirt and glanced up at the back window of the bus, where he caught Marianne, Annie, Beth and the two Glavin sisters watching him. Marianne, Beth and Annie laughed – they were caught and they knew it – but the poor Glavin sisters looked utterly mortified.

Kevin saw what happened and started joking when Conor got back on the bus. 'Hey, Conor, they're filming a new Diet Coke commercial out there, huh? 'Cause you sure got the ladies' attention!'

Erin and Shannon had no idea what he meant and looked perplexed.

Marianne enlightened them. 'You remember that commercial for Diet Coke where all the girls in the office are watching some hot guy out the window?'

Erin swallowed, her face puce with embarrassment. 'No... I never saw that, but we weren't... I mean, we were only admiring the scenery...' Shannon was about to back her up when Jimmy gave a rare interjection.

'That's exactly what you were doing, Erin.' And he grinned.

The whole bus descended into laughter, Conor and Eddie included, and even Erin and Shannon had to give in in the end.

CHAPTER 29

The shower that had drenched the entire peninsula seemed to have revealed the landscape in bright light and vivid colours. Not just the green fields and the stone walls, but the white fluffy sheep dotted everywhere, the red lead paint on a corrugated iron roof of a shed, the whitewash on the cottages, all seemed in such brilliant Technicolour.

They stopped at the furthermost point on the peninsula, the Atlantic stretching out before them all the way to America. There was a clifftop with a small footpath to its edge, and Conor suggested they walk out there and scatter Bubbles's ashes.

'I can't imagine anywhere more beautiful.' Marianne sighed.

'And it's facing the US as well, his other home. It's perfect. Bubbles's heart always was somewhere between the two,' Beth said. Everyone gathered themselves and got out of the coach.

'You coming, Conor?' Annie asked as she passed the driver's seat.

'No, I'll let ye at it, this is yer time. Take as long as ye need. I'll be here.'

Eddie led the group across the field to the edge, while Conor waited in the bus. He wanted to call Ana and fill her in on everything that had happened. He watched them all walk, much more solemnly now than before. This was their time to say goodbye to their friend. The sun was out again, and the ocean was wild and crashing far below. He could see a school of basking sharks a little way offshore, and gulls circled noisily.

* * *

THEY STOPPED at the cliff edge and automatically huddled together. Miguel held the urn tightly to his chest.

'Now,' Eddie said, 'I thought we would begin by each person saying goodbye to Bubbles in his or her own way. We're a small group, so you may do it silently or aloud, whichever feels right for you. I didn't ever have the pleasure of knowing him, but I would like to say something, so I'll break the ice and go first.

'Bubbles O'Leary was a name I had never heard before, and one that conjures up all sorts of images. None of these images I imagined when Conor first rang me turned out to be true. He has come to life, through your stories for me, and so we are gathered here on this beautiful day to say our final farewell to this extraordinary man. Bubbles touched so many lives, many of which I'm sure we know nothing about. It seems that though he tried his best to help everyone he met, he did not seek praise or even recognition for it. In fact, some of you explained to me that if you tried to thank him, he wouldn't allow it and would brush your thanks aside.'

Several people nodded and smiled.

'Everyone here today has a personal story, whether you met him late at night in a hospital beside a homeless man he'd befriended, or at the Irish Centre where he encouraged others to volunteer as he did. Or maybe you knew him through your job, or you worked with him, or just that you stumbled across his bar one day and you never stopped going there, whatever the circumstances. However your relationship with Bubbles began, each of you has told me how welcome he made you feel. Bubbles made you all feel special and wanted. And so, I'll invite you each now to say goodbye to Bubbles in your own way.'

He smiled and nodded at Miguel.

Marianne wiped a tear from her eye, and Kevin gave her a Kleenex.

Annie linked Miguel's arm with hers as tears flowed unchecked down the man's cheeks. He still held the urn. Nobody had asked him for it, and he was glad. He knew it was stupid – Bubbles was dead – but this felt very final. He cradled the urn to his chest and didn't care what anyone thought. He wished for the millionth time he'd had the courage to say something before it was too late, to tell Bubbles how much he loved him, to hear him say those words in return, even if only as a friend.

'Goodbye, my love,' he said, loud enough for everyone to hear. He reached into the urn, took a handful of ashes and threw them into the wind.

Jimmy thought about his prayer for the big, audacious and warm Irishman. He stepped up and took a handful. 'Farewell, old friend. Thank you for making me welcome, for understanding how I am. For accepting me.' He put his arm around Miguel.

Marianne stood beside Kevin as he held Tess in his arms. She stepped forward and took a handful. 'So long, Bubbles.' She tried to focus on her memory of his face. 'Thanks for making a place for us to go, and especially thank you for sparing my pain. Only you would start a rumour that was a lie to protect someone. You'll be so badly missed.'

Kevin was next. 'Bubbles, we loved you, man, we really did. Enjoy the craic up there.' A single tear ran down his face. Marianne put her arm around his waist, and Tess snuggled into his neck.

Annie went next. 'I did what you said, Bubbles, and you were right – there is nowhere on earth like Ireland. Rest in peace, big guy. I love you.'

Beth scattered a handful and whispered, 'Thank you for everything, Bubbles, and mostly for looking out for me and Maddie. I'll never forget you.'

Erin and Shannon stood together, clinging, crying. They stepped towards the urn. 'Erin and I don't go out much, we don't have friends, but Bubbles, you made two ladies like us welcome. We'd never been in a bar before, and we weren't sure it was a good idea when you made us promise we would come to your Irish dancing night.' Shannon's voice cracked so Erin continued.

'You gave us a life, you gave us friends, you gave us so much. We can't imagine life without you – where will we go?'

Kevin extended his big arm and they moved closer.

Eddie waited until he was sure everyone was finished, and then he spoke once more. 'And so we have come to the part where we must say goodbye. We will scatter the remainder of Bubbles's ashes here in the land where he was born, but facing out to the ocean in the direction of the land that became his home, where he made such a wonderful life for himself, surrounded by dearly loved friends. Now, we will pray for his soul, which I am full sure is already at the right hand of the Lord.'

Eddie blessed himself and placed a silver and purple stole around his neck. He bowed his head, and the others did as he did.

'Eternal rest grant unto Bubbles's soul, oh Lord, and may perpetual light shine upon him forever. May he rest in peace. May his soul, and the souls of all the faithful departed, through the mercy of God, rest in peace.'

The gathered group spoke as one. 'Amen.'

As they stood, gathered and bereft, Kevin began to sing. *'Oh Danny Boy, the pipes, the pipes are calling...'*

Before he got to the end of the first line, they all joined in.

From glen to glen, and down the mountain side, the summer's gone and all the roses falling, 'tis you, 'tis you, must go and I must bide. But come ye back when summer's in the meadow, or when the valley's hushed and white with snow, 'tis I'll be there, in sunshine or in shadow, oh Danny Boy, oh Danny Boy, I love you so.

Conor looked at the gathered crowd in amazement. He got out of the bus and heard their song rise up on the wind. He'd never seen anything like it. He got out of the bus and took several pictures with his phone.

Slowly, they all walked back to the bus, arm in arm, holding hands, everyone connected to everyone else.

CHAPTER 30

*C*onor drove the bus around impossibly tight bends while relaying a hilarious story about a couple he'd once had on a tour who were supposedly husband and wife until they ran into their neighbours from home in an ancient ring fort on that very peninsula. They were husband and wife all right, but not each other's. As everyone laughed at the incongruity of that situation, Jimmy wondered whatever became of Will. He knew very little of him prior to the trip, apart from the fact that he was a regular at the bar.

Bubbles had mentioned that while he was in hospital for something, he met Will, a porter, and they struck up a conversation. Of course, Bubbles invited Will to the bar. The thing that struck Jimmy as odd though was that Bubbles always attended Mount Sinai in Queens; he'd told him so on a few occasions.

Will and Beth had been on the seat opposite him; now it was just Beth on her own.

Once Conor stopped talking, Beth leaned over. 'Jimmy, how well do you know Will?' she asked.

He looked at her, sensing she was upset about something. 'Not very well. I knew him from coming into the bar, but only to say hello.'

'Okay.' She smiled, uncertain how to continue.

'Can I help you, Beth?' he asked.

She exhaled, as if trying to formulate the words. 'Well, he... I don't know. When we got off the bus in Dingle earlier, I wanted to just stroll around on my own and said so to him, but he got very...well, not angry exactly, but kind of upset. It's my fault, giving him the impression that I was looking for something...' She coloured with embarrassment. 'I'm sorry, I must sound like a teenager. Forget I said anything.'

'Beth.' Jimmy stopped her. 'Did Will ever mention to you that he works at Mount Sinai, Queens?'

She looked confused. 'No, he doesn't, does he? I... He said he works as a porter in a warehouse or something...'

He paused. 'No, I'm fairly sure he is a porter at Mount Sinai, Queens.'

'But...that's where I work. He knows that, so why would he not say it?'

'I don't know,' Jimmy replied.

Now that Beth had confirmed what he suspected, that Will never admitted they worked in the same hospital, his behaviour seemed even more odd. He liked Beth; she was a nice person and had a lot on her shoulders. She was worried about her sister, and she seemed to be kind of alone in the world.

'As I said to you before, trust your intuition.'

'But that time, I said I thought Maddie was in trouble, and it turns out she's fine – she sent me a text.'

He nodded. 'I know that. But still, I think you should trust your instincts. If you are not interested in a relationship with Will, then you're perfectly entitled to say so.'

She looked at him, bemused. 'Okay. I think I need to have another talk with him, explain things. And ask him why he didn't say we worked at the same place, as that's just weird. But I don't think it's anything sinister. Maybe he thought I wouldn't be interested in him because he was a porter... But then he did tell me he was a porter, so that doesn't make sense either. Anyway, I'm not interested. He's a nice guy, just a bit intense for me. I guess I was so distraught over Maddie,

I kind of leaned on him a bit over the past couple of days. I just need to straighten that out.'

'Just be careful, Beth,' Jimmy said.

'I will,' she replied with a smile.

* * *

WHEN THE GROUP got back to the hotel, there were several messages waiting for them, all from Paudie Mac, with potential dates lined up.

Miguel opened his. He was sad, but actually the scattering of Bubbles's ashes had given him some kind of closure, and he seemed a little better. He even had a joke with the others at Paudie's ideal companion description.

He read the email aloud. 'Dear Miguel. I have found the perfect lady for you.' He smiled sheepishly at the group, who if they had suspected before, they now all knew that there was no such thing as the perfect lady for him.

'She is from Australia, and she is a tree surgeon. She is a beautiful woman with a very nice personality. She is quite tall, but don't let that put you off – she says she doesn't mind that you are a little shorter than her. Call by the office as soon as you can, and we'll set it up. Regards. Paudie Mac.'

'Sounds perfect, Miguel.' Kevin nudged him with a wink.

The other man grinned and shook his head. 'I suppose you all know anyway, but ladies are not really my thing.'

They all smiled, and Marianne gave him a one-armed squeeze.

'How about you, Annie? Did you get someone?' Marianne asked, knowing she was the only one of the group who saw this as anything more than a bit of fun.

Annie scanned the single sheet that Katherine had printed out. 'Yes, he thinks he has someone.' She tried to keep her voice light, but Marianne could see the hope in her eyes. 'Look!' She handed Marianne the email.

Dear Annie,

As luck would have it, I have a man for you to meet that I think might work out very well. He's a farmer, and he seems like a grand, lovely man altogether. He's a biteen older than you, but not that it makes a difference when it comes to love, I've always found. Call into the office soon, and we can talk some more about it.

Fondest regards,

Paudie Mac

Katherine looked sceptical from behind the reception desk but kept her own counsel. She caught Jimmy's eye.

As Katherine handed out room keys, Jimmy waited until last.

'You're not a believer in the powers of the matchmaker,' he said, a statement not a question.

She gave nothing away. 'I'm sure Mr Mac has many years' experience, but I think human relationships are a little more complex than he might imagine.' She smiled professionally. 'Though I might be wrong of course.'

'Rarely, I imagine.' He was rewarded with one of Katherine's rare smiles.

'I'm enjoying the book. I started it last night and stayed awake too long reading. I will finish it tonight,' she said.

'I'm glad. I enjoyed it too.' Jimmy hesitated. He was in unchartered waters here. He had never asked a woman out in his entire life. When he was young, he was such a maelstrom of emotions, feeling everything so acutely that he felt he could only survive by distancing himself from people. As he grew older, it just became his way. His father died eventually, and it was one of the few times in his life when he felt nothing. Relief maybe. When his mother died a few years later, he thought he would die from grief. The pain of her loss was so intense, so raw, for so long. The night he buried her was the night he met Bubbles.

He wasn't much of a drinker, and he didn't enjoy socialising, so he avoided places like bars, but Bubbles had been standing at the back of the church during the funeral Mass. He came up and sympathised, though he had never met either Jimmy or his mother. They got talking, and Bubbles invited him to his bar for a drink. Jimmy didn't want to be alone; the pain was too much. So they went back to the bar. It was closed despite being mid-afternoon, and Bubbles showed no signs of opening up.

The big Irishman had a way of striking up a conversation – not intrusive but not pointless small talk either. Jimmy found himself talking all about his mother, his father, how his loss was nothing but how much he would miss his mother, the only person on earth who understood him. He cried, and Bubbles was there. He didn't do anything, didn't offer platitudes of comfort that society had crafted for just such occasions, but he shot the bolt on the inside of the door, locking them in, poured Jimmy a large whiskey and let him cry for his mother.

Jimmy turned to face him. 'My father was violent. He beat me up all the time, my mother too. I wish I could have killed him.' He took a small silver ring out of his pocket, twisting it round and round in his hands. 'My mom could never afford jewellery, but this was her wedding ring. It's a symbol of her marriage to that brute, but she wore it all her life. It's all I have left really.'

'Then it's hers and you should wear it.'

Jimmy slipped the ring on his pinkie finger; it just about fit.

Bubbles lifted his glass in a toast. 'May your mother rest in peace now.'

It was the nicest thing anyone had ever done for him, so that was why he was here. He knew how much Bubbles wanted to come home.

He'd thought about Bubbles a lot since he got here, but he also thought of his mother and what she would think of this fancy place. The intensity of that pain of her loss was as sharp as ever. It did not dull with time as people thought it did.

He had learned to shield himself from others over the years, taught himself how to protect his heart, how to stay aloof and read the signs, but something drew him to this woman. They stood there, her on one side of the desk, he on the other, awkwardly.

'Well, I must get on…' Katherine began. She seemed a little flustered, and he sensed she was uncomfortable.

'Would you have dinner with me?' he asked, not even sure if that was the correct way to ask a woman out. He never watched films and didn't have a TV, so his knowledge of how one did these things was limited.

'I... Well, I normally don't... Well, I...' She was embarrassed.

'I'm sorry. That was inappropriate, I'm sure you're busy and anyway it's not...' He wasn't often lost for words – he used so few of them every day – but he too was embarrassed and felt stupid.

He remembered the sensation, how he felt when he was fourteen and his father grabbed one of his books. It was Plato, describing the attractiveness of the youth Charmides at the wrestling school and how Socrates himself 'catches fire' when he sees inside the boy's cloak.

His father had called him a faggot that day. He'd screamed into his face how no son of his was going to be a poof, how he'd rather Jimmy would die than admit to being a homosexual. His father broke his hand that night, cracked four ribs and tore off a piece of his ear, and he shattered his wife's jaw when she tried to stop him.

Katherine looked at him and seemed to regain her composure. 'I'm sorry, you took me by surprise. I actually would like that. I finish here in forty-five minutes. But if you don't mind, we will go into town. I'll drive.' She looked up and suddenly flushed red. 'Or did you not mean tonight? Perhaps you meant...' Her face burned.

Jimmy smiled a warm, genuine smile. A rare sight. 'Tonight would be perfect. I'll meet you outside at seven thirty-five, then.'

'Very well,' she said, and escaped into the back office.

Conor watched the entire exchange from his office behind the reception desk. He'd texted Jamsie as soon as he got back, and his father told him that Gerry was having more tests and wouldn't be available to speak for a few hours. Jamsie had checked into a hotel near the hospital and was going to have a rest; it had been a very long day. They arranged to meet at the hospital later.

He knew the staff called Katherine 'The Rottweiler'. She took no prisoners, that was for sure, and she made it close to impossible to see Conor. That was fine because he did a walkabout each morning, calling to all the various departments, so anyone with anything to ask or tell him got their chance. But he was so fond of her; he was glad she was going out to dinner. And Jimmy seemed like a nice man.

Jimmy left, and Conor called her into his office. He knew she lived a short drive away. 'Knock off now. I'll manage the desk till Meghan gets here.'

'I will do nothing of the kind...'

'Katherine.' Conor came out from behind his desk and shut the door. He placed his hands on her shoulders. He was the only one in the whole castle who would ever dare to touch her. 'Go home, change your clothes, take down your hair, and be back here in forty-five minutes, okay?'

'Get off me, for goodness sake, Conor. I have work to do...' She tried to shrug his hands off her shoulders, but he wouldn't let her.

'Listen to me,' he said gently, his eyes never leaving hers. 'Jimmy seems like a nice man, and you deserve some fun. You're a lovely woman, Katherine. Now, how about the blue dress you wore to the barbeque at our house two weeks ago? That was really lovely, and you had your hair down as well, and you looked great. Ana said it too, just in case you don't trust my judgement when it comes to women's clothes and hairstyles.' He winked and was rewarded with a tiny smile.

'I suppose I do look a little like an undertaker.' She sighed. One of the disgruntled waiting staff had called her a dried-up old undertaker before storming out last week.

'You don't. You look efficient and professional, but this is a date, so you can let that off for tonight.'

'It is not a date... For goodness sake, Conor, I'm fifty-six years old, not sixteen.' Her cheeks burned. 'This is madness. I'll just tell him I can't go...'

'Over my dead body.' Conor was determined that she wouldn't backtrack. 'Come on, Katherine, we're cut from the same cloth, you and me. 'Twas you who made me lower my guard and see what was in front of my face with Ana all those years ago. You know that for all my flirting and messing in those days, I never let anyone in because I was so hurt when I was young. But that doesn't have to be the story of your life.'

'Yes, Conor.' Katherine sighed. 'Except there is one slight difference. Every woman for six counties wanted you on her arm. I'm not exactly a catch now, am I? I mean, look at me.'

His heart melted to see his friend so vulnerable. 'Will I tell you what I see? Will I?' He kept his hands on her shoulders.

She lowered her face, embarrassed, but he lifted her chin with his finger, forcing her to look into his eyes. 'I see a fine-looking woman with a great figure and a pretty face if she'd only stop scowling at me.' He grinned. 'But more than that, I see a smart, intuitive, kind, loyal friend, and that's what Jimmy sees too.'

'I don't know...'

She was coming around, he could tell, but years of a protective wall were not going to crumble in an instant.

'Well, I do. So just trust me on this one, okay? Just go with me – it will be fine. Now go home and change.' He wrapped her in his arms and held her tightly for a moment.

'All right.' She exhaled and took a step back. 'I'll go. But where should I take him? I don't want every tongue wagging in the morning.'

Conor chuckled. 'So what if they are? What you do and who you do it with is nobody's business but yours. I'd go to the Lobster Pot – the food is great, and the tables are all in alcoves and are discreet.'

'Good idea.' She nodded. 'Should I offer to pay?' she asked.

'Jimmy strikes me as an old-fashioned guy, so no, I wouldn't. Now, get out of here,' he ordered.

As she turned the handle on the big oak door, he said, 'And Katherine?'

She turned.

'If you are late in the morning, we'll manage it.' He gave her a cheeky wink, and she shook her head, dismissing his outrageous suggestion.

Once Katherine was gone, he sat at his desk and dialled Ana.

'Hi, Conor.' She sounded bright.

'Hi, love, how're you feeling?'

'Not bad. Good actually. I just made some soup with the vegetables my father bring from hotel garden.'

He smiled. It was great to see her doing normal things. She'd had chemo yesterday, so these were the good days. By the weekend, he knew, she would be flattened again as the poison that was saving her life ravaged her already weak body. It was torture for him to watch it. He could only imagine what it must feel like for her, but she was so tough. He was in awe of her.

'Listen, pet, I need to talk to you. Jamsie rang me earlier, and he's in Ireland, and he's got my brother Gerry with him. He contacted me first thing this morning – I assumed he was in America – saying Gerry wanted to talk to me, to apologise for everything, it's part of the recovery from the addiction programme he's doing, but I said I had too much on at the moment to deal with that.'

Ana didn't interrupt, but he could sense she didn't agree.

'Anyway, he called me again, around lunchtime, this time telling me they were in fact in Ennis and they were heading back to Dublin since I refused to meet them. Gerry is sick, but I don't think Jamsie knew just how sick he was, because he collapsed on the platform at the train station and now he's in the hospital.'

'Sick from what?' Ana asked.

'Cirrhosis of the liver. It's something people get if they abuse alcohol for many years,' Conor explained. 'Gerry was an alcoholic and a drug addict. He's been in and out of jail in America all his life...'

'And what do the doctor say?'

'It's not treatable – he's going to die. Maybe if it was caught sooner, they say something might have been possible, but at this late stage, it seems not.'

'Oh, Conor, I'm so sorry.' She sighed. 'I can take taxi, come to you?'

'No, that's okay. I'll go in and see him. I can't let Jamsie manage all of this on his own – he sounded exhausted.'

'I'm coming too. No arguing.' She knew he was going to refuse.

'No way, Ana. You are immune compromised as it is. The last thing you need...' He tried to shut her down.

'Conor, I go in that hospital every few days, I go to cafés, I go to shops. This liver thing is not contagious, no?' she demanded.

'No, but...'

'So no reason I don't go. Conor, we are team, we do this together. I won't let you do this on your own.'

'But, Ana... Really, my love, I don't think...' Conor knew there was no point; she'd made up her mind.

'Collect me on the way. I'll ask my mother to come over to watch the boys.'

'Fine, I'll see you in twenty minutes.' He hung up. One part of him was glad Ana would be by his side, but a bigger part of him was worried. God alone knew what condition his brother was in, and she was so frail and weak. He allowed himself to think about Gerry properly for the first time.

For so long he'd held such anger, such bitterness towards his brother, but somehow it had evaporated. He'd had such a horrible life – his father leaving when he was only a toddler, then Mam being sick and finally dying. He hated school, and he didn't want to work; he was a troubled soul from the off.

Conor remembered him as a teenager. All the local girls loved him because he was so good-looking and charming – he looked like John Travolta in *Grease*. He loved America and all things American; he couldn't wait to get there. By the sounds of it, the American dream didn't work out for him.

Ana and Eddie were right – he could afford to be generous. He had so much. It was time to let it all go.

CHAPTER 31

*J*immy headed back to his room, hardly believing what he had done. He passed Will's room, which was next door to his, just as the other man was coming out.

'Hi, Will.'

'Hi, Jimmy, did you have a nice day?' Will asked with a smile. It was as if nothing odd had happened.

'Well, we scattered Bubbles's ashes, and the ceremony was very nice,' he said pointedly.

'Oh yeah, that was today.' The other man seemed a little distracted.

'Okay, see you later.' Jimmy put his key card in the lock.

'Sure, sure.' Will waved. 'By the way, how was Beth? She was a little upset earlier... I think she got the wrong impression...' As he spoke, he was scrolling on his phone as young people seemed to do incessantly these days.

'She was upset,' he said quietly.

The other man rolled his eyes and shrugged. 'Chicks, eh? What are you gonna do? I'm gonna hit the gym. See ya later.' He slung his gym bag over his shoulder, put his phone in his pocket and sauntered off.

The beautiful room had been serviced, though Jimmy always made his own bed. The double doors leading onto a small balcony with easy chairs were slightly ajar to air the room. He woke early and loved to sit out there in the mornings. It was Will's balcony as well – a small wall was all that separated the two – but in the mornings, Will's curtains were always drawn, and Jimmy had never seen him use it. He stepped out to enjoy the view and to steady his nerves about his upcoming evening. Will's door was slightly ajar as well.

He heard a phone ringing inside; the other man must have forgotten to take it downstairs. Maybe one didn't take a phone to a gym – he had no idea as he'd never set foot in one in his life. Then he remembered – Will had been scrolling on his phone when he was talking to him just moments ago. That was odd.

He could have two phones, or maybe the thing he heard was another device of some kind. Still, something rankled with him. Should he tell someone? What was there to tell? Will had two devices? Hardly a crime. But yet the feeling lingered.

He tried to put it to the back of his mind. He was taking a woman out for the first time in his life, and he needed to focus on that. Katherine intrigued him. There was something deep about her; he felt he could recognise her as a kindred spirit. She had one face for the world, and he could see how jealously she guarded her private self, but there were glimpses.

He showered, shaved and dressed in his best dark trousers and a charcoal-grey button-down shirt. He didn't have a tie, so even if he wanted to wear one, he couldn't. He'd only brought two jackets: a tweed one that he'd had for years and a cream one that he'd picked up in a thrift store before coming. He'd packed it and unpacked it before leaving home, feeling foolish. Where would he wear such a garment? But he was glad he had something different to wear.

As he waited for the elevator, Beth and Annie arrived.

'Oh, Jimmy, you look great,' Annie gushed. 'I love that jacket. It's a Tom Ford, isn't it?'

Jimmy smiled. 'I've no idea.'

'May I?' Annie pulled the jacket slightly open to reveal the Tom Ford logo.

'That's a very nice jacket. I never had you down as a guy for labels...' She grinned.

'I got it for twenty dollars in a thrift store,' he said as the elevator arrived.

'Well, you look a million dollars.' Beth smiled kindly and kissed his cheek.

He was a little early, and he was unsure what to do. She wasn't on the reception desk, Conor was.

'Hi, Jimmy.' Conor greeted him with a cheerful wave.

'Hello, Conor.' He walked over. 'I want to thank you for organising that today. It was a very moving tribute to Bubbles, and your friend Eddie did a really good job. It meant a lot to us.'

'I'm glad. Bubbles sounded like a remarkable man.'

'He was. And it would have meant the world to him to come back to Ireland. He always wanted to, but for some reason, he felt he couldn't.'

Conor considered his next question. 'Do you know why?'

He shook his head. 'I don't.'

'So I hear you're off out on the town tonight?'

Jimmy looked a bit sheepish. 'Yes... I invited Katherine to join me for dinner. She's a very nice lady. We met in the library the other day.'

'She most certainly is. And there's a lot more to her than meets the eye, no more than yourself, I'd say. Ye are well met, as we say here, but I will tell you this – a more decent, kind, loyal person you won't meet, so be sure to treat her well.' Conor felt like Katherine's father, marking the card of a young buck coming to the door to take his daughter out despite both Jimmy and Katherine being older than him. It was silly probably, but he felt so protective of her. He'd hate her to be hurt.

'I will.' Another man would have been indignant or made a joke, but Jimmy was sincere.

'She's just popped home to get herself out of her work gear and all that stuff women need to do.' Conor gave a gentle smile. 'But she should be here any minute. Can I get you a drink or a coffee or something?'

'No thanks. I'll wait outside for her. The grounds are so beautiful, and so many unusual plants.'

The Irishman nodded, thinking of Nico, the Russian garden restorer who had fallen for Ana while he worked there last year. How he nearly went out of his mind with grief and pain at the thought of losing his wife to this man who spoke her language and seemed to share so much with her. He dismissed the painful thought and explained to Jimmy, 'The wife of one of the owners back in the fifties was an Australian lady, and she was an expert in horticulture. She planted an amazing garden here. Because the Gulf Stream actually reaches the coast of Ireland, it warms the soil slightly, allowing us to grow tropical plants. Over the years, the castle became derelict. It had all become a tangled, overgrown mess, but we had a garden restorer work here last year to bring it back. He did a great job.'

'He did,' Jimmy said. 'I enjoy sitting out there.'

The phone rang again, and Conor answered it as Jimmy moved away. He crossed the expansive lobby with its terracotta tiles worn down by years of feet. The huge fireplace was filled with a gold and cream dried-flower arrangement, and beside it stood two suits of armour. On the mantelpiece, scented candles burned. The place looked bright and airy now in summertime, but in the winter, he could imagine it as equally inviting, with log fires and décor to match.

The enormous door was the original, Conor told them, and though there was a very sophisticated security locking system in place, you couldn't see it. The door looked like it was opened with a big black key that fit into an ornate cast-iron lock. The door itself was made of oak planks, held together by iron studs that were painted black. Every detail was pleasing, from the brass umbrella and walking-stick holder to the walnut hatstand. Nothing had been overlooked, and the overall effect was lovely.

He walked outside and went in the direction of the car park. There was a large van open, and from it came the sweetest female voice he had ever heard. The young woman singing was inside the van, coiling up electrical cables.

The lyrics rang clear in the still evening air, and Jimmy stopped to listen as her voice rose and fell.

OF ALL THE *money that e'er I spent*
I spent it in good company
And all the harm that e'er I've done
Alas, it was to none but me
And all I've done for want of wit
To memory now I can't recall
So fill to me the parting glass
Good night and joy be with you all
Oh all the comrades that e'er I've had
Are sorry for my going away
And all the sweethearts that e'er I've had
Would wish me one more day to stay
But since it falls unto my lot
That I should rise and you should not
I'll gently rise and I'll softly call
Good night and joy be with you all
Good night and joy be with you all

SHE EMERGED, and Jimmy recognised her as the musician who Conor had been speaking to on the first day, the one who had helped to do Tess's hair. He had seen her perform, and she was wonderful on the harp and the fiddle, but there was something so pure about her voice now, with no amplification or music behind her.

She seemed to be wearing a kind of black pinafore held together at the sides by large safety pins, under which he could see a hot-pink tiny T-shirt that barely reached her ribcage. On her legs, she had green and black tartan tights, and on her feet were what looked like lumberjack boots.

She spotted Jimmy. 'Oh, hi. I didn't see you there.' She flashed him a mischievous grin and began throwing leads and connections into a large plastic box she'd placed on the ground beside the van. 'You'd never think I'd a boyfriend, would you? Leaving me to load all the gear on my own!' She sighed with mock exasperation.

'That's a beautiful song you were singing.'

'Thanks. I'm practising it because I'm singing it at a funeral tomorrow. My mam's uncle died, but he was like ninety-eight or something, so hardly a tragedy. But he loved that song anyway, so they asked if I'd sing it.'

'I like the sentiment. It reminds me of a friend who died recently.'

'Oh, are you part of that group Conor is minding? Ye brought someone's ashes over to scatter him here?' She paused what she was doing.

'Yes, the man was named Bubbles O'Leary, and he owned a bar in New York. We all used to go there.'

Laoise laughed. 'Great name. He'd have to be Irish with a name like that.' She resumed packing up. 'I think that's a lovely idea that all his mates brought him home. Fair play to ye, he must have been a great guy to say ye went to so much trouble.'

'He was.' As Jimmy spoke, he heard a vehicle enter the car park behind him. It was Katherine.

As she pulled up, Laoise looked in amazement. Katherine was transformed. Her chestnut hair, thick and glossy, fell to her shoulders. She wore a baby-blue dress that showed curves nobody ever knew she had, and she even looked like she might have a bit of lipstick on.

'Miss O'B! Looking smokin', girl!' Laoise grinned, and Katherine coloured but looked pleased.

She smiled. 'Hello, Laoise.' Despite the younger woman's mad hair, piercings and tattoos, Katherine knew she had a heart of gold. 'No sign of Dylan?' They were usually inseparable.

'No, he's had to go up to Dublin to see Corlene. It's her birthday, so they are going to some black-tie thing in the mansion house – the president's going and all. You know Corlene will love that. Sounds like a total yawn-fest to me, so I let him off. He was allergic actually, but she's his mam, and I have to do enough old folk stuff as it is. My mam has me singing at my old Uncle Richie's funeral tomorrow, in flippin' Wexford.'

'You'll be rewarded in heaven,' Katherine said with a chuckle.

'Ha! I hope I get rewarded before that! We need a new van. This one's giving up the ghost, and Dad and Conor said 'tis I have the engine wrecked, but they're mad. I'm a great driver.'

Jimmy remembered the erratic way she drove the first time he met her and guessed Conor and her father were probably right. He caught Katherine's eye as he walked towards her car. They both smiled.

'Of course you are,' Katherine said, not meaning a word of it. Laoise was famous around Castle Dysert for being a terrible driver. Artur was constantly complaining about her driving over kerbs and destroying flowers; just last month she backed the van into a pillar at the front gate.

'You two are playing again at the weekend, isn't that right?' she asked, changing the subject since she didn't want to lie again.

'We are, the party for the opening of the new wing. Though Conor isn't calling it that. It's hard to believe that whole thing was a year ago, isn't it?'

A cloud passed over Laoise's normally happy face. That night, a year ago, Dylan's father had set a fire in the castle. The man had hated Corlene so much, he was determined to destroy everything she'd worked so hard to build up. And when Dylan saw what kind of man he was and cut him off, he decided to hurt his son too, by hurting the person in the world who meant the most to him. Conor had found Laoise in a stable. Thankfully she was able to fight Dylan's father off, but not before he really gave her a terrible fright. Katherine was the person Conor called that night to look after Laoise, and the two women had a bond ever since.

Katherine nodded. 'It certainly is, but thankfully, we all escaped relatively unscathed. When I think of what might have happened...'

'It wouldn't do you good, would it?' Laoise was pensive but soon shook herself out of it, bouncing back like she always did. 'Anyway, listen to us going on like a right pair of misery guts, and you off out on a date...'

'It's not a date for goodness sake… We are just having dinner…' Katherine was mortified.

Laoise winked at Jimmy, who had said nothing during the entire exchange.

'Enjoy your *not-a-date* night so!' She laughed at the other woman's discomfort. 'And don't do anything I wouldn't do!'

Katherine waited for Jimmy to get into the car, her cheeks flaming. She ground the gears in her haste to get away from the incorrigible Laoise, terrified in case her young friend said anything else embarrassing.

Neither Katherine nor Jimmy normally minded silence – in fact they enjoyed it – but the silence between them in the car was suffocating and Jimmy wondered if this was a terrible idea. He wanted to talk to her but didn't know what to say. What did people discuss in these situations?

Instead, she took the lead. 'I think Gaarder's handling of the core of existentialism in *Sophie's World* was a little patronising. Sophie is able to understand the other main philosophical ideologies, the Renaissance, romanticism, Darwinism, Marx even, so I don't understand why he took that approach to existentialism.'

She never took her eyes off the narrow road. Both hands on the wheel, in precisely the ten and two positions.

'I thought that initially as well,' he responded easily, 'but perhaps because the entire book is about that – existentialism, where Sophie is supposed to be a free and independent individual but is in fact having her existence determined by Knag, her whole world is a construct of his imagination – the author takes a different approach?'

Katherine relaxed. It was going to be okay.

CHAPTER 32

*K*evin lay on the bed as Tess did some colouring at the table. His phone was on his chest, and he had half a text written. Conor told him that there was a childcare service in the playroom in the evenings, where between seven and ten parents could drop the kids off. They were fed from a specially prepared kids' menu, and games and activities were arranged. For the last hour, the kids could continue playing or they could lie down on beanbags and watch a movie or read. He had run the idea by Tess, and she was happy to go. She'd wanted Laoise to work there as she was very taken with her, and was disappointed to discover she didn't.

The only reason he'd send her there was if he was going to ask Marianne to have dinner with him. He had written and rewritten the text four times now, and he didn't know if it sounded okay.

Tess looked up from her colouring. 'So am I going to the play place?'

'I don't know, honey. You okay with that?' Kevin asked, half hoping she'd say no so he would not be in this dilemma.

'I told you, Daddy, I'm fine. Why don't you call Marianne? She's nice and I think she likes you.' The girl giggled.

He didn't know what was holding him back. Marianne was nice, really nice, and she was so easy to be around, not like walking on eggshells with that head wreck Debbie. How he stuck with her for so long remained a mystery to him, but he could never regret it, because that marriage gave him Tess. Marianne was lovely too, such a warm open face, and she was the shape of a woman, not a twelve-year-old boy. And she was great with his daughter.

He knew what it was, and he had to admit it. As a social worker all these years, he saw the underbelly of life – the domestic violence, the child abuse, the gun crime, the bitter divorces – and he was afraid. Marianne was hurt by that guy she was married to who was now a woman – he couldn't begin to imagine what that must be like – so she was going to be nervous too. He'd never had a successful relationship in his whole life. He was forty years old, and he wasn't sure he was even able to do it. The odds seemed so stacked against a happy ever after.

His old man was okay – not great but okay – but his mother was so religious and obsessed with heaven that she had no time for what was going on under her nose on earth. Kevin and his brothers kind of raised themselves.

Before Debbie, he'd gone on dates over the years and had a few that turned into physical things, but to call any of them a relationship would have been stretching it. After Debbie, there hadn't been anyone. He worked a lot, he hung out with Tess, he went to Bubbles's, he went to see the Red Sox when he could, and that was pretty much it. He was happy enough, but the thought of having Marianne in his life was so appealing. There was something about her; she made him feel protective, but she was also this really strong person. It was an intriguing combination.

Tess finished her drawing – it was a picture of him and her. He smiled and gave her a cuddle.

'Can we go to the pool, Daddy?' she asked.

'Sure, sweetheart.' He got up and gathered their swimming things. Maybe it was best just to leave it. This trip was about him and Tess, and they were getting on so much better now. Keeping Marianne as a friend was the best thing. He could do friendship; he wouldn't make a mess of that. It was when things got emotional that he was a disaster. He deleted the half text.

* * *

MARIANNE STOOD UNDER THE SHOWER. Annie had gone out to meet the guy that the matchmaker had set up for her, and Marianne warned her to stay in touch by phone. It all seemed innocent enough, but Annie was a little naive in lots of ways. She wanted to meet someone so badly and seemed convinced for some reason that Ireland was where it was going to happen. Marianne hoped she wouldn't get carried away with the romance of it all and be taken for a fool by some guy.

She wondered what everyone else was up to this evening. Miguel was so cut up when they scattered the ashes. She'd had no idea that he loved Bubbles in that way. She didn't think Bubbles was gay, but then he was never with anyone as far as they knew, so perhaps? She was really fond of Miguel. He was such easy company, and he seemed better this evening, like the lovely ceremony gave him a bit of closure.

She hoped Bubbles could see them all standing on that cliff. An image of him behind his bar popped into her mind, the big booming voice welcoming her into the bar, like she was just the person he was hoping to see. Bubbles really was unique, like some kind of big Irish fairy godfather – solving people's problems, keeping their secrets, offering support to anyone who needed it – and yet he spent his life alone.

Marianne wrapped herself in a towel. Thankfully, the hotel supplied decent-sized ones, not the kind that would hardly wrap around a lamppost. She dried her hair.

She was trying not to think about Kevin. He was such a nice guy, so funny and straightforward. And he was attractive in that big-guy kind of way. After all the emotional angst with Warren, it was nice to hang out with a guy who worked hard, liked baseball and a beer and didn't overthink everything. It had been so long since she felt attracted to someone, it took her by surprise. She had met Kevin lots of times in the bar and always liked his company but never saw him like that. He was a million miles away from Warren in so many ways. Warren was slim and kind of intellectual, and he loved nothing better than philosophical debate. In hindsight, she remembered she found that kind of exhausting. Warren would talk at her more than to her, lecturing her about global warming or some geopolitical crisis in the Middle East. And it wasn't that she didn't care; it was just there was nothing she could do about the UN's role in Syria, for example, so she tried not to get too het up about it. Warren got het up. All the time.

Kevin, on the other hand, dealt with real-life problems, things he could actually change or help with, and she liked that enormously. He was a social worker with a heavy caseload. But he seemed to do his best. He really did care, but he was able to leave it in the office. He said it would make you crazy if you took it home, and she could see why.

She would like to have dinner with him and Tess, but she hesitated to make the call. Would it come across as too pushy? Or worse, desperate? The poor woman whose husband was transgender and she never even knew, developing a crush on a friend? How mortifying. She felt her cheeks burn even though she was alone. She flicked on the TV, as her own thoughts were annoying her.

Her phone beeped. A text.

Hi, Marianne – this is Tess. My daddy and me are going to the pool, do you want to come?

She smiled. Tess was such a sweet kid. Kevin was right about the screens – they made her so irritable – but now that they were gone, she was adorable.

She wondered at the parenting of Kevin's ex, who saw no issue with her eight-year-old having a tablet stuck to her face all day long but would not let her have a candy bar.

This was perfect. It was just a swim, no big deal, and if he suggested they have dinner together, so much the better.

I'd love to, she texted back. *See you there.*

She threw her swimsuit in her bag and went down quickly before the terror of Kevin seeing her in it stopped her.

They were already there when she arrived, and there was only one other swimmer, doing lengths at the other side. The entire leisure centre was as gorgeous as the hotel, but this was totally modern. There was a children's pool with toys, several bubble pools and an infinity pool as well as the main swimming area.

Marianne slipped in as quickly as she could and swam over to them.

'Hey, thanks for inviting me, Tess. This place is great,' she said, anxious to let Kevin know she was invited and not stalking him.

'I didn't know she did that!' Kevin grinned. 'Did you call Marianne?' he asked his daughter.

'I texted her. Not all technology is evil, Dad.' She giggled as he tried to catch her to tickle her. She swam over to the kids' pool and started playing on an elephant that spouted water out of its trunk.

'It's nice here, huh?' Kevin relaxed on an underwater seat in the bubble pool, and Marianne took the seat beside him.

'It really is. I'll never forget this place.'

One wall of the leisure centre was entirely glass, and it looked directly out to the ocean. The landscaping was clever in that you could only see the gardens outside from the deep end. Where they were, at the shallow end, the ocean was like an extension of the pool.

Marianne tried not to react to the fact he was naked from the waist up. His chest was covered in dark curly hair. Warren had waxed the little bit of chest hair he had, and Kevin was twice the width of him. He had a tattoo of the Boston Red Sox on his shoulder, and he caught her looking at it.

'One night in Atlantic City, when I was twenty-one. I may have been drunk.' He chuckled, and she tried to relax.

It was hard to be semi-naked with a guy you found attractive but who had never given the slightest indication that he felt the same. She tried to be cool, but inside she was in jitters. He was so… She couldn't really find the right words, but so *male*. Not macho, and he probably didn't take too much care over his appearance – she couldn't imagine him preening in front of a mirror – but he just exuded manliness, and she found it compelling.

'You got any?' he asked as they watched Tess wave from the top of a little waterslide.

'No.' She said. 'We tried, but no luck. Though I do think I should have idiot tattooed on my head sometimes.'

He smiled. 'It's not your problem y'know? The thing with Warren.'

'I know,' she said, putting on the non-committal half-smile she used whenever people brought it up. She braced herself for yet another person's interpretation of why her husband was a woman, why it wasn't her fault, how it was better in the long run, how lucky that she didn't have kids, if you love him let him go. She'd heard it all a hundred times.

'You're gorgeous. Forget about him. Move on.'

'I'm trying to.'

'Good. You know, Marianne, stuff happens all the time, to everyone. The difference is how we deal with it. We're only getting one shot at this, and nobody knows when it's all going to be over – look at poor Bubbles. So we should just live in the now and let crap from the past go.'

'You're right.' She leaned back against the contoured wall of the bubble pool.

'You still love him?'

She looked at him, unsure if it was a statement or a question.

'No. I don't,' she admitted. 'I guess I'm just a bit hung up on what everyone thinks. Like, I was sure everyone knew and that was mortifying. But now that I realise Bubbles told them a lie for me and nobody knows, it's better. I know I shouldn't care what people think, but it's just so… I don't know… I feel like a failure.'

'I get it.'

'You do?'

'Sure. The feeling like a failure bit anyway. I'm forty years old, and I've never been able to make a relationship work. I've got Tess, and she's the best thing, but to have her, I need to deal with Debbie and all of that. What a train wreck that relationship was. We only got married because Tess was on the way and her parents are Italian and very

Catholic. I think I would have woken up with a horse's head in the bed if I didn't marry her, y'know?'

Marianne laughed.

He went on. 'It was carnage from the start. And since then, look, I'm not saying I live like a monk, but I just don't seem to be able... I don't know.'

'And is a relationship what you want?' she asked, trying to keep her voice steady and praying he didn't think she was propositioning him.

'Yeah, it is. I'd like to have someone, y'know, to wash my clothes and cook my dinner...' He laughed as she punched him playfully.

'Ow! Hey, lady, you're packing some punch there! I'm kidding... I'm kidding!' He splashed her back.

'Okay...now this is war.' She splashed him mercilessly. Tess saw the fun and ran over to join in. She and Marianne chased Kevin around the shallow end, splashing him until he grabbed both of them and started tickling.

Conor finished his laps and jumped out of the pool, happy to see what he hoped was the start of a new family.

CHAPTER 33

*E*rin and Shannon sat on the two king-sized beds. They'd had a fright when they checked in, as they had only paid for a twin, but the room they were allocated was almost a suite. They had wondered if they should mention it to the lady on reception but decided against it, fearing they would look silly. They were relieved the next morning when everyone commented on how luxurious their rooms were, so much more sumptuous than they had expected. They knew from Kevin that Conor had cut them a deal, but it must have been an exceptionally good one.

The young woman at the front desk had been most accommodating and was amazingly able to locate the number for Seamus Glavin of Carrick-on-Shannon, County Leitrim, in just a few clicks of a button. She printed it out, and now the white sheet of paper lay on the locker between the two beds.

He would be in his sixties or even seventy now. He was their father's youngest brother, so he was about ten years younger than Daddy. There were three children in that family: Daddy, Seamus and the youngest, a girl called Cait. Daddy always said he wanted his daughter called Shannon after the town he was from on the River Shannon. And he called Erin after the Irish word for Ireland. Mammy always said she would have preferred they were called something more American, like Susan or Linda, but the girls loved their Irish names.

'What if Uncle Seamus has no idea who we are?' Shannon asked fearfully.

'Or they know who we are but don't want to hear from us?' Erin countered.

'Or what if there was some terrible argument that Mammy and Daddy never told us about, and we are just stirring up the hornet's nest, as Mammy used to say?' Shannon was working herself up now. 'Or what if he's like that old guy in the café the other day?'

Erin put her hand on her sister's leg. 'Look, we can just call them, say we are in Ireland, and we –'

'And we what? Wanted to stop by? Wanted to be invited for tea?' Shannon said, her voice rising in panic.

'Look, should we forget it? It might be better...'

The words hung between them. They looked at the sheet of paper again. They were one phone call away from having a family. When their father died, the girls were bereft, and their mother so angry at life for taking her husband from her. Mammy never had any contact with her Irish family; they were never mentioned. Losing Mammy was awful too, but in some ways, it was liberating. They were able to do things that their mother would have flatly refused to allow. But the emptiness of their lives was hard. And now that Bubbles was gone, they really felt like they were totally alone. It was finally admitting that they felt lost. What if something happened to either one of them? The other would be left with nobody. They were really enjoying the trip – it was the most exciting thing they'd ever done – but there was an air of finality to it. Not only were they saying a last farewell to Bubbles, but the friends they knew from the bar would all disperse, find someplace else to go. The Glavin sisters were not going to trawl the bars of New York City trying to find somewhere they felt welcome. Bubbles's place was as unique as the man himself; there would be no other.

'Well, we leave on Saturday, so what's the worst that could

happen?' Shannon asked, coming down from the precipice of panic. 'If it doesn't work out, then we can go back home and at least we'll know. They did go to the trouble of sending a Christmas card every year, so we must be in their thoughts somehow, mustn't we?'

'Now I feel like we should have put a letter in with ours. Just our names seems cold, but that's what Mammy always did.' Erin was hesitant.

'Look, let's give it a try. We'll never know if we don't.'

'Good point.' Erin gave a half-smile. She lifted the receiver and offered it to her sister. 'Will you talk?'

Shannon was older, but Erin was probably braver.

'Can you?' Shannon said with a wince. 'I would probably choke and say nothing.'

'Ok.' Erin sighed. 'What should I say?'

'Try to imagine you're at work and you are just calling a client – be polite and deliver the message. We are your brother's daughters, we're on vacation in Ireland, and we thought we'd call to say hello.'

'And they say hello… And then what?'

'I don't know. You'll have to improvise. But they're Irish and Irish people talk…' She was anxious to reassure her sister but glad she didn't have to do the talking.

'If I can understand them. Some of these accents are so thick and then they talk so fast…' Erin was panicking again.

'Didn't Mammy say that Seamus was a school teacher? So he is probably a bit more used to talking to people…'

'Okay. Let's do it now before I change my mind.' Erin picked up the piece of paper and punched in the number on the hotel phone.

'It's ringing,' she hissed, suddenly terrified.

She was about to hang up when a man answered, his voice deep and perfectly intelligible.

'Hello, Seamus Glavin speaking.'

She froze.

'Hello, is anyone there?'

She heard a sigh and then managed to blurt, 'Yes, hello, hello…

Um... My name is Erin Glavin. My sister, Shannon, and I... Shannon Glavin... We are your nieces...'

'Donal's girls, from America?' He sounded incredulous.

'Yes...' Mammy always insisted on calling Daddy 'Daniel' instead of the name he was known by back in Ireland.

'We are... We're actually in Ireland right now, on vacation,' Erin said hesitantly.

'Well...you could knock me down with a feather, ye are here in Ireland? And where are ye at?' He gave a chuckle.

At least he sounded pleased, she thought. 'We're staying at a place called Castle Dysert, on the west coast,' she said, relaxing a little.

'Well, isn't that something now?' Seamus asked, but it would seem he did not require an answer, as he went on. 'I was only watching a programme on the telly about that place a few weeks ago, and Eileen says to me, would we go there sometime. It looks lovely altogether.'

'Oh, it really is. It's just beautiful. We've never stayed anywhere as grand,' she said, though she and Shannon had never stayed anywhere at all, grand or otherwise, apart from the odd trip to a motel when Daddy was alive.

'And what has ye over here at all?' Seamus asked.

'We're over with some friends on a trip...' Erin didn't really want to get into all about Bubbles.

'Well, isn't that something else now? We often wonder how yer getting on. We look forward to yer Christmas card every year.' There was no hint of animosity in his voice, though the lack of contact was definitely more from their side than the Irish side.

'I was sorry to hear your mother passed on,' he said, and they were struck how comfortable the Irish were talking about death and dying. Conor had explained about Irish funerals and how they were really a community affair. It sounded much nicer than the cold sterile service they'd had for each of their parents, but the trouble was they didn't really know enough people to make it into a celebration.

'How old was she?' he asked.

'Seventy-nine. She got cancer,' she told him, though Mammy

would have had a fit if anyone knew her age. It was one of her many closely guarded secrets.

'Ah, sure, that's a bad lad. I had a touch of it myself last year, but I'm grand again now – they caught it in time.'

Erin tried to hold the receiver out from the side of her head so Shannon could hear too. 'I'm glad to hear that,' she said.

'So will we come to ye or will ye come to us?' Seamus asked, and the sisters smiled at each other. Their uncle just assumed they would meet up.

'Well, it would be wonderful to meet you. We'd love it. I don't know how we could get to County Leitrim, maybe a bus or something like that?' Suddenly the reality of what they were doing hit her, and she was exhilarated.

'Oh, have ye no car?'

'Oh, no.' She laughed. 'We're on a tour. We don't drive.'

'Ah, I see. That's probably just as well anyway, the way them young bucks drive around the roads like lunatics. Ye'd be killed stone dead before ye got out the gate.' He paused. 'How long are ye here for?'

'Until Saturday,' Erin answered with a grin. The way he spoke was so reminiscent of their father, it was like he was back with them.

'Righto. Myself and Eileen – and I'll see if I can get Tony and Cait too, as they'd love to meet ye as well, I'm sure – we'll drive down to ye in the next few days. Give me yer number there, and I'll talk to the others and we'll make a plan.'

'Wonderful. I hope it's not too much trouble though, and we totally understand if you can't do it as it's very short notice –'

'Ah, will you stop it girl,' he interrupted. 'Our two nieces home from America? Sure this is a great excitement altogether – 'tis only a pity it took this long – but sure we'll make up for lost time when we see ye.'

She gave him the contact number of the hotel and their room number.

'We're really looking forward to meeting you,' she said. 'Thank you so much for making the trip all the way here.'

'Not a bother. 'Twill be great to meet ye. Mind yerselves now.'

They said their goodbyes and hung up. Shannon and Erin looked at each other incredulously. They were going to meet their uncle and aunt. This trip was turning out to be so much more than they'd imagined.

CHAPTER 34

$\mathcal{A}$nnie tried to still the butterflies in her stomach. She was the only one of the group who had taken Paudie Mac up on his offer of a date.

Okay, Bubbles, I don't know where you are or what you're doing, but if you're around, I could use you right about now. She offered up a silent prayer to her old friend.

She pushed open the door of the bar that served as Paudie's 'office' and caught a glimpse of herself in the large mirror over the bar. She looked good, she thought, in that all-American way Bubbles talked about. Blonde hair assisted a little by a very expensive hairdresser on Eighth Avenue, blue eyes, tanned skin and very even, very white teeth. She worked out and took care with what she ate, so she was in good shape, but she knew what Bubbles meant – girls like her were a dime a dozen at home.

She wore skinny jeans and strappy sandals – not too high but enough to lift her up – and a white top. She would have liked Marianne's opinion on her outfit, but she was gone swimming with Kevin and Tess. She hoped that worked out; they were both nice people.

As she approached Paudie's desk in the corner of the pub, she paused. He was on the phone again.

'Of course she won't, my dear man. Have you lost the run of your-self entirely?' Paudie ran his hands through his hair in frustration. 'Well, if it was a farm labourer you were after, then you should have said so!' he barked. 'She's a fine woman with a grand job above in Dublin in the bank. And she was willing to jack all that in to live a life of wedded bliss with you, and now she's in here telling me you have her pulling calves and cutting silage and drawing bales and all sorts! Would you have a hair of sense and treat that woman properly, or she'll hightail it back to Dublin, and who could blame her?'

Annie immediately regretted the whole thing. None of Paudie's matches appeared to be working out, and every time she saw him, he seemed to be dealing with some ridiculous situation. She was about to leave when another woman came in behind her and asked, 'Are you waiting for Paudie?'

Her instinct was to say no and flee out the door, but she didn't get the chance.

Paudie was off the phone and walking towards them. 'Well, ladies, what a delight it is to see you both, and looking so radiant.' He was about to go full-charm offensive when the woman opened fire.

'What class of a clown was that you set me up with, Paudie?' She was in her forties and looked tough. She stood with her hands on her hips, challenging him. She had short, spiked scarlet-red hair and six earrings in each ear. She was short and squat and dressed in black combat pants and a Grateful Dead T-shirt.

'Ah, Margaret, my dear woman.' Paudie went to place his hand on her shoulder, but the look she gave him made him think better of it. 'Sure Toss Quinlan is considered the catch of not just this parish but of the county, and a finer man, nor a more courteous gentleman, you'd struggle to find on a day's walk, and that's the truth.'

'Paudie, he's eighty-six! Seriously, eighty-six, and he's deaf as a post,' Margaret burst out in indignation.

'Ah, but sure, didn't your mother always tell you that the older the fiddle, the sweeter the tune?' Paudie ventured, less sure of his ground now but brazening it out.

'My mother, Lord have mercy on her, would even be too young for that auld fossil!' the woman exclaimed as Annie backed away and sat down.

'But you said you didn't mind a bit of an age gap, and sure we even laughed about it at the time – better be an old man's darling than a young man's slave and all of that?' Paudie was conscious that his reputation was at stake here as more and more customers in the bar were turning to watch the floor show.

'A bit!' Margaret spluttered. 'I said I didn't mind a bit, like five years, ten at a push, but this fella is only fit for a nursing home. Or maybe he should just go straight up to Donald McNamara's Undertakers now and get himself measured for the box and embalmed and the whole lot because he's definitely not long for this world.'

Paudie scratched the side of his head and winced. 'Well, he has a fine big farm and no child to take it, so maybe 'twould be the way that you wouldn't need to stick at it too long, if you see what I'm driving at,' he murmured out of the side of his mouth.

'And what do I want with a farm?' The woman was going red in the face now. 'I'm after a man, not a corpse. How you get away with this year in, year out is a mystery, Paudie Mac. I swear it is.'

Paudie caught Annie out of the corner of his eye. She was trying to discreetly make her escape.

'Annie, please accept my apologies.' He went over and held her hand. 'A fickle business, affairs of the heart, and as Bing Crosby used to say, the course of true love never did run smooth.' He grinned to reveal a gold tooth.

'That was Shakespeare, you muppet,' Margaret spat as she walked out past them both and slammed the door behind her.

'You can't please all the people all the time,' he said with a sigh of resignation. Annie wondered if he had a cliché for every occasion.

'Now, my dear Annie, you got my email –' he began, but Annie interrupted him.

'Yes, but I just wanted to say I'm no longer interested... I...ah...I met someone else, er...today...so I... Well, I'm not available.' She blushed; she was terrible at telling lies.

'Ah well, I'm glad you met someone, and you are a beautiful lady if you don't mind me saying so. And you'll forgive me if I say you are easier to match than some others I could mention.' He glanced at the door through which the disgruntled Margaret had just recently stormed.

'But if you'll just indulge me a moment, I have a man for you. Now, he's a real find. This is his first year applying even.' Paudie sounded so pleased with himself at that. Clearly he had a lot of repeat offenders on his books. 'And I think ye will really hit it off.' The fact that she was allegedly no longer available seemed to carry no weight whatsoever.

Annie was too polite to storm out like the other woman, but she dreaded to think what kind of person Paudie would deem suitable. She had yet to encounter a happy customer of his.

'Now, my dear girl, you'll come with me up the street there to the Hydro Hotel, where there is a dance about to start. And there we will meet the man I believe will be your soulmate.'

Annie cringed, and several people in the pub suppressed a smile or a snigger. 'I really don't think…' she began again, trying to channel her assertive side, but she just couldn't.

Paudie turned her around and placed his hands on her shoulders. His grey sprouting eyebrows almost covered his eyes, and his skin was leathery from years of exposure to the wild Irish weather. A tuft of silver hair was peeping out from the top button of his shirt.

'Trust me,' he said quietly.

He offered Annie his arm, and reluctantly she took it as they waltzed out of the bar.

CHAPTER 35

*E*ddie was waiting in the car park for Conor when he came out of the hotel. The little priest had left in a taxi immediately upon returning with the group because he'd got word he needed to see a very ill parishioner, but he promised he'd be back.

After Conor spoke to Ana, he texted Jamsie. According to him, the immediate panic was over for now. Gerry's condition had been stabilised in the hospital, so there was no imminent danger of him dying.

'How was Mrs O'Sullivan?' he asked as he walked towards his car. Eddie fell into step beside him. Conor knew her grandson; he was a friend of Artie and Joe's.

'Fading fast. She won't see the morning,' Eddie said as Conor eased the car out of the car park. 'Did you speak to your father since?'

'Yeah, I texted him. Gerry is stable. I called Ana as well. She's insisting on coming with us, so we can pick her up on the way.'

'She should. You need her, and she needs to know you need her. People can feel like a terrible burden when they're ill. Let her help if she can.'

'I'm afraid she might pick something up…'

'She'll be fine. Sure isn't she out and about all the time on the days she's well?'

Conor smiled at his old friend and sighed. 'I can only fight one of ye at a time. When ye gang up on me, I don't stand a chance.'

His phone beeped – a text.

'Check that, would you, in case it's Jamsie.'

Eddie picked up the phone. 'It's from Ana.' He smiled.

'What does it say?' Conor asked, navigating around a herd of cattle being brought in for milking.

'You're doing the right thing. I'm proud of you. I love you.'

Conor smiled. There was a time a text like that would have embarrassed him in front of someone else, but not any more. He was such a lucky man to enjoy her love, and he didn't care who knew it.

'Can you just text back the number two, please? When the twins were small and I or Ana would say "I love you", they would simply reply "two", meaning "I love you too".'

The priest did as his friend asked and then put the phone back on the dashboard. 'How are you feeling now?'

'Nervous? Like I don't know what to expect. I haven't seen my brother for over thirty years. I don't know what to say to him, you know?' His mind was racing.

'Don't worry, or try not to anyway. It sounds like he has something to say to you, not the other way round.'

Conor pulled in outside his home, and Ana was already there. He got out, and Eddie insisted on letting her take the front seat while he sat in the back.

Jamsie had given them instructions as to where to go, and they found the place easily. Gerry was in a room on his own rather than a ward.

Conor hesitated at the door; suddenly, he didn't want to go in. Eddie stood back and Ana took his hand. 'It's okay, my love. I'll be here, and Eddie too. It will be okay.'

He looked down into her green eyes. Her tiny elfin face was thinner now, but she was so strong and determined. If she could face this illness, he could face his brother. He nodded, squeezed her hand gently and knocked on the door.

Jamsie appeared, looking old and exhausted.

'Hi, Jamsie.' Conor greeted him quietly. 'This is my friend Father Eddie and my wife, Ana.'

Ana leaned over and kissed his cheek, and Eddie shook his hand warmly.

'Come in. He's awake now.'

The room was small, but there were two chairs beside the bed. Eddie stood in the background as Jamsie led Conor and Ana in.

Conor didn't recognise the person in the bed as his brother. His hair was thin; the bit that remained was brushed into a ponytail. He had a tattoo of a snake on his arm, and around his neck he wore a wooden cross. He had a yellow tinge to his skin and could not have weighed more than 100 pounds.

He struggled to sit up, and Jamsie helped him. He had an oxygen mask on the bed beside him. Just the effort of sitting up took its toll, and the pain was written all over his face. A set of rosary beads was wrapped around his fingers.

Conor stepped forward first. He felt huge beside his tiny brother. 'Hi, Gerry,' he managed.

'Hey, Conor, it's so good to see you. Thank you for coming.' The effort of talking seemed to tire him, but he went on. 'I know you didn't want to, and I don't blame you, but I prayed you'd change your mind.' He lay back on the pillows.

Ana moved forward, and stood beside her husband.

'And this is Ana, my wife.'

'I'm so happy to meet you.' Gerry managed a smile.

'And me to meet you. Welcome home,' she said, and Conor marvelled at how his brother seemed to grow a bit stronger in her presence.

He stood back to allow his brother to see Eddie. 'And this is our friend, Father Eddie.'

Gerry smiled again. 'Hello, Father.' He turned his head slightly to address Eddie. 'Would you give me the last rites, please?' he managed, but the effort of the sentence took so much out of him, he sank back onto the pillow and closed his eyes.

They stood there, listening to his rattling breath, incongruous with the jubilant sounds coming through the open window from the hurling match being held in the football field beside the hospital.

Conor watched his brother fight the urge to sleep. He was really struggling to keep his eyes open. Gerry took another rasping breath and spoke again. 'I'm so sorry, Conor, for what I did. It was unforgiv-able, after everything' – he paused, trying to gather his strength to go on – 'you did for me. You were my parents, and I behaved so badly. Not just with Sinead, but I was so ungrateful for all you did.' He let out a long, ragged sigh.

Conor sat on the chair and took his brother's hand in his. 'It's okay. I forgive you. I forgave you a long time ago. Sinead would have made me miserable, and if I'd married her, I would never have met Ana, so you did me a favour.' He smiled and Gerry smiled back.

'I'm dying,' he said matter-of-factly.

'I know.' Conor locked eyes with his little brother, and all the years and all the pain melted away. He wanted to look after him, like he'd always done. 'But soon you'll be with Mam, and until then, me and Jamsie will be here, and Ana and Father Eddie, so you won't be alone. You'll have your family around you, and I know Mam will come for you, so there's nothing to be afraid of, okay?'

Gerry's eyes closed once more. But again he fought it.

'Take him.' He gestured at Jamsie. 'Get him a pint. He needs a break.'

Conor caught Eddie's eye. The unspoken question – was it safe to go? Would he die while they were gone?

Eddie nodded slightly. He'd seen so many people die in his long life as a priest, he had a feeling for these things.

'Good plan, Gerry.' Eddie took out his oils and placed a stole around his neck in preparation for administering Gerry's last sacra-ment, as the others made their way out. 'We'll be fine here.'

* * *

ANA INSISTED on going to the bar and ordering while Conor and Jamsie sat down. She joined them as Jamsie was recounting Gerry's collapse at the train station, the ambulance ride and how they were sure it was over, and how he rallied a bit. Conor thought his father looked wretched.

'This must have been so hard for you to see,' Ana sympathised, placing her hand on his.

The barman delivered not just two pints for the men but also two large plates of Irish stew.

'You both did not eat much today, I know... You must stay strong.'

Conor shot her a thankful glance. She was right. He was hungry, and judging by the way Jamsie tucked in, so was he.

'So now what?' she asked.

Jamsie sat back and sighed, the exhaustion of the last few days showing on his face.

'Well, my plan was to take him home with me to my place in Dublin. I knew he was sick, but I had no idea it was this bad. I don't think Gerry did either, to be honest.'

Conor heard the crack in his father's voice.

'But now, I don't think he's well enough to go anywhere. The doctors are saying he should go to the hospice, but he doesn't want to... He said he spent his life in institutions and doesn't want to die in one.'

'What are they doing for him?' Ana asked.

'Not much really. They give him medication, and he has a tank of oxygen that he's supposed to use, but sure he takes the mask off as much as he can.' Jamsie took a long welcome draft of his pint, wiping the froth off his lip with the back of his hand.

'Then he must come to us,' she said, as if it were the most logical thing in the world.

'Ah, Ana, I don't know. You need to rest and –' Conor began.

'Conor, listen to me. He is your only brother, and we must take care of him. What if it was Artie and Joe, and something happen, and one has a good life and the other a bad one. You tell me you don't want they look out for each other, even to the very end?'

He thought for a moment. He wanted to take Gerry home as much as Ana did, but he was fearful it would be too much for her, for the lads. 'Of course I would want that, but I just wonder, with the timing and everything... And having someone they never met dying in their house, it might be scary for the boys...'

'How it scary? People are born and people die. This is not scary – this is life. We must do this. If it was Artie and Joe, I would want this, and your mother wants it too. We can care for him. The doctor can come and Eddie and my parents. We can do this.'

Conor looked at her and doubted he had ever loved her more. He knew everyone thought he fell for Ana because she was gorgeous and so much younger than him and all of that, and while those things were true, that wasn't why he fell in love with her. It was this, her genuine raw goodness.

'What do you think?' he asked his father.

'I think if you could do it – and it won't be for long – it would be the kindest thing you could do for him. The doctors say they should get him a bit better once they stabilise his medication again. He's not a bad man, Conor. I know it's hard to believe that with his track record, but he was a victim, and this is my fault. If I hadn't taken off and left my family, he might have turned out all right and that whole path of self-destruction might never have happened.'

Conor didn't disagree.

'So...will we take him home?' Ana asked, and he looked from the face of his wife to that of his father.

'I suppose we will,' he finally agreed.

CHAPTER 36

he waiter showed Katherine and Jimmy to a corner table with a window looking out to sea. The sun was setting as it glowed red over the Atlantic. The sky was streaked with red and gold – it was spectacular.

The restaurant was busy, and there was a general hum of chat, but the soft furnishings, dark heavy wood and thick carpet seemed to muffle the sound.

'Coming to spy on the opposition, Ms O'Brien?' joked the young waitress as she handed them their menus. Katherine recognised her as an employee she had let go a few weeks back for being cheeky to a guest.

'Not at all' – Katherine made a point of checking her name badge though she remembered the girl's name perfectly well – 'Kayleigh. I am merely enjoying a meal with a friend.'

'Well, I recommend the trout,' the young woman said with a catty smirk and turned on her heel.

Jimmy looked confused.

'I had to fire her from the castle a few weeks ago for being extremely rude to a guest. When we spoke, she called me a dried-up old trout.' She smiled to show she wasn't upset by it.

'Well, I don't think you look anything like a trout, or any other fish. You look lovely, in fact,' he said, entirely without guile.

'Thank you,' she replied, reddening slightly at the compliment.

'I might as well come clean, Katherine, if it's okay to call you Katherine?'

'Of course.'

'This is the first time in my life I have ever taken a woman out to dinner. I'm not sure what the protocols are, so if I do or say something wrong…well, you can tell me.' He cleared his throat.

'Well, I don't do much in the way of going out to dinner with men myself, so let's just do our best, shall we?' She smiled and he responded.

'Great.' He relaxed.

They chatted effortlessly, and Jimmy found himself speaking more to Katherine in that one night than he had in the entire month previously. She was so easy to talk to and was really interesting. She explained how she took classes by night. She had a degree in Greek and Roman civilisation and archaeology, and another in German and politics. She was currently in her third year of a degree programme in archaeology and sociology.

'And you never wanted to find a job in those fields?' he asked.

'No. The study is for my own entertainment. I like the hotel, and Conor has been very good to me. I worked for many years in another hotel, when Conor was a tour driver, and when that was sold to a soulless chain, I found myself unemployed. A lady of my years unemployed is not a pleasant prospect, and while my administration skills for running a hotel are excellent, my face would not fit everywhere, if you understand what I mean. Conor spared me the humiliation of going to interviews where I would no doubt be rejected as someone from another era. The chain that took over the Dunshane, where I worked for twenty-three years, wanted me to wear a yellow T-shirt with "Hi, I'm Katherine, How Can I Help?" emblazoned on the back. They had all sorts of insane notions, nobody had a title, and guests were supposed to check themselves in and out of the hotel using computers in the lobby. It was horrific. Conor saved me from all of that and gave me a job at Castle Dysert.'

'I'm similar,' he said. He never spoke about his personal life, such as it was, and he knew people found him odd. 'I studied for a degree in philosophy, and then went on to do a masters and a PhD, but I work in the New York City sanitation department. I'm a garbage man.'

She never flinched. 'And what did you write your PhD on?'

'Well, philosophy and anthropology are my favourite things, but I did my doctoral thesis on the function of the highly sensitive brain. It was a review of the brain circuits underlying sensory processing of sensitivity and seemingly related disorders.'

She seemed unfazed. He'd never discussed his research with anyone apart from his supervisor and when he'd had to defend his thesis in order to be awarded his doctorate.

'Why did you choose that?' she asked.

Before he had a chance to reply, a different waitress arrived. They both ordered the John Dory on the bone.

When she left, he debated telling Katherine the truth, something he'd never revealed. 'I chose it because I'm a highly sensitive person. I'm also socially kind of awkward, and the two are interlinked. I feel things deeply and absorb the emotions of others, and so I wanted to understand what was happening on a neurological level as well as on a philosophical one.'

'Intriguing. Go on,' she said, sipping her sparkling water. He'd ordered a glass of red wine.

'Well, since I was a child, I have been sensitive. I can't watch sad or violent things on TV or in the movies, or even hear sad stories. I distance myself from people for that reason. It can be overwhelming sometimes,' he said quietly.

'Did your parents understand?'

The question struck him. It was the last question he would have guessed anyone would ask, and yet it was the most pertinent.

'My mother did. My father didn't. He was violent and abusive, and he regularly used both my mother and me as a punching bag, both physically and emotionally. He died in 1989, and my mother and I lived peacefully from then on. She died two years ago. I miss her every day.'

She held his gaze. She said nothing; she didn't need to.

'I was reared by my aunt,' Katherine revealed. 'My parents thought it would be better for me, so they sent me to live with her. She wasn't married and had no children, so I was company for her.'

Jimmy sensed the pain as acutely as if it were his own. 'But you didn't want to be there?' he asked.

'Well, I suppose I never understood why I was chosen. I have brothers and sisters, and they stayed at home with our parents.' She was matter-of-fact, but the hurt was there behind the words.

'And did you have a relationship with them?' he asked gently.

'No. Not really. When I came back home on the rare occasion, I didn't fit in. I was different, not used to the rough and tumble of family life. They thought me odd, and I suppose to them I was. My aunt was a good person but aloof. She cared for me, educated me, provided for me in every way…'

'Did she love you?'

She shook her head, not trusting herself to speak.

'And what about later, when you were an adult? Did you stay with her or leave?'

Something about the way he asked questions didn't feel like prying. She had never been so open – even Conor didn't know about her past.

'I stayed with my aunt until she died. I was in my twenties then, and she left me her house. It's the house I still live in. I had a brief relationship with a man I believed to be decent and honest. He was neither. He left me at the altar. My whole estranged family were there to witness my humiliation.' The words were tight and hard to say.

Jimmy reached for her hand. He normally moved away from people with sad stories to tell, but he found himself drawn to Katherine.

She would normally flinch at such kindness, but she didn't move her hand.

The rest of the night went by in a blur of confidences and revelations, and by the time they were sipping coffee, having shared dessert, both knew they would be close for the rest of their lives.

He told her all about Bubbles and what he meant to everyone, especially what the man meant to him. He told her about his conversations with Beth, about her sister's disappearance, about how Beth wasn't as into Will as Will would like. He told her about him storming off when Beth said she wasn't looking for a relationship, and about the phone ringing in his room, when he clearly remembered Will having his phone with him when he left.

Katherine thought for a moment. 'Do you have a feeling about it?'

He felt foolish. It wasn't as if he had any evidence. But something about the way she asked made him think she would take him seriously.

'I could be wrong – I hope I am – but I think he had something to do with Beth's sister's disappearance. That night, the night she went missing, there was a quiz on in Bubbles's. I didn't participate, so I was sitting in my usual spot, reading. Maddie was talking with a bunch of guys at the bar. They probably thought they were onto a good thing, but she wasn't like that. Maddie is friendly with everyone – there's a kind of innocence to her if anything.'

'Go on.' She was intrigued.

'Well, they were talking, and then the guys were going to another bar or a club or something, and Maddie said she didn't want to go. Being in Bubbles's place made her feel safe, I think. He was kind of like a father figure to her and Beth – he was that kind of man. So there was just her and Will left. Beth had gone home earlier. I couldn't hear what they were saying, but it looked serious. Like Will was trying to get her to see his point of view. Maddie was drinking a lot, and he kept buying her more drinks. Miguel had gone off shift by that stage, and a new guy was working the bar. I went home not long afterwards, but nobody's seen or heard from Maddie since that night.'

'But all the stuff about this Will person, especially now that he's acting so strangely…' She spoke quietly but urgently. 'Have the police talked to him?'

'I don't know. I'm not sure the police are treating it as a missing person case, as Maddie has taken off before. They never came into the bar, to the best of my knowledge, asking about her. If they had, I would have told them what I saw. I never thought it was anything significant until now.'

Katherine was still curious. 'And Beth thinks she is okay now?'

'Yes.' Jimmy was trying to seem logical. 'She got several texts from Maddie, saying she was fine.'

'Hmm.' She wasn't convinced. 'Still seems odd behaviour though.'

They carried on talking until they were the last people left in the restaurant. Jimmy insisted on paying the bill and refused to even allow her to leave a tip. They walked in the warm night air together to the car, the night sky twinkling with stars. Katherine's was the only car in the car park, and the lights had been turned off in the restaurant. By the time they realised it was time to leave, everyone but the owner who lived upstairs had gone home.

'The skies here at night are amazing,' he observed, looking up at the inky sky glittering with many thousands of stars.

'Very little light pollution,' she agreed, looking up beside him. 'The childcare staff sometimes organise star gazing for families late at night. They lie on the lawn and watch the sky and often see shooting stars.'

Jimmy walked over to the lawn beside the car park and took off his jacket, laying it on the grass. He held his hand out.

'I'm too old now for star gazing.' She laughed nervously.

'Please?' he asked. 'I'd love to lie beside you and watch the stars.'

She paused, wrestling with her conscience. She had been so proper all of her life, never doing or saying anything remotely wild, but just because she never had, did that mean that she never could?

'If anyone sees me, I'll be carted off to the county home as simple in the head. You do know that, Jimmy Burns, don't you?' She smiled as she took his hand.

'Well, Katherine O'Brien...' He chuckled. 'They'll take me too, so I guess we could enjoy institutional life together?'

He helped her down and then sat beside her; they were barely touching. Then he lay back, and she eased herself down beside him.

'There's the plough,' she pointed out.

'And the Milky Way,' he responded.

And then, as if it were the most natural thing in the whole world, Jimmy reached for Katherine's hand as he lay beside her on the lush green grass. The scent of jasmine and late summer roses filled the warm night air, and he wound his fingers though hers. He relaxed when he felt the pressure of her hand gently squeezing his.

CHAPTER 37

*M*oving Gerry from the hospital to Conor and Ana's house went much more smoothly and quickly than they imagined it would. They met with the doctors, who assured them that there was no risk to Ana but that she could not take on his care because she would not be strong enough.

Conor arranged for a nursing service to do a twenty-four-hour rotation at the house. Artur moved a special bed they rented from a medical supply company into the boys' playroom downstairs. The boys helped and even tidied up all the toys and stacked them neatly in one corner of the room.

The day they brought Gerry back to their house, the boys were fascinated. Gerry was actually in good spirits as the medical team had managed to do as they promised and got the correct cocktail of medication to maximise his energy and manage his pain. Ana and Conor had sat the boys down and explained everything, leaving out the reason their dad and his brother were estranged and where Gerry had spent most of his adult life. And in the manner that always fascinated Conor, they just accepted it.

He mentioned to Artur how surprised he was at their reaction as they set the room up according to the nurse's instructions.

'It is not so strange I think,' Artur said in his heavily accented English. 'You and Anastasia is for Joe and Artie what is safe and what is okay. If they think is okay with you, then is okay with them.'

They heaved the heavy bed into position, and as they rested, Artur said, 'You happy with this?'

'The bed? Yeah, the nurse will tell me how to rearrange it when she gets here if it's not right.' He pushed the locker into place beside the bed.

'No, not this, with all' – he waved his hand – 'this, your brother coming here...'

Conor sat on a chair and exhaled. 'To tell you the truth, I don't know how I feel about it. He hurt me badly years ago, but I'm well over it, so that's not my issue really. I want to help him – he's my brother. I just didn't want to draw anything else on Ana, you know? Or the lads. They're just about coping with Ana being sick, but now to have a man they've never met come to our house to die – it's the timing really.'

Artur nodded and patted him on the back. 'You are a good man. Always I say this. You look after my daughter when she here on her own, all those years ago. And then when she call me and Danika in Ukraine and say you and her getting married, I am happy.'

Conor looked up and smiled. 'You make it sound like I was doing you a favour. Ana is the best thing that ever happened to me.'

'I know. It is true, but for her too. And you make it so we can come here, you get me a job, you make us welcome in your house. Ukraine now, it is bad. We are so happy to be here in Ireland. I think we don't say thank you enough.'

'Ah, will you stop?' He hated this kind of talk. 'You and Danika are my family too. And I'd have cracked up these last months if ye hadn't been there to help with the boys and everything. And we'd have to close down the hotel if you ever left – Katherine is always saying it.' He laughed.

Artur looked pleased. He was a proud man, and when he was sick two years ago in the Ukraine and there was no way to have the proce-dure he needed, Conor brought them both over. It was a bit of a palaver to sort out visas and all the rest of it, but they did it, and now the Petrenkos were Irish residents and entitled to stay. In truth, Conor had just given his father-in-law a job in the hotel to keep him busy once he'd recovered, but he had proved himself invaluable. Between Carlos running the hospitality end of things, Katherine overseeing all the paperwork and Artur managing the grounds and all the maintenance, they had everything covered. The hotel employed over 200 staff, and none of them would dare to cross any one of the three of them.

'You're a good man,' Artur repeated. 'Your mother is proud of you.'

'I hope so. She was a lovely lady, and she did her best in very hard circumstances.' He rarely talked about his childhood – it was a sad one and it didn't do anyone any good to dwell on things – but he told Artur now. 'When my father left, it was devastating. Apart altogether from the heartbreak, we had no money and no way of making any money. Gerry and I were just kids, and Mam was like all mothers in those days – at home looking after us. We lived in a small town, and even though my mam did nothing wrong, there was a kind of a blame there, like she must have been a bad wife if she couldn't keep her man. I heard all kinds of rumours, that he had women everywhere and all the rest of it – some of it true, more of it not. The truth was he was after getting some young one pregnant, and she would have been sent to the nuns and the child adopted in America if he didn't take her to England. That's his story anyway. My poor mam couldn't face going to claim the deserted wives' allowance – a small payment the government made to people in her position – so she went to work. She cleaned houses, she did laundry, mending, anything she could to keep a roof over our heads and food on the table. She had great faith, you know, went to Mass every day, all that, and she believed that God would provide for us. She did most of the providing though. The church were notable by their absence.'

He was getting emotional just thinking about her. He remembered the old parish priest and him sticking his nose in the air when he came to collect the dues. His poor mother scraping together her few pennies to give him, and he swanning around in a fancy car. She was much more in need of it than he was, but that didn't stop him. Conor's dislike of the Catholic Church began then. But his mother was devout and dedicated to her church, so he never voiced his opinion. He wished he had a photo of her to show Ana and the boys.

'So I left school as soon as I could, got an apprenticeship with a local mechanic, and he was really good to me. Joe is named after him actually. And then Mam died. She got cancer, and she was dead within five months of diagnosis. She probably had it for much longer but didn't say anything. Gerry was only a kid, still in national school, and the authorities wanted to take him into care, but my mam's friend Mary Harrington, and Joe and his wife and me, we fought it. We knew what those places were like, and we managed to convince them that I could take care of Gerry. It was what my mam would have wanted.'

Artur placed his hand on his son-in-law's shoulder. 'She was a good lady, and she reared a good son. Danika and me always say a prayer for her when we go to Mass, and Joe and Artie always light a candle for her.'

Conor looked at him in surprise. 'Do they?'

He hadn't been to Mass in years. He went when it was absolutely necessary, for funerals and so on, but never of his own accord. Ana went and so did her parents, and they took the boys.

'Yes,' Artur said with a nod.

'Anyway, Gerry didn't give a monkey's about anyone, never did. And he was lazy and got into all kinds of trouble, first at school, then with the guards. It got to the stage where I was working and he would lounge around the house all day, and then he'd spend whatever money I gave him in the pub. The girls were mad about him – he was good-looking, and great craic and all that, but a nightmare to live with. I was at the end of my rope with him, and I was going out with this girl – I was going to ask her to marry me actually. Until one day I came home from work, ring bought and everything, and found a note from both of them saying they had run away together. I never heard a single word from him all these years.'

Artur was silent, but Conor knew what he was thinking. He was the kind of father Conor aspired to be. Ana loved her dad with all her heart, and he was the protector and provider for their family. He loved her but was not blind. Last year, when that Russian gardener was sniffing around, it was Artur who called Ana to task about it. Ana did nothing wrong, but she missed having someone her own age to speak to in her own language. Artur said it wasn't appropriate.

Ana wasn't that close to her sister and brother, but Artur called them each week to check they were okay. He and Danika never forgot a birthday or Christmas and always sent presents for their other grandchildren. Conor had tried to get the family to come on a visit, but they didn't ever take him up on the offer.

Joe and Artie simply adored Artur and Danika. He let them work with his tools but showed them how to be safe and how to take care of the items as well. He was the perfect granddad as far as the boys were concerned. And Danika just spoiled them rotten.

'The boys like Jamsie. He is good with them,' Artur said eventually.

'He's a novelty I suppose.' Conor shrugged.

'I think he would like to be in your life, in their life, after' – he nodded at the bed and the medical equipment – 'all of this is over.'

Conor looked at him directly. 'I needed a father when I was eight years old, and he wasn't there. He never taught me to drive a car, or shave, or change a plug, or anything fathers are supposed to do for their kids. I'll do this for Gerry, but I just don't need a father at this late stage.'

Arthur held his gaze. 'Maybe he needs you though.'

CHAPTER 38

*A*nnie felt ridiculous being paraded into a hotel lobby with Paudie Mac. Everyone knew what he was doing, and suddenly she became a person of great interest.

'Now, I'll just call our man to see where he is... His name is Fergal, and he's a fine man altogether...' Paudie said, scanning the lobby. Just as soon as he reached for his phone, a loud altercation coming from the bar area to the right distracted everyone.

A woman was seemingly assaulting a man. The man was in his fifties and appeared ridiculously overdressed in a three-piece suit and a red tie with matching handkerchief. His dark hair was a suspicious colour of blueish-black. The woman bashing him looked older, with bleached-blonde hair in a tight ponytail. Her face was caked in make-up, some of which was smudged now as a result of her exertions. Her weapon was a very heavy-looking handbag, and she was screaming all kinds of obscenities. The hotel manager was trying to break it up, but the woman was so incensed with rage that nobody else dared approach her, and she was totally ignoring the entreaties of the manager. The man she was attacking was trying to cover his head from the blows. Annie only caught every third word.

'Thought you could get away with it...'

Something unintelligible.

'After the last time, Fergal Dunne...'

More words she couldn't make out.

Then a second woman, who looked very like the first one, joined in – she kicked the man. 'I'll give you matchmaking, you disgusting auld tomcat...'

Paudie looked horrified and was trying to shuffle Annie out the door when the man shouted, 'Paudie, save me... She'll kill me...'

Annie looked from the man to Paudie. 'Please tell me he wasn't the guy...'

'Ah no, no...not at all. Sure he's well and truly shackled elsewhere by the looks of things...'

But Annie knew he was lying.

The next thing they knew, the fight was bursting through the open door from the bar to the lobby as the man tried to escape his attackers. Annie jumped out of their way as a table with a large glass vase smashed on the tiled floor. Splinters went flying in every direction, one catching her just below her eye – she felt blood.

As she tried to stem the flow, the Irish police came bursting through the door and immediately brought the whole melee under control. The two women were arrested and handcuffed, though they were practically spitting with rage, and since Fergal tried to throw a punch at the guard who was arresting his wife, he was taken into custody as well. Within moments, calm was restored, and two cops went with the three detainees and two remained. One took statements, while the other one, a younger policeman with reddish-brown hair, scanned the room for other casualties.

Spotting Annie trying to stop the blood flowing from the cut on her face, he crossed the lobby. 'There's an ambulance on the way, but will I just take a look at that for you?' he asked.

Of the intrepid Paudie, there was no sign. He must have taken off at the first sight of trouble. She wasn't surprised.

'I'm fine. I don't think it's deep,' she said.

The guard stopped a young man who worked in the hotel.

'Can you bring some water and a clean cloth, please?'

Within moments, the young man came back with the requested items as well as a big square Band-Aid, and Annie started to clean her face. Her white top was ruined.

'Do you know these people?' the guard asked, and she looked up, seeing him properly for the first time. He was tall and slim and had the most amazing dark-blue eyes. He sounded just like Bubbles.

'No... I was just... I'm here on vacation,' she answered, too mortified to tell him the real reason that had brought her into the hotel.

'Well, is there someone I can call to come and collect you? I don't think that cut is deep, but you probably want to go and change.'

She was flustered. She figured she must look awful. 'No...no thanks, I'll take a taxi back to my hotel. I'm travelling with a bunch of friends.'

'Which hotel are you staying at?' he asked.

'Castle Dysert.'

'Well, that's on my way back to the station. I could drop you off if you like? My colleague lives here, and we were just knocking off when we got the call, so he'll probably stay here.' He noted her trembling fingers having trouble opening the Band-Aid.

'Can I help?' He bent down beside her, and she gave him the plaster. He peeled off the paper backing and gently applied the bandage to her face.

She was about to refuse and say she'd take a taxi, when something stopped her. 'That would be great, thanks.'

He walked over and said something to the other policeman, who was deep in conversation with the hotel manager. The manager then followed the younger guard back to where Annie sat.

'I'm so sorry about that... We don't usually have that sort of carry on, but during the matchmaking festival, well...it's a bit wild. Are you all right? Can I get you anything? A drink?'

'No... Thanks, I'm fine,' she said.

'Well, let me at least compensate you for your clothes. This is a terrible thing to happen... I'm so sorry.' He scurried to the main desk and spoke rapidly to the receptionist, returning moments later with an envelope.

'Look, this is just a voucher for dinner. Please come back whenever suits, with a friend or whatever.' He pressed the envelope into her hand, and as he did, his phone rang.

'Thank you,' she said. 'Please, take your call. I'm fine, honestly.'

The younger guard appeared again beside her, having consulted with his colleague, and said, 'Are you right so?'

She nodded and followed him to the police car, its lights flashing. He opened the passenger door for her and went around to the driver's side.

'I thought you were going to put your hand on my head,' she said, and was instantly mortified by how it sounded.

He looked perplexed but smiled. 'And why would I do that?' he asked in that gorgeous soft accent.

'Just...' She coloured with embarrassment, her cheeks burning. 'You know, on TV shows, when the police put people in cars, they put their hands on their heads as they get in.' She wanted the ground to open and swallow her. He must think she was the most ditzy person he'd ever met.

'Ah, no... We only do that for hardened criminals, murderers, drug barons, that sort of thing. We'd hate them to hurt their little heads. You law-abiding citizens just have to get in like a normal person.' He laughed and she relaxed a little. 'So what's your name?' he asked as he drove out of the hotel.

'Annie... Annie deLancey.'

'Well, I would say welcome to Ireland, Annie deLancey, but that was a bit of a rude introduction. Most people are normal – well, normal-ish anyway. What has you here?' He was very direct, just the way Bubbles was.

'My friend was Irish and he died, so a bunch of us, friends of his, brought his ashes back here to scatter them.'

'That was nice of ye.'

'Yes, well, we are all single, so we thought we would come to the festival at the same time.' She went puce again – what was wrong with her? She sounded insane.

He looked over at her and smiled as they waited at a red light. 'My name is Darragh, Darragh O'Murchú. It's nice to meet you, Annie.'

'Do you spell that D-A-R-A?' she asked.

'No, it sounds like that, but it's an Irish name, so it is spelled nothing like it sounds. We did it on purpose long ago to bamboozle the English.' He grinned and his whole face crinkled into a smile. 'And my surname is in Irish too, but translated, it would be Murphy. I'm from the Gaeltacht, the Irish-speaking part of Ireland, so when I was growing up, we only spoke Irish.'

They chatted easily for the twenty-minute ride to the hotel, and as they pulled up, causing more than a few raised eyebrows from guests enjoying a pre-dinner cocktail on the lawn, she dug inside her bag. 'Um… The hotel manager gave me this voucher, and I'm going home on Saturday, so maybe you could use it?' She offered him the envelope.

'Ah, that's not fair – you were the one who sustained the injury.' He grinned. 'How about we go to dinner together some evening before you have to go?'

'Um…sure… I'd like that.' She couldn't believe this was happening. Was this cute cop actually asking her out on a date?

'Great, you can tell me all about New York. I'm taking a career break to study forensics at NYU next year, and I'm moving over there in April. At least this way, I'll know one person.'

'Sure, that sounds great.' Annie smiled though it hurt her face.

'How about tomorrow night? I'll pick you up – in a normal car this time. Around seven?'

'Perfect.'

Annie moved to get out, but Darragh jumped up, went around the car and opened the door for her from the outside. 'I can't have you thinking all Irish fellas are desperate altogether,' he said with a grin.

On impulse, as she turned to leave, she asked him, 'Where in Ireland are you from?'

'Kerry, out near Dingle. It's like the incubator for guards.' He laughed, a lovely gurgling sound, and she melted. 'Why do you ask?'

'Oh, it's just you sound exactly like my friend, and he was from out near there as well.'

''Tis a sign so.' Darragh winked at her and hopped back in the car. 'See you tomorrow night, Annie.'

She didn't care about all the strange looks she was getting as she emerged from a police car covered in blood with a large Band-Aid on her face.

She turned to wave as Darragh drove off and gave a beep. As she climbed the stone steps to the castle's huge entrance door, a robin landed on the stone urn that decorated the balustrade beside her. She stopped and looked at the little bird with its signature red breast.

'Thanks, Bubbles. I never doubted you,' she said, not caring who heard her.

CHAPTER 39

ill lay on the bed. The group had a free day today. Conor had given lots of options, places to go, but he thought he'd just stay in the hotel. Beth had said she wanted to sleep late, and he was hoping to get back in her good books today. He had, in hindsight, come on too strong; he needed to take it more slowly.

He probably should not have abandoned the group yesterday either, but Beth was so ungrateful, and he hoped to get her to realise what she was missing. So often he had tried in the bar to talk to her, and she did converse with him but no more than with anyone else. She was so damned aloof, and that was what he loved about her. She wasn't dumb like Annie or fat like Marianne; she was perfect.

She seemed to be a bit unstable emotionally. Whenever she got a text from her sister – and there had been several over the last few days – she was elated, but after a period of time, she seemed to get anxious again. It was so strange. The texts should reassure her, but they seemed to only work temporarily.

She really was remarkable – if only he could get her to feel about him the way she felt about Maddie. Maddie was okay. She was a bit of an attention seeker though, always flirting and joking with the guys in the bar. Beth never did that.

* * *

BETH SAT on the bed and tried to get through to the cops once again. She'd been trying to reach the detective dealing with Maddie's disappearance, but he was away on another case. She wanted to thank him for his patience and diligence and let him know personally that Maddie was okay. There had been lots of texts in the past few days, jokey ones, just like Maddie, and Beth was now finally assured that she was safe.

One thing kept niggling her though. She replied right away and always tried to call but never got through. She begged Maddie just to call her once, from another phone if hers was broken, just to hear her voice. She dismissed it; she was starting to sound crazy.

She was holding for the police officer, fully expecting a voice to tell her he was unavailable, when she heard him answer.

'Lieutenant Bowers.'

'Oh, hi, Lieutenant, it's Beth Anderson. I'm calling from Ireland.'

'Hello, Beth, I was just going to call you actually...'

'Maddie's been in touch, and she's fine.' She wanted him to know as soon as possible.

'How did she get in contact with you? Did you speak to her?'

'Er...no. She texted, several times.'

'From her own phone?' he asked, and Beth was surprised he wasn't happier.

'Yes, she sent several texts saying she was fine, she just needed some space... You were right all along. I'm sorry for wasting your time.'

'So you're together now?' Lieutenant Bowers sounded confused.

'No,' she replied. 'We're not together now. I'm in Ireland, and she's out west somewhere – she didn't say exactly where – but she's okay.'

The lieutenant paused. 'But *you* are in Ireland?'

'Yeah, remember I told you I was taking a trip...' She wondered if this guy listened to a word she said.

'Yes.' He paused again. 'Beth, I don't know what's going on, but we've run a trace on Maddie's phone – it was hard because it is rarely switched on – but it is in Ireland.' She heard papers rustling. 'Let me see...' He was reading. 'Positive identification of the location of the cell phone of Miss Madeline Anderson to... it gives a bunch of GPS coordinates. So we ran it through our mapping system, and it's a hotel, Castle Dysert, I think, on the west coast of Ireland, County Clare.'

'What?' She was totally confused. 'But how can Maddie's phone be here? That's where I am! I didn't bring the phone with me – I haven't seen it since the night she left. Remember I told you, we went to the bar, Bubbles O'Leary's, and I left early. Maddie wanted to party, so she stayed on, and I never saw her again.'

'I don't know what's going on, Beth, but Maddie's phone is there and you say she isn't. Okay, take me back to what we know about that night again.'

She sighed; she'd been over this and over it.

'Maddie and I went to Bubbles. There was a quiz on, and everyone, all the regulars, were there. I was on a quiz team, but Maddie didn't want to play, so she was up at the bar just talking.'

'To who?' Lieutenant Bowers interrupted.

'I don't know, a whole bunch of people. Will, some of the guys from a shoe store up the street, Miguel was behind the bar, I think Jimmy was there, a few more...'

'And of that group she was talking to, how many are on this trip?' the detective asked.

Beth thought for a moment. 'Just Miguel, Jimmy and Will.'

'What are their last names?'

'Um... Miguel Sanchez, Jimmy Burns and Will Munro.' She was bewildered. Surely he didn't think Maddie taking off had anything to do with the three men?

'Okay, let me run a check on those, and I'll get back to you.'

'A check for what?' she asked.

'I don't know, but what we have so far is those three guys were with Maddie on the night she disappeared, you left early and she stayed there, and she never showed up again.'

'But she did... She texted...'

'But you haven't spoken to her?' Bowers sounded ominous.

'No, her phone is broken – the microphone isn't working – but the texts are definitely her…' Beth was starting to panic now.

'Oh, the texts might have come from her phone – in fact they probably did – but we don't know if it was Maddie who sent them.'

'But I don't understand… Are you saying Miguel or Jimmy or Will –'

He interrupted her. 'I'm not saying anything yet. Let me just run a check on these three and get back to you. But don't do or say anything to alert anyone, okay?'

'Okay,' Beth said, and the line went dead.

She tried to quell the churning in her stomach. Maddie's phone was here? In this hotel? But she wasn't. It made no sense.

She decided to phone Jimmy. She stopped, thinking about what Bowers had said, but that was crazy. Jimmy wouldn't have anything to do with Maddie's disappearance. He was her friend, and he was the one she wanted.

There was a group WhatsApp for the trip, and Jimmy's number was on it. She pressed Call.

'Hello?' he answered.

'Jimmy? It's Beth. I need to speak to you.'

'Of course, I'm in my room.'

'What number?' she asked urgently.

'405.'

'I'll be right there.'

She ended the call and headed straight to Jimmy's room. He was next door to Will. She remembered that because the night she and Will slept together, he joked that they should go to her room in case they shocked Jimmy.

He opened the door, fully dressed. The bedroom was tidy.

Quickly she told him what the cop had said. As she spoke, her phone beeped – another text.

Hey B! Hope Ireland great 'craic' C ya soon. Can't wait to hear all about it!!! M xxxxx

The by now familiar relief she experienced when she got a text had changed to something terrifying. She showed it to Jimmy.

He took the phone and went to the open sliding door to the balcony and went out. It was after ten, so Will must be up, and his door was slightly ajar. Jimmy pressed the Return Call button. A phone rang in Will's room. Beth crept out behind him, all colour draining from her face.

The phone call was rejected after just a few rings. Beth's screen darkened. Jimmy led her back into his room and quietly closed the door to the balcony.

'That was Maddie's ringtone.' She tried to steady her breathing. Surely there must be some other explanation. Will could not have Maddie's phone; he could not have been texting her all this time. Beth felt like she was going to throw up. She'd slept with him, and all the time, he had her sister's phone.

'Where is she, Jimmy? Where's Maddie?' She couldn't stop the tears. This was a nightmare. She made to go.

'What are you doing?' he asked.

'I'm going in there, make him tell me why he has my sister's phone...' She was torn between terror and fury.

'Hold on. If you go in there shouting and demanding, he'll know he's been discovered. I think we need to be a bit clever here. Please, just wait a moment, okay?'

Jimmy thought. He had Conor's mobile number in his phone, and he called him. 'Conor, it's Jimmy. Can you come to room 405 right away? It's urgent.'

Conor was just pulling into the hotel. He'd got the boys breakfast, put on some laundry and run a few errands in town. He was only planning on popping in to the hotel for a few minutes, as he needed to get home. Gerry was installed, and while there was a nurse there, he wanted to make sure Ana wasn't overdoing it.

'Sure... Is everything okay?' He knew that Jimmy was not a man for dramatics, so this was very out of character.

'I don't think so. I'll explain when you get here. If you meet any of the others, don't say anything.'

'Right.' Conor hung up, perplexed.

He took the service lift from the back entrance and met nobody. He knocked on room 405 and was surprised to see Jimmy looking grim and Beth in tears.

They filled him in as quickly as they could.

'We need to get the guards,' Conor said definitively. 'Beth, if you can give me the contact details of the detective you are dealing with, I can ask the guards here to get in touch.'

Beth and Jimmy looked at each other. 'Conor is right,' Jimmy said.

Conor called the front desk and Carlos answered. 'Get the guards – fast. Room 405.'

'Very well,' Carlos replied, no questions, unflappable.

They stopped as they heard a door being opened in the corridor outside. Conor put his finger to his lips, indicating they should be quiet. He pulled up the CCTV app for the hotel from his phone. He selected the camera on that corridor.

'It's him. He's leaving.'

'Now what?' Beth asked, wild-eyed.

'We go in and check if Maddie's phone is in there. He's not expecting anyone now, so it might not be hidden, but once the guards get here, things could be different. If it's not her phone, we spare everyone, and if it is, then the guards are on the way. Beth, you come with me, see if you recognise it, okay?'

She nodded, unable to speak.

'Jimmy, can you phone Carlos Manner on the front desk, explain what's going on and get him to brief the guards when they come?'

'Of course.' Jimmy turned to his task.

Conor used his master key card, and the lock of Will's room clicked open. They quickly went inside. Beth immediately fixed on an iPhone on the locker. She picked it up and the home screen flashed to life, a picture of her and Maddie. It was her sister's phone.

Before they had time to process it, the door opened. They spun around.

'Hey!' Will shouted. 'That's my stuff! What the hell do you think you're doing?'

Beth held tightly to the phone as Will approached, his eyes glittering chips of blue. Conor stood between them. 'Leave her alone, Will.'

Before he knew where he was, Will had punched him hard in the stomach, doubling him over. Conor was winded but managed to stand up. Will punched him again, this time on the jaw, and sent him reeling backwards, knocking over the coffee table.

'Give me my phone!' Will roared, furious now.

He grabbed the terrified Beth and tried to prise the phone out of her hand. Conor got up and pulled Will round by the shoulder, landing a punch to his jaw with the other hand. Will grunted and fell backwards, but he came at Conor again within seconds. Beth screamed as Will pulled the heavy brass bedside lamp from its socket and swung it. Conor ducked, and the base of the lamp missed his head by an inch. He drove forward, his head making contact with Will's chest, and then he was on top of him on the floor.

Jimmy heard the screaming and ran in. Thinking quickly, he stamped on Will's hand with his foot, and the younger man howled in pain. Conor used the distraction to flip Will onto his front and pinned his arms painfully behind his back.

Jimmy placed his foot firmly on the back of Will's neck.

'Aargh...' Will protested, but Jimmy increased the pressure.

Jimmy never let him go, and though the other man was struggling, he and Conor managed to restrain him. Will became totally disabled, but it didn't stop him from shouting.

Three guards arrived in moments, followed by Carlos.

'Right so,' the older policeman said, helping Conor up after he placed handcuffs on Will, who was kicking and shouting in protest. The two younger cops restrained him, and the older one approached him. As he did, Will kicked him hard in the shin.

'My name is Sergeant Clancy, and you'd want to cop on fairly fast now. I believe, Mr Munro, you have some questions to answer on this side of the Atlantic and considerably more on the other, so be a good man now and don't give us any trouble, do you hear me?'

Will spat, and a glob of saliva slid down the sergeant's cheek. The younger guard put pressure on Will's arms, causing him to cry out in pain. The officers exchanged a look, and the younger one increased the pressure.

'This is police brutality!' Will screamed. 'You could break my arm.'

'Your powers of observation are truly astounding,' the sergeant remarked as he wiped his face. 'Take him in, lads.' He nodded and they manhandled Will out the door.

Jimmy smiled at the condescending manner of the Irish cop.

Beth ran and followed them down the corridor, frantic now. 'Will, where's Maddie? What have you done? Please, please tell me – where is my sister?'

Will just smiled.

'If you know anything about this young woman's disappearance, I'd suggest telling us now,' Sergeant Clancy said. But Will just gave a snort of derision.

Beth launched herself on him, crying and screaming and scratching his face. 'Tell me!' she screamed, hysterical now. 'Tell me what you've done to her!'

He seemed to be enjoying her distress, the smirk never leaving his handsome face.

Jimmy could see he wasn't going to tell her anything. He gently put his arms around her as two policemen pushed the man out the door. Carlos was on the phone, asking for medical assistance – Conor was bleeding.

'William Munro,' the sergeant said, 'I am arresting you on suspicion of grievous bodily harm and larceny. You do not have to say anything, but it may harm your defence if you do not mention when questioned something you later rely on in court.'

'What have you done?' Beth shouted as Jimmy held her in his arms. 'Where is Maddie? Please just tell me... Where is she?' Tears streamed down her face. 'Please tell me you didn't hurt her... Please... Don't say she's...'

Will's face softened into a gentle smile. 'I wasn't enough for you, was I? You, the big high-flying doctor. I would have been good to you, Beth, but you were too stuck up to take me seriously.'

She made another dive for him. 'Where is my sister, you creep?' she screeched.

He started to laugh, and the police shoved him roughly in the service lift as Beth sank to her knees on the carpet in uncontrollable sobs.

Jimmy helped her up and put his arms around her, and she sobbed into his chest as one of the onsite first aiders arrived with a kit to patch Conor up.

The sergeant stayed to take statements. Jimmy filled him in as quickly as he could.

'And this is an open investigation in the States?' the sergeant asked Beth.

'Yes. Here's the number of the detective in charge.' She tried to get the number from her phone, but her hands were trembling so much she couldn't do it.

'Don't worry, I'll get it from you later. This is a terrible shock to get, Miss Anderson. Take it easy there, and I'll make a few calls and get back to you.'

'Are you all right?' Carlos asked Conor. His shirt was torn, and blood was trickling from a gash over his eye.

'Grand. How about you, Jimmy, you okay?' Conor asked.

'Yes, fine. But I'm too old for fighting.' Jimmy smiled ruefully.

CHAPTER 40

*C*onor knew he probably should have stayed and talked them all down, but he wanted to get home. Ana and the boys would get a fright if they saw him with his shirt torn and his face cut, so he asked Carlos to find him a shirt. His wound was cleaned and some Steri-Strip bandages applied. He suspected he might have a broken rib, but he'd had one before, so he knew he'd survive.

Beth was being comforted by her friends, and now it was just a case of waiting. The American police were liaising with the Irish Guard, and hard as it was for Beth, she would have to be patient.

He arrived home to a peaceful scene. Jamsie was telling the boys a story, and they were absolutely riveted, whatever it was. They were all sitting on the patio outside, Ana wearing one of Conor's fleeces, with a woolly beanie hat on her head, the boys listening to Jamsie. Danika was baking in the kitchen, and the aroma was wonderful.

'How's everyone?' he asked as he approached.

'Conor!' Ana looked up but her face fell. 'What happen to you? You have cut?'

'Long story, but I'm fine. I'll tell you later. Bit of drama up at the castle, but it's all okay now.'

'Did you get in a fight, Dad?' Joe was wide-eyed.

'I did, Joe, but then the guards came and took the baddie away, so all is well.' His boys left their seats and stood beside him; he put his arms around them.

'How's Gerry?' he asked Jamsie.

'Sleeping again. He won't eat.'

'Will we go into him?'

'Sure.' Jamsie stood.

'But Granda, you never finished the story,' Artie said, dismayed.

Conor looked at his boys. They were very taken with Jamsie, calling him Granda now and everything. Six months ago, he might have been horrified, furious even, but not any more. His father was an old man, and he just wanted a bit of comfort in his old age. He took to the twins immediately, and he was so considerate of Ana and the situation. Conor had no complaints.

'I'll finish it just as soon as I go and check on your Uncle Gerry, okay, lads?' He patted them on the head.

'Okay,' they chorused.

He went in and Gerry opened his eyes. Jamsie sat on one side and Conor on the other.

The nurse was discreet and considerate when they wanted to spend time together. She only appeared when Gerry needed medical attention.

They ate dinner in the room. The boys came in, and Gerry managed to stay awake to talk to them. They were all full of questions about America, and he answered them as best he could. It was so touching; they drew pictures to decorate his bed, and after the first few hours, they were used to him being there. They wandered in and out, and Gerry seemed happy to have them around.

Jamsie was shattered. Ana too was looking pale and drawn, though she insisted she was fine. Conor asked Artur to convince her to go to bed; she was so stubborn but usually did as her father asked. Conor sat with Gerry all through the night.

It was a long night. Gerry slept fitfully and woke often. They exchanged little bits of conversation, memories mostly.

On one occasion, long after everyone was in bed, Gerry woke and said, 'She's a beautiful person, your wife. She has a kind of glow.'

'She has. I'm a lucky man.'

'And Artie and Joe are great boys.' He lay back, exhaling heavily. 'You're a wonderful father. I should know, you were the closest thing I ever had to one, long before you should have had to be.'

He swallowed and Conor saw him wince.

Conor held the cup of water to his lips, giving him a drink. Once, when he seemed relatively peaceful, Conor went to the kitchen to find something to eat. He opened the fridge and saw a bowl of borscht, a delicious soup Danika made with beets and potatoes and tomatoes and garlic. He heated a bowl up for himself and cut a slice of bread and buttered it before going back in to Gerry. His brother was awake when he returned.

'Smells good,' he managed to croak.

'Danika makes it. It's Ukrainian soup, delicious.'

Gerry sniffed appreciatively.

'You want some?'

Gerry nodded, and Conor helped him into a more upright position. Slowly he spooned the soup into his brother's mouth as he swallowed it.

'More?' Conor asked after four or five spoonfuls.

Gerry nodded again. 'Please.'

He finished the entire bowl and lay back on the pillows and fell asleep once more. Conor was too tired to get himself another bowl, so he ate the bread and butter, reclined the chair as much as it would go and dozed off himself.

He woke a few hours later to find Danika and Artur there. Ana and the boys were still sleeping.

'Go to bed,' Danika whispered. 'We watch him. Go now.' She shooed Conor out. Gratefully, he climbed the stairs and went into his and Ana's room. He checked his watch – it was five a.m. She was sleeping peacefully, so he took off his trousers and shirt and got in beside her as gently as he could. In her sleep, she turned to him and rested her head on his shoulder while she flung one arm across his chest. He kissed the top of her head and was asleep in seconds.

CHAPTER 41

*M*iguel knocked on the red front door of the small terraced house in the centre of Killarney, having first checked with the local post office that he had the right address. There were several entries in the phone book for a Kathleen O'Leary, and through that and Facebook, he had managed to narrow it down to this one. The age profile was right; she was younger than Bubbles, and he was only in his fifties, so she was in her late forties. She was single, but the photo on her Facebook profile was the best bit of evidence – she was the absolute image of her brother.

He was nervous, and while he'd tried to work out the potential conversations they might have, he was just going to have to wing it.

A boy of about fifteen opened the door. He was red-haired and dressed in a football kit. He had a sports-gear bag in his hand.

'Hi,' he said as he opened the door.

'Oh, hi. I'm looking for Kathleen O'Leary?'

'Oh, right. I'm actually late for training,' the boy said before yelling back into the house, 'Mam! Someone at the door for you.' He passed Miguel as he dashed out the door and up the street.

A woman with red hair tied back in a ponytail came to the door.

She looked harassed and tired, and while she wasn't rude, he could tell she didn't really want to engage with any callers.

'Don't worry, I'm not selling anything,' Miguel opened.

'It wouldn't matter if you were – I can't afford it.' She gave a half-smile.

'My name is Miguel Sanchez,' he began. There was no point in beating around the bush. 'And I'm just wondering if you had a brother named Finbarr who went to America?'

The woman looked stricken. 'I do,' she managed after a few seconds. 'Do you know him?'

'Yes. May I come in?' he asked.

Kathleen stood back to let him enter the small hallway. 'First door on the left there,' she said as Miguel turned into a little living room. Sitting on the end of a sofa was an elderly woman.

'Mam.' Kathleen raised her voice; the old lady was clearly hard of hearing.

The woman gazed at Miguel with rheumy eyes, and he wondered if she was senile.

'This is Miguel…' Kathleen was trying to keep her voice steady.

'Miguel, Finbarr's friend?' the old lady asked, her voice thin and reedy. 'I know your face. Finbarr sent me lots of postcards of the two of you. Is he with you?'

Miguel was stunned. He knew Bubbles sent postcards home once a year, but he didn't realise he'd sent ones of the two of them. The thought made his heart burst with pride. He knew Bubbles saw him as more than an employee, but this touched him. He swallowed the lump in his throat.

'May I?' Miguel indicated the armchair beside the fireplace.

'Of course.' Kathleen took the newspaper and TV remotes off the chair.

'No, Mrs O'Leary. I am so sorry to tell you that Finbarr died three months ago.' Miguel hated having to give her this news.

'My boy is dead?' the woman asked, and Miguel nodded sadly.

'He was only fifty-seven – what happened to him?' Kathleen asked, her voice cracking.

Before Miguel could answer, his eyes rested on a photograph on the mantelpiece. It was of a young red-haired man, and initially he thought it was Kathleen's son who had just left. But as he looked more closely, he realised it was a very young Bubbles. There was no beard, and his face was much leaner, but the same twinkly eyes, the same broad grin. Beside it was another, a photo of Bubbles and Miguel, taken last Christmas Eve in the bar. Miguel felt tears prick his eyes.

'He had a heart attack. He owned a bar in New York, and everyone who went there knew him. Bubbles died in the bar, surrounded by his friends who all loved him so much that we had him cremated. And now we are here – we scattered his ashes a few days ago out on the Dingle Peninsula.'

'I don't understand… What did you call him?' Kathleen looked totally confused.

'Oh, I'm sorry. He was known to everyone as Bubbles. Most of his friends never even knew his first name. I only do because I worked for him.'

'Finbarr changed his name?' The old lady spoke again.

'No, ma'am, he didn't change his name. He just had a nickname, and it was Bubbles.'

'He was called that here, remember, Mam? The lads on the football team he played on always called him that.' She smiled sadly at the memory. 'I remember Michael Jackson had just got his monkey, Bubbles, and Finbarr was so hairy, one of the lads said he was like the monkey, and the nickname just stuck.'

'I do remember.' Her eyes shone with unshed tears. 'I'm so glad he had his friends over in America. I haven't seen my boy for thirty-five years, but every year I'd get a postcard…'

Miguel hated to hear the pain in the old woman's voice. Bubbles was still her son, and she was losing him once again.

'Get my box there, Kathleen, would you?'

Kathleen handed her mother a tin box with a picture of a kitten on the front. She opened it, and sure enough, there was a whole bundle of postcards, tied together with a blue ribbon.

'I remember how important posting those cards was to him.' Miguel tried not to tear up. Every postcard had a photo and just 'I love you' on the back. No address, no details, just that.

'Do you know why he left?' Kathleen asked Miguel.

'I do. Bubbles – I mean Finbarr – told me one night years ago.'

She sighed. 'The case is still open, I presume, though to be honest, the local guards here might not have gone to too much trouble to find Finbarr. Kit Mulligan was well known to them anyway, and apart from his sister, Bridie, nobody thought he was any loss at all. It suited them that Finbarr took off.'

She tried to keep her voice steady. She sat beside her mother and held her hand. Silent tears flowed down her wrinkled, age-worn face. 'We wrote to him at the first address we had for him. It was in Tumbler Street in Brooklyn, but apart from the postcards, we heard nothing.'

Miguel could see the raw pain on the women's faces. 'He never forgot you, and he talked about Ireland all the time. He didn't give you his address or any way of contacting him because he was afraid it would get you into trouble with the police. If you didn't know where he was, then you couldn't be implicated.'

Kathleen nodded. 'The postcards were a comfort, but we would have loved to have seen him again.' She fixed her gaze on the wall above the fireplace, trying not to break down.

'Bridie Mahon said she'd make sure he went to jail for life the minute he set foot in Ireland again. And her other brother was very high up in the guards, so she probably could have done it. Finbarr didn't kill that man – it was an accident – and anyway, Kit Mulligan was no good to man nor beast.' Mrs O'Leary was adamant, still fighting in her son's corner after all these years.

Miguel wondered about his own mother. He kept in touch, sent the postcards just like Bubbles, but now it was time to go home. His mother would love to see him – he knew she would – but just how much he was missed he didn't understand until that moment.

The rest of the afternoon went well. Miguel told them all about

Bubbles and what he was like, all the kind things he did for people, how everyone loved him, how fondly he spoke of home. They told him stories of Bubbles as a boy, the crazy stunts he pulled. He sounded just the same.

He had kept back some of Bubbles's ashes. It felt silly, and he didn't want to tell the others in case they thought he was putting himself in the position of chief mourner ahead of them. He had taken a few spoonfuls out of the urn and placed them in a Ziploc bag; he'd planned to keep them for himself. When he found Kathleen's number, he went out and bought a small marble box and placed the ashes inside. He hoped they didn't think it morbid or stupid, but he was going to give them to Kathleen and her mother. They had a far greater claim to them than he did; these people were Bubbles's flesh and blood.

When Kathleen came in with tea and biscuits after they had been talking for a while, he reached into his bag and pulled out the small green box. It was Connemara marble, and the lady in the shop had assured him it was very authentically Irish.

'I hope you don't think I am being... Well, I don't know... Even after all these years, sometimes my English lets me down.' He smiled apologetically. 'But I want to give you both this.' He handed Kathleen the box.

'Those are some of Bub – Finbarr's ashes.' He stopped, not knowing what else to say.

Kathleen explained to her mother, who wasn't sure what a cremation even was. While it was becoming more popular in Ireland, Conor had explained, it was still relatively rare. Most people were buried.

Kathleen handed the box to her mother, who held it reverently. She eased herself up slowly and walked to the mantelpiece, where she had the photograph of her son as a young man on display for decades, never knowing where he was. She ran her gnarly old hands over the glass, as if caressing his face, and then placed the box lovingly beside it.

She then crossed the room once more to where Miguel sat and put one of her hands on his.

'Thank you for bringing my boy back to me. I was waiting for him. I can go home myself now – he'll be waiting for me.' The matter-of-fact way she said it touched Miguel. He had done the right thing. It was time to let Bubbles go; he was home.

CHAPTER 42

The Glavin sisters eyed each other urgently. The entire group, apart from Miguel who had left early this morning for some unknown reason, were absolutely distraught at the developments around Will. Conor had provided a private room, and there were tea and coffee available, so at least they were not on public display. The events of the morning had shaken everyone. Could Will really have had something to do with Beth's sister's disappearance? It was hard to believe; he seemed like a nice enough young man. Though they had noticed how he could be a little dismissive sometimes, as if he secretly thought they were ridiculous. But so many people at the bar thought them an oddity, they were used to it. Bubbles made them welcome, and that was all that mattered.

Erin and Shannon both felt for Beth – she was very nice – but they were torn. Today was such a big day for them.

They were due to meet their uncle at midday, and he was going to collect them and take them to see where their daddy had come from. They had even had his name added to the family gravestone, though he was buried in Yonkers, the cheapest plot their mother could find. Apparently, Seamus had arranged to bring them back to his house afterwards, and other aunts, uncles and cousins were going to visit. It was so exciting, and Seamus had been so welcoming and seemed genuinely delighted they were there, that any fears they had about not being wanted or there being some kind of feud dissipated. They should really be up in their room, getting ready. It was ten forty-five already, but everyone was still around Beth, trying to offer her comfort.

They had mentioned their uncle's offer to Conor last night when they ran into him as he was leaving for home, and he was really happy for them, touchingly so when he had so many other calls on his time. He listened to them tell him the whole story and about how Seamus was coming to collect them and everything.

Kevin also knew of their plans, and he approached them as they stood at the edge of the group around Beth. 'Don't you two have a big day today? Seeing your Irish family?' he said quietly.

'We do, but...' Erin was unsure.

'Ladies, Beth would want you to go. We'll stay with her – we don't all need to be here. Go on, get yourselves organised.' He nodded encouragingly.

The Glavin sisters were so relieved, and they didn't need to be told twice. They gave Beth a hug and told her they would be praying that everything worked out all right and that the truth was discovered as soon as possible. The poor girl just nodded, and the tears shone in her eyes.

Kevin had taken Tess to the childcare centre. There was baking going on that morning, and she was excited to take part. She didn't need to witness any of this craziness. Marianne sat on one side of Beth holding her hand, Jimmy on the other.

'I should have said something sooner. I don't know how, I just had a feeling...' Jimmy was upset.

'It's okay, Jimmy...' Beth turned to him, her tear-stained face pale. 'It's so hard to accept that he has done something to Maddie. I thought we knew him, you know? He was one of us...and a friend of Bubbles's too, but you warned me to trust my intuition, and I didn't. When you told me he worked at Mount Sinai in Queens, and he'd never mentioned it to me, that should have set alarm bells going. And when

I said I didn't want to have a relationship, he got really mad – like really mad – and just stormed off.'

This was news to everybody except Jimmy.

Beth's phone rang, and she sprang to answer it. 'Hello? Yes, Lieutenant Bowers, it's me...'

They waited as she listened. You could hear a pin drop.

'And you're sure?' Beth's voice cracked. Marianne caught Kevin's eye. *Please, God, no. Let them not have found her body.*

'Okay... What should I do?'

Another pause while the detective spoke.

'Okay, thank you.'

She pressed End, and all eyes were on her.

'They've searched his apartment and his car. There is evidence of a fight or something in his place – there's blood, but no body. They're running tests on the blood now to see if it matches Maddie's.'

Jimmy put his arm around her, and she broke down. 'I think he killed her...' was all she managed to choke out.

They all sat there, not knowing what to say but all thinking exactly the same thing.

They looked over at the door, where a grey-haired man in his fifties entered. He introduced himself as Detective Joseph O'Riordan.

'Could I speak to Ms Beth Anderson, please?'

Beth rose. Then she looked back at Jimmy and held her hand out. He took it and they went with the detective.

'Miss Anderson, I just wanted to fill you in on what we know so far. We've spoken to the detective who is dealing with this in the States, and he has run a check of this Todd William Munroe. He's an ex-convict, served eleven years in Texas for larceny, GBH, impersonating a police officer... To be honest with you, he has a charge sheet as long as my arm.'

'Has he said where Maddie is?' Beth asked.

'No, I'm afraid he hasn't. He says he knows nothing about it and, apart from that, refuses to cooperate with us in any way. He's had a state solicitor appointed to him now, so they are in conference, but it's going to take time. Either way, we'll charge him with assault of the manager here, and he'll face court for that. But ultimately, he'll have to be extradited back to the States, and they'll continue the investigation.'

'I spoke to the detective who was dealing with her as a missing person just now. He said they searched his apartment and car and they found blood, but they are waiting on test results to see if it's Maddie's.'

Detective O'Riordan nodded. 'Right. Well, I'm sorry that is all I have for you at the moment, but of course we'll keep you updated as it unfolds.' He shook her hand and left.

Beth looked back at her friends, Marianne and Kevin, Annie and Jimmy. They all meant so well, and she was lucky to have them, but she wanted to be alone.

'Please, guys…' She seemed a little more like herself. 'Please go and do whatever you had planned. There's no point in all of us hanging around all day. I really appreciate it, but there's nothing to do but wait.' She noted the doubt in their faces. 'Honestly, please… I'll put a message in the WhatsApp group once I know anything.'

Kevin took out his phone and opened WhatsApp. He was the admin, so he removed Will from the group, though he would not be given access to his phone in custody anyway. Shannon and Erin had bought a smartphone between them just to be able to access the group chat, and Kevin had spent a full hour explaining to them how to use it.

'Are you sure?' Marianne asked. 'Annie and I can stay with you. We could go for a walk or something?'

Beth gave a weak smile. Annie had mentioned her date that was to take place that night when she met everyone in the bar for a nightcap the previous evening.

'Definitely not. Annie needs to get herself even more gorgeous, if that's possible, for her date later, and I know you and Kevin planned on taking Tess to that funfair today. So, please, go.' She shooed them all out and sat down again, her eyes never leaving the screen of her phone.

Jimmy was the last one there.

'Thanks, Jimmy. I don't know what I would have done without you.'

He nodded. 'I'm glad I was there.'

She willed her phone to ring. 'I should call my mother,' she said. She had explained about the fractious relationship she and Maddie had with their mother to Jimmy before. 'I don't want her hearing about it on the news.'

As she scrolled to find the number, the phone lit up again.

'Lieutenant Bowers?'

Jimmy stood and waited, his heart thumping. Beth's face was impossible to read as she listened.

'And you're sure it's her?' Beth breathing was ragged.

'Thank you, thank you...' She pressed End and looked up at Jimmy.

'They've found her.'

CHAPTER 43

$\mathcal{A}$nnie was in the hair salon having her hair blow-dried when she got the message on the group's WhatsApp.

Maddie in hospital, but she's alive. Will imprisoned her and beat her up and left her to die in his apartment. She managed to escape somehow and was found unconscious on the street two days ago. She's still in an induced coma because of her injuries, but doctors say she is going to make it. Beth x

What a relief. Poor Maddie. It was mind-blowing to think that good-looking, charming Will was capable of something like that.

* * *

KEVIN, Marianne and Tess were having great fun riding the stomach-churning rides at the funfair set up for the festival. Tess was munching a huge cloud of cotton candy, which they learned the Irish called candy floss, and having the time of her life. As she dashed around a hall of mirrors, giggling at how they made them so tall and elongated or short and squat, Kevin felt his phone vibrate in his pocket. He took it out, read the message and relayed it to Marianne while Tess danced in front of one of the mirrors.

'Oh, that's great. Well, not great that he injured her like that, but that she's alive. That poor girl. What an ordeal. I really was afraid he'd killed her,' Marianne said, finally airing the fear they'd both had but didn't want to tempt fate by even saying.

'Yeah, me too. He seemed okay, but now that I think back, even Bubbles had his reservations about that guy. He invited him to the bar, but I always got the impression he wasn't Will's biggest fan. When I put the notice up about the trip, I was surprised he put his name down. I mean, he used to come in, sure, but he wasn't exactly one of the gang, was he?' Kevin asked.

'No, but then neither is Jimmy. He keeps to himself too,' she said reasonably.

'Yeah, but Bubbles loved Jimmy. Those two had a connection.'

Just as Marianne was about to reply, Kevin's phone rang again.

'Hello?' A pause. 'Speaking,' he said.

She knew by his face he didn't recognise the number.

Then his face cracked into a huge grin. 'Well, that's just great, really, really great. Congratulations, Deshane. I'm so happy for you. Sure, put her on.'

He listened and then said, 'Mrs Fisher, I'm delighted. It was my pleasure, and I'm so happy it all worked out. Of course, I'll do the endorsement this afternoon. I'm on vacation at the moment, but I can send the email easily from here.' Another pause. 'No… It's no problem. Happy to do it.' He smiled from ear to ear. So rarely in his job was there good news. 'Take care. I'll speak to you soon. Bye.'

Marianne grinned. 'The kid got the scholarship?'

Kevin had told her all about his work, including Deshane Fisher.

'He will. He got an A plus on all of the exams, and they are so hard. He must have hardly stopped studying since I met him.'

She looked up at him. 'You're a good man, Kevin Wilson.'

'I'm an average man, Marianne, a very average man, and my ex would say I was considerably below average actually.' He smiled ruefully but put his arm around her shoulder.

'I think she's hangry,' she quipped, and he burst out laughing.

'You got it. She needs to eat something, then maybe she wouldn't be so ratty all the time.' He gave her a gentle squeeze.

'Not a problem I've ever had – clearly.'

'I think you're perfect.' All the joking was gone this time. She cast a sidelong glance at him.

'You do?' She sounded sceptical.

'Yeah, I do. You are gorgeous, with curves in all the right places. And what's more, you're interesting and kind and funny and I... I really like you, and I'd love to see more of you when we get back to the States.' The whole sentence came out in a rush.

'I'd like that too,' she replied.

He gestured towards the mirror in front of them. They were both no higher than three feet tall and both were wider than they were tall.

'Look at us – we're perfect together.' He grinned and they both dissolved into helpless laughter.

SHANNON AND ERIN posed for pictures, their smiles broad. They were back at their uncle's house, a lovely old farmhouse in the middle of the countryside, having spent the day visiting places their father frequented as a boy. They saw the school and the farm where he grew up, and they walked the streets of his home town before climbing up the hill to the graveyard.

They wept as they saw the names of their grandparents, Julia and Daniel Glavin, their infant daughter, Teresa, who died when she was only six months old, and their father's older brother, Frank, who died back in the '70s. Carved beneath those names was, *Their son Donal, who went to God on the 3rd of April 1981, buried in New York, USA.*

'He would love that,' Shannon whispered to her uncle, who had arranged for it to be done. 'Thank you.'

'We always hoped he'd come home, just for a visit. But having you two turn up is just great altogether,' Seamus said gruffly, not wanting the emotion of the occasion to get the better of him. 'Now we better get home because there's enough cake and sandwiches to feed an army at our place and cousins and second cousins twice removed crawling out of the woodwork waiting to meet ye.'

Everyone made them feel so welcome – it was overwhelming and wonderful simultaneously. And as the stars twinkled in the Irish night sky, Seamus dropped them back to the hotel. Erin and Shannon stood on the steps, waving him off as the clock struck three a.m., with the promises of their family to stay in touch ringing in their ears.

CHAPTER 44

The rest of the trip was uneventful, and everyone relaxed and enjoyed the sights of ancient castles and stunning landscapes. They were all invited to attend the opening party for the new wing. Beth caught the first flight she could back to New York, where she was assured her sister had been taken out of her coma and was awake. Recovery would be slow, and Will would most likely never again see a free day, but Beth tried not to think about him. She would concentrate on getting her sister better.

She'd video-called her mother and told her what had happened, and to Beth's surprise, her mother broke down. She had never seen her so emotional, and Melanie even asked if she could come to see Maddie. They were meeting at the hospital. Beth had no idea how that would work out, but she was glad for Maddie, as she missed her mother, even after everything that had been said.

The music and noise of the opening party wasn't really Jimmy's scene, though he could see everyone was having a good time. Katherine was behind the front desk, insisting on being there for this event – which was a big one for the hotel – but he couldn't go out and bother her while she was working.

He did ask Laoise to sing 'The Parting Glass' for Bubbles, and she promised to do so at the end of the night.

Conor joined him as he stood at the bar. 'Hi, Jimmy, how's things?' he said, his eyes never leaving a woman with a headscarf tied around her head, who was dancing with two blonde boys.

'Good. Are they your family?'

'Yeah, that's Ana, my wife, and my sons, Joe and Artie. We just came up for an hour. My brother is not well, and he's staying with us, so we can't leave him for long. But I needed to show my face here.' He saw the other man's look of surprise. 'My father and a nurse are with him.'

'I'm sorry to hear about your bother.'

'We were estranged, as they say, for a long time, until very recently actually. But well, that's all water under the bridge now.' Conor thrust his hands in his pockets.

Silence settled between them.

'She is lovely,' Jimmy said, his eyes on Ana as well.

'She is that.' Conor sighed. 'I don't know if you're a religious man, but if you are, say a prayer for her. She's going through cancer treatment, and it's hard on her.'

'I will. I hope you get a long and happy life together, you and Ana and your boys.'

'And what does the future hold for you?'

Jimmy turned his head, catching the other man's eye.

'That, I'm afraid, I am less certain of,' he replied.

'She won't ever make the first move – it's not in her,' Conor said, watching his family once more.

Jimmy wasn't going to be coy or pretend he didn't know what was meant. 'I don't know what to suggest,' he said simply.

'What do you want?'

He thought for a moment. What did he want? He never allowed wants to enter his existence. He had no real ambitions. He did his job, he read, he ate, he went for a glass of wine or two in the evenings. His apartment looked the same since the time he lived there with his mother; he didn't buy new things, not until the old thing broke or was no longer usable for some reason. He had the same clothes for years. And even books – he mostly borrowed them from the library. So up to this week, he thought he had everything he wanted.

'I want to never leave her, to have her with me for the rest of my life,' he said, the words sounding strange even to his own ears.

'Do you want her to go to New York?' Conor asked him. 'I'm not saying she'd go – I've no idea if she would or not. And if you took her away from us, then it would want to be for a fairly fantastic life you were offering her. But is that what you'd want?'

He doubted his time-warp apartment would constitute a fairly fantastic life. 'I don't have anything to offer her. I live in a small apartment, do a poorly paid job. I don't really have family or friends. I don't travel – apart from this trip, I've never left the United States. I read all the time... So no, it would not be remotely fantastic.'

'Well, she has a magnificent house, you know that. And a well-paid job that she loves. She doesn't have family, but she has great friends who love her –'

'I know,' Jimmy interrupted uncharacteristically. 'I don't have anything. It is foolish of me to think I could –'

'Let me finish,' Conor said. 'She has all of that here, and you don't have that at home. But I've never seen anyone make her light up like you do. As you probably know, Katherine is very important to me, not just at work, though this place would be lost without her, but she's as close as family. I love her, though she'd probably give out to me for saying it. That's why I'm interfering at all.'

Jimmy was silent, absorbing what the other man said.

'I know this sort of thing doesn't happen every day. I mean, for young ones like Annie there' – he nodded at Annie, who was now dancing closely with Darragh – 'maybe it does, but for the likes of us, it just doesn't.'

Jimmy smiled at the idea that the handsome Conor O'Shea put the two of them in the same category.

'That woman over there' – he pointed at Ana – 'took a chance on me when I wasn't husband or father material at all. But she took a chance, and would you believe it, she had a job convincing me. And every single day of my life I thank God that she did.' He turned to Jimmy. 'Come over, live here. Or at least suggest it to her. All she can say is no, and you'll be no worse off than you are now.'

'Would she even want that?'

'I don't know, maybe she wouldn't. She's a bit of an enigma, our Katherine. But a dumb priest never got a parish, as my mam used to say. You have nothing to lose but your dignity, and that's a small price to pay if it does work out, isn't it?'

The dance ended, and Joe and Artie each took one of Ana's hands as they left the dance floor. Conor went to join them.

Jimmy ruminated on the man's advice. He'd tried to spend as much time as he could with Katherine. Conor insisted she take some time off – she had lots of holidays accrued that she had never taken – so they had spent a wonderful few days exploring the countryside together. Jimmy felt he was living his entire lifetime in those few days. The idea of saying goodbye to her was intolerable, but he didn't know what to say to stop it happening. He was a garbage man in New York; she was a hotel receptionist in Ireland. In theory, they should have nothing in common, but he'd never felt closer to anyone. Maybe Conor was right; he should offer to move here, see how she reacted. The thought made his stomach churn in terror.

Kevin and Marianne were finally open about their relationship, and everyone was thrilled for them, Tess included. She and Miguel were having such fun as Laoise called out instructions for a very complicated dance that involved spinning your partner until their feet left the ground. Tess screamed with delight as Miguel swung her around. Annie was dancing with her cop and seemed very taken with him. Jimmy watched as the young red-haired Irish man threw his head back and laughed at something she said.

Shannon and Erin were looking at photos on their phone. They'd had a marvellous time with their relatives, and he was glad. The sisters struck him as a bit like himself, an oddity in New York. The fast-paced, impossibly glamorous, trendy, cutting-edge place that it was often seemed like an alien planet to people like him and the Glavins, and yet they were just as much a part of the fabric of that city as the hipsters with their fancy coffee and art-house music.

He knew they were bereft without Bubbles; he had given them a social life, friends, as well as the friendship they had with him personally. He was glad their little world had expanded to include their Irish family.

Jimmy walked past them, out into the reception area. The place was a hive of activity, press and people milling about to witness the sumptuous party to celebrate the reopening of the wing destroyed by fire.

He spotted Katherine, back in her work mode. Dark suit, white blouse, hair tied back and held in place with a clip. His heart lurched, followed closely by his stomach. He couldn't do it. He turned to go back to the party, but as he did, his eye caught hers and she smiled at him. A rare, genuine smile of joy. He smiled back.

He walked over to the desk and waited until she was finished dealing with the guest at the counter. He felt more like a fifteen-year-old kid than an almost sixty-year-old man. Not that he ever spoke to a girl when he was fifteen, or any other age. He was ridiculously inexperienced in the art of seduction, never anticipating a need for it. Eventually, the guest moved away, problem solved.

'I'm taking a break in fifteen minutes,' she murmured as he approached the desk. A younger receptionist was just a few feet away.

'My room?' he asked, and immediately realised how crass that sounded. It was somewhere they could be alone, but his intentions were honourable even if he sounded like some kind of lounge-lizard creep. He blushed puce. 'I didn't mean...' he began.

'It's all right.' She smiled. 'See you there.'

Jimmy almost ran from the desk in an effort to hide his embarrassment. What on earth made him suggest a bedroom? They had never gone anywhere near a bed. She slept in his arms that first night, on her sofa. In her beautiful house. What if she thought he was just a fortune hunter? He knew Conor said he had nothing to lose, but that wasn't true. He had her to lose if she thought he was after her house and her money. He opened the bedroom door and saw the pile of library books beside the bed. All the wisdom of the ancient world was no good to him now. For the first time in his life, he felt all he had learned was irrelevant and useless.

He paced. Should he forget the whole thing, just go home as planned? He was happy before. He could be so again. What if this was nothing more than a stupid old man's infatuation? He was going to make a total fool of himself, in front of someone who was essentially a stranger. He had guarded his sensitivity all his life, never getting close and never getting hurt. It had served him well, and yet here he was risking all that pain. If Katherine rejected him, it would be unbearable. But would walking away and never stating his case be any less so? Round and round the various scenarios went in his head, and he tried to rationalise it. She would be there any moment. He had to decide.

Long before he was ready, a gentle tap brought him back to reality. He opened the door and stood aside for Katherine to enter. There was nobody else on the corridor.

'When I suggested here, I didn't mean anything...' he began.

'I know that,' she said. 'We can talk here uninterrupted.'

So she wanted to talk. He recalibrated his thought process with this new information. What did she want to talk about? Conor said she would never take the initiative – what should he do? He took a deep breath. 'Katherine, I have never met anyone like you. I've never enjoyed anyone's company as much as yours.'

She bristled. 'I sense a but...'

Jimmy was startled. Did she think he was giving her the brush-off? 'No...the complete opposite. I don't want to go back to America and never see you again.'

'Well,' she said matter-of-factly, still on her guard, 'we could visit. You could come back, and I could go to New York possibly.'

'Would you be happy with that?' he asked.

'Would you?' she countered.

It was time. He could protect himself no longer. He could sense her reticence was born out of a deep need to protect herself. He understood that better than anyone, but if they were to have any chance, he would have to open up and accept his fate, whatever it might be. He thought to all the men he admired: Aristotle, Plato, Nietzsche, Marx. None of them were lily-livered. They were each brave in their own way. It was his turn.

'I would give up all I have – which is not much, I can assure you – to come and live here with you. I am not after your money or your house, though your home is one of the loveliest places I've ever been, but I want to be with you all the time. I feel like you are the answer to all the questions that have plagued my life. Many people who claim to have near-death experiences say there is this sudden realisation, a full knowing, the world makes sense. That's what I feel when I'm with you, Katherine. I have never had a relationship, nor anything even approximating one. I have avoided close connection with others. I sense others' emotions, the good – but all the more keenly – the bad. I've known I was different since I was a child, and my mother was the only one who understood. I loved her so much, and when she died, I thought I would never recover. Maybe I never did until now. I was told to toughen up, to grow a pair, to be a man, but I couldn't help it. I would cry often. I hated to see pain, in anyone or anything. I hated it when children burned ants with a magnifying glass, or when boys in my class talked about catching rabbits or whatever. That's what made me study philosophy, looking for an answer to why I was the way I was.

'I'm not much of a catch, Katherine. I'm a garbage man, and I don't have any friends or anything other than myself to offer you. I'm awkward in company, and I find most social situations really difficult. But you are the other half of me from where I'm standing. I totally understand if you don't feel the same – in fact, it would be sensible not to – but I can't leave this country without telling you the truth.'

Jimmy realised that was the longest speech he had ever made in his whole life. Katherine stood before him, looking stunned. The answer was going to be no – he could sense her trying to find the kindest words to let him down.

His instinct was to leave, just to go and spare them both the agony of that conversation. He headed towards the door.

'Where are you going?' Her voice was like a whip.

'I'm going to join the others. There's no need to explain, and I apologise if I've embarrassed you.' He took another step.

'That's what you do, is it? When you are unsure, or if it gets a little difficult, you bolt for the door?' There was none of the previous tenderness in her voice; in fact, she sounded angry.

'I… I wanted to spare you…'

'Don't give me that old nonsense. I got a letter once, three weeks after I was to marry, from a man who never turned up to marry me, because he wanted to *spare* me the misery of discovering he loved someone else.' Pain and bitterness dripped from the words. 'I have no room in my life for people who leave when the going gets tough. So if that's your default position, Jimmy Burns, then you better keep on walking and don't look back.'

He stopped and returned to stand square in front of her. 'And what if it wasn't how I was? What if I swore to you that I would never leave, never disappoint you, never let you down? That I would rather die than hurt a hair on your head? If I gave you my word that I would be yours and yours alone till I took my last breath?' His voice was more forceful than he intended, but he knew he was only getting one shot here.

'So what do you want?' she asked, still all defences up.

'I want to be with you, you infuriating woman. I'd really like to marry you actually, if that was something you'd consider. But if you don't want that, then I would simply want to be with you. If you don't want me, say so, and I won't ever bother you again, but as I said, I had to tell you.' Jimmy's eyes were downcast. The emotional charge of looking her in the eye was too much for him to bear.

'Why though? Why do you want to move over here?'

He was confused. 'I thought I explained…' Then he realised there was something he forgot to say. 'I want to move over, to be with you, because I love you, Katherine O'Brien.'

'And you promise you're telling me the whole truth? I swore I would never be burned like that again…'

'I swear on my mother's life,' he said quietly.

Katherine's face softened. He had spoken often of his mother in the days since they met, and she knew that was not a vow given lightly.

'So ask me then,' she said, a slight smile playing on her lips.

He knew what she meant, so he slipped his mother's simple silver wedding band from his pinkie, the one Bubbles had convinced him to keep, and got down on one knee in front of her. He took her hand in his and looked up. His eyes locked with hers. 'Will you marry me, Katherine?'

She allowed him to slip the ring on the third finger of her left hand, and she sighed as all the pain of years and years seeped out of her. 'I will.'

They walked downstairs together, and Katherine went back to the desk. He returned to the party just as Laoise was saying, 'Now, folks, I've had a very special request. This is a song for a man with the wonderful name of Bubbles O'Leary.' The group were gathered around one table and cheered loudly. Jimmy sat down with them.

'This is a song called "The Parting Glass", and it's a song of farewell. Bubbles passed away a while ago, and his friends loved him so much, they brought his ashes all the way from New York back here to Ireland. Now, I'm sure you know it, so if you'd like to stand, we'll sing this one together. *Slán go foill*, Bubbles, till we meet again.'

Dylan fiddled with a laptop on the side of the stage, and in a moment, the words of the song were projected onto the backdrop behind them.

Everyone stood, and one could hear a pin drop in the room as Dylan played a lonesome-sounding introduction on the uilleann pipes. Then Laoise's voice rang out sweet and clear.

Of all the money that e'er I had, I spent it in good company, and all the harm I've ever done, alas 'twas done to none but me…

To the amazement of Bubbles's friends, everyone sang along, their voices rising in a melodious crescendo. They sang the entire song, and the last line seemed so poignant.

But since it fell, unto my lot, that I should go and you should not, I'll gently rise and softly call, goodnight and joy be to you all.

Bubbles's friends wrapped their arms around each other, singing the words as best they could, tears streaming down their faces.

CHAPTER 45

*C*onor pulled out of the driveway with the group for the last time. Jimmy waved to Katherine, who stood on the lawn, tears in her eyes. Conor stopped and wound down the window, leaning out to her, making sure only she heard him.

'He'll be back in a few weeks, ya big eejit.' He winked and grinned. The morning she told him her news, they had stood together in his office and he had hugged her with such ferocity, she gasped for air. He was absolutely thrilled for her. If anyone deserved happiness, it was Katherine.

Beth had sent Kevin an email to be read out to everyone, which he did before they boarded the bus while Tess was having her hair done by Laoise one last time.

Will was being extradited to the United States to answer questions about everything, and his criminal past was not going to do anything to help him. Conor was not going to press charges here for assault, which meant the case in the US could go ahead more quickly. Lieutenant Bowers seemed confident that Munroe would be going back to jail for a very long time.

Maddie was recovering and was awake all the time now. It would be some weeks before she was discharged, and she would need a lot of therapy, physical and emotional, to get over her ordeal. Apparently, the blood they found was hers. After he assaulted her, Will had tied her up and left her unconscious, his plan being to never return to that apartment. Maddie woke up and managed to crawl out onto the street, where she passed out. The next thing she knew, she was being told her sister was on her way.

Kevin looked across the aisle, his heart bursting out of his chest with love. Marianne was helping Tess to read the book Jimmy had bought for her. Her voice had the entire bus enthralled.

'There once was a king called Labhraidh Laoiseach' – she'd had to get Conor to explain it was pronounced like 'louree linshig' – 'who had donkey's ears, but it was a huge secret and nobody knew. To make sure nobody ever found out, he had to have every barber who cut his hair killed immediately afterwards for fear they would reveal his secret. Every barber for miles around lived in terror of being picked.

'Nobody knew why barbers never came back from the castle, they just knew that they were never seen again. One barber, called Fionn, was afraid he would be next. Soon enough, his turn came, and he was selected as the king's barber. He kissed his wife and children, fearful he would never see them again, but he had no choice. He went to the palace and immediately saw, with his own two eyes, the reason the king had all the barbers killed. With trembling fingers he cut the hair, and the king told him, with tears in his eyes, that now the poor barber had to die. Fionn begged and pleaded for his life, and the king, tired of so much killing, agreed to spare him, provided the barber gave him his word to never reveal the king's embarrassing secret. Fionn agreed, but over months and months, he found himself getting sick because of holding the secret inside. In desperation, one day he went deep into the woods and whispered the secret into the bark of a willow tree. "Labhraidh Laoiseach has donkey's ears." Immediately, he felt better.

'Several years later, the king's musicians were ordered to make a new harp, so they went in search of the perfect willow tree. They found one deep in the forest and cut it down. The harp maker made the finest the country had ever seen. There was a huge banquet arranged for the unveiling of the new instrument, and the king's best harper had been practising day and night. The evening finally arrived, and everyone from the entire kingdom was invited to the party. The harper was finally called upon, after all the feasting, to play. But to the horror of the king and the hilarity of the crowd, the harp, instead of the tune the harper was plucking, cried out in a melodious voice, "Labhraidh Laoiseach has donkey's ears!" The king went red, then he went purple, then his face turned black with rage, and he roared in a thunderous voice, "Bring me that harper!"

'The harper was dragged to the foot of the throne, and he was crying, "I didn't know, I swear… I didn't know…"

'The king looked down at the frightened faces of his subjects and realised the monster he had become, all to save his blushes. He made a decision. He took off his crown and pulled back his hair to reveal a pair of grey donkey's ears. He started to laugh, then the queen laughed, then all the little princes and princesses laughed, until eventually everyone at the banquet was howling uncontrollably. The secret was out, and everyone lived happily ever after.'

'Again… Marianne, read it again, please,' Tess begged, making elaborate praying gestures.

Erin and Shannon dabbed their eyes self-consciously. When Kevin asked them if they were okay, Shannon replied, 'Our daddy told us that story often when we were little girls. We hadn't heard it for years.'

As they watched the green fields speed past the coach window, the land where they felt like strangers just a week earlier felt much more like home. Seamus had invited them to stay with him and his wife for Christmas – they had plenty of room as all their kids were grown and married – and they were going to do it. They had already looked up the flights, and they were so looking forward to it. Late into the night, they pondered what sorts of things they could buy as gifts, and the idea that the one candle from Dr Mills and a small token for each other would not be the entirety of their Christmas gifts was something that brought the sisters untold joy.

Annie took her phone out of her pocket, feeling it vibrate.

Miss you already. FaceTime when you land? Darragh xxx

She smiled. He was so cute, and maybe he was Mr Right, though she suspected he might not be. He certainly was Mr Right Now, and that was enough. She thought about Bubbles and his promise that she would find someone – it just might take a bit. And for the first time, it didn't feel like she needed to be in such a rush.

Miguel stared out the window, not wanting to engage with anyone. He was happy for them that everything worked out. He liked Bubbles's friends – with the exception of that Will guy, of course – but he knew that while they all were so fond of Bubbles, not one of them felt his loss as keenly as Miguel did. He was going home to Mexico. He'd changed his itinerary, and when the rest of the group boarded the United Airways flight to JFK, he would take Aer Lingus to London and from there catch a plane to Mexico City. Maybe open a bar. He'd saved pretty much all his wages over the years, and yesterday, he got an email to say Bubbles had left him the bar. The lawyer had scanned the note Bubbles had left for him with his will.

Miguel,

Thank you for everything you've done for me. I value your friendship above all others. I'm leaving you the bar to do with as you wish – don't feel you have to keep it going. I'm gone if you're reading this. Keep in touch with your family – it's my biggest regret that I didn't.

Until we meet again, my dearest friend,

With love,

Bubbles

The rest of his considerable estate was going to his sister and his mother.

Miguel realised he might have been able to negotiate a green card – as a business owner, he had some chance – but he couldn't stay there without Bubbles. The bar was going on the market next week. He was really glad Kathleen was going to benefit, as she needed help taking care of Bubbles's mom and she was a single parent; this money would be life-changing for her. He called his own mother from the hotel, something he only did at Christmas, to tell her he was coming home for good, and she was so happy. It made him feel bad that she'd had to live with the knowledge that all her son ever wanted was to get away. He would do his best to make it up to her now. He hadn't said anything to the rest of the group; he'd tell them in the airport.

Conor pulled the bus into the airport car park and stood up. They had plenty of time to check in.

'Now, folks, this is goodbye – for some of you at least – but I don't think I've ever had a group with such a high proportion coming back to Ireland.' He grinned and the group responded in kind. 'Now, to say this has been an eventful trip is to say the very least of it. And believe me, I could tell you some stories – maybe someday I will. But if you'll just indulge me for one minute, I want to show you all something.'

He opened the bus door.

'You're not stripping at the back of the bus again, are you, Conor? You caused a bit of a commotion the last time you did that,' Kevin joked. The Glavin sisters tittered at the memory.

'No...nothing like that.' Conor rolled his eyes.

'Pity...' Annie nudged Marianne and both women giggled.

He went to the boot of the bus and extracted a large envelope and then got back in again.

'Now, there's a story here...' he began.

'Isn't there always a story with you?' Jimmy quipped.

'Well, that's true, I suppose, but anyway, here we go.' Conor winked and went on. 'The day we scattered Bubbles's ashes, that feels like about five years ago, to be honest, but anyway, you all walked out onto that headland. As you recall, it was after a huge thunderstorm. You all walked out with Eddie and were gathered there saying your goodbyes. You were all holding hands, and I waited on the bus. Well, just as you all sang "Danny Boy", you don't realise what happened, but a huge rainbow appeared, and you were all standing in it. I took a photo with my phone, and I got one printed for each of you.'

He handed a photo to each of them, and sure enough, there they were, Bubbles's urn in Miguel's arms, Eddie's hands joined in prayer and the group of them all huddled together standing in the most glorious Technicolour rainbow arcing out of the sky. None of them had ever seen anything like it.

Marianne was the first to recover, the others too emotional to speak. 'Conor, this is the coolest gift any of us could ever have asked for. Saying goodbye to our friend was so hard, but seeing this, I don't know… It's like he was with us. Bubbles was such a colourful character, really – colourful was the best word for him – I know each and every one of us will cherish this picture forever.'

Miguel spoke too. 'I know, Conor, that this week could have been a very different experience if anyone else was helping us. We met your lovely wife and your boys, and we all hope that she gets better really soon. And I think you now have someone else in heaven working for you. Bubbles had a way of fixing things for people, and he'll do all he can for you now, I'm sure of it. Thank you, on behalf of all of us.'

The group burst into spontaneous applause.

'My pleasure.' Conor smiled.

As each of them took a trolley and loaded their bags, they turned to say goodbye.

He hugged each one in turn and waved as they walked through the entrance doors of the airport.

CHAPTER 46

onor and Ana sat in the oncologist's waiting room, every minute feeling like an hour. The chemotherapy and the radium treatment were both complete, and now they needed to meet with Ana's consultant to review the results.

Each week, the radiation consultant gave Ana feedback about how the treatment was progressing, and it was always positive, but this meeting was with Dr Sunita Khatri, and they were nervous.

Ana reached for Conor's hand, and he squeezed it gently. She gave him a weak smile, and he whispered, 'It's going to be grand – I know it is.'

She nodded, her green eyes locked with his. Her hair had begun to grow back, and her head was covered in curls. She had been blonde with straight hair, but the doctors explained that it was not uncommon for it to grow back much curlier after treatment. He told her she looked adorable. She was eating normally again and had also put up some weight, which he was relieved to see.

'Jamsie is taking the boys into town to buy them guitars this morning for their birthday,' Ana said.

'I know. They were full of it yesterday. Apparently, he's going to teach them. I never even knew he could play.' Seeing his father and his sons interacting over the past few weeks had been so inspirational. Artie and Joe held no grudge, nor did they know anything about the past where their grandfather was concerned, so the relationship was developing organically.

Conor and his father had been spending a lot of time at Gerry's bedside, and so they were getting to know each other. The story of Jamsie's life was a sad one. The girl he'd left Cork with had no interest in his previous family and forbade him to ever make contact. Conor had been honest with him when he heard that, saying that he should have done it anyway, and Jamsie agreed. He was sorry; that was all he could say. She had a baby girl, called Elizabeth, so Conor learned he had a half-sister in England. Jamsie and her mother didn't work out. She married someone else with better prospects and more money, and the happy couple made it clear that they would be raising her daughter. Having Jamsie hanging around was surplus to requirements.

He sent her Christmas and birthday cards though, and persisted in seeing her as much as he could, even though her mother and stepfather obstructed it every step of the way. He even went to court to get access. She was a grown woman now, with kids of her own. Jamsie spoke about her warmly.

'It was she who encouraged me to find you and Gerry. Liz never knew about you until recently. I had a bit of a health scare, and I decided to tell her the truth. She said it wouldn't be right for me to end my days on earth without at least trying to make it up to you.'

Conor felt a stab of pain. His father would fight for this girl, and yet he had just walked away from his wife and sons without a backwards glance. 'Why didn't you try before now?'

Jamsie gazed at one son while the other lay in the bed between them, sleeping. The drugs to manage the pain meant he was only awake for short periods.

'I don't know. I wish I had a better answer for you, I really do. Fear of rejection? Not willing to face the music? I don't know. I wish so much that I had.'

Conor sighed. 'I wish you had too.'

After that conversation, things were easier, and the family's days fell into a kind of routine: caring for Gerry, looking after the boys, managing the hotel, and spending valuable time together. Danika and Artur were there, and the boys were so sweet, making sure Artur didn't feel left out because of the new granda.

'Yes, Joe thinks he's going to be like the Jimi Hendrix man. Jamsie was showing him YouTube yesterday, playing American – what is word, you know, the special music of a country?'

'National anthem?' Conor smiled.

'Yes, this. Jimi Hendrix play American national anthem at Woodstock, and now Joe says that is what he will be when he is big.' She chuckled. Throughout this gruelling process, the boys and their antics were a constant source of joy and laughter.

The door opened and Dr Khatri appeared. 'Anastasia, Conor, please come in.'

Conor had a flashback to the day they were in that very office being told about the treatment Ana would need. It had felt like his whole world had come crashing down.

'Have a seat.' She opened a buff-coloured folder on her desk. She glanced over the file and then looked up. 'I'm happy to tell you that the treatment was very successful. Of course we can't say you are free of cancer at this stage – we will need to monitor everything over the coming months and years – but for now, everything is looking good.' She smiled.

Conor recovered first. 'So she's all clear?'

'Well, the chemotherapy and radium combined removed all traces of cancer, so there is no cancer at the present time. However, I cannot guarantee it won't come back. Words like "all clear" and "cure" are mentioned in the media, but I prefer not to use such terms. They suggest a finality I could not stand over. But this is a great day. The treatment has worked, and you no longer have cancer. We will be keeping a very close eye on you in the future, and we will hope for no further recurrence.'

'Thank you.' Conor stood and shook the woman's hand.

Ana gave her a hug. 'Yes, Sunita, thank you so much for everything. I feel like I could fly.' She smiled through her tears.

'Well, don't do that,' the doctor said with mock sternness. 'We don't want to see you back in A&E. Now, I need to go. I apologise, but we are very short-staffed at the moment. So go home and celebrate. This is a great day.'

Conor and Ana walked hand in hand to the car. As he opened the door for her, she stood on her tiptoes and kissed him. 'You are stuck with me for longer now.' She grinned.

Conor hugged her like he would never let her go.

Once they were sitting in the car, he turned to her. 'I was so scared,' he finally admitted.

'Me too, but they were so great in the hospital. From the start, they say they can fix it, and they did.' She was philosophical.

'I know, but you hear such stories, and then worry about the worst happening, or if it spread. I…'

Ana leaned over and wiped the tear from the side of his face. 'You are so strong, such like a rock for us all, and I know it is so hard for you, me being sick and Jamsie coming from out of green…'

'Blue.' He laughed.

'What?' She was perplexed.

'Out of the blue, not out of the green.' Conor wiped his eyes.

'Oh yes, blue, green, whatever.' She dismissed it. 'What is important is now we focus on you and the next while. Gerry will not live much longer – nurse say any day now. And then, after everything, maybe we can take holiday?'

'That sounds wonderful.' Conor smiled, reaching over to cup the side of Ana's face in his hand. She turned her head and kissed his palm. 'You are my whole world, Ana, you know that?'

'I do. Now take me home to my boys.'

As Conor drove out of the hospital car park, Ana opened the sunroof. The autumnal breeze filled the car with weak warm sunshine.

She stood up, put her head out, and screamed, 'Woo-hoo!'

* * *

THAT EVENING, Conor invited his parents-in-law, Laoise and Dylan, Katherine and the newly arrived Jimmy, Valentina and a few of the neighbours in for a barbeque and a drink. It was still warm enough to sit outside, and Artie and Joe were playing football on the lawn with Dylan and a few of their friends.

As she surveyed the scene, Ana chatted animatedly with Laoise and Valentina. Jimmy and Katherine were talking to Artur and Danika, Katherine trying out her Ukrainian. Jamsie said he would come out later, as he was spending most of his time with Gerry. The medical team were there that afternoon and assured them that he was comfortable. Ana had wondered if it was right to have a party with Gerry so ill, but Jamsie assured her it was what he would want.

Jamsie appeared.

'Granda!' Artie threw himself at Jamsie. 'Mammy's cancer is gone, she's better...' he blurted, trying not to cry, Joe hot on his heels.

'I know. Your daddy told me earlier. Isn't that just brilliant news, really, really brilliant.'

Ana moved towards him. She hadn't seen Jamsie all day, and over the last weeks, they'd become very close. Jamsie adored her. She gave him a hug, drawing him into the family.

'It is...the best news I could ever have imagined,' he said, making room for the boys to wriggle into the hug too.

Danika produced salads to accompany the steaks and burgers and a mouthwatering array of cakes for afterwards – the woman was incredible – and the noise levels rose with excitement and delight. Joe and Artie reminded their father that he said they would go to Disney-land when Ana was better. Conor had no recollection of such a prom-ise, but Ana backed the boys, so he reluctantly agreed to make good on the deal.

They took turns to go in and check on Gerry. It felt so strange to have someone dying in the next room and such jubilation everywhere else.

Jamsie did by far the lion's share of the bedside vigil during the day. Conor had been doing nights, and Artur and Danika arrived very early in the morning to allow him a few hours' sleep before work. It was a gruelling schedule, but it was working. The nurses were there, unobtrusive and helpful, to attend to Gerry's medical needs.

As Conor came back from checking on him, he found his father outside, leaning against the garage wall smoking a cigarette. 'They say it won't be long now,' Jamsie said.

'You'll be following him if you don't pack in those things.' Conor nodded at the butt Jamsie ground under his heel, taking care to pick it up and put it in the bin.

'I'm smoking so long now, I'd say the shock would kill me if I stopped,' Jamsie replied with a yawn.

'You're exhausted. Why don't you go for a snooze?' He was watching his father age almost before his eyes. The strain of the last few weeks was really taking its toll.

'Nah, I'm okay. I'll stay with him tonight. Enjoy the time with your family – they are what matter the most. It's a great day, and ye all got such fantastic news, ye should be allowed to enjoy it without thinking about me or Gerry. Letting him stay here, it really was an act of great kindness. You're like your mother that way – she was so good. She deserved so much better than me. She'd be so proud of how your family turned out.'

Conor stopped his father as he went to go back to Gerry, his hand on his arm. 'You and Gerry are my family too.'

Jamsie smiled, patted Conor's hand and went back in.

Hours later, everyone was gone home and the place tidied up. Conor and Ana went to Gerry. His breathing was laboured, and he seemed distressed, but the nurse assured them he wasn't in pain. When she saw them come in, she said she was going to get a cup of tea to give them some time. Jamsie was dozing in the chair beside the bed.

Eddie had called in earlier, congratulated Ana on her great news and went in to say a prayer with Gerry. He stayed for a coffee and a big slice of one of Danika's legendary cakes, theatrically hiding it from his doctor, who was a neighbour of Conor and Ana's and whose boys were friends with the twins. Apparently, Gerry had asked Eddie to pray for him when he could still communicate. Eddie called every day since.

Ana took Gerry's hand in hers and sat down.

'Hi, Gerry. I hope you are sleeping peacefully. Today I get great news – I am getting better. You said a prayer for me, I know, so thank you.' She stood up and kissed his forehead. Conor marvelled at the sheer humanity of his wife, that she could feel such affection for someone she hardly knew.

He at least had some good memories of his brother to offset against the reality of his adult life. He reminisced as Gerry lay unconscious; the nurse had explained that often those in a coma could still hear. He often sat at night, remembering incidents and people from their childhoods. He talked a lot about their mother, and in a weird way, it was oddly comforting.

'Good night, Gerry. Jamsie is staying with you tonight, but I'll be back on duty tomorrow night, boring you to tears with stories from the past. Just you relax there and take it easy. Everything is fine.' He laid his hand on the sheet that was neatly pulled up over his brother's chest. There was hardly anything left of him, his body wasted away, just skin and bone remaining.

There were no machines as one might expect in a hospital, just a drip feeding him morphine to keep his pain at bay. The room was quiet and peaceful.

Jamsie woke with a start as they turned to leave.

'It's okay,' Conor whispered, holding Ana's hand. 'We just came to say good night.'

Jamsie sat up and turned towards Gerry. His son's breath had normalised, no longer laboured. As the three of them stood around the bed, Gerry's eyelids seemed to flutter slightly and a small smile played around his lips. He breathed in deeply, and then exhaled in a long, slow breath.

They waited for another, but there was none. Gerry was gone.

Ana leaned over and kissed his forehead again. 'Safe home, Gerry,' she whispered.

'Goodbye, son,' Jamsie said, emotion choking his words.

Conor put one arm around his father's shoulder and another around his wife's waist. 'Good luck, Gerry. Say hello to Mam for me. She'll be delighted to see you.'

The nurse arrived and confirmed what they already knew. 'I'm sorry for your loss. But he had a very peaceful end, and he was happy and secure in his final weeks, so you all did right by him. There's nothing more to be done tonight. I'd suggest you all get some sleep. I'll record the time of death and finish up here. The doctor will come first thing.'

Conor nodded.

'Should we stay?' Jamsie asked.

'No. He'd want you to get some sleep. We'll have a busy few days ahead. Gerry's gone. He doesn't need us any more.'

Conor led Jamsie to the spare room that he'd moved into weeks ago, and Ana helped to settle him into bed. They tucked him in like he was a child, and Conor realised his father was crying.

'I'm so sorry. I made such a mess of everything. Gerry's life, it was my fault...'

Conor sat on the edge of the bed. 'You were there for him when he really needed you. That's what matters. There's no point in what might have been. Gerry is at peace now, and he died surrounded by his family. Go to sleep now, Dad. We'll all be here in the morning.'

He left his father to rest as Ana took his hand in hers and led him up the stairs. Tomorrow was another day.

THE END

Thank you for reading my novel, I sincerely hope you enjoyed it. This is the fourth book in a series so if you'd like to read more about Conor and the gang, check out my website. www.jeangrainger.com

If you had a moment, I would really appreciate a review on Amazon.

If you would like a free Jean Grainger novel, go to my website, www.jeangrainger.com when you can download a free copy of my book *Under Heaven's Shining Stars*.